Deborah Challinor MNZM has a PhD in history and is the author of fifteen bestselling novels, including the Children of War series, the Convict Girls series and the Smuggler's Wife series. She has also written one young-adult novel and two non-fiction books. She lives in New Zealand with her husband. In 2018, Deborah was made a member of the New Zealand Order of Merit for services to literature and historical research.

Books by Deborah Challinor

FICTION
THE RESTLESS YEARS Series
From the Ashes

THE SMUGGLER'S WIFE Series
Kitty
Amber
Band of Gold
The Cloud Leopard's Daughter

CONVICT GIRLS Series
Behind the Sun
Girl of Shadows
The Silk Thief
A Tattooed Heart

CHILDREN OF WAR Series
Tamar
White Feathers
Blue Smoke

Union Belle

Fire

Isle of Tears

My Australian Story – Vietnam

NON-FICTION
Grey Ghosts

Who'll Stop the Rain?

Deborah
CHALLINOR

FROM
the ASHES

A Restless Years novel

HarperCollinsPublishers

HarperCollins*Publishers*

First published in Australia in 2018
This edition published in 2019
by HarperCollins*Publishers* Australia Pty Limited
ABN 36 009 913 517
harpercollins.com.au

Copyright © Deborah Challinor 2018

The right of Deborah Challinor to be identified as the author
of this work has been asserted by her under the *Copyright
Amendment (Moral Rights) Act 2000.*

HarperCollins*Publishers*
Level 13, 201 Elizabeth Street, Sydney, NSW 2000, Australia
Unit D1, 63 Apollo Drive, Rosedale, Auckland 0632, New Zealand
A 53, Sector 57, Noida, UP, India
1 London Bridge Street, London, SE1 9GF, United Kingdom
Bay Adelaide Centre, East Tower, 22 Adelaide Street West, 41st Floor,
  Toronto, Ontario, M5H 4E3, Canada
195 Broadway, New York, NY 10007

A catalogue entry for this book is available
from the National Library of Australia.

ISBN: 978 1 4607 5413 9 (paperback)
ISBN: 978 1 4607 0853 8 (ebook)
ISBN: 978 1 4607 9945 1 (audio)

Cover design by Alissa Dinallo
Cover images: Woman by Giorgio Magini / stocksy.com / 1080202;
Auckland by Travelscape Images / Alamy Stock Photo
Typeset in Sabon LT Std by Kelli Lonergan
Printed and bound in Australia by McPherson's Printing Group
The papers used by HarperCollins in the manufacture of this book are a natural,
recyclable product made from wood grown in sustainable plantation forests.
The fibre source and manufacturing processes meet recognised international
environmental standards, and carry certification.

This book is for Summer Rose Harete Paul

Part One

Part One

Chapter One

Hawke's Bay, June 1955

The late afternoon sun sat just above the line of bald poplars between the tractor shed and the house, almost blinding Ana Leonard as she peered out the kitchen window. Oh God, he was at it again. She rapped smartly on the glass.

'Jack!' she shouted. '*Jack!*'

He didn't even look up. Should she go and get him, or let him wander inside in his own time? She opened the range door, eyes narrowed against the escaping heat, and poked a skewer into the roast. Nearly done. She sighed: if she didn't fetch him he might never come in. She wiped her hands on a tea towel then went out, flapping across the yard in her slippers.

As she watched her seventy-five-year-old father-in-law shuffling about in shirtsleeves, gumboots and a pair of baggy underpants, crumbling up Weet-Bix and feeding them to the chickens, she had to admit he really was getting worse.

She said, 'That's our breakfast you're chucking on the ground.'

'Well, I don't bloody well like Weet-Bix. I'd rather have bacon and eggs.'

'You get bacon and eggs, every morning. I make them for you.'

'Do you?' Jack looked genuinely surprised.

'Yes, after your Weet-Bix, which you do so like. You have them with hot milk and sugar.'

'Do I?'

'Come on, come inside, it's getting cold.'

The sun was dropping behind the hills now and, although the day had been fine, outside at dusk in the middle of a Hawke's Bay winter was no place for a half-dressed old man. Also, David and the children would be back soon and the kids would only laugh — not cruelly, but they were likely to find the sight of their grandpa wandering the yard in his underpants highly entertaining. Then again, they were used to his odd behaviour, so perhaps they wouldn't.

'I'm not cold,' Jack said, hurling two whole Weet-Bix at a chook.

'Well, I am.' Ana took him gently by the sleeve. 'Come on, in you come.'

Jack allowed himself to be led. 'Where are the kids?'

'Out with David.'

'But where are they?' he demanded, sounding a little panicky.

'Up in the top paddocks, moving sheep. The grass is getting a bit low.'

Jack relaxed. 'That's true.' He toed off his gumboots at the back door and arranged them neatly beside the wood box. 'What's for dinner?'

'Lamb roast.'

'And kumara?'

'Always.'

'My favourite.'

Jack gave Ana the empty Weet-Bix box and headed towards the kitchen.

'Go and wash your hands,' Ana reminded him.

He changed direction.

'And put some trousers on!' she called after him.

*

'Pass the carrots, Peter,' Rowie said.

'Pass the carrots, Peter, please,' Ana corrected. Rowie was nine and because of that believed she could order her younger brother around like a lackey.

'Yeah, please,' Peter echoed.

David said mildly, 'That's enough from you, Mr Smart Aleck.'

'She started it.'

'And I'm finishing it. Eat your dinner.'

They ate in silence for a minute, then Jo said, 'I fell off Misty today. In the top paddock.'

Alarmed, fork poised halfway to her mouth, Ana stared at her youngest daughter. She rode very well for a five-year-old, was fearless and fell off her pony with apparent impunity. Usually she bounced, but one day she wouldn't.

'Did you hurt yourself?'

'No.'

'Did she?' Ana asked David.

'She said she didn't.'

Jack said, 'Pass them kumaras, will you?'

David passed his father the roast kumara. 'Anything in the post today?'

These days the mail arrived once a week at the farm gate via rural delivery van, which was a marked improvement on the war years, when someone had to drive into Kereru, the closest little settlement twelve miles away, and collect it from the general store.

Jack shrugged. 'Bits and pieces.'

'Nothing important?

'Didn't look. Been too busy.'

'Doing what?'

Jack stared at his plate. After a minute it became clear he was struggling to remember his day.

Ana rescued him. 'You read your book, tidied up in the yard, helped me with the washing and fed the chooks. That's right, and you fixed the fence behind the tractor shed.'

'Full day,' David agreed.

'And we got through over a thousand sheep,' Jack added.

No one blinked an eye though obviously that was completely made up; shearing wouldn't start till November.

'Did you?' David said. 'Good on you.'

Ana sent David a fond glance across the table. Jack's deteriorating state of mind was the only fly trapped buzzingly in the ointment of her family's happy existence on the farm. She'd been a land girl working for Jack during the war when David, a veteran, had arrived home in 1944. She'd stayed on and married David two years later, then the children had arrived. Jack's mind had been fine then, but over the last couple of years his behaviour had become increasing erratic, to the point that David couldn't work with him on the farm any more. He had enough to cope with without babysitting someone who was becoming forgetful, unpredictable, irrational and foul-tempered. David, however, flat out refused to take Jack to the doctor in town in case the doctor recommended a mental hospital, which, David knew, would be the end of his father.

Instead, she and David kept a close eye on him at home. In the mornings she helped the children with their correspondence school lessons, as the farm was many miles out in the Hawke's Bay hills, so it was relatively easy to watch Jack, and in the afternoons they all often rode out and worked on the farm with David, though today she and Jack had stayed home as it had been washing day.

In a year or so, though, Rowie would have to be sent to boarding school in Napier, and when Peter and Jo — who refused to answer to Joanne — grew older, they'd go off to town, too, which saddened her. But they had ambitions they'd never achieve if they stayed on the farm. Rowie wanted to be a nurse, and Peter, even though he was only six, was desperate to be a soldier — just like his father, and his grandpas Jack and Joseph Deane, Ana's father, and half a dozen men on the Murdoch side of his family, not to mention all the warriors on the Te Roroa

side. Jo's current goal in life was to be a shearer because she
had so much fun when the gangs — made up mostly of Ana's
Maori relatives — came out to the farm at the end of the year.
Ana wasn't too concerned — there were worse things to aspire
to than being in a shearing gang. Besides, up until the Christmas
just past Jo had wanted to be a horse.

It was an isolated life, living this far out, but very rewarding
living and working on the land. Some days it was heaven on
earth, and on others it was a grind — freezing, miserable and
filthy — but they loved it. They didn't own the farm, they leased
it and always had, but they were doing really quite well from
their sheep, which they did own. David had lived here all his life
and Ana came from both sheep-farming and shearing families,
so it was everything to them. They grew almost all their own
food, and only went into Napier once a month for other supplies,
or perhaps to the store at Kereru for anything urgent. The
electricity was on at the house now, albeit somewhat unreliably,
and up at the shearing shed, and they even owned a refrigerator
and a radiogram. There were regular district dances and sports
events, neighbours close enough to ride to, and the great sheep
station Kenmore, which Ana's parents ran, was within driving
distance. It was a good life.

Rowie cleared the plates while Ana fetched pudding, hot
from the range. It was apple and blackberry crumble, which she
served with cream — also Jack's favourite.

'Lovely-looking crumble, Mary,' he said.

Ana smiled. 'Thank you.'

It was his long-deceased wife's name — and he used it so
often these days she no longer bothered to correct him. Though
she did tap his wrist to stop him pouring mint sauce over his
pudding, and pointed instead to the jug of custard.

Pudding finished, David pushed his plate away and let out
a long, satisfied burp, which never failed to make the children
laugh. 'Open the post, will you, love?' he asked Rowie, pointing
to the small stack of envelopes propped on the kitchen mantel.

It was usually the kids' job to open the mail, a feat David couldn't manage with only one arm, though Jack collected it from the letterbox at the end of their long driveway. Actually, Ana suspected David probably could open the mail, but he let the kids do it to make them feel important.

Rowie carefully removed the contents of each envelope, unfolded them, smoothed them flat and passed the small pile to her father.

'Bill, bill, advertisement for sheep wormer,' he muttered, shuffling through them, and then stopped, his gaze snagged. As he read a few lines his mouth opened but nothing came out, then he abruptly scraped back his chair, stood and left the room.

Alarmed, Ana stared after him. She wondered if she should go after him. 'Clear the table, please, Rowie.'

'But it's not my turn, it's—'

'Just do it, will you?'

Grumbling, Rowie began collecting plates while Pete and Jo smirked at each other.

Ana snatched up the fruit crumble dish and shoved it into the range.

Rowie said, 'Mum, there's nothing in that.'

Ana took it out again, dumped it in the sink and chipped furiously at the baked-on crusty bits around the edges with a knife. Little lumps of crispy oatmeal flew everywhere.

Jack laughed, and so did Pete.

'What's so funny?' Ana demanded. 'Get off your backside, Peter, and help your sister.'

Peter looked as though she'd slapped him and Ana felt awful because she hardly ever spoke to the kids like that.

Then David came back. They all stopped what they were doing and looked at him. His face was white.

He dropped the letter in front of his father. 'What's the meaning of this?'

Jack fumbled his spectacles from his shirt pocket, put them on and slowly read the letter. Ana could hear the dogs yipping at something outside and the night wind rattling the poplar branches, but the silence in the room was total and went on and on until she thought surely her head would burst.

Finally Jack said, 'I don't know.'

'What do you mean you don't know?' David almost but not quite shouted. His face had gone from white to red now. 'It's addressed to you! Mr Jack Leonard!'

Ana was shocked. Her tall, handsome and, above all, usually imperturbable husband hardly ever lost his temper, and especially not with his father. 'Who's it from?' she asked. 'What does it say?'

David glared at her, making her think *she'd* done something wrong. 'It's about the lease on the bloody farm. It hasn't—' He stopped. 'Hop off, you kids. Go to your rooms. Now. Go on.'

They scuttled off, frightened.

David closed the kitchen door behind them. 'The bloody lease payment hasn't been made.'

'Yes it has,' Ana said. 'Ages ago.'

'Not according to that, it hasn't,' David snapped, snatching the letter off Jack and handing it to her. 'See?'

She read quickly.

> *1 June 1955*
> *Mr Jack Leonard*
> *Maunganui Road*
> *RD*
> *Napier*

Messrs Larkin, Scott and Picard
Barristers and Solicitors
Hastings Street
Napier

Dear Mr Leonard,
We have been instructed to contact you on behalf of the lessor of your farm, Mr Charles Johnston. You will be

*aware that a lease payment is payable every five years,
and that a payment was due in December of 1954.
Reminders were sent in February and in April of this
year (1955).*

*As the lease payment is now six months overdue, and
reminders have been sent with no apparent response on
your behalf, we regret to inform you that Mr Johnston
feels he has no option other than to terminate your lease
contract.*

*Therefore would you please vacate the farm within a
period of two months, i.e. by 1 August 1955, removing
all your stock and any farm equipment purchased by
you, but leaving the house and farm buildings, fences,
etc, in good order.*

*Please note that Mr Johnston does not wish to enter
into any personal discussion regarding this matter, please
therefore direct any questions, in writing or in person, to
the above address. Thank you.*

*Yours sincerely
GA Scott
Solicitor
(Messrs Larkin, Scott and Picard)*

'But we did pay it,' Ana insisted. 'In December. I sent Jack down
to the letter box with the cheque for the postman. I know I did.
You *did* put it in the letter box?' she asked Jack.

He stared helplessly back at her. 'I must have, if you gave it
to me.'

'Well, you bloody well *can't* have!' David roared. 'For
Christ's *sake*, Dad!'

Jack's arm shot out, a shaking finger pointing angrily. 'Don't
you take that tone of voice with me, boy. You're not too old for a
hiding, you know. Fucking cheeky little sod!'

'Jack!' Ana exclaimed. It wasn't the bad language — he'd been coming out with that for a while now — it was the nasty, bullying sentiment that accompanied it.

'You keep out of this, Mary.'

David turned on her next. 'Didn't you notice the cheque hadn't cleared?'

Ana felt sick. It had been shearing time and money had been going out of the farm account to the shearing gang, and coming in from wool sales. Financially it was a very busy time of the year. 'No, I didn't. I just assumed ...'

David thundered out of the kitchen, yanking the door open so hard it bounced off the wall. Ana followed him to Jack's room, where he started going through the drawers in his father's bureau. It didn't take him long to find what he was looking for because they weren't hidden, just shoved in among the socks, underwear and bits and pieces: the missing cheque still in its envelope, and the reminder letters (opened), together with a handful of other bills Ana had thought had been lost in the post but which had since been paid anyway.

David turned to Jack, now standing in the doorway, and brandished the cheque and reminder letters. '*Why*, Dad?'

Jack's anger seemed to have left him. He was just a confused old man again. 'I don't know. I can't remember.' A lip-quivering silence, then, 'I'm sorry.'

David rubbed his hand across his eyes and breathed out an enormous sigh. 'God almighty. I'll go into town first thing tomorrow.'

*

As David drove off the next morning Ana watched him all the way down the long driveway until she could no longer see him. No rooster tail of dust followed him as it was raining and the day was grey and miserable, just like her mood. They'd had an awful night, neither of them getting much sleep, and he probably felt as ragged as she did. He'd taken the new car, a Chevrolet they'd only had since February, when they'd bought it second-hand. It had cost them a packet nevertheless, but it was definitely worth it. However, he was that stroppy this morning, in a terrible frame of mind, and she was worried about him.

She was worried about all of them.

In the kitchen Peter and Jo were clearing the breakfast table in silence. The children all knew something was wrong. They hadn't been told what, but they were on edge. Only Jack, out feeding the chooks — in the rain, getting soaked — seemed oblivious. Ana very much wanted to shake him until his false teeth flew out of his head and make him tell her why he hadn't put the cheque in the letter box for the postman to collect, and, even more baffling, why he'd opened those reminder letters and then just shoved them in his sock drawer, but she knew it would be pointless. And cruel. He possibly hadn't known why himself, at the time, never mind knowing now. It was her fault, really, for giving him the cheque to take to the letter box in the first place.

Rowie came in from feeding the horses. 'When will Dad be back?'

'Sometime this afternoon, I expect.'

'Do we still have to do our lessons?'

'Well, yes. Why wouldn't you?'

Rowie stared at the floor. 'I don't know. Because things feel funny.'

'I'll make cheese scones for lunch, shall I?' Ana suggested, then bit her lip. Her children were upset and she couldn't think of anything better to offer them than cheese scones.

Peter said, 'Has Grandpa done something wrong?'

'No. He's just ... no, he hasn't.'

Jo stood on tip-toe to put the Marmite back in the cupboard. As usual, she couldn't quite reach. 'Can we go for a ride this afternoon?'

Taking the jar off her and putting it in its customary place, Ana replied, 'If it's stopped raining. I don't fancy riding out in all this, do you?'

'I don't mind. I'm not scared of rain.'

Jack came in then, his socks squelching on the kitchen lino. 'Fucking rain.'

Ana winced, though the kids all giggled. 'Well, you shouldn't have gone out without your gumboots, should you?'

After that the morning seemed to drag on and on. Jack stayed in his room and the children plodded through their schoolwork, then Ana made the promised cheese scones and cold meat sandwiches.

During lunch Jack asked, 'Where's David?'

Ana told him, 'In town.'

'What for?'

'Business.'

'What business?'

Taking a deep, calming breath, Ana said, 'Just business, Jack. He'll be back this afternoon.'

'Bloody waste of time.' Jack bit into a scone. 'Should be out with the sheep.'

At the word 'sheep', crumbs flew out of his mouth and landed all over the lunch things.

'You've got terrible table manners, Grandpa,' Jo observed.

'Sheep farmers don't need table manners.'

Jo took a bite of her sandwich and deliberately spat it onto her plate.

'Stop that!' Ana exclaimed.

'Grandpa did it.'

'I don't care what Grandpa did! Bloody well behave!'

Jack reached for the butter. 'Don't be so hard on her. She's only wee.'

Ana turned on him. 'Shut up, Jack. Don't you think you've caused enough trouble?'

Looking astonished, Jack stared at her. 'Have I?'

Ana put her elbows on the table and rested her head on her hands. He was unwell, she knew that. He couldn't help it and she shouldn't lose her temper with him. But that didn't stop him from being unbelievably annoying. God, where had the old quietly strong, unerringly reliable Jack gone? She might as well be raising four children now.

Everyone was silent for a long time.

Then Jack said, 'Where's David?'

*

It had stopped raining so they all went out to check the sheep David had moved yesterday. Oddly, Jack didn't need any help saddling Rex, his horse, or riding him, even though Rex was a bit of a bad-tempered bugger. David thought it was because being on horseback was so ingrained in his father it was automatic. He didn't even have to think about it. It was only when he stopped to open a gate, or to do some other farm-related task, that things started to go wrong.

When they got back to the house at a little before three o'clock, the Chevrolet was in the driveway.

Ana rushed inside to find David at the kitchen table. He'd buttered a scone but hadn't eaten it, and had made a pot of tea. She touched it: cold.

She didn't need to ask — she could see it in his face.

'I'm sorry, love,' he said. 'We've lost it.'

She sat down, feeling suddenly sick. 'We truly have lost it?'

'Apparently Johnston won't change his mind. According to his solicitor he's already got new tenants lined up.'

Ana couldn't believe what she was hearing. 'But we've been leasing off him for years. You have, at least. And Jack leased off his father.'

'I know, but it's something to do with being able to put up the rent if he gets in new tenants.'

'Well, we can pay more, can't we?'

David closed his eyes briefly, and Ana could see this was hurting him horribly.

'It doesn't matter, Ana. It's too late. We have to sell up — the stock, the horses, the dogs, everything.'

'But ... what will we do?'

'I don't know, love. I really don't.'

Chapter Two

The room was full of blinding, acrid smoke and she could feel the searing heat of flames all around her, though they hadn't quite reached her yet. But they soon would. The noise was terrific but above it rose the piercing screams of people she knew she *had* to save — Daisy and Terry, Irene, Miss Willow and Miss Bourke, and dozens of others. She staggered around in the swirling hot darkness, reaching, reaching for them but never quite connecting, then realised with an awful soaring panic that she never would.

With a cry of despair Allie Manaia sat bolt upright, her nightie stuck to her body with sweat. She swung her legs over the side of the bed and leant forwards, coughing to clear her throat and lungs of non-existent smoke.

She felt her husband's gentle hand on her back. 'Another bad dream, love?'

Allie nodded.

'What about?' Sonny asked.

Without looking at him, Allie croaked, 'Not sure.'

Though she was. It was always the same horrible nightmare — being trapped in Dunbar and Jones department store while it burnt and not being able to save anyone. But that had happened over eighteen months ago, so why was it still haunting her? Surely she should have put it behind her by now? Everyone else who'd survived the fire had. Even the wreckage on Queen Street where Dunbar and Jones had stood had been razed and a smart new building was going up, as though a terrible tragedy had never even occurred there. So she couldn't tell Sonny she still often dreamt about the fire, or anyone else, either. They'd think there was something wrong with her.

'Do you want some water? Or a cup of tea?'

'Just water. Thanks.' Her mouth was as dry as sand.

Sonny padded out to the kitchen, flicking on the hall light. Don't leave me, she wanted to blurt, afraid of being left alone. Twenty-two and still frightened of the dark. She might see poor little Daisy sitting in the chair in the corner, or sexy, loud Irene. She glimpsed them on the street sometimes, but not really, of course: they were dead and buried in Waikumete Cemetery. Would they be bones yet, lying cold and abandoned in their coffins?

She heard Sonny open a cupboard door, get a glass and fill it with water from the tap. He was such a good husband. It was a pity she was turning out to be such a useless wife. She glanced at the bedside clock: Christ, a quarter to four. Thank God it was the weekend.

*

She couldn't get back to sleep and wanted a cigarette, but they were in the sitting room and she couldn't be bothered getting up to fetch them. Instead she lay next to Sonny, listening to his gentle snoring. They'd got engaged not long after the fire, even though they'd only been going out together for about three months. Everyone — especially her mother, and Sonny's mother, Awhi — had told her it was far too soon, and that it wouldn't last. But she and Sonny had seen the terrible mess the fire had made of people's lives, and didn't want to waste any more of theirs not being together. She didn't care that she hadn't known

Sonny long, or that she was Pakeha and he was Maori, or that he only drove a delivery truck for Smith and Caughey, or that neither of them had any money, and she knew he didn't care about any of that, either.

They'd married in April the previous year. She was working in the cosmetics department at Smith and Caughey, a job she'd got straight after Dunbar and Jones burnt down, and she'd used her staff discount to buy some nice material from the drapery department for her wedding dress. They'd had a church service, then a reception in a hall at Orakei, near where both her family, the Robertses, and Sonny's extended family lived. They'd invited several hundred people and served hangi food, sandwiches, pies and cakes, with lots of beer on the tables, laughter and shouting, a live band, dancing, kids sliding around the floor in their socks, and a few unplanned fights outside in the carpark. Some of the Pakeha guests hadn't stayed long, but on the day Allie hadn't had time to worry about that. Then everyone had waited for the early baby. She'd arrived — remarkably early, in fact — in August and they'd called her Irene Hana, after Irene Baxter, who'd perished in the Dunbar and Jones fire. But Irene had seemed such a grown-up name for a baby, so everyone was soon calling her Hana.

She was beautiful, healthy, thriving, bright and utterly adored, and then, just before she was four months old, the unimaginable had happened.

Allie had been woken by the discomfort of swollen, leaking breasts: Hana had slept right through the feed she usually demanded at two in the morning. She'd risen and gone to the baby's bassinet and found her still sleeping. Pleased, because perhaps Hana was weaning herself off her night feeds, Allie had turned away, but then she'd looked back — Hana had seemed very, very still. Her eyes had been closed and she was on her belly with her head to one side on the little pillow, exactly as Allie had left her when she'd put her down.

She'd touched her baby's cheek and her skin had been as cold as marble. That was when Allie had screamed.

Their beautiful little girl had gone, and no one had been able to tell them why.

After the funeral she'd returned to work at Smith and Caughey. It had been better than sitting around the flat floundering in misery, crying, and wishing things were different. By February Sonny had packed up Hana's things and taken them round to his mother's house because she couldn't cope with seeing them every day. She suspected he couldn't, either. They'd decided to try for another baby straight away, but it was nine months down the track now and nothing had happened. Why not, they wondered, when she'd so effortlessly, and accidentally, fallen pregnant the first time?

So now she was back to being just ordinary Mrs Sonny Manaia, which wasn't as easy as she'd thought it would be. Sonny was lovely. He was handsome, bright, funny, honest, a hard worker and he loved her, but she'd quickly discovered that some people were offended by a Maori being married to a blonde and very fair-skinned white girl. They took it out on her too. She'd been told she could 'do better', often by women, and some men treated her with less respect, pinching her backside and making snide remarks. She'd once even been called a whore, which was ridiculous because she'd only ever been with one man, who she'd married!

She really didn't think she did need to do better. Sonny probably could, though, and that knowledge hurt her very much. She tried so hard to be the cheerful, energetic girl he'd first gone out with, but it was so difficult when some days she could barely drag herself out of bed, she felt that low. The gloomy predictions made by their mothers that the marriage wouldn't last were coming true already, and she had no idea what to do about it.

And it was all her fault.

*

She held on to Sonny, her thighs pressed against his, her arms wrapped around his waist, leaning over hard as he took the tight corner off Kepa Road a little too fast, then tore along Coates Avenue, the engine of his Indian Chief roaring. Her hair whipped behind her in tattered streamers and crisp air bit at the bare ankles below her capri pants, reminding her of why they went to work in Sonny's battered old truck and not on the motorcycle, but she loved the bike almost as much as he did — unlike her mother, who never stopped making digs about it being a death trap.

They pulled up outside her parents' house with a minimum of unnecessary revving (no point rubbing it in), opened the garden gate, parked the motorcycle on the lawn, and went round the back. Hardly anyone used the front door.

'Mum's hydrangeas could do with a prune,' she remarked, pushing past enormous caps of blue and lilac flowers leaning over the path.

The house, a state house rented by Sid and Colleen Roberts ever since it was built, sat on a sloping quarter acre on a ridge overlooking Okahu Bay and the site from which the Ngati Whatua — Sonny's people — had been evicted by the government several years earlier. The Roberts family had lived in the Coates Avenue house so long — since 1939 — that, of the children, only Allie vaguely remembered living anywhere else.

Allie and Sonny climbed the ten scoria-red concrete steps to the back door. Allie knocked lightly and went in.

'Morning! Something smells nice.'

'Hello, love,' Colleen Roberts said from the kitchen bench. She set down her knife and wiped her hands on her apron. 'Hello, Sonny.'

'Morning, lovebirds,' Sid said from behind *The Truth*.

Allie's sisters said nothing, Donna busy reading a magazine and Pauline concentrating intently on painting a toenail, a sweep of her fair hair falling across her face like Veronica Lake's. Allie frowned; she'd been wondering where her bottle of Revlon 'Cherries in the Snow' nail varnish had gone.

'You look tired,' Colleen said, peering at Allie.

'I'm OK. Is that my nail varnish?'

Pauline looked up. 'This? I dunno. It might be. Can we go for a ride on the Indian?' she asked Sonny.

'Maybe, after lunch.'

'No,' Colleen said emphatically.

'Fancy a beer?' Sid asked.

'No, he does not,' Colleen said, 'and neither do you. It's not even twelve o'clock. I can make you a nice cup of tea, though.'

'That'd be lovely, thanks,' Sonny said.

'Do you need a hand, Mum?' Allie asked.

'Someone could pick some leeks. There's a lovely crop just come on in the garden.'

When her father showed no indication of moving, and neither did Donna nor Pauline, Allie exclaimed, 'You lazy buggers. Mum's not your slave, you know!'

'You're the one who offered,' Donna countered.

Sonny asked, 'How many do you need?'

'Oh, you're a love,' Colleen said. 'Three or four?'

Allie followed him outside, grumbling, 'God, they're lazy. Mum works five days a week, and then comes home and has to wait on them hand and foot!'

She didn't expect a response because Sonny had heard all this before. He knew Sid, an ex-watersider, had been more or less unemployed and on the invalid's benefit since badly breaking his leg (on the way home from the pub) four years earlier, and that both Donna, seventeen, and Pauline, a year younger, could be handfuls. They both worked — Pauline in The Cedar Room, Smith and Caughey's tearoom, and Donna as a nurse aid at Bethany Maternity Home in Grey Lynn. To everyone's amazement — because until recently she'd been the real tearaway — Donna had decided she wanted to be a nurse, had applied and been accepted but couldn't start her training until she turned eighteen, so was gaining work experience at Bethany. Now Pauline was the problem, being cheeky and rude, sneaking out at night, hanging around with milk-bar cowboys and generally behaving in a way that sorely tested Colleen and Sid. Allie was amazed some days that her mother didn't just walk out on her family, but she knew she never would. She wasn't that sort of woman.

Sonny made a sympathetic 'mmm' noise.

'I mean, I know the girls work, but Dad could put the tea on, or at least get the veggies started.'

Sonny looked at her as though she were mad.

Allie laughed. 'It's not *that* hard to peel a carrot. He can grow them — why can't he peel one?'

It was true, Sid's vegetable garden was magnificent. At the moment it was replete with neat rows of celery, broccoli, silverbeet, cabbages and cauliflowers, leeks, onions, potatoes, parsnips, pumpkins and carrots. Far more than one family could eat, so he gave at least half the produce away to neighbours. He had a little orchard too, though at the moment only the apple and lemon trees were fruiting.

Sonny took a garden fork and eased a few fat leeks out of the ground.

'Rex!'

Allie and Sonny looked at each other.

'Rex! Here, boy!'

The voice was coming from next door. Allie stuck her head over the fence. An elderly man was wandering around the lawn, looking agitated. Must be the new neighbours her mother had mentioned.

'Lost your dog?' Sonny called.

The old man stopped and stared at them. 'No. My horse.'

'Oh. Right,' Sonny said. Then, 'What does it look like?'

'Don't,' Allie whispered.

'Can't miss him,' the man replied. 'Got a red blanket under his saddle. Rex!'

A woman appeared at the house's back door. She spotted the old man, trotted down the steps and hurried across the grass.

'Hello, I'm Ana Leonard. We've just moved in. I see you've met my father-in-law, Jack. I hope he's not being a nuisance.'

'No, no,' Allie said quickly. 'I'm Allie Manaia and this is my husband, Sonny. We're visiting my mum and dad. You've met them?'

'Oh, yes. Your mum brought some baking over the day after we arrived. A cake. So lovely of her.'

'She's like that.'

Sonny said, 'Er, Jack says he's lost his horse.'

Kindly, Ana said to Jack, 'I think I saw him down by the feijoas. Why don't you go and have a look?' Off Jack went. When he was out of earshot, Ana said, 'He's not very well. We had a farm before this. He misses everything about it, especially the horses.'

'Whereabouts?'

'Sorry?'

'The farm,' Sonny said. 'Where was it?'

'Oh. Hawke's Bay. We ran sheep.'

'You must be finding Auckland a big change, then,' Allie remarked.

Ana just nodded, looking at a complete loss for a moment.

'Are you Ngati Kahungunu, then?' Sonny asked — a bit bluntly, Allie thought.

Ana smiled. 'I am. Well spotted. Most people can't even tell I'm Maori. My father is Joseph Deane. His father was Kepa Te Roroa and his mother was Tamar Murdoch, nee Deane, from Cornwall. My mother is Erin Deane, whose parents were Jeannie and Lachlan McRae from Scotland. They were all sheep farmers. My mother and father still are.'

Sonny rattled off his own family tree, which was something Allie had learnt a lot of Maori folk did when introducing themselves to other Maori. She'd done it herself, once, to one of Sonny's many uncles, listing the names and Irish and English birthplaces of her parents and grandparents. The man had stared at her for several long, silent seconds, then walked off. Maybe he'd thought she was being cheeky.

'So what brings you to Auckland?' Sonny asked.

Reappearing, Jack said, 'Not in the feijoas. Fucked if I know where he is.'

Ana turned scarlet. 'Jack! I do beg your pardon.'

Sonny grinned and waved away her apology.

'I don't know what you're laughing at, Sonny Jim,' Jack grumbled. 'You haven't got a horse missing in your garden.'

'It's just Sonny, not Sonny Jim,' Sonny said.

Jack scowled. 'What?'

Sonny opened his mouth, closed it, then said, 'Never mind.'

Ana took hold of Jack's arm. 'I think we'd better get you inside. We'll look for Rex later, shall we? Lovely to meet you two.'

'And you,' Allie replied.

She and Sonny watched as Ana frog-marched her father-in-law across the grass, up the steps and into the house.

Back in her mother's kitchen, Allie ran the leeks under the tap to get the dirt off and laid them on the chopping board. 'What do you want me to do with these?'

'Just take the ends off and chop them,' Colleen said. 'I'll do them in a white sauce.'

'We met your new neighbours.'

'All of them? Even we haven't met the husband yet.'

'That old bloke's not the full quid,' Pauline said, screwing the lid back on Allie's nail varnish. 'I saw him outside in his underpants the other morning. Dirty old bugger.'

Allie shook her head. 'No, it was just the old man and Ana.'

'Mrs Leonard to you,' Colleen corrected. 'There're three children as well, and Mrs Leonard's husband.'

'What does he do?' Sonny asked.

'Something with the Wool Board, apparently.'

'Is it time for a beer yet?' Sid said.

'No!' Colleen exclaimed. 'Allie and Sonny are here. You're not spending the day sitting behind the paper drinking beer!'

'But I always have a beer with me Sunday roast.'

Donna yanked *The Truth* out of her father's hands, folded it, and sat on it. 'There, now you'll have to talk to us.'

'*You're* not talking,' Sid grumbled. 'You're reading your blimmin' woman's magazine.'

'Well, I've finished now.'

'Pauline, get Sonny and your father a beer,' Colleen ordered, apparently changing her mind, 'then come and help me with the veg. Do you want one, Allie?'

'No, thanks. I'll have Sonny's cup of tea.' The pot was on the table, its sides still hot to the touch.

'Can I have a beer?' Pauline asked.

Colleen flicked her with a tea towel. 'No you can't.'

Once Sid was happily settled with a bottle of DB he said, 'I've met the husband. The bloke next door. Name's David.'

Peeved, Colleen said, 'You didn't tell me that.'

'Had his head under the bonnet of that flash American car of his. It's a Chevrolet Styleline. You don't see many of them about. I was coming past on me way home from the pub so I stopped and introduced myself.'

'I love Yank cars,' Pauline said. 'D'you think he'd take me for a ride?'

Donna gave her a scathing look. 'Why would he want to take you for a ride?'

'He might.'

'Seemed a decent bloke,' Sid remarked. 'Only got one arm.'

Pauline pounced. 'Then how does he drive the car?'

'It's automatic. No gear shift.'

'Did you ask him why they moved to Auckland?' Colleen asked.

'No, because I'm not nosy.' Sid laughed at the look on Colleen's face. 'But he told me anyway. They had a nice little farm down in Hawke's Bay but they lost it. Didn't say why but I gather they didn't want to leave. Had to sell up all their stock and everything. He's doing wool inspections all over the North Island now and won't be home much, which I don't think he's too happy about.'

Colleen glared at him. 'And you knew all that but didn't think to tell me?'

'You didn't ask, love.'

'I can't ask if I don't know you know, can I?'

Sid shot an exasperated look at Sonny, who looked quickly at his DB bottle.

Allie smiled to herself. Her parents bickered constantly but she knew their love for each other was like concrete.

'And what else did he say? What's wrong with the old man?'

'I don't know,' Sid said, winding his finger in a circle next to his temple. 'Mental?'

Donna and Pauline both laughed.

Colleen let fly with the tea towel again. 'Stop it, you two. You'll both be old and doddery one day.'

'I won't,' Pauline said. 'I'm dying young and beautiful. Like Carole Lombard.'

'You have to *be* beautiful to die beautiful,' Donna pointed out.

'Bugger off.'

The milk wasn't on the table so Allie fetched it from the refrigerator — her mother's pride and joy. Recently purchased, it had cost seventy-nine pounds and she'd saved long and hard for it, pinching pennies from wherever possible. Colleen was the primary earner in the family as Sid's benefit only paid one pound ten shillings a week, though he did quietly do a bit of house painting on the side with his mate Bill, and her 'refrigerator jar' had been slowly filling up for several years. It had been a toss-up between a refrigerator and an electric washing machine, but the fridge had won as it could get quite hot in Auckland during the summer. Privately Allie thought it a bit of an indulgence, as milk was delivered daily and everyone could find time to nip to the butcher's two or three times a week, but her mother was thrilled with it so she kept her thoughts to herself.

'Is Nan not coming for lunch today?' she asked as she sat down again.

Colleen didn't turn from the bench but Allie could hear the frown in her voice. 'Her hip's giving her gyp. I popped round to see her on Friday after work and she was already in bed! I wish she'd go to the doctor.'

'She'd have to unlock her purse to do that,' Sid said.

Colleen did turn then. 'My mother is not cheap, Sid Roberts, and well you know it.'

'You need to get the phone on,' Allie suggested.

'And who's going to pay for that?' Sid asked.

'You, if you got a proper job,' Colleen replied, but there was no malice in it. She knew Sid really couldn't work full time. 'And what would be the point? Mum hasn't got the phone on, either.'

'Should I go and see her this afternoon?' Allie asked.

'She'd like that. You could take her a bit of dinner on a plate.'

Allie thought she would maybe while Sonny was visiting his mother. She wanted to talk to her nan but not while he was there. He'd think she was losing her marbles. She was worried too. It wasn't like Nan to miss a Sunday lunch.

Chapter Three

Polly Manaia stood naked in the staffroom of Flora's brothel on Ring Terrace at St Mary's Bay, digging through her carry-all for her underpants and bra, smoke from her cigarette curling up from an ashtray on the table. 'Christ, I can never bloody find anything in this bloody bag!'

'Well, hang your things up in the lockers like everyone else,' her colleague Roxanne remarked as she rolled a stocking up her leg.

'I hate the lockers. They remind me of school.' Finding her pants at last, Polly yanked them on, followed by her bra, then a flared skirt and a jumper, both black. She took a deep drag on her cigarette then shoved her feet into pointy-toed flats. 'God, I smell like a monkey.'

'Did you wash?'

'Yes I bloody washed.'

They all had — no one wanted to go home smelling like what they'd been doing for the past twelve hours.

Roxanne suddenly yawned so widely her face almost turned inside out. '*Christ*, I'm tired. I hate the Saturday late shift.'

Polly fought a yawn of her own. Why was it when someone yawned, it made you want to too? 'But think of the money.'

'We took enough last night,' remarked Sherri, slumped at the table next to Roxanne. 'I can hardly bloody well sit down.'

'Home for a Sunday roast?' Roxanne asked Polly. 'I am. I'm starving.'

'I don't live at home. Anyway my mother doesn't really do one. We're Maori.'

'No Sunday roast!' Sherri was aghast. 'God, you're hard done by.'

Polly gathered her heavy black hair into a high ponytail and shrugged. 'It's just a feed. Who cares?'

'I bloody do,' Sherri said. 'I love my Sunday roasts.' She slapped her belly and laughed. 'Can't you tell?'

The back door opened then slammed shut, followed by the sound of shoes clattering down the hallway. Polly stuck her head briefly out of the kitchen: Suzanne and some girl she didn't know, half the day shift.

'Morning,' she muttered.

Suzanne grunted.

Roxanne went on poking her nose in. 'Home for a sleep then, Pol?'

To shut her up Polly nodded, though she wasn't heading back to the Grafton house in which she rented a room, she was going to her mother's place at Orakei. She'd lie to Awhi as usual and say she'd been working last night waitressing at the Hi Diddle Griddle restaurant on Karangahape Road, or maybe the Gourmet on Shortland Street, both of which she actually did do sometimes, on a casual basis, but neither brought in much money. She made more modelling clothes at Smith and Caughey and Milne and Choyce, and working at Flora MacKenzie's brothel was the most lucrative of the lot, though she'd never tell Awhi that. She thought prancing about on a catwalk was shameful enough. She wasn't stupid, though, her mother — she must wonder where the money Polly spent on her daughter, Gina, was coming from. And that was nowhere near all of it: the bulk was going into a special bank account in Gina's name.

Flora herself bustled in, dressed in something weird and wonderful she'd designed herself, and clapped her hands.

'Right, my lovelies, here are your funds. Now, off home with you.'

Taking her little brown envelope of cash, Polly thought how it was never 'money' or 'pay' with Flora, it was always something like 'proceeds' or 'earnings' or that 'renumeration' word she could never pronounce. Just because Flora's family owned a horse farm and she had a posh wedding dress business didn't mean she could lord it over the girls who worked for her. She was still a brothelkeeper.

Outside the day was bright but the wind sharp, and Polly pulled on her coat as she walked to the nearest tram stop. Going over to Orakei was such a bloody trek, especially all the way from St Mary's Bay on Sunday mornings after a long night's work, but she visited at least twice a week to see Gina, who'd lived with Awhi most of her short life.

She smoked two more cigarettes waiting for the tram, then rode into town and waited for another one that took her up the hill to Parnell then Newmarket, where she bought and scoffed a pie. Then she caught a bus over to Orakei, got off on Tamaki Drive and traipsed up Kitemoana Street, by which time it was nearly one o'clock.

Her heart sank as she neared her mother's home. It always did. The house, a fairly new rented state house, was fronted by a bit of patchy lawn featuring a concrete path and two immature lemon trees, and separated from the street by a hurricane wire fence broken by an unpainted metal gate. The house was boring and soulless, and exactly like the others on Kitemoana Street. Her heart dropped even further when she saw Sonny's motorbike on the lawn. He was probably the most easy-going of all her brothers but she still nearly always managed to end up arguing with him. He didn't criticise and he didn't judge — unlike her mother — but she picked fights with him anyway. Sometimes she wished he would give her a hard time; then at least she'd know why she was being a bitch to him.

He was round the back, digging in their mother's enormous vegetable garden.

'Hey, Polly. Come to see Gina?'

'No Allie today?' Polly asked.

'Visiting her nan. She's laid up.'

'Mummy! *Mummy!*'

At the piping little voice they both turned to watch Gina coming down the back steps sideways like a crab.

'You be careful there, sweetie!' Sonny called.

Polly met her daughter halfway and picked her up, swinging her into the air so she squealed and laughed. 'How's my beautiful little girl?'

'Booful, booful, *booful*!' Gina shouted.

A dark shape appeared at the top of the steps.

Polly glanced up, settling Gina on her hip. 'Hello, Mum.'

'I've just put some tea on,' Awhi said, turning away.

Polly followed her into the kitchen. It was, as always, spotless, sunny and sparsely decorated, though a scrubbed kitchen table and chairs filled the centre space where everyone — family, friends and newcomers — was welcomed. The house was superior to the one in which they'd grown up, but Awhi didn't like it because it reminded her every day of the way the government had forced them off their land, which still rankled bitterly. *And* she had to pay rent to live in this one.

'How's she been?' Polly asked, sitting Gina on her lap.

'You'd know if you came to see her more often.'

Polly stared at her mother's broad back as she stood at the bench readying the tea things, her long, greying plait, her bare legs and the feet in worn slippers, and held her tongue for several long seconds. 'I would if I had time. I've been busy working.'

'She misses you. She asks for you.'

Oh, shut the fuck up, Mum. 'Does she? Do you, sweetheart?' Polly kissed the top of Gina's head. 'Well, Mummy misses you too.'

Awhi opened a window and bellowed, 'Sonny! Tea!' Then she carried the tea things to the table, sat down, snapped a biscuit in half and gave a piece to Gina. 'She's turning into a very pretty little girl. But then she was a beautiful baby.' She looked up slyly. 'She's got your good looks, but there must be a bit of her father in there too.'

Dig away but I'm not telling you who he was, Polly thought. I'm never telling you.

Sonny came in, washed his hands at the sink, and sat down. 'Are these your hokey-pokey biscuits, Mum?' He took two and stuffed a whole one in his mouth, making Gina laugh.

'Don't do that,' Awhi scolded. 'You'll teach her bad habits.'

Sonny drew in a breath to respond, choked, and violently coughed soggy crumbs all over the table, making Gina laugh even more wildly.

'For God's sake, boy, don't be such a pig!'

Sonny rolled his reddened eyes at Polly while his mother rose to fetch a tea towel. As she fussed about wiping up bits of half-chewed biscuit, Polly reached into her bag and produced a wad of folded notes.

'This is for Gina.'

Awhi counted the money. 'Twelve quid? That's a hell of a lot for a week's work.'

'Been doing a lot of waitressing?' Sonny asked.

Polly narrowed her eyes at him. He knew bloody well what she'd been doing, and that she'd made a lot more than that.

'Have you been working behind one of those bars down the waterfront?' Awhi demanded. 'Shame on you, girl, if you have. Your father would turn in his grave.'

'Half the cops in town drink in those places, and they don't give a bugger if there's a girl behind the bar. It's not against the law if you don't get reported for it. Anyway I wasn't, I've been waitressing, and doing a bit of modelling. I had a good week. And you said she needs some new clothes.'

Awhi raised a finger as though she'd just remembered something, stood and left the kitchen.

Polly lit a cigarette. 'Thanks a lot, big mouth.'

Affronted, Sonny said, 'What?'

'The way you said, "been doing a lot of waitressing". You might as well have just bloody said "been whoring".'

Uneasy at the aggression in her mother's voice, Gina gazed up at her, her hands over her ears.

'Never mind, sweetie,' Polly soothed. 'It's all right.'

She wanted a drink. Beer would do, though rum or bourbon would be better. She hadn't had one since early this morning and she was gasping.

Sonny said, 'I didn't, though, did I?'

'She'll work it out, you know. She's not stupid. So just shut the hell up about it.'

Sonny reached for another biscuit. 'Well, seeing as I didn't say anything in the first place ...'

'I mean it. Just keep your sticky bloody beak out of it. It's none of your business.'

Awhi returned holding a child-sized dress. 'I made this for her. For going out.'

'That's pretty,' Sonny said.

Polly felt her anger bubble up even further. Awhi was always doing this. 'Mum, I've *told* you, you don't need to make her stuff. I can afford to pay for nice things, from the shops.'

Awhi looked down at the little pink gingham dress, decorated with broderie anglaise. 'Nice things? What's wrong with this?'

'Nothing. But bought things are—'

'You'll spoil that child, Polly Manaia,' Awhi interrupted. 'She'll forget where she comes from.'

Good, Polly thought.

'Like you have,' Awhi added.

Sonny got to his feet. 'Got to go. Have to pick up Allie.'

'But you haven't finished your tea,' Awhi complained.

'Next time, eh?'

Polly could see he'd had a gutsful of the bickering. 'I'll bring Gina round soon for a visit, shall I?'

Sonny grinned at her. 'Yeah, that'd be good. Allie wanted to come today and see her, but, you know, her nan.'

'She all right, Mrs Murphy?' Awhi asked.

'Probably. Tough as old boots, that old girl.'

*

Sonny had dropped Allie off at her nan's house in Almorah Road, Newmarket, the roast dinner nestled carefully in a biscuit tin, because a plate just wasn't practical on a motorbike. Rose Murphy actually lived very near the flat Allie and Sonny rented in Crowhurst Street, but they'd not seen her for a week. She was fit and spritely for seventy-five, and was frequently out and about, playing bowls, visiting or doing her shopping, and Colleen went to see her at least once a week. If Allie had known she was under the weather she'd have been round there like a shot and now she felt guilty.

She went round the back of the little worker's cottage her nan had owned and lived in for decades and knocked on the door, calling out, 'It's only me, Nan, Allie!'

There was no answer but she went in anyway. The house felt different, damp and cold, and smelt musty and devoid of its usual homely scents of cooking and baking. Actually, it not only smelt musty, it smelt bad, especially in the kitchen. Mr De Valera, her nan's cat (named for Eamon De Valera, hero of the Irish Easter Uprising of 1916, whom Rose fervently admired), was nowhere to be seen and his bowl was empty.

'Nan! Where are you? It's me, Allie!'

'In here, dear.'

Allie wandered down the hallway, peering into rooms and frowning at a vase of drooping, shedding dahlias here and some unopened post there, till she reached the front room and stopped, shocked to see that her nan was still in bed. Rose had long ago hung a curtain over the alcove created by the small bay window and moved a single bed into the space to catch the warmth of the sun.

She was such a small woman, made even less substantial by age, that she barely made a lump under the covers. She sat propped against pillows, was wearing several cardigans, a scarf and a knitted hat, and was reading a library book from a pile on her nightstand.

'Hello, dear. I saw you come past the window,' Rose said.

Allie put down her tin. 'Why are you still in bed?'

Rose flapped her hand. 'Oh, my damn leg's giving me gyp.'

'Well, for God's sake, put the heater on. It's freezing in here! Here, I'll do it.' Allie bent to drag a one-bar heater out from beside the sofa.

'No, leave it, really, I'm fine,' Rose protested.

Trying to save your pennies as usual, Allie thought. 'Have you had your lunch yet?'

She sniffed the air, but not so her nan would notice. There was a bad smell in this room too.

'Oh, well ...'

'You haven't, have you? God, Nan, you'll starve to death. Well, lucky I brought you some roast from Mum's. It's mutton, carrots, leeks in white sauce, broccoli and potatoes. Will that do you?'

'Sounds lovely. I'll save some for my tea.'

'No, you'll have it now. I'll just put it the oven for a few minutes, shall I?'

'Right you are. Thank you, dear.'

Allie went back down the hall to the kitchen, decanted the roast into a Pyrex dish and slid it into the oven. The whiff at that end of the house, she discovered, was coming from the meat safe — a raw lamb shank definitely on the green side. Frowning, she wrapped it in newspaper and took it out to Rose's garden incinerator.

Back in the front room she said to Nan, 'Now, tell me what's wrong with your leg?'

'Oh, it's nothing. Just a twinge.'

'A *twinge*? I've never known you to take to your bed, Nan. *Ever*.'

Rose blew out a big breath, making an annoyed horse noise with her lips. 'I fell when I was bringing the washing in. On Wednesday, on the back steps. They were slippery. I just …' She scowled. 'Oh, it was just so *stupid*! And now I have this pain in my hip whenever I try to stand.'

'Have you been to the doctor?'

Raising a bony hand and twitching a gap in the lace curtains at the front window, Rose said, 'There goes that lad again, tearing along. He'll come a cropper off that bicycle one of these days.'

'Don't change the subject. Have you been to the doctor?'

A sigh. 'No.'

'Why not?'

'I never go to the doctor.'

Allie felt like snatching Rose's book off her and hitting her over the head with it. 'That's because you're never sick. But now you are. Did you tell Mum your leg hurts when you stand?'

'Not in so many words.'

'Why not?'

'She's got enough to worry about.'

'How long have you been in bed?'

Rose made a show of having to think. 'Perhaps Thursday morning?'

Allie was appalled. 'You've been in bed since you fell over?'

'Possibly.'

'But what about your meals?' A worse thought occurred. 'And the loo?'

'I haven't really felt hungry,' Rose replied. 'And there's the po. I've been putting it up on the bed.'

With much trepidation, Allie crouched and lifted the bedcover. There was indeed a potty under the bed — a full, extremely smelly one. She gingerly eased it out, careful not to spill the contents.

She didn't say anything, not wanting to embarrass her nan, and carried it warily outside to the toilet, emptied it, rinsed it in the washhouse tub, washed her hands, then put it back under the bed.

She'd smelt the roast dinner on the way past the kitchen so she transferred it to a plate on a tray and served it, careful where she placed it across Rose's skinny thighs.

'Oh, I don't think I can eat all that, love.'

'Well, do your best.'

'There're some pikelets in the cupboard if you're still peckish, and some of my raspberry jam.'

Allie hesitated. Rose Murphy was famous for her raspberry jam, but as her eyesight had deteriorated her ability to distinguish between raspberry seeds and ants had too, resulting in 'Nan's Ant Jam'. 'I'm right, thanks.'

They both looked up as muted galloping sounded along the hallway, then Mr De Valera burst into the sitting room, shot across the rug and launched himself at Rose, landing squarely on her lap. She squawked in pain and batted him off, though he still managed to snatch a piece of meat off the plate on his way to the floor.

Watching him tear into it, Allie said, 'He's starving.'

'I *know*,' Rose said crossly. 'But I couldn't get up, could I? I left the kitchen window open for him, though, and he's had a few mice.' She pointed at several stains on the rug. 'See where he's brought them in? Clever old Dev.'

Vaguely disgusted, Allie said, 'Eat your lunch, Nan, while I feed him. What do you normally give him?'

'Meat and a bit of fish, but I've nothing in for him. Here, give him some of this mutton. With gravy. He loves gravy.'

'No! That's for you. You're not giving it to the cat!'

Allie glared at her nan. Rose glared back.

'Allie, dear, that cat is my live-in companion. He's here with me when no one else is. He listens to my grizzles and groans, he gives me affection when I need it, he never judges me, and all he ever asks for is a feed twice a day. Do you understand what that means to me?'

Not really, Allie thought. She didn't much like cats, especially stroppy great tabbies like Mr De Valera.

'Now please get his bowl and put some mutton and gravy in it.'

Grumbling, Allie fetched the cat's bowl and served him his lunch, saying, 'Here you are, Your Majesty.'

'Sarcasm is the lowest form of wit, you know,' Rose remarked.

'I'm sure.'

Pushing the tray farther down her legs, Rose said, 'I've eaten all of this I can. Tell your mum it was lovely, thank you.'

Allie saw she'd managed a sliver of meat, half a carrot and half a potato. 'That's not going to keep you going.'

'I'd love a cup of tea.'

'Well, I'm not getting you one unless you show me your hip.'

'What for?' Rose yanked the bedcover up to her armpits. 'There's nothing to see.'

'Which leg is it? It's the left, isn't? Come on, show me.'

'Don't you be so damn bossy, girl.'

Allie whipped the tray off the bed and clattered it onto the floor. 'Nan! Why are you being so stubborn? I'm trying to help you!'

Rose's cheeks went pink and her eyes reddened behind her glasses, filling with tears. Then she got control of herself. 'All right. But please don't touch anything. It's just too sore.'

She folded back the bedclothes revealing veined white legs, a winceyette nightie and a sour waft of unwashed body and urine. Dismayed, Allie forced herself not to lean away. This wasn't her cherished nan: that Rose Murphy smelt like talcum powder and rose water, not pissed pants.

Carefully, slowly, Rose pulled the nightie up her leg, groaning as she lifted herself off the fabric beneath her. As she slid the garment higher a huge bruise appeared on her thigh, a bilious yellow colour then a pinky-red deepening to dark purple as it neared her hip, where it disappeared under her pants.

Allie felt sick. She'd seen worse, of course, in the fire, but this was her nan. 'What's it like under your pants? The bruise?'

'It's right across my belly.'

'I really think you should go to the hospital, Nan. I think you've broken something.'

'And how do you suggest I do that?' Rose snapped. 'Walk?'

Allie stared at her, realising Rose knew she was in trouble and that she was really quite frightened.

'Shall I call an ambulance?'

'None of my neighbours have telephones. You'll have to go all the way down to the other end of Broadway to find a telephone box. And I don't know if I can afford to pay for an ambulance.'

'They're free, aren't they? And it's only round the corner to the Mater, isn't it?'

'I don't know what they cost, and the Mater's private. I'd have to go to Auckland Public.'

'Well, what about a taxi? You could lie on the back seat, couldn't you?'

'Allison,' Rose barked, 'I can hardly flaming well move!'

They sat in awkward silence for a few moments. Allie didn't know what her nan was thinking, but she felt awful. So often the old lady had been a source of strength and comfort to her, and now Rose was the one needing help and all she could do was dither and make unhelpful suggestions. Her nan was old. What if she had a heart attack or a stroke from the effects of the broken hip? What if Rose died right now, in front of her, like the other people she'd loved but hadn't been able to save?

Then Rose said, 'I'm sorry, dear. I'm not helping, am I?'

And then Allie heard the most welcome sound she'd heard in ages — a motorcycle rumbling along the street. 'That's Sonny. He'll know what to do!'

Grimacing, Rose eased her position slightly and muttered, 'I'm damned if I'm going to the hospital on that contraption of his.'

Stifling a wild urge to giggle, Allie hurried down the hallway and met Sonny at the back door, rubber-legged with relief. 'You're back early, but thank God because Nan needs help.'

'Why? What's the matter?'

'I think she's broken her hip, or maybe her leg. It looks awful. I think she needs to go to the hospital.'

'Right-oh, I'll get the truck.'

'No, I don't think she can get in it. I'm not sure she can sit up properly, and she can't walk at all.'

'Not in it, *on* it. And we'll carry her out.'

Imagining everything that could go wrong — Nan getting dropped in the gutter, Nan rolling off the back of the truck, etc — Allie began, 'But—'

Sonny interrupted, 'No buts. You organise her things and some blankets and I'll get the truck. Go on.'

He pecked her on the cheek and was off around the side of the house. A few seconds later she heard his motorbike start and roar off down the street.

'He's gone to get the truck,' she said to Rose.

Rose looked worried. 'I doubt I could sit in a truck, Allie.'

'We'll work something out. What do you want to take to the hospital? You might be in there for a little while.'

By the time Sonny returned Allie had packed a small bag with Rose's necessities and fetched her beloved cloche hat, which Rose put on. She never went out without her cloche hat. Allie also collected several blankets off the beds in the spare rooms and folded them in readiness. Looking out the window she watched Sonny back the truck up to the garden gate. The house didn't have a driveway and was fenced, and that was as close as he could get.

'What's he doing?' Rose asked suspiciously.

'Not sure,' Allie said.

Sonny hopped out of the truck, disappeared for a moment, then they heard him clomping up the hallway.

'Hello, Mrs M. Had a bit of a fall?'

'It appears so, doesn't it?'

'Well, don't worry, we'll soon sort you out.'

'I don't think I could walk anywhere, dear, or sit in your truck,' Rose said.

Sonny shook his head. 'You won't have to. We'll carry you out.'

Rose looked horrified. 'Oh, I don't know about that. I think that might be rather painful.'

'Not if we put you on a stretcher.'

'Oh, what a shame. I think I might have given all my stretchers to St Michael's last jumble sale.'

Allie eyed Rose; she was getting snippy again. 'It's all right, Nan. Sonny was a soldier, remember? Korea? He knows about these things.'

Sonny said brightly, 'I'll have a quick look around, if that's all right. Everyone has something in the house they can use as a stretcher.'

'You won't find anything,' Rose warned.

He was back a minute later, carting a clanking great ironing board. 'See?'

Rose said, 'I haven't used that in years. It's too heavy and I can't get it to stay up.'

'A few blankets and you'll be snug as a bug on the back of the truck.'

'But how do we get her on it?' Allie asked.

'The truck?' Sonny said. 'Easy, lift and slide.'

'No, the ironing board.'

Sonny explained that it was a matter of raising one side of Rose, sliding the ironing board beneath her, then lifting her other side and pushing the board all the way under, which they managed to accomplish but with an unavoidable level of discomfort to her.

While Rose was catching her breath, she suddenly said, 'What about Dev? Who's going to feed him? He'll get lonely too, you know, here by himself.'

Lonely my backside, Allie thought. He'll have the fire going, the radio on and piles of dead mice all over the place.

'The cat?' Sonny said. 'Don't worry about him. He can stay at our place. I like cats.'

Allie glared at him.

'What?' he asked. 'He'll be OK.'

'Oh, thank you, Sonny,' Rose said. 'You're *such* a good lad. That's really taken a weight off my mind, that has. And you too, Allie.'

Allie's heart sank. She couldn't refuse to take the bloody animal now, could she?

'We'll come and pick him up tonight,' Sonny said, in what Allie thought was an unnecessarily jolly tone. 'But first let's get you to the hospital, eh?'

*

'On an ironing board?' Colleen stared at them, aghast. 'On the back of the *truck*?'

'But it was all right,' Allie said quickly. Her poor mother's face had gone completely white when they'd told her Rose was in hospital. 'I held onto the legs so it wouldn't slide around.'

'Mum's legs?'

'No, the legs of the ironing board.'

Colleen launched herself out of her chair. 'Where's my purse? Allie, get my coat. Sid, get yourself properly dressed. We're going up to the hospital.'

Allie glanced at Sonny: that meant they were driving her parents to the hospital, jammed into the truck. She glanced at her watch. 'I think visiting hours might be over soon, Mum. You might have to leave it till tomorrow.'

'Like hell. I have to work. I'm not waiting till tomorrow evening.'

'But the doctors said she's quite comfortable now,' Allie said. 'They gave her an injection and she did seem a lot happier after that, didn't she?' This to Sonny, who nodded.

'How can she be comfortable with a broken hip? No, we're going up,' Colleen insisted. 'You'll take us, won't you?'

'Course,' Sonny replied.

Allie stifled a sigh. Her nan would probably be asleep by now. But she knew what was wrong — her mother felt guilty. She'd visited Rose on Friday and not really noticed that much was amiss, but that had been her nan's fault, not her mother's.

So off they went, shoe-horned into the cab of the truck, arriving at Auckland Hospital forty minutes before visiting hours ended. By the time they found Rose's ward there were only fifteen minutes left.

She was dozy, and looked like a little wrinkled doll parked in the middle of her pristine white hospital bed, and was pleased to see her visitors.

Then Sid bent down to kiss the pale skin of her forehead and said, 'Get out of bed, you lazy old trout.'

Raising a hand to his cheek she replied in a voice slowed by morphine, 'I know, it's your job to lie around and do nothing, isn't it?' And they both had a good cackle.

'Have the doctors said anything else?' Colleen asked. 'Apart from the hip being broken?'

'I'm dehyderated,' Rose mispronounced, 'but I had one of those Murphy drips.'

'What's a Murphy drip when it's at home?' Sid said.

'Fluid up the back passage.'

Sid looked horrified: Allie nearly laughed.

'The doctor says my skin's too fragile so I can't have one of those needle under the skin things with the tube,' Rose explained. 'Plus I'll be needing an operation.'

'So you'll be in here a while?' Colleen asked.

'Could be, but that's all right because Dev's staying at Sonny and Allie's.'

Colleen said, 'For God's sake, Mum, I think there're more important things to think about than the flaming cat!'

'Such as?'

'Such as where you'll go when you get out.'

'Well, home.'

'No, you'll come to us,' Colleen insisted. 'And that's final.'

Both Rose and Sid looked dismayed.

A nurse approached, telling them that visiting hours were over. In a garbled rush, Rose explained to Allie and Sonny that Mr De Valera had to be fed twice a day, his meals consisting of fresh red meat five times a week, and fresh fish (scaled and deboned) twice a week. He drank water, not milk as it upset his bowels, and he enjoyed between-meal treats of cheese, buttered toast, and plain biscuits, though he probably wouldn't eat a whole one in a single sitting.

'Christ,' Sonny muttered, 'he eats better than we do.'

'Have you got him yet?' Rose asked anxiously.

'We're picking him up on the way home,' Sonny said, adding to Allie, 'Aren't we, love?'

'Certainly are,' she replied with as much enthusiasm as she could muster.

Which wasn't much at all.

Chapter Four

Allie arrived at work the next morning in quite a bad mood, mainly because during the night Mr De Valera had done an enormous shit in the bath. They'd decided not to let him outside for a couple of days so he wouldn't run off, and had made him a sandbox for a toilet, but clearly he'd decided not to use it. Sonny thought it was a great joke but she didn't. It stank and it was disgusting, so she'd made him clean it up. God knew what they'd find when they got home at the end of the day.

She put her things in her locker in the staffroom and sat down, her hands in her lap. Every day — every single day — when she walked into the Smith and Caughey building her heart raced, she broke into a sweat and she felt dizzy. But she'd discovered that if she sat for a minute or two and breathed deeply, she could calm herself and the panicky feeling would start to ebb. Then she straightened and smoothed her uniform and took her place in the Beauty Hall on the ground floor. At Dunbar and Jones she'd worked in Fashions, but Smith and Caughey had offered her a position in cosmetics so she'd taken it, though she'd started first on general toiletries, moved to Helena Rubinstein, and now she was on the Elizabeth Arden counter.

'Have a good weekend?' her friend and colleague Peggy asked.

Peggy was a hoot. She was pretty, clever, unnaturally blonde and applied her make-up with a trowel, but with so much skill she got away with it. They were there, she reckoned, to flog powder and rouge and mascara and lipstick, so why not demonstrate them?

'Not really,' Allie replied. 'My nan ended up in hospital with a broken hip.'

'God, really? Is she all right?'

'She's comfortable but she has to have surgery.'

'That's awful.'

'I know. And nearly as bad, we're stuck with her bloody cat till she's better again.'

'But you don't like cats.'

'I *hate* this one. It did the *biggest* poo in the bath last night. Stank the whole flat out.'

Peggy shrieked with laughter. 'Sounds like our dog. He's always shitting on our lawn. I wish he'd go and shit at the neighbour's.' She pushed a cardboard box across the counter. 'Here, you need cheering up more than me. It's the new lipsticks. You can unpack them.'

'Ooh, really?'

Allie found the scissors, slit the tape on the box and began extracting a series of smaller boxes, inside which were packed row after row of lipstick tubes, like golden bullets. She lined them all up on the counter in order of colour, then selected a tester, bent to a mirror and tried it on.

'Pure Red. Does it suit me? It doesn't, does it?'

'Not really,' Peggy said. 'It's not right for your skin tone.' She wound open a few more testers, her mouth pursed in thought, then handed one to Allie. 'Wipe that off and try this. Pink Violet.'

Allie did as she was told.

'That's better,' Peggy said. 'It's much softer.'

Allie agreed — it was. She'd discovered fairly quickly that selecting the right cosmetics for a woman's complexion wasn't that different from helping them choose the most flattering colour of clothing, and she'd been very good at that. Of course, they didn't all listen, but if the occasional woman wanted to go around looking like a clown, that wasn't her look-out.

She'd just finished building a counter display of some of the new lipsticks using a Perspex stand and a square of gold satin when she smelt smoke. Her heart thumped wildly as she scrambled to establish whether it was just someone's cigarette or something far, far worse.

She relaxed shakily as a woman approached the counter, her cigarette in its long black holder wafting a plume of smoke. She wore a beautifully tailored two-piece suit in dark blue wool with a black fur collar, black gloves, a black sculpted half hat in felted wool with a tiny net veil, and black suede heels. Her face was expertly made up and, beneath the cigarette smoke, Allie caught a whiff of some exotic floral scent she didn't recognise.

'Good morning, madam. May I help you?'

The woman smiled, revealing even, white teeth. 'I expect so. Which one of you is Allie?'

'That's me,' Allie said.

'Oh, good. You were recommended to me by my nanny, Evelyn Palmer. She says she knows someone who says you're very good with cosmetics.'

'Really?' Allie wondered who that could be.

'Yes. I need face cream and also face powder, please. I seem to have run out.'

The woman's accent was posh New Zealand, overlaid with something else.

'Do you usually use Elizabeth Arden?' Allie asked.

'Actually, no. I prefer Payot for skin care.'

Allie had never heard of it. 'I'm afraid we don't carry Payot.'

'I didn't think you would,' the woman said. 'It's a French brand. I used to buy it at Harrods when we lived in London.'

'I think you'll find Elizabeth Arden is also very good. Our customers seem very happy with the results and we do sell quite a lot of it.' Before the woman wriggled off the hook, Allie forged ahead. 'We have Elizabeth Arden's full Ardena range, including the Cleansing Cream, Skin Tonic, Velva Cream, Orange Face Cream, Eye Lotion, Hand Lotion, the Featherlight Foundation Cream, and, of course, the Eight Hour Cream. And some of those come in sets, which is handy.'

The woman took a long drag on her cigarette, causing the ash to droop then fall to the floor. 'They're not always full-sized in the sets, the bottles and jars, are they?'

'Well,' Allie began.

'I'll take three of everything,' the woman interrupted. 'Of the full sizes.'

Allie stared at her. 'Pardon?' She was aware Peggy had been having a good eavesdrop farther along the counter, and was now openly listening in.

'I'll take three of everything, thank you.'

'Oh. Well, yes, of course.' Christ almighty, that would cost her a *fortune*.

'Now, face powder,' the woman said. 'Nothing too cakey.' She laughed brightly. 'I don't want to look even older than I do already!'

Allie thought she didn't look very old at all, probably somewhere in her early thirties, but changed the subject as she reached for their lightest powders. 'Have you been home from London very long?'

'Oh, London. No, just a couple of months, though I miss it dreadfully already. We lived there for some years. My husband's English, ex-RAF. He's a senior pilot for NAC now.'

From the corner of her eye Allie saw Peggy mouth, 'Well, lah di dah', but smiled at her customer.

'Could I show you the Ardena Invisible Veil?'

'Lovely. I quite like the floral box. Very pretty.' The woman looked around and stubbed out her cigarette in an ashtray stand then permitted Allie to dust some of the powder onto her hand. 'Yes, that's acceptable. I'll take three of those as well, thank you.'

Peggy said, 'I'll package everything while you're writing the docket, if you like.'

Allie nodded her thanks and asked the woman, 'May I please have your name?'

'Mrs Kathleen Lawson. That's Kathleen with a K.' Mrs Lawson offered a hand. 'Thank you, Allison, you've been very helpful. It is Allison, isn't it, your proper name?'

Feeling rather uncomfortable Allie shook the proffered hand, then went back to her docket. 'Er, yes. May I have your address, please?'

'Three Eastbourne Road, Remuera. Such a nice part of town and with lovely views.'

'I'm sure,' Allie said. From her flat they had a stunning view of the neighbour's clothesline and some sheds on the property behind them.

As she wrote Mrs Lawson's purchases on the docket, Peggy packed them into a smart Smith and Caughey shopping bag, then Allie discreetly advised Mrs Lawson of the total cost.

'Not as bad as I thought!' she said with a laugh, and handed over a wad of notes.

Allie folded the money and the docket into a capsule, inserted it into the Lamson tube and fired it off to Miss Cato at the cash desk. While they waited for the change to come back, Mrs Lawson chattered on.

'Are you married, Allison?'

'Yes, I am.'

'No children, I gather?'

Allie shook her head, thinking that was a bit of a nosy question. Actually, they both were.

'Good. I don't approve of mothers who work. Except for charity work, of course.' She turned to Peggy. 'And you, er ...?'

'Peggy Mitchell, ma'am. No, I'm not married. Haven't met the right man yet.'

'Oh, I'm sure someone will come along. I have three children myself, two boys and a girl, ages nine, seven and five.'

She paused, and Allie thought she might be expecting either her or Peggy to say something, but Allie had no idea what might be expected, so she kept quiet.

'Of course, being a mother is a full-time job in itself, isn't it? We had a nanny in England and she was worth her weight in gold. My husband insisted I hire another nanny here— Evelyn, of course — and I really don't know what I'd do without her. He's away quite a lot flying, you see, my husband. Not on long trips, usually just overnight, but it's wonderful to have someone to help get the children off to school in the mornings and what have you. We were considering boarding school, but, really, there are some very good schools in Remuera. She cooks too, the nanny. She's marvellous.'

Allie, who knew Peg took a dim view of people who skited, dared not catch her eye. At last the change came whistling down the Lamson and she counted it out.

'Thank you very much for shopping at Smith and Caughey, Mrs Lawson. I hope you enjoy your purchases.'

'I'm sure I will. Thank you for your help, girls!'

And off she went.

As soon as she was out of earshot, Peggy said, 'What was all that in aid of, telling us about her home in fancy Remuera and the nanny and all the rest of it? Posh cow.'

'I don't know. Do you think her teeth were real?'

Peg shrugged. 'I'm thinking of having all mine out. They keep giving me gyp.'

'Nice clothes, though. And beautiful accessories.'

'Just because you worked in Fashion.'

'I can't help having a good eye.'

Peg got out the inventory book and wrote down the sales Allie had made. 'I think she might have taken a shine to you. What's the bet she'll be back?'

'Well, it won't be for ages, the amount of stuff she bought.'

'*And* you were impressed,' Peggy added slyly. 'Go on, admit it.'

'I was not!' Allie protested, feeling herself going red.

Peggy laughed. 'Yes, you were. You can't fool me, Allie Manaia.'

'Oh … shut up!'

*

Rose had her surgery two days after she was admitted to hospital. Colleen took a very rare day off work and, with Sid, caught the bus to spend the day with her. While Rose was coming round from the anaesthetic, her surgeon explained to Colleen that the break had been complicated as it had involved a significant femoral neck fracture including tearing of the blood vessels, on top of osteoporosis, which meant they'd only been able to 'patch' the break, not mend it completely.

'I see,' Colleen said.

Sid said, 'I don't. What does that actually mean?'

'I'm afraid it means she won't be very mobile any more,' the surgeon replied. 'And no longer independent.'

'Oh God,' Sid groaned.

'Well, can she have a wheelchair?' Colleen asked.

'We can arrange that.'

Sid said, 'I'm not putting her on the bog.'

Colleen turned on him. 'Will you shut up! No one's asked you to!'

'Fracturing a hip at your mother's age also means there's a greater risk of her dying earlier than she might have,' the surgeon went on. 'Complications can arise, such as a pulmonary embolism, or an infection, or heart failure. You need to bear that in mind.'

'How much earlier?' Colleen asked.

'Well, sometimes it makes no difference, sometimes it's a year, and sometimes …' The surgeon spread his hands, palms up. 'We just can't make a judgment. It depends on the patient.'

Colleen said, 'So now she's living with a death sentence?'

'We're all living with a death sentence, Mrs Roberts.'

'That's bloody cheery, isn't it?' Sid remarked.

'I'm sorry I can't give you better news,' the surgeon said.

'Have you told all this to Mum?' Colleen asked.

'She wasn't sufficiently awake when she came out of surgery. I thought I'd leave that to you, as her family.'

'Thanks very much,' Sid said.

'I'll see her on my rounds in the morning, and answer any questions she has then.'

Colleen and Sid were sitting with Rose when Allie and Sonny arrived after work. Rose was awake, but exhausted and still faintly groggy.

Allie gave her a kiss. 'How are you feeling, Nan?'

'As though I've been run over by a bus. But the doctor said he fixed everything all right.'

'Did he?' Allie pulled up a chair. It made a terrible scraping sound on the linoleum and she winced.

'He had a good talk to you, didn't he?' Rose said to Colleen.

Allie looked at her mother expectantly.

Colleen got that expression on her face that Allie knew meant she wasn't telling the whole truth. 'Yes, he said the operation went very well and Mum should be back on her feet in no time.' Her father, Allie noticed, was staring hard at his hands.

'Well, that's good news, isn't it? You must be pleased, Nan.'

'You bet I am. The food in here's atrocious.'

'That reminds me.' Allie opened her bag. 'Here. Cadbury Milk Tray. I know they're your favourite.'

'Ooh, you do spoil me, love.'

Allie checked her watch. 'What time do you get your tea? I hope they don't kick us out while you have it.'

'Been and gone,' Rose said. 'They bring it round at a quarter to five. Far too early.'

'Then who's that?' Sonny asked, nodding at a woman slowly making her way down the ward with a trolley.

'Tea lady.'

Sid rubbed his hands together. 'Good, I could do with a decent cuppa.'

'Well, you won't get one in here,' Rose grumbled.

*

In the ward directly on the floor below, Kura Apanui poured the last cup of tea from her enormous enamel pot for the patient in the bed nearest the door.

'Milk and—' the man began.

'Two sugars, I know. And a couple of super wines, Mr Stewart? We're out of gingernuts.'

'Yes, please. Can't eat gingernuts anyway. My teeth, you know.'

'Oooh, I know, they're hard, eh? But you can always dunk them.'

'That's true,' Mr Stewart said, wriggling up the bed into a sitting position.

Kura set the cup of tea on his nightstand. 'There you go. Mind it's not too hot.'

'Thank you.'

'See you tomorrow.'

Her teapot empty now, Kura wheeled the rattling trolley into the service lift, pushed B for Basement, then eased off a shoe and wriggled her aching toes as the lift descended. Then she followed a warren of corridors to the hospital's enormous and busy main kitchen, where she unloaded stacks of dirty cups and saucers from the trolley into an outsized sink. Not her job to wash them, fortunately — some other lucky person would be doing them today.

'You nearly done?' her cousin and best friend Wikitoria Irwin asked. She was standing there with her hat on and her handbag, looking grumpy. 'Come on, you should've clocked off.'

'I got held up.'

'Well, hurry up. We'll miss the bus.'

'Wait on, I'll only be a second.'

Wiki could be bossy and bad-tempered sometimes, Kura knew, but she was loyal and had a huge heart, and she loved her.

'Give me your locker key,' Wiki said. 'I'll get your bag and things.'

By the time she came back Kura had finished unloading the dishes and put on her hat. She clocked off and they hurried out of the hospital towards the bus stop just outside the main gates.

'Bugger,' Kura said as the bus they hoped to catch started to pull away.

'Well, I'm not waiting for the next one,' Wiki declared and ran after it, banging with all her might on its shiny painted side.

Embarrassed by all the faces peering out the bus's windows and too shamed to join in, Kura nevertheless couldn't help laughing, and the driver must have heard because he slowed to a stop and the door opened again.

'Come on, get on!' Wiki called.

Kura did, following her cousin up the steps, her face a blaze of heat. They got some dirty looks too when they moved down the aisle looking for seats. No one shifted over for them and she didn't manage to sit down till Queen Street, where a lot of people got off. She cared because it was insulting and because her feet hurt, but she didn't let it upset her, not these days.

They stayed on the bus as it went up Wellesley Street then up College Hill to Ponsonby, where they got off opposite Hargreaves Street and walked the last few hundred yards.

'You coming over for tea?' Wiki asked.

'You got enough?'

'Plenty. We've still got some of that pork. If we don't eat it tonight it's just going to go off. You got any bread?'

'Did some rewana last night. I'll bring that.'

'Lovely. See you soon.'

They lived on opposite sides of the same short street, so Kura wouldn't have far to herd her husband Joshua and seven children. There was an eighth child, her youngest, Alice, who was eight years old, but she and Joshua had left her with her grandparents at Maungakakari because she needed extra care. The family missed her desperately. She was a mongol child, and when she'd been born Kura had had trouble, though she'd popped the other seven out at home as easy as pie. She'd had to go to the hospital with Alice and the doctor had told her she shouldn't have any more babies because Alice was a retard, and had tied her tubes, and that was the end of that even though Kura had only been thirty-three at the time.

Wiki herself had her husband Henare and five kids, which had put an end to any ideas they'd had about sharing accommodation when they'd all come to Auckland to seek their fortunes. They'd heard that Auckland was full of big old houses for rent, but when they'd got here they'd discovered they weren't for rent to the likes of them. The advertisements in the papers often said straight out, *No Dogs, No Maoris*, and if they didn't say that, when they turned up at a house they were told time and again the place had just been let. So they'd had to settle for two houses in the same street, and they were dumps, nowhere near as nice as the whares they'd lived in back home.

Kura's rented house had three bedrooms and a front room, a kitchen tacked onto the back, but no bathroom. There was an outhouse with no light that stank so badly you couldn't take a breath in it, and a laundry in a shed out the back with no water supply. There was no running hot water in the house though there was electricity; there were holes in the floor, which was on a lean; the walls were bare scrim in places and had the paper hanging off in others; and some of the windows had been boarded over. The four boys shared one bedroom, the girls shared another and she and Joshua the third, which barely had space for their bed. The house was infested with cockroaches no matter how carefully Kura cleaned the kitchen, and rats lived under the floorboards. But at least the rent was cheap. Wiki's house wasn't any better, and only had two bedrooms so her kids — three girls and two boys — were jammed into one so she and Henare could have the other.

But they were making money, more than they had back home. In Hawke's Bay there was good money to be made during the shearing season, but that didn't last long and apart from that there was only labouring for the men, which didn't pay well, and not much at all for the women. So if you wanted to get on you had to leave. Plenty of young people and families were moving to the cities these days, where the jobs were. The world was changing too, and the old ways didn't seem to work so well any more, and that's another reason they'd come — to give their kids a better chance at fitting in with the Pakeha way of life.

Wiki and Henare had given their kids Pakeha first names and Maori middle names, so they'd sound like they were Pakeha — which Kura thought was silly because all the Irwin kids were a beautiful shade of Cadbury's Dairy Milk. But Joshua had put his size twelve foot down and insisted on giving their own kids Maori names first followed by Pakeha names, though, Huriana, his mother, had stubbornly insisted on calling them all by their Pakeha names — 'To help them get on,' she reckoned — and they'd stuck. But they were still brown and had Apanui for a surname, so what was the point of that?

They were what they were, Kura thought, and that was good enough, but that didn't mean they couldn't live like Pakeha if they wanted to. And there were plenty of Pakeha in Ponsonby, and even some Islanders. There were labouring and service jobs and work in the factories but, like her family and Wiki's, folk in her area seemed to be stuck at the bottom of the pile. Things just cost more in the city. On the other hand there were more opportunities, especially for the kids. Joshua worked, Henare worked, her three eldest — Johnny, seventeen, Patricia, sixteen, and Mary, fifteen — were working, and Wiki's eldest, Rena, fifteen, was working. So in her house there were five wages coming in, but nine mouths to feed and nine bodies to clothe. Wiki, Kura thought, was probably worse off because Henare, as a labourer, didn't earn as much as Joshua did on the railways, so she gave her food and a bit of money whenever she could. But then Wiki would turn around and give it back some other way, which defeated the purpose, but you couldn't stop her without offending her and sending her into a shitty liver. Kura knew her own budget didn't have any leeway but the Irwins were family, and that's what you did for family.

Joshua's mother, Huriana, and Wiki's father, Haimona, were brother and sister. *Their* parents had been Kepa Te Roroa and his wife, Parehuia. That made Kura and Wiki cousins, Kura by marriage, and their children second cousins, which was close enough to consider themselves first cousins. So now there was a little outpost of the Maungakakari hapu taking over Ponsonby, a thought that always made Kura smile. And they'd heard recently through the grapevine that another branch of the family had lately moved to Auckland — Ana Leonard and her husband and kids.

Ana's father was Joseph Deane, Kepa Te Roroa's illegitimate son to Tamar Deane, so that made Ana a first half-cousin. But no one cared about the halfness and to everyone she was a full cousin. Ana had married David, a sheep farmer, and it had been his family's sheep the Apanuis and Irwins had shorn every season for years, among others. But apparently the Leonards didn't have the farm any more — no one seemed to know why not — and were living in Auckland now. Kura had been meaning to find out where exactly Ana was and pay her a visit, but hadn't got around to it yet. But she would — it was important to keep up with family.

Kura entered the front door of her house, which opened no more than two feet from the footpath. All the houses round here were like that — no grass out the front, no garden, nowhere for the kids to play except on the street. There was a broken old path leading round to the back of the house but it was covered in dirt and slime and they were all sick of falling over on it, so now they went through the house instead of round it. She toed off her shoes and added them to the tidy, but very long, row of footwear already in the hall. That was the rule — no shoes on in the house, but they couldn't leave them outside in the porch in case someone pinched them.

The only member of her family not home was Sam, her nine-year-old. According to Joshua he was out somewhere playing with Eddie, Wiki's nine-year-old and her youngest. They were as thick as thieves, those two. Sam was a bright, happy boy, and slow to anger, but when he did, boy, did he do a haka. Kura wasn't too worried, though — there was time for him to grow out of it.

'Go and find them, will you?' she said to Johnny. 'We're going over to Auntie's for tea.'

'I'm going out.'

'No you're not. You're getting Sam and Eddie then you're coming to Auntie's with us. Plenty of time to go out after.'

'Ah Jeez, Mum!'

'Ah Jeez yourself. And don't take the Lord's name in vain. Go on, off you go.'

Johnny slouched out, probably thinking he looked like that Marlon Brando from the pictures with his hair slicked back, his collar turned up and his peaked cap on.

Kura took off her work uniform, put it on a hanger and sat on her bed in her petticoat, massaging her aching feet. She *did* worry about Johnny. He was a good boy and always had been, and his boss at the Destructor said he was a good, hard worker, but Johnny hated the job. Kura didn't blame him. The Destructor was the incinerator that burnt the rubbish for all of Auckland city, casting a massive pall of smoke over Ponsonby, Freeman's and St Mary's bays, and Johnny complained it made him stink, which it did, but he got paid reasonably well for burning everyone else's crap and Kura thought he should stick with it. But Johnny had ambitions and wanted to move on — he just hadn't decided what to, yet. And Kura feared he was running around with the wrong crowd. He desperately wanted a motorbike, though there was no chance of him ever affording one, and now he'd bought one of those portable record players and was listening to that new wild music, that greasy American boy mumbling his song 'That's All Right, Mama' or some such. Worse, Wiki reckoned you couldn't buy those records from the USA in New Zealand and Johnny was probably getting them off sailors down at the docks, so what was he doing hanging around down there? What was so wrong with Ruru Karaitiana singing 'Blue Smoke' anyway? Or Bill Sevesi, or Billy Wolfgramm and His Islanders — they were good. And when Johnny had told her the record player hadn't cost much she hadn't believed him, and had spent nearly an hour looking through his things (when he was out) and had discovered a hire-purchase docket. Forty-three pounds and ten shillings! How many times had they told their kids never to buy anything on tick, that HP was a fool's game and that if they wanted something they had to save up and buy it? God, she'd been ropeable. And on top of that they'd had to listen to Elvis bloody Presley day in and day out ever since

And as well there were the outlandish clothes, the silly cap and turned up collars and the denim trousers. The other week he'd come home from town with a pair of boots so clompy she wondered how he could walk in them. She'd told him he looked like a train driver from the 1920s, but he only ever smiled, kissed her cheek and told her he loved her too!

But it wasn't all hopeless. He went to the Maori Community Centre two or three times a week, to the dances and some of the Maori cultural events, and that made her feel better. They were run by decent people, folk from other marae who knew what was what. They'd keep his feet on the ground.

Sam flitted past the bedroom door.

'Come here, boy!' Kura called.

He slunk back.

'Where have you been?'

'Nowhere.'

'Look at your feet! Go and give them a wash. With soap!'

Finally everyone was organised and they arrived at Wiki's. She had a huge pot bubbling away on the stove.

'Boil-up?' Kura asked as she placed four large rewana loaves wrapped in tea towels on the little kitchen table, which was far too small for a family of seven.

'Cabbage, though,' Wiki apologised.

It was a common problem — there wasn't a lot of puha or pikopiko to be found in the middle of Auckland. Not these days.

Kura shrugged. Cabbage was still a green vegetable. Close enough.

'And there's some steamed pudding and cake for after.'

'Sure you can spare it?'

"Course,' Wiki replied, then turned and vomited into the sink.

Kura said, 'Shit!' and rushed to her side.

Wiki threw up again, spat and leant on her arms, head down. Kura ran the tap into the sink to clear it, squirted in some dishwashing liquid, gave it a good wipe down, then handed Wiki a cup of water. Then she stood gently patting her back, waiting.

Wiki's daughters Rena and Vicki came into the kitchen and Kura shooed them out.

Finally Wiki said, 'I think I'm hapu again.'

Kura didn't congratulate her because she knew Wiki didn't particularly want any more kids. 'Oh, well.'

'I thought I was past it.'

'You're only forty.'

'But nothing's happened for years.'

'Haven't you been using anything?'

Wiki gestured towards the doorway with her head. 'He wouldn't and, well, I couldn't be bothered sometimes. You know how it is.'

Kura said, 'Mmm,' though she didn't. She'd never worried about it and after Alice she didn't have to.

'There'll be such a big gap,' Wiki said.

For a moment Kura was confused. 'Where?'

'Between this one and Eddie. Nearly ten years. And I won't be able to work. I'll be showing soon.'

'How far along are you?'

'Over three months.'

She was right, Kura thought, she would be showing soon. Unlike herself Wiki was a small woman — only five feet two and the size of two Topsy sticks tied together with cotton. 'Why didn't you say something?'

'I don't know.'

'Have you told Henare?'

'Not yet. I don't know if I want this one, Kura. We can't afford it.'

Kura gave her a squeeze. 'You can, you wait and see. Anyway, us Maungakakari women never get rid of our babies. We keep them and we do our best for them.'

'I know. It's just that …' Wiki got her hanky out of her sleeve, dabbed at her eyes then blew her nose. 'I know.'

'All right, then?'

Wiki nodded. 'It'll be all right.'

*

When Allie and Sonny got home that night, Allie opened the back door with considerable trepidation, sniffing theatrically. Sonny laughed.

'*You* go in first, then.'

'Don't be a twit,' Sonny said and gave her a gentle shove.

She stepped into the kitchen. No smell of cat shit, but she did see Mr De Valera sitting in the middle of their little two-person dining table, staring back at her.

'Look at him!' she exclaimed. 'He's got his bum all over the tablecloth!'

'Well, get him off it.'

Allie grabbed the cat round his plump middle, which made him immediately roll over. Out came his claws, so that when Allie picked him up the tablecloth came with him. What a little bastard. Over went the salt and pepper shakers, the sugar bowl and the sauce bottle.

'It's not *funny*. Come and unhook him.'

Grinning hugely, Sonny disconnected Dev and smoothed the cloth back over the table.

Dumping the cat on the floor, Allie said, 'Don't bother, that'll have to be washed now. I'm not eating off where his bum's been.'

Sonny picked up Dev, who gave him a smoochy cuddle and rubbed his furry face against Sonny's neck. 'I think he can tell you don't like him.'

'Good.'

'But if you tried it might make things a bit easier. He might be here for a while.'

'No he won't. Nan'll be home soon. Mum said so.'

'Did she?'

Allie filled the kettle with water and put it on the stove. 'Well, you heard what she said. Nan'll be back on her feet in no time.'

'I know that's what she *said*. But, Allie ...'

He had his serious face on now, and she didn't want to hear what he was going to say. She moved the upended condiments from the kitchen table and carried the sugar-scattered tablecloth to the back door.

'Allie, sit down for a minute.'

'I'll just shake this out.'

'No, sit down.'

She sighed, and did, the tablecloth in a ball in her lap.

He said, 'I know your mother said your nan will be better soon, but old people often don't get better after a bad fall. Sometimes they stay bedridden, and sometimes it's just too much for them and, well, they die.'

The ember of dread and fear that smouldered constantly in Allie's belly flared into painful brightness. 'How do you know?'

'Because I've seen it, with our kaumatua.'

'But why would Mum say she's going to be all right if she isn't?'

'Well, no one really knows right now, do they? And because I'm sure she doesn't want it to happen.'

Allie said, 'But just because some old people die after a fall doesn't mean Nan will.'

'No, I know.' Sonny took her hand. 'I'm just saying this … just in case. And because, well, you know, I love you.'

Allie burst into tears.

Chapter Five

November 1955

Ana Leonard stared out the kitchen window at her back lawn as she washed the breakfast dishes. The kids had left for school, Jack was in his room pottering about, and David had gone for another week, though they'd all had a nice weekend together.

She hated living in Auckland. She missed the farm, she missed her parents and other family, she missed the horses, the dogs, the sheep, the hills, the weather, the glorious solitude — she missed everything. She particularly missed hopping on her horse whenever she felt like it and riding miles out over the hills by herself, the wind in her hair, just thinking her thoughts. She couldn't do anything by herself in town and the only time she got the wind in her hair was when she walked down the hill to the butcher's, which wasn't the same at all.

She really should make an effort to get in touch with some of her relatives. Her cousins on her grandfather's side, Wiki Irwin and Kura Apanui and their families, whom she knew well, lived in Auckland now. It would be wonderful to see them — if only she could leave Jack. She'd also heard from her mother that her cousin Kathleen on her grandmother's side had lately moved back to New Zealand from England with her family and was also living somewhere in Auckland, though she wasn't in such a rush to visit her. Kathleen seemed to think she was a cut above everyone else, and had never been too keen on mixing with the 'native' side of the family, which suited everyone, actually. Oh, she'd probably call on Kathleen one day, for the sake of propriety, but she'd much rather spend time with Kura and Wiki, and so would her kids.

They hadn't liked it here to start with, either, and had missed their horses and dogs dreadfully, but she suspected they were beginning to enjoy making new friends at school and in the neighbourhood, which was nice for them. Peter had joined the local branch of Cubs and was loving that, marching about in his uniform and going on campfire outings and what have you, and David had built a hutch on the back lawn so Rowie could keep rabbits, which she tended adoringly and frequently bandaged in order to practise her nursing skills. Ana had never seen such tolerant, and indeed stoical, rabbits in her life. Jo, though, had discovered the school library and spent hours reading when not outside tearing about. Perhaps she was destined to become the family intellectual, and not a rouser in a shearing gang after all. David wasn't too keen on his new job and was still quietly bitter about losing the farm — though he seemed to have forgiven his father — but the wool inspector's position paid well, and at least he got to spend time out on different farms. As for Jack, he didn't know where he was half the time now. She couldn't even leave him alone to pop down to the shops and had to drag him along with her, which was often more trouble than it was worth, so now she usually did her shopping after the kids got home from school and they could watch him, which she realised wasn't ideal.

She wondered how long they could keep going like this. She wondered, in fact, how long *she* could keep going. She felt trapped, with nothing to look forward to and nothing to look at, except a couple of tatty feijoa trees and a gone-to-seed veggie garden no one had had time to dig over and replant.

Feeling tears coming she sat at the table and dabbed at her eyes with a tea towel. It smelt of sick and needed a good boil and she hurled it across the kitchen in frustrated despair.

'Is this a bad time?' someone asked.

It was Colleen Roberts at the back door.

Wiping quickly at her face with the back of her hand, Ana said, 'Oh, no, you're right. Please, come in.'

They'd chatted over the fence and progressed to calling each other by their first names, but Colleen had been very busy lately and Ana hadn't seen much of her.

Colleen set two jars on the table. 'Lemon curd and strawberry jam, made from our garden. Thought you might like some. Oh, look at the size of your fridge! I've got one too, but not that big.'

'Lovely, thank you very much. Yes, we had it on the farm. We lived such a long way out it was essential, really. No work today?'

'I'm not on till twelve. It's a part-time job, but a lot of days it might as well be full time.'

'I'll put the kettle on,' Ana said. 'How's your mum?'

'Still in hospital. Six weeks now, it's been. She had an X-ray the other day and they say the bones aren't mending yet.'

'I'm sorry to hear that.'

'Thank you. Still, it's early days,' Colleen said.

Ana didn't think six weeks was early days for bones to mend, especially when you were old and running out of days, but said nothing.

'And how's your father-in-law?' Colleen asked.

'Oh, you know. Jack's just being Jack.'

'Yes, er, Sid saw him the other day. Out by the clothesline.'

Ana winced. 'That day he went out in the nude?'

Colleen nodded.

'I'm *so* sorry. I was hoping no one saw.'

'Well, I don't mean to be unkind,' Colleen said, 'I really don't, but Sid said it was the funniest thing, you running round after him and him ducking and diving.'

'Yes, the kids thought it was hilarious too.'

'It must be so difficult, having to keep an eye on him all the time. Like having an extra child, I should imagine.'

'He is like a toddler, but in a grown-up body.' Ana was very tempted to tell Colleen how aggressive Jack could also be at times, but couldn't quite bring herself to share that. Jack being a clown because he was mentally unwell was almost acceptable, but his rage and nastiness wasn't. To her it felt shameful, a secret that should be kept. She poured hot water into the teapot.

'It's tricky, isn't it?' Colleen went on. 'There comes a point when your parent stops being a parent and becomes a child again.'

'I suppose you're right. Though I expect that doesn't happen with everyone's parents.' Ana couldn't imagine her mother and father ever reverting to childhood. 'How old's your mum?'

'Seventy-five.'

'Oh, right.'

'I hope you don't mind me asking, but have you given any thought to what will happen if your father-in-law —'

'Oh, look, you've seen him in his underpants and your Sid's seen him in even less. You might as well just call him Jack. He won't care and I certainly don't. You take sugar, don't you?'

'Yes thanks. Have you thought about what you'll do if Jack gets worse?' Colleen asked.

Ana put cups and saucers, milk, sugar and the teapot on the table. 'I'll let you pour when you're ready. I like my tea really strong so I'll wait. We haven't really, no. David won't even take him to a doctor. He dreads the idea of him being put in a mental hospital.'

'But they can't *make* you do that, can they?'

'I really don't know. I wouldn't think so. I'd say only we could do that.'

'Does he know there's something wrong?'

Ana glanced towards the hallway, and sighed. 'Before we moved up here I would have said yes, but now I don't think so. I think we've just about lost the old Jack.'

'That's very sad.' Colleen reached across the table and touched Ana's arm. 'I feel for you, I really do.'

'Thank you. I appreciate that.'

Colleen sighed. 'And while we're being honest, my mother isn't doing too well.'

'Oh, I am sorry, Colleen. That *is* bad news. But I'm sure your—'

'Rose. Her name is Rose Murphy.'

'I'm sure Rose is getting the best care possible.'

'So am I.'

Ana poured her own tea and they drank in companionable silence.

Then Colleen asked, 'Have you made many friends here yet?'

'Not really. It's hard to get out with Jack. I imagine I will eventually.' Ana hoped she sounded more convincing than she felt.

'You're lonely, aren't you?' Colleen said.

'The kids are good company.'

Colleen said, 'Mine aren't, pair of madams. Oh, Donna's not so bad these days, I suppose, and she'll be moving into the nurses' home in January anyway. But Pauline's a proper little witch. I really worry about her. She's only sixteen and she's sneaking out at night and running round with all sorts of lads, thinking she's one of these Wodgie girls.'

'I think it's Widgie.'

'Eh?'

'Widgie. Bodgies and Widgies.'

Colleen nodded. 'Them on the motorcycles.'

'Does she work?'

'In the tearoom at Smith and Caughey, but she's got this grand idea of being a stewardess for TEAL. The airline?'

'There's nothing wrong with having an ambition.'

'Except you have to be twenty-one before you can do that, and that's nearly five years away. She'll have changed her mind by then and want to fly rockets to Mars, but she won't be able to because she left school at fifteen. She hated school. She'll end up like me, still slogging away in a tearoom at the age of forty-eight, with kids and a husband who doesn't work.'

'He puts a lot of time into your garden, your Sid,' Ana said.

'I see him out my kitchen window, digging and planting away. Must save you a lot of money, that garden.'

'Oh, that's right, I meant to say, come and help yourself, any time.'

Ana felt her face redden. 'Oh, I wasn't hinting!'

'No, I know, but Sid gives half of it away anyway, so you might as well take your pick. I didn't want to suggest it before, in case your husband was insulted, but, well, I know you a bit better now.'

'David wouldn't mind.' Actually, he might, Ana thought. He didn't like the idea of receiving charity, but she doubted he'd even notice, he was so seldom home. And it wasn't charity; it was just the Robertses being neighbourly.

'Well, come and grab a few veg now. Might save you going down the shops.'

'Thank you very much, Colleen. I'll just tell Jack I'm popping out.'

He was still in his room, walking round and round in a circle, following the outline of a floor rug.

'You'll get dizzy doing that,' Ana warned. 'I'm just going outside for a few minutes, all right? Stay in here, please. Don't go out the front door, and don't go in the kitchen. I'll only be a few minutes. Jack? Did you hear me?'

'Yes, yes, yes,' Jack replied, still going round and round.

'What did I just say?'

'Stay here, no front door, no kitchen.'

'Good. I'll only be a few minutes, all right?'

No response. Ana watched him a moment longer, then shut the door on him.

She grabbed a shopping bag (not her biggest, as she didn't want to appear greedy), and met Colleen by the tall wooden fence separating their properties. At some point several slats had broken away, and Collen squeezed through to her side.

'We were going to fix this,' she said over her shoulder, 'but I don't think we'll bother now. Saves going all the way up to the street when we want to visit.'

That gave Ana a nice, warm, neighbourly feeling and she happily ducked through after Colleen. The Robertses' vegetable garden was indeed magnificent, better even than the plot she'd grown herself at the farm. The soil here must be really rich. Of course, a green thumb helped and clearly Sid had two of those, plus eight green fingers. She filled her bag with beetroot, radishes, broccoli, swedes, peas, carrots, celery, silver beet, courgettes, even sweetcorn, but, sadly, no kumara.

Colleen was jamming some rhubarb into the top of the bag when suddenly she let out a strangled yelp. 'Christ, Ana, your kitchen!'

Ana glanced back towards her house to see dark smoke billowing from an open window and the back door, and dropped her bag and ran, Colleen close behind. Arriving at the top of the steps minus her slippers, which had slipped off and she'd barely even noticed, she tore inside to find the kitchen filled with acrid black smoke, and on each of the stove's three red-hot elements a slice of incinerated bread. She quickly grabbed each piece and tossed it into the sink, ran the tap, then turned off the stove. Then she opened all the windows and stood back, hands on hips, breathing heavily.

'Bloody hell, that was close,' Colleen exclaimed. 'Are you all right?'

Ana nodded, then shouted, '*Jack! Jack! Come out here!*'

Colleen said quickly, 'I'll get your bag of veggies, shall I?'

'Thanks. I'm sorry about this, Colleen.'

But Colleen waved her apology away as she headed off. Jack appeared in the doorway and Ana glared at him, then took a deep breath as she reminded herself that he was ill. It didn't really help. 'Come here, Jack.'

'I'm not allowed in the kitchen.'

'But you came in anyway, didn't you?'

'No.'

'You did, and you turned the stove on, which you *know*

you're not allowed to touch, and put bread on the elements. Bread! What on *earth* did you think you were doing?'

'Making toast.'

'What for?'

'Breakfast.'

'But you had breakfast, with me and the kids.'

'No I didn't.'

'You did.'

'I didn't.'

Ana lost her temper. 'You bloody well did, Jack! I bloody well made it for you!'

'Don't you talk to me like that!' Jack said, stepping towards her.

Ana could see Colleen standing in the porch, looking embarrassed, clutching the vegetables, but it was too late now, so she ploughed on.

'I'll talk to you however I like. You could have easily burnt our house down!'

'Not my house,' Jack shot back. 'This isn't my house. I don't even know you, and I don't know her, either,' he added, pointing at Colleen. 'So get out, both of you. Or I'll get my gun.'

'Shall I get Sid?' Colleen said from the doorway.

'That'll only confuse him more,' Ana said without taking her gaze off Jack. She moved towards him. 'Go back to your room. Go on.'

He took a few steps in her direction, his eyes narrowing and his lips pressed together in a hard line. Then he raised a fist at her.

'Touch me and I'll knock your block off,' Ana warned.

Several long seconds passed, then he turned and walked away. A moment later Ana heard the door to his room close. She sat down at the table as she didn't trust her shaky legs.

Colleen crept in and put the vegetables on the bench. 'My God, Ana, is he always like that?'

'No, usually he's fairly manageable. Just now and again he gets a bit unpleasant.'

'Has he got a gun? I'd take it off him, if I were you.'

Ana managed a smile. 'No. He had several on the farm, but we took those away ages ago.'

'And he doesn't know who you are?'

'Not often, not these days. Sometimes he thinks I'm his wife.'

'Does he recognise your children?'

'Not really.'

'How awful for them. And you. What about your husband?'

'He does seem to know who he is, on and off, but of course David's hardly here, so that's not much help, is it?'

Colleen bent and gave Ana a quick hug, and Ana felt herself responding with real gratitude.

'Well, any time you need help,' Colleen said, 'you just yell out or send one of the kids over, all right? Or come over yourself. Any time, day or night. I mean that. Sid might be useless in some departments and he can't run very fast because of his leg, but I expect he could be quite handy if you needed help with Jack. And I can swing a mean handbag myself, so don't hesitate, all right?'

'Thank you very much, Colleen. I really do appreciate that,' Ana replied.

Then she turned away, so Colleen wouldn't see the tears in her eyes. When her neighbour had gone she stood and thought for a moment, the assurance that she could ask for help already easing her despair and frustration. She had a little weep, then let out a huge, wobbly sigh, padded down the hallway to Jack's room and knocked on his door.

'Jack?'

No answer.

She opened the door and peeped in. He was sitting on his bed, staring at the floor. 'Jack, I'm sorry I yelled at you. I know you didn't mean to do it.'

But he wouldn't even look at her, and after a while she closed the door and left him to it.

*

Donna Roberts held her nose as she emptied yet another bedpan into the sink in the Bethany Home's sluice room, wondering how anyone could do a poo while they were lying down. She knew she certainly couldn't. But the owner of this one hadn't had much choice as she was in labour and confined to bed — nurse's orders. She shouldn't have been doing a poo at this late stage anyway as she'd had an enema four hours ago, but sometimes there was too much soap in the enema water and the girls got the runs, which was a bit of a nightmare.

Poo aside, she quite liked working here, though she was doing all the lackey work and none of the glamorous stuff, but she was only getting work experience so she supposed that was fair enough. The girls in the home were nice. Most of them were around her age, or even younger, though there were a couple of older ones, who you'd think would have known better than to get caught out. She'd only met two so far who planned to keep their babies; the rest were giving them up for adoption. She didn't know if she could do that, either. If you didn't want a baby you should make sure you didn't fall for one, or you should do something about it before your pregnancy got too advanced, that was her opinion, even if she had been raised a Catholic. Not that she'd ever been in that position herself. True, she had run around a bit when she'd been younger, but she'd kept her legs firmly shut when it had mattered.

She felt sorry for the girls giving up their babies. They were so lovely and no matter how determined the girls were to be brave, when the babies went, or when they went without their babies, there were nearly always tears and sometimes a lot more than that. It must be so tempting for the girls at the last minute to grab their children and tell themselves it would be all right, that the stares and the nasty comments and the stigma and the lost opportunities wouldn't matter. But they would.

And they were just ordinary girls. Not sinners, not sluts, just the sorts of girls you might have gone to school with. Sometimes the staff at Bethany could be a bit judgmental, she thought, especially some of the real dyed-in-the-wool Salvation Army ones, who told girls off for reading Mickey Spillane books and gave them a Bible instead. But others weren't, and treated the girls almost like friends, asking them about their families and where they came from (hardly any of them lived in Auckland, and were only there to have their babies), and what their hobbies and interests were. That was the sort of nurse she wanted to be.

And she liked Bethany Home itself. It was cosy, like a real home. It was in Grey Lynn and was a big old multi-storey wooden house with dormitories and a lounge for the girls where they lived while they waited for their babies to arrive. Some were there for months, sent away from home when they really started to show. And there was a delivery ward and a nursery and all the bits you'd expect in a standard maternity hospital, so she was getting real nursing experience, if only just the basic bits.

In December she'd turn eighteen, which meant she'd be old enough to join the January intake of trainee nurses at the Green Lane School of Nursing at Green Lane Hospital, and she couldn't wait. She'd live at the nurses' home at Green Lane, do her introductory training at the Market Road Preliminary School, her ward training at Green Lane, and attend lectures at the Central School of Nursing at Auckland Hospital. Thank God for public transport! The course was three years long and she'd been warned the pace was hectic for the entire time, but she thought she could manage that. She was even looking forward to living in the nurses' home because it meant she wouldn't have to live with her family any more. She loved them but sometimes — often, actually — they drove her around the bend with their boring, nit-picking, go-nowhere behaviour.

Her mother was lovely but she worried so much it was stifling. And the things she cared about — making preserves, the buttons on her cardigans matching, her refrigerator, what other people thought — were things she, Donna, just didn't give a toss about. *She* wanted a career, a proper job that would earn her enough money to be independent, so that when she met the right man she wouldn't have to rely on him to bring in the money. That way if he turned out to be like her father — that is, very lovable and a laugh, but, let's face it, not really a provider, not these days — she'd still have a job she enjoyed and not be forced to go out and make egg sandwiches and sausage rolls to keep the family afloat.

And as for Pauline, she'd had just about enough of her. She needed a bloody good boot up the toot, but it didn't matter how much you tried to give her one she just smirked at you and kept on being a bitch. She was going to get into real trouble one of these days: Donna was sure of it. She was either going to fall off one of those motorcycles she loved and hurt herself badly, or possibly even get arrested. And if she got her name in the papers, there went her job at Smith and Caughey, and all the rest of her pie-in-the-sky dreams. But apparently that hadn't occurred to Pauline; she never seemed to think any further than the weekend. Honestly, what was wrong with her?

And yes, she'd been guilty of a fair bit of tearing around herself a couple of years ago, and possibly, on her worst days, even of being a bitch, but she'd never been as bad as Pauline. She'd had itchy feet, that was all. She'd grown past that. She was far better off now, being sensible and practical and mature, and concentrating on her nurse training by cleaning up other people's shit. So yes, much better off.

She did envy Allie, being married to Sonny and having a flat of her own and all that freedom, though it was pretty rude the way some people acted towards her for marrying a Maori. He was such a lovely bloke. Sid and Colleen thought he was the bee's knees and so did Nan, though Donna knew her parents worried a bit about the mixed marriage side of things. But who cared, really? Times were changing, if more slowly than people liked to go around saying. She'd love to be married to a decent bloke, have a good job and be living in a modern flat with a proper bathroom and an indoor loo like Allie. What luxury!

'Are you going to stand in the sluice room all day, Miss Roberts?'

'Sorry, Matron. Off with the fairies.'

'Well, would you please re-join us. Miss Elliott's baby seems imminent.'

'Right away, Matron. I'll just finish up here.'

Josie Elliott was the owner of the poo, and Donna liked her a lot. She was seventeen, from Te Awamutū, smoked like the Destructor at Freeman's Bay, swore loudly and frequently, and liked a beer when she could sneak out and get one. Josie clashed constantly with Matron Arnold, though Donna thought the matron was a very good nurse, if a bit starchy and abrupt. She was a major in the Sallies, and definitely acted like one. Cleaning the bedpan thoroughly, Donna dried it and hung it on the wall rack, then washed her hands with disinfectant soap and hurried down the hallway.

She could hear Josie turning the air blue even before she reached the delivery room. Opening the door she heard Matron say, 'Kindly refrain from using that sort of language, Miss Elliott. It's offensive and of no help whatsoever.'

'It's bloody well helping me,' Josie shot back.

She was propped against a pile of pillows, her knees up and her heels against her bare buttocks. Tendrils of damp, burgundy-dyed hair stuck to her gleaming face and sweat stood out on her forehead and top lip in beads.

'I can assure you it isn't.'

'You try shoving a fucking watermelon out of your fanny, see how you like it!'

Matron flicked out a hand and slapped Josie across the leg. 'I said that's enough!'

Donna gasped and shared a quick, shocked glance with the other Sister in the room.

'Don't you dare hit me!' Josie exclaimed, then lowered her head and went purple in the face as she gave an almighty, extended push. As the contraction passed, and as though it hadn't occurred, she went on, 'You've no right to hit me. You're just a nurse. You're supposed to be helping me. I didn't ask for this.'

'Didn't you?' Matron snapped. 'Miss Roberts, please fetch towels and a wrap, and prepare the scales.'

Donna busied herself collecting a small pile of fresh towels and a wrap for the baby when it finally appeared, and lined the scales in which it would be weighed with a nappy. And as she did, she realised with sudden clarity that Josie Elliott wasn't just in pain, she was angry. More than that, she was furious.

'Jesus fucking *Christ*!' Josie roared as another contraction surged through her.

This time Matron ignored her, then cupped her hands to receive the baby's head as it emerged. 'One more push, please, then baby will be out.'

Josie bore down again, groaning like a cow, and the baby slid out, all wrinkled and bloody and covered in vernix. It cried immediately.

'A boy,' Matron said, then prompted, 'Sister Tapp.'

The sister clipped the umbilical cord and cut it, then placed the infant, still bawling, on the scales.

'Five pounds six ounces.'

Sister Tapp wiped him down, swaddled him in a wrap and brought him across to Josie on the bed.

Josie turned her head. 'Take it away.'

'Don't you want to see him?' Sister Tapp asked.

'No I bloody don't,' Josie barked, tears coursing down her face now. 'Take it *away*.'

Sister Tapp looked at Matron, who said, 'Take baby to the nursery. It's for the best. Now, Miss Elliott, let's see about tidying you up, shall we?'

*

December 1955

'Oh look,' Peggy said, 'your favourite customer.'

Kathleen Lawson was approaching the Elizabeth Arden counter in full sail, clutching a small girl by the hand and trailing two young boys behind her.

'Good afternoon, girls,' Mrs Lawson trilled, as though they were all the best of friends. 'And how are we today?'

'Good, thank you,' Allie replied.

Peggy said nothing, just smiled without showing her teeth and waggled fingers tipped with fuchsia nail varnish.

'I'd like you to meet my children,' Mrs Lawson said.

Allie wondered why.

Peggy said, 'It's not school holidays yet, is it?'

'No, but we're off to Hawke's Bay for a few weeks. My people live there. My family has owned a very big sheep station there for generations. You may have heard of it. Kenmore?'

Peggy and Allie shared a glance: No.

'And I thought it wouldn't matter if the children missed a few weeks of school. You don't do much this close to Christmas anyway, do you?' Mrs Lawson went on, looking down at her brood. Obedient shakes of the head from the two boys. 'Anyway, this is Geoffrey, he's seven and doing very well at school. Geoffrey hopes to become an officer in the New Zealand Army and also to train at Duntroon in Australia.'

'Good afternoon,' Geoffrey said politely.

He was a nice-looking boy, tall for his age with very nice posture, and beautifully dressed in pressed shorts, a blazer, shirt and tie, and long socks and extremely shiny lace-up shoes.

'Hello, Geoffrey,' Allie said, wondering what Duntroon was.

Peggy gave another little wave. 'Geoff.'

Allie bit her lip.

Mrs Lawson frowned slightly. 'And this is Terence, our eldest, who is nine. He's very artistic. His paintings have been exhibited at his school.'

Terence nodded a bit distractedly, Allie thought, as though he were wool-gathering. Other than that he was *beautiful*, with pale golden skin, full lips with a perfect cupid's bow, eyes the rich brown of smoky quartz, ridiculously long eyelashes, very fair curls, and dressed identically to his brother.

Allie declined to say hello, as Terence hadn't bothered.

'And this is dear little Rosemary,' Mrs Lawson wittered on. 'She's only five and hasn't started school yet, have you?'

'No,' Rosemary said in a tiny voice.

Rosemary was wearing a child's version of her mother's outfit. Whereas Mrs Lawson's three-quarter-sleeved, polished cotton dress hugged her torso and waist then flared into a crisp, full skirt, Rosemary's was short-sleeved and cut in an empire line. The tan patent leather of her Mary-Janes matched the colour of her mother's suede heels, and they carried matching purses, though Rosemary's was pint-sized. She was a lovely-looking little girl and Allie thought mother and daughter looked adorable.

'Hello, Rosemary,' she said.

'Good afternoon,' Rosemary said barely audibly.

'Hello, sweetie,' Peggy offered.

Rosemary waved and smiled, still hanging grimly on to her mother's gloved hand.

'But what I've come to tell you,' Mrs Lawson said excitedly, 'is some really very exciting news.'

Allie waited, hoping her expression made her look more interested than she felt. Usually Mrs Lawson's visits to the Elizabeth Arden counter — and there had been, as predicted by Peggy, quite a few — involved drawn-out discussions about the merits of one cream over another, or the impact of a certain lipstick shade on your complexion in relation to what you were wearing, etc. She knew it was her job to advise on that sort of thing, but, really, it didn't have to take forty-five minutes every time, did it? She'd come to the conclusion a while ago that Mrs Lawson was bored to death.

'You're aware of the fashion parade your store is having in February?'

'Ye-es,' Allie said cautiously. Everyone knew about. It had been advertised in the papers and in the store for the past couple of weeks.

'Well, I'm going to offer my beautiful garden as the venue! The roses will still be in bloom and we've a very large and manicured lawn and it will be perfect. What do you think of that!'

Allie forced a smile. 'Very nice.'

That was never going to happen. Fashion parades were almost always held in-store, and certainly not in someone's garden, never mind how nice their roses looked.

'And I'll put in a good word so that you girls are the make-up artists, shall I?' Mrs Lawson added.

Allie shifted uncomfortably from foot to foot. 'Er, thank you.'

'I'm very much looking forward to it,' Mrs Lawson said. 'I've never been involved with a fashion parade before. Although of course I shopped at Selfridges and Harrods regularly when we lived in England. And John Lewis and Harvey Nichols. Marvellous stores.'

Peggy said, 'You must find it a bit of a come down being back in New Zealand.'

'Oh, well, needs must. As I think I might have mentioned, my husband was offered a rather prestigious position as a senior pilot for NAC, and my family are all here. That's important.'

Yes, it is, Allie thought. She and Sonny were off to visit Rose after work, and Mrs Lawson's comment reminded her she wanted to buy some flowers.

After Mrs Lawson and her children had gone, Peggy shook her head and said, 'That woman is *completely* batty. The cheek of her.'

'I think she's just lonely.'

'No, she's mad,' Peggy said. 'You mark my words.'

*

Kathleen sat with her legs crossed at the ankle, smoking, watching the woman behind the desk tapping away at a typewriter. Terence, Geoffrey and Rosemary sat beside her, in that order, ducks in a row.

The phone rang and the woman picked it up, said, 'Yes, sir, right away,' then returned the handset to its cradle. 'Mr Holmes will see you now, Mrs Lawson. Please go in.'

'Will you please watch my children?' Kathleen asked as she stood and stubbed out her cigarette in an ashtray. 'I shouldn't be too long.'

The woman looked very taken aback. 'Er, I—'

Changing her mind, Kathleen took Rosemary's hand. 'My boys are very well-behaved, I assure you.'

Before the woman could respond Kathleen knocked on Mr Holmes's door and swept into his office, Rosemary trotting to keep up.

George Holmes stepped out from behind his vast desk and offered Kathleen his hand. 'Mrs Lawson, very nice to meet you. I'm George Holmes, store manager.' He bent down to Rosemary. 'And you must be ...?'

'Rosemary, my daughter.'

'What a poppet. Please, do take a seat.'

Kathleen sat. So did Rosemary, wriggling onto a chair, her arms on the armrests and her legs straight out in front of her.

Back behind his desk, Mr Holmes asked, 'Now, how may I help you?'

'I hope you don't mind me being forward,' Kathleen said, not really caring if he did, 'but it concerns your February fashion parade.'

Mr Holmes raised his eyebrows.

'My father, James Murdoch, was in banking and horticulture, though he's semi-retired now. You may have heard of my family? The Murdochs of Hawke's Bay?'

'Er, the name does ring a bell,' Mr Holmes said vaguely.

'Well, as the daughter of a banker I couldn't help but learn a thing or two about business and it occurs to me that you might score a march over your competitors by staging your parade at an exciting new venue.'

Mr Holmes remained politely silent.

Kathleen went on. 'My husband and I would be more than willing to host the event in our beautiful, extensive gardens at our home in Remuera.' She hadn't mentioned her idea to Jonathan yet, but was sure he'd agree. 'My husband is Captain Jonathan Lawson, a senior pilot at NAC, and of course held the rank of captain in the RAF during the war.'

Sitting back in his squeaky leather chair, Mr Holmes smiled and said, 'That is indeed a most generous offer, Mrs Lawson. Thank you.' Then he leant forwards again, his stylish, Anthony Squires-suited forearms on the desktop, hands loosely clasped. 'However, I'm very much afraid that won't be possible.'

Kathleen felt her smile slipping, and fixed it back in place.

'You see, audiences for our fashion parades are very often considerable, and they require seating, refreshments and, er, comfort facilities. That's why we hold our parades in The Cedar Room, our public tearoom, which is already configured for large groups and can provide catering. The models have access to changing rooms on the nearby Fashion floor and the clothing to be shown is also on hand. I'm sure your garden, and home, are absolutely delightful, and I thank you very much for your offer, both you and Captain Lawson, but the logistics simply preclude our moving the event off site.'

Forcing her shoulders to remain back and keeping her head high, Kathleen felt ill. This would ruin everything. She'd told so many people. 'Oh. Well, then.'

Mr Holmes picked up a gold pen and fiddled with it. Kathleen waited, knowing he would find the lengthening silence embarrassing. People usually did.

'But if you'd like to be involved with the event in some way I'm sure we can find you some part to play. I take it you're a regular customer at Smith and Caughey?'

'Oh yes, I shop here frequently.'

'Have you met Miss Weaver, our Head of Fashion?'

'I believe so.'

'Why don't you pop down and have a word with her? I'll let her know you're coming. I'm sure she'll be delighted to talk to you.'

'I'll do that.' Kathleen stood. Rosemary scrambled off her seat. 'Thank you very much, Mr Holmes. I do appreciate your time.'

'My pleasure entirely, Mrs Lawson.' George Holmes scribbled something on a piece of notepaper, leant across his desk and handed it to Kathleen. 'A chit for the toy department. Young Rosemary might like to pick something out for herself, courtesy of the store.'

'How generous. Say thank you, Rosemary.'

Rosemary did.

As soon as Kathleen had closed the door, George Holmes was on the phone to the Fashion department several floors below.

'Edna? Oh, can you get Edna Weaver for me, please?' While he waited he drummed his fingers on his blotter. 'Edna? It's George Holmes. Listen, I've just had a Mrs Lawson in my office very keen on having some sort of role in the February parade.' Pause. 'No, she's just a customer.' Pause. 'Well, at first she suggested having the parade at her home in Remuera.' Pause. 'Well, of course I did. But she *is* very keen so I've sent her down to you.' He moved the handpiece slightly away from his ear for a moment. 'Yes, I know. The thing is she had her daughter with her, about five, and the cutest little thing. You're always looking for kids to model the children's wear, aren't you?' Pause. 'Well, I don't know. You're the expert on frocks, not me. Can you at least talk to her?' Another pause, then he laughed. 'All right. Thanks, Edna. I owe you one. Cheers.'

*

Kathleen didn't in fact know Miss Weaver, but she was easy enough to find — she just asked a salesgirl to point her out. She was behind the main counter in the Fashion department, sorting through some paperwork. She looked as old as the hills but was very well groomed and Kathleen thought she'd probably worked at Smith and Caughey forever.

'Good afternoon, Miss Weaver. I'm Mrs Kathleen Lawson. I believe Mr Holmes might have mentioned me?'

'How do you do, Mrs Lawson. Yes, he did. How can I help you?'

This brought Kathleen up short. She'd expected Miss Weaver to provide her with a range of options from which to choose, not to have to make suggestions herself. 'Yes, well, Mr Holmes and I were discussing the February fashion parade. He felt there may be a role there for me.'

'Did he?'

Kathleen's temper was already close to boiling over. She was deeply disappointed, and, yes, humiliated, by Mr Holmes's rejection of her offer of her home as a venue, and to make matters worse Terence had thrown a tantrum when he'd discovered Rosemary had been given a gift voucher for the toy department. She'd itched to slap him but had refrained, one of her rules being that she never, ever hit the children in public. Now here she was confronting an uppity old shop woman who clearly didn't know how to deal with a person from a superior class — who was accustomed to spending money in establishments *far* grander than Smith and Caughey — or that the customer is always right.

'Yes, actually, he did,' she replied frostily.

Miss Weaver tapped her horsey front teeth with a short fingernail varnished the most insipid beige colour Kathleen had ever seen. 'You purchased your mother and daughter outfits here, didn't you?'

Kathleen looked down at her polished cotton dress, then at Rosemary's 'Little Miss' version. 'That's right. They were from the summer range. And the shoes. And my hat.'

'Well, you both look charming. Would you be interested in modelling mother and daughter outfits in the parade?'

Perhaps Miss Weaver wasn't such a bitch after all.

'Oh, I couldn't walk in a parade!' Kathleen protested. 'Wouldn't you rather use a professional model?'

'We hire professional models for the glamour outfits, but we like our mother and daughter ensembles to appeal to a wide range of women, not just the physically blessed. And you have a very nice sense of style.'

This wasn't the answer Kathleen was looking for. She knew she wasn't stunningly beautiful, but she was attractive and spent a lot of time and money on making the most of what she did have. Mentally, she moved Miss Weaver back into the bitch category.

'We have some gorgeous autumn ensembles arriving just after Christmas exclusively for the parade,' Miss Weaver went on. 'I think you'd enjoy yourself. Your little girl would look divine. But if you don't think it's for you ...'

Kathleen waited several beats so she wouldn't seem too eager. 'Well, I wouldn't want to deprive Rosemary of such an exciting experience. Would you like to be in a fashion parade, sweetie?'

'What's a fashion parade?' Rosemary asked.

Miss Weaver bent down to her. 'It's a sort of show where you walk up and down in front of nice ladies and you wear the loveliest new clothes, so that the ladies can decide what they want to buy for their children and for themselves.'

Rosemary looked at her, then up at Kathleen. 'No, I don't want to.'

'You'll be with me the whole time,' Kathleen said. 'I'll be holding your hand.'

'No.'

Kathleen said quickly, 'She's a little shy but I'm sure she'll be very good at it when the time comes. Thank you, Miss Weaver, I think we'll accept your invitation.'

Wait till she told everyone she was walking for Smith and Caughey. That would show them.

*

'How are you feeling?' Allie asked as she wrestled the enormous bunch of white, pink and lilac stock into a vase. They were her nan's favourite, smelt gorgeous and would go a long way towards covering up the less pleasant smells in the ward, like bedpans, sick people and boiled cabbage.

'Oh, I'm coming along.'

She didn't look *too* bad, Allie thought. Her teeth were in and someone had combed her hair, though it seemed far wispier, like candyfloss, now she wasn't having it curled and set, and you could easily see her pink scalp. She was really thin, though. Her wrists were like sticks, her cheeks were hollow, her eyes seemed like they were sort of sinking into her head, and there was a rasping noise every time she took a deep breath.

No, actually, she did look quite rough.

'Have you caught a cold?' Sonny asked, pulling up a chair.

'I don't think so.'

'You sound a bit chesty,' Allie said. 'Shall I help you to sit up a bit?'

Rose was lying almost horizontal, her head on two uninspiringly flat pillows. Allie had a look at the mechanism that raised the head of the bed, put her foot on the lever, struggled and swore for a few moments and managed to jerkily ratchet Rose into more of a sitting position.

'That's better. Thank you, dear,' she said, rearranging the bedclothes.

And then she coughed, hard. Out of her mouth flew a massive lump of green phlegm that sailed through the air and landed wetly on the white bedcover. They all stared at it.

'Yuck,' Allie said.

Grabbing a flannel off the nightstand she scraped it off, though it left a nasty mark.

'Has anyone said anything about your chest?' Sonny asked.

'Oh, I don't know,' Rose replied, leaning back against the pillows. She suddenly seemed to Allie to be exhausted. 'I get told this and I have pills and injections for that. I can't remember.'

Sonny said, 'I think you might have a chest infection.'

Rose closed her eyes. 'And when did you become a doctor?'

'He's just trying to help, Nan.'

'How's Mr De Valera?'

'Don't change the subject.'

'I'm not. Is he missing me?'

Allie exchanged a look with Sonny. Apparently not. He'd made himself very much at home in their flat, monopolising the sunny window seat in the kitchen nook during the day, if the fur all over the cushions was anything to go by, and the armchair in the evenings, leaving the couch to her and Sonny, which was all right with her. He'd conceded to doing his business out in the back garden, miaowed a greeting when they came home, and even stooped these days to rubbing against her legs when he was hungry. He cost a fortune to feed, though, and absolutely *refused* to eat cat meat from a tin. Spoilt little bugger.

'Lots,' Sonny said. 'And he sends his love.'

Allie gave him another look, this one full of pity. Or was he just trying to cheer Rose up?

'Well, tell him I love him back,' Rose said.

'I will.' Sonny suddenly waved out to a passing nurse. 'Excuse me!'

She stopped, looking harassed.

'Could you please tell us what's happening about Mrs Murphy's chest? Does she have an infection? We're a bit concerned.'

The nurse frowned. 'Are you relatives?'

'She's my nan,' Allie explained.

The nurse whipped Rose's chart off the end of her bed and flicked through it. 'She started antibiotics this morning and she's scheduled for a chest X-ray tomorrow.'

'Thank you very much,' Sonny said.

'You're welcome,' the nurse replied and marched off, her shoes squeaking on the linoleum floor.

Full of admiration, Allie said, 'I'd never have thought to do that. Or had the guts.'

'We could have found out ourselves if we'd known those're her notes hanging on the end of the bloody bed,' Sonny said.

Rose erupted into another fit of coughing. No phlegm flew out this time, but her teeth did. Allie handed them to her and she and Sonny both looked away while Rose put them back in.

'Thank you, dear. I think my gums must be shrinking,' she said eventually. 'They're not fitting as well as they used to. I don't know what's wrong with them.'

'Well, you still look a picture,' Sonny said.

'That's very kind of you to say so, but I know I look a dog's breakfast. In fact, I doubt I'll be seeing in the new year.'

Allie was genuinely shocked. 'Nan! Of course you will!'

'I don't think so, love. My hip isn't healing, I can feel it, and now there's my chest. I think God's calling me home.'

'Don't say that!' Allie couldn't believe what her nan was saying. Hot tears pricked at her eyelids and she furiously blinked them away.

Rose laid a thin-skinned hand over hers and said gently, 'It's my time. Nobody lasts forever, Allison. And I'm not frightened. God's kingdom awaits me.'

Bugger God and his bloody kingdom, Allie thought. That was all right if you were a staunch Catholic like Rose and believed in all that, but she wasn't and she was the one who was going to be left behind without a precious nan. Well, all right, her parents and sisters would be left without her too. But why couldn't Rose fight a bit harder and hold on? It might make the difference between whether she lived or died.

'Well, I don't believe you,' she said. 'I think your chest'll clear up and your hip'll come right and you'll be home before you know it.'

Rose squeezed her hand but there was no strength in it at all. 'I hope you're right. We'll see, shall we?'

Chapter Six

The Apanuis and the Irwins shared their Christmas, just as they shared almost everything. They would have liked to have gone home to Maungakakari but neither family could afford it, so Henare put down a hangi in his backyard using the special stones he'd brought with him when they came to the city. Before breakfast he heated the stones in a fire and, when they were white-hot, he and the older boys moved them to the hangi pit then lowered in wire baskets filled with potatoes, kumara, pumpkin, chicken and pork, all wrapped in cabbage leaves and wet mutton cloth. Then in went the puddings in the big fruit tins and the whole lot was covered with a clean wet bed sheet, then carefully layered wet sacks, then a layer of soil to stop the steam escaping, and left to cook for five hours.

While everyone waited for the hangi they went to church in their Sunday best (which they would have done anyway because it actually *was* Sunday), except Henare and Joshua who stayed at home to tend the hangi — to Kura and Wiki's disapproval. They felt it could look after itself, especially on Jesus's birthday.

On arriving home everyone had a snack then exchanged presents. No one could afford to give expensive or frivolous gifts, so in both families the children received shoes, or clothing that Kura and Wiki had made in secret, mostly knitted garments as both women were very accomplished knitters, while the children gave their parents small tokens or something they had made at school. However, Kura's eldest girls, Patricia and Mary, had chipped in together and bought Johnny a copy of Lloyd Price's song 'Lawdy Miss Clawdy' to save the family from Elvis (Kura shuddering to think where they'd got it), which delighted him. But presents weren't the highlight of Christmas Day, Christmas dinner was, and at four o'clock, with much anticipation, the hangi was brought up. It was cooked perfectly and the Apanuis and Irwins enjoyed a long and leisurely picnic in the Irwins' derelict backyard.

After the feed Johnny plugged in his record player and everybody, even the grown-ups, danced to Elvis and Lloyd among the cast-off sheets of rusted roofing iron, the rubbish, the dirt and the weeds.

*

At the Leonards', David was home for the Christmas break. They had a beautiful roast leg of lamb, which David had brought back from his travels, and new potatoes and peas from Sid's garden, and trifle and Christmas pudding. Ana had tried making a pavlova but it hadn't really worked, though the kids had eaten it anyway under piles of whipped cream. Still feeling horribly guilty for uprooting the children from the farm, she and David over-compensated and went mad with their Christmas presents. While David stayed home minding Jack on the Friday night before Christmas weekend, Ana went out and, spending *far* too much money, bought bicycles for each of them, which they'd never had before (why ride a bike when you owned a horse?), and books, and clothes from Farmers. She bought gifts for Jack too, and she and David stayed up late on Saturday night wrapping everything, except for the bicycles, which were parked on the back lawn at the bottom of the steps.

On Christmas Day Jack seemed to be on his best behaviour — Ana thought probably because David was at home — and ate his dinner mostly using his knife and fork, hardly swore, and even offered to help with drying the dishes, though he couldn't remember the word for dishes and wandered off before he got round to it. But he didn't seem to know it was Christmas and asked why there was a tree in the front room and what the presents were for. The next day, while out in the garden, he shat his pants and didn't appear to notice till he came inside and Rowie asked what the horrible smell was. It was a first for him and left Ana praying it wasn't going to happen again. But she suspected it would.

*

Everyone in the Roberts family trooped up to the hospital to visit Rose on Christmas morning. She wasn't doing very well. Her breathing was shallow but raspy and bubbly, and her eyes seemed glassy and a bit unfocused. A nurse told them they had to give the antibiotics time to work and that they shouldn't expect miracles.

Sid said, 'I thought antibiotics *were* a miracle drug.'

Colleen shushed him and got out the gifts she'd bought for her mother: a tin of her favourite Cashmere Bouquet rose talcum powder, a pretty new floral nightie, and a bed jacket she'd knitted. Donna and Pauline had gone in together for a boxed set of 4711 toiletries, and Allie and Sonny produced a gift basket of chocolate and biscuit treats from Smith and Caughey, plus a tiny cat ornament from Mr De Valera (purchased by Sonny). They all knew Rose was getting the best presents this year, and none of them begrudged her.

She seemed pleased with her gifts, said she was sorry she hadn't been able to get anything for them, but was so tired she fell asleep fifteen minutes after they arrived. They sat around her bed for a while but she didn't wake up so they left, piling into Sonny's truck for the ride back to Coates Avenue. Pauline, Donna and Allie sat in the back laughing, saying they felt like the Joads in that book by that bloke John Steinbeck.

They exchanged gifts, ate an enormous Christmas lunch of roast chicken, garden vegetables and assorted puddings, then slumped around the kitchen table, Allie and Sonny wondering how they were going to fit in another feed at Awhi's place, where they were due for a family Christmas dinner in about an hour.

'Walk up there,' Colleen suggested.

'All the way to Kitemoana Street?' Allie exclaimed, her hands resting on her distended belly. 'Up that hill? I'm just about vomiting as it is.'

'Do you good,' Sid said, not quite stifling a burp.

Pauline said, 'A vomit? God, I could really do with one. I shouldn't have had all that trifle.'

'No, the walk, you silly girl,' Colleen snapped.

Shrugging, Pauline picked a cherry out of the Christmas pudding and ate it.

'I think we'll probably take the truck,' Sonny said. 'Would you like a hand with the dishes?' he asked Colleen.

'No thanks, love. You finish your beer, Pauline and Donna can do that.'

'Not me,' Pauline said. 'I'm going out.'

Colleen looked at her. 'Out where? It's Christmas Day, *and* Sunday. Everything's shut.'

'I dunno, just out.'

'That's what you think, young lady. It's Christmas. You're going to stop in and enjoy being part of this family whether you like it or not.'

'But—'

'But nothing. You're stopping in and that's that.'

Her expression foul, Pauline stalked from the kitchen and down the hall into her room, slamming the door so hard that elsewhere in the house other doors opened.

'Ho, ho, ho,' Sid said.

*

The Lawsons were back in Auckland for Christmas Day, as Jonathan had to fly the day after Boxing Day. They had a twenty-pound turkey for their Christmas dinner, a ridiculously over-sized bird for a family of five. Kathleen had to cook it herself along with the rest of the meal, as to her irritation Evie, the nanny-cum-cook, had asked for Christmas Day off and Jonathan had given it to her, but at least she'd made Evie brine the damn thing the day before. At lunchtime she stuffed the bird, trussed it and put it in the oven so it would be ready by about six o'clock, and got on with the rest of the dinner, which was new peas and assorted roasted vegetables, and gravy for the turkey, all while drinking her way through five sneaky gin and tonics. Evie had also pre-made a trifle, a pavlova and brandy snaps, to which Kathleen only had to add cream and fruit, plus serve a cheese board, the cheese already prepared and waiting covered in muslin in the refrigerator. She'd add savoury biscuits and some dried fruit to the board before serving.

The children had opened their gifts in the morning, having been banned from getting out of bed before seven o'clock, and were busy playing with their new toys so the house was relatively peaceful. Jonathan was in the garden drinking vodka martinis and reading, where he'd been since lunchtime, so she had the kitchen to herself.

The turkey looked perfect, lovely and golden. While she let it rest she set the dining table with a white damask cloth, her flatware with the gold rim, crystal stemware, her best silver, two candelabrum with white candles, a floral centrepiece Evie had made with red roses and carnations, red berries, little pine cones and greenery, and placed a gold foil Christmas cracker on everyone's dinner plate. She stepped back, very pleased with the effect. It was the sort of table arrangement you might see in a magazine featuring homes of the wealthy.

Then she called everyone together and told them to wash their hands and get changed, which Jonathan refused to do, insisting there was nothing wrong with eating Christmas dinner in casual slacks and an open-necked shirt. But she changed into one of her nicer dresses, and made the children put on smarter clothes. She wasn't going to let Jonathan spoil *her* Christmas dinner.

The turkey, when she brought it into the dining room almost staggering beneath its weight, elicited gratifying oohs and aahs from the children, and Jonathan carved it skilfully, complimenting her on her cooking skills. But then Terence decided he didn't like it and said he would have preferred roast lamb and wasn't hungry anyway, which encouraged Rosemary to declare she wouldn't eat her pumpkin or peas. Rather than tell them off, Kathleen ignored them. Geoffrey told his siblings they were being selfish and she felt absurdly grateful to him.

Then Jonathan eyed the turkey, laughed and said, 'Looks like we'll be eating turkey sandwiches till March, kids! Except your mother's too posh to actually eat sandwiches.'

Which stung, so she glared at him, and he only laughed harder and opened another bottle of wine. He was always doing this. She *did* eat sandwiches — she ate club sandwiches. What was wrong with being 'posh'? He said it as though it were an insult. *He* came from money but it was as if his family's money was different from her family's money. Just because his was generations old and English didn't make it any better than hers, which came from sheep farming. He never called himself posh — he just said his 'people' were upper-class, if he ever said anything like that about them at all. It *really* irritated her.

She cleared away the mains plates, wishing Evie were here to do it for her, and brought out the puddings, to discover they'd all pulled their Christmas crackers without her. Jonathan declined pudding, patting his belly, which was as flat as a washboard (which Kathleen had never used but she'd seen one), but poured himself more wine and helped himself to the cheese. Terence, suddenly hungry now, had three servings of pavlova and brandy snaps, then declared he felt ill. Kathleen had one brandy snap, making it last.

'Do you know your flight schedule for February yet?' she asked.

'More or less,' Jonathan said, cutting a wedge of cheddar. 'Why?'

'I'd just like to know.'

'Why?' Jonathan said again.

'I'd like to know whether you'll be able to come to the fashion parade.'

Jonathan was still for a moment, then his face flushed red and he thumped the table mightily with a fist, making the cutlery and glasses rattle. 'Do you know something, Kathleen? I am sick to bloody *death* of hearing about this fashion parade. Even if I am home I won't be coming. Why would I want to come and watch you prance around wearing some God-awful bloody frock?'

Terence and Rosemary both burst into tears.

'And you two can both pipe down. Go to your rooms if you can't act like adults. Go on.'

'Jonathan, don't! Leave them alone.'

But Terence and Rosemary didn't have to be told twice and ran out of the dining room, bawling. Geoffrey went as well, walking stiffly, his head held high.

'You bastard,' Kathleen said. 'Now look what you've done. You've *ruined* their Christmas.'

'*I've* ruined it? *I'm* not the one who's made us sit round a table with more bloody china and silver and crystal on it than the captain's table on the fucking *Titanic*, when we could just as easily have had a picnic somewhere.'

Kathleen's skin prickled and a stab of dread pierced her, as it always did when they argued like this. 'Well, *I'm* not the one who's been drinking since ten o'clock this morning and has now terrorised the life out of his children. And I just wanted to make our Christmas nice.'

'No, you didn't. You wanted to make our Christmas better than anyone else's. It's what you always want, Kathleen, to be better than everyone else. For God's sake, I've never met anyone so obsessed with class and status as you. It's just so ... *common*.'

'You bastard, Jonathan. You're drunk. You're always drunk.'

'No, only when I'm home. I never drink when I'm flying. I wonder what that could mean?'

'So you *say*.'

Jonathan threw a piece of cheese at her, hard. It hit her right between the eyes and bounced onto the table. 'You know, Kathleen, sometimes I really don't like you.'

'Well, if you don't like me perhaps you shouldn't have married me,' Kathleen snapped, though she could hear the wobble in her voice.

Jonathan stood and snatched up a bottle of wine. 'Perhaps I shouldn't have,' he replied, then marched out through the French doors and into the garden.

Kathleen sat for a while, surveying the shambles on the table. Then she carefully took the damask napkin off her lap so that crumbs wouldn't fall on the floor, and started the clearing up.

*

Sonny and Allie arrived at Awhi's place at about half-past four, still uncomfortably full after their meal at the Robertses'. There were quite a few vehicles parked out the front, kids shouting and laughing and chasing one another around on the lawn and a lot of noise coming from the back.

Allie knew that just about all of Sonny's brothers and sisters and their families would be there, plus various aunts and uncles, so it would be crowded. He had five brothers, aged thirty-two to twenty-four, who had nine children among them, and five sisters, aged twenty-eight to seventeen, who had eight children. The only sibling missing would be Gilbert, who was in Mt Eden gaol serving a long sentence for manslaughter. Awhi would have been to visit him that morning. There wouldn't be any presents as gift-giving in such a large family was prohibitively expensive and complicated (though she had bought something for Gina, which she'd leave on her bed), but everyone would have brought along food, which she thought was quite a good idea. At least that way you didn't end up with a present you didn't particularly want but had to pretend you really liked, like the salmon pink bloomers Nan sometimes gave her, Donna and Pauline and which they wouldn't be seen dead in.

The back lawn was packed and everyone was talking at the tops of their voices. The marquee was up, the hangi was in its usual spot and someone was yelling at the kids not to run all over Awhi's veggie garden. There was a table set up in the shade and laden with snacks, and underneath were several half-gallon drums holding bottles of beer in ice. Alongside the table was another drum for the empties. Allie sighed. Parties at Awhi's place were always the same: the same marquee, the same hangi, the same faces, the same beer, the same noise, the same drunken behaviour later on, the same fights. Mind you, you didn't even have to add alcohol at her parents' house to start a fight, just a stroppy sixteen-year-old.

Sonny waved at everyone on his way to grab two beers, then cracked off the lids with his teeth. Allie winced.

'Don't do that. We can't afford the dentist!'

'You tell him, Allie, the useless bugger.'

This was from Polly, reclining in a deckchair, drink in hand, gin bottle beneath her seat. She was wearing black capri pants, a white sleeveless top and enormous black sunglasses, and looked fabulous. But then it didn't matter what she threw on, she always managed to look effortlessly stylish.

'Hi, Polly. How's things?'

Polly shrugged. 'Same as usual. You?'

'Good.' Allie made a face. 'Though we just had lunch at my parents' place and I'm still stuffed.'

'Go and have a spew,' Polly suggested.

'My sister said that. Where's Gina?'

'Running round here somewhere.'

Allie spotted her, racing around after some other little kids, laughing and screaming her head off, her feet bare though she was wearing the most beautiful frothy, lacy confection of a dress. 'We've got that little dress at work.'

'I know. That's where I bought it.'

'You must have robbed a bank, the price of it.'

Polly shrugged again, drained her glass and stared into the bottom of it for a moment, then felt around under the deckchair for the bottle. 'She deserves it.'

'Steady on with that gin, sis,' Sonny warned.

'Bugger off.'

Sonny grinned. 'Bugger off yourself.'

Allie remembered a party she'd attended here at Awhi's, when she first started seeing Sonny, and Gina was just nine months old. Polly had been really drunk and hadn't wanted to give her her bottle — hadn't wanted much to do with her at all, in fact. Gina had been living with Awhi more or less full time even then. Polly had been hopeless, apparently incapable of looking after her and, unforgivably in Allie's eyes, also incapable of loving her. But she loved her now, that was obvious, even though Awhi was raising her. Allie didn't know what had happened to make Polly suddenly start loving Gina but she had, and by the time the baby had turned one, Polly was round at her mother's at least a couple of times a week, taking Gina out, lavishing gifts on her and promising her the world. Privately Allie thought Polly had always loved her but wouldn't admit it even to herself, though God only knew why. Who couldn't admit to loving a beautiful little girl like Gina?

Awhi appeared at the back door, balancing a huge tray of sliced and buttered bread, and made her way carefully down the steps. Sonny took the tray off her and carried it to the table under the marquee, which appeared to be a signal for the hangi to be brought up. The kids all crowded round and were shooed away as the dirt was scraped off the top of the mound and the sheet and sacks were carefully lifted, in case someone fell in and got burnt. There were loud expressions of appreciation as four large baskets of food were raised, wafting their distinctive aroma.

Actually, Allie didn't like hangi food. It was too smoky and sometimes it tasted greasy to her, and she found the meat in particular to be unpleasant. But she always managed to nibble some potato and the steamed puddings could be nice, especially with cream. She wondered whether it was because she wasn't used to hangi food, or because she was a Pakeha. She said this to Sonny once, who laughed his head off and said that was like saying only Pommies liked fish and chips because the English invented them. And that wasn't true, was it, because everyone liked fish and chips.

To avoid being handed a big plate of hot, smelly food, she slipped into the house straight after the karakia. As always she had to check, and there he was in the sitting room, resplendent as was customary every Christmas. Not in person of course, that would be horrifying, just his photograph — Sonny's late father, Major Pera Manaia, hero of A Company, 28th (Maori) Battalion, 2nd New Zealand Expeditionary Force, and pillar of the Ngati Whatua community. Across the top of the photo frame hung the velvet ribbon displaying his seven war medals, and cascading across that were ropes of silver beads held in place at the corners by red velvet bows. At the base was a carefully arranged selection of painted glass Christmas ornaments, including bells, balls and pinecones. Nothing else in the room — or the house, in fact — was decorated, just this photograph. Allie had once asked Sonny why, and he'd shrugged and said his mother did it, as though that was an answer in itself. Perhaps it was.

She waited a good fifteen minutes, sliced and buttered some more bread, and took it down to the table under the marquee.

'Thanks, dear,' Awhi said. 'Did you get plenty of kai?'

'Lots, thanks,' Allie replied.

In the end she didn't eat anything, just chatted to people and drank beer, which was possibly a mistake, because by the time they went home she was really quite pissed, but the sex was so good — despite Mr De Valera sitting in the bedroom doorway watching them with avid interest — that she didn't care, even though she knew for a fact she'd have quite a rough hangover the next morning.

*

The very early hours of the last day of December 1955 are quiet at Auckland Hospital, the sun nowhere near the horizon and the birds still all fast asleep, like most of the patients in Rose Murphy's ward. Some snore gently while the breath of others struggles through respiratory systems failing gradually from age and disease. A lone nurse sits at her station at one end of the ward, working beneath the light of a desk lamp, listening now and then in the dimness of the room, her ear attuned for changes in breathing, for chokes and splutters that might indicate assistance is required. Occasionally she stands and walks the length of the ward, her shoes gently squeaking, glancing down at her patients, but mostly she stays where she is, writing notes, yawning and waiting for the end of her shift at eight o'clock — a long way off yet.

But Rose doesn't see or hear the nurse, though she isn't asleep; she's somewhere else altogether. She's slipped back in time, back to her beloved Emerald Isle — not that her bit of Ireland is particularly green. Dublin, in fact, is the shitty grey of tenements and bricks and cobbles and soot, and of bone-scraping poverty. She's always lived in a dank, cold tenement and after she marries the absolute love of her life, Patrick, no matter how hard they both work, they still can't earn enough to afford anything better. Then when Colleen comes along Rose shocks everyone by handing her baby to her mother and carrying on working at the brewery. Patrick works on the wharves and they're both bloody lucky to have jobs.

They love Ireland, though, and want the English out. Not even Home Rule will do. Patrick joins the Irish Republican Brotherhood and she joins the women's movement Cumann na mBan, but both in secret of course or the Black and Tans will be on them and gunning them down in the street, because that's what they do, the dogs. Her mother tells her she's asking for terrible trouble but she doesn't care, she can't just stand by and let the English carry on pillaging her beloved country.

Then comes the Easter Uprising in 1916. She's thirty-three and it's the most exciting event of her life, even though it fails and so many of their friends are killed. But it does change things — she knows that even as it's happening. Things will never be the same in Ireland again. Then someone dobs Patrick in to the Black and Tans so they take Colleen, who's nine by now, and run. They go from Dublin to Liverpool, then, after the war ends, to Australia, then finally arrive in New Zealand. Patrick gets work on the Auckland wharves, she finds a job in a luggage manufactory, and Colleen settles in at school. She and Patrick make more money than they ever could in Ireland and their standard of living is far better than they'd hoped. When the second war starts Patrick doesn't volunteer. Of course at fifty-nine he's far too old for the proper forces, but he won't even sign up for the Home Guard because he refuses to serve under a British flag. Fair enough, she thinks, though she doesn't mind knitting socks for the boys overseas. Feet get cold and wet whether they're English or Irish — or German, for that matter.

And then, just after that war ends, Patrick dies. At work, pushing a trolley-load of goods off a ship. His heart. Apparently he just dropped. It takes her a long time to get over that.

But she's had a good life, and an interesting one, and now it's over. She doesn't mind, not really. Colleen and Sid will be all right. Sid can be a clown and sometimes talks shite, but he loves Colleen dearly and that's the most important thing. It always is. The girls will be all right, too. Pauline will stop fighting and settle down eventually and Allie will sort out whatever's been bothering her. She's a clever girl and that lad of hers will stand by her.

The minute hand on the clock above the nurse's station moves around. The nurse takes another walk down the ward, checking each bed, then ducks out to the staff toilet, smelling of Knight's Castile soap when she returns. She takes a moment to blow her nose, then settles again at her desk.

Rose tries to open her eyes, but can't. She listens to her own heartbeat pulsing faintly in her ears, like a gently outgoing tide. She feels as though Mr De Valera's sitting on her chest but she doesn't think he actually is. It's just that she can't breathe any more. She'll miss Dev a lot.

She isn't in pain and she isn't frightened.

She knows where she's going and she knows Patrick will be there to meet her.

She lets go.

Part Two

Part Two

Chapter Seven

January 1956

Colleen didn't have a black dress — well, not one that fitted properly any more — and hadn't been able to bring herself to buy a new one, thinking that if she held off, her mother might not die.

'You could wear your grey one,' Allie suggested, looking through Colleen's wardrobe.

'I don't want to wear my grey one,' Colleen snapped. 'It's a funeral. My *mother's* funeral. Don't young people know anything about etiquette these days?'

Allie ignored her. She was allowed to be upset. They were all upset, going around with swollen red eyes and dissolving into snivels all over the place. Even her father looked like a blinky little pink-eyed mouse, blowing his nose all the time and pretending he had a cold. Hearing the news from the hospital yesterday had been such a shock. Rose had said she wouldn't see in the new year but neither she nor Sonny had actually *believed* her. Well, at least she hadn't. Her poor mother was devastated. She hadn't even said goodbye.

She, Allie, hadn't said goodbye, either. She hadn't said a lot of things. She'd so wanted to tell Rose about the vague, unformed sense of dread that ate away at her every day and blighted her sleep. Why couldn't she relax? Why did it seem so hard just to get from one end of a day to the other? Why was she so bloody *frightened* all the time? What was wrong with her? She had been sure her nan would know because Rose was old and wise and seemed to know everything, and even better she never judged, especially if she saw you were in pain, but now it was too late. It was too late to ask, and it was too late to thank her nan for always being there, and it was too late to say goodbye.

They'd been to see the funeral director that morning, a man Allie hadn't liked at all. His name was Grimwade — what a name for an undertaker. But he was Irish and he'd organised Granddad Patrick's funeral and her mother thought he should do Nan's as well. He was tall and skinny and pasty-skinned and looked like he should be in a coffin himself. He was exceedingly polite and solicitous but cracked his knuckles all the time, as though he couldn't wait to get stuck into whatever undertakers did to dead bodies when no one was looking.

He was bad enough but there'd already been some unpleasantness before that. The funeral wouldn't be till Wednesday, three days away, because her mother was worried people would be on holiday until then and no one would come. Her father had said what did it matter if it was only them — Nan wasn't going to be there to care. Which was true but it had really upset her mother. Then the priest from Nan's church, Father Noonan, who'd turned up at her parents' house yesterday afternoon, pointed out that if they wanted to delay the funeral Nan would have to be embalmed, given that it was the height of summer. And bloody Pauline had said, 'Why? Will she start to stink?' And her mother had marched across the front room and belted her on the arm, in front of the Father. Then, while everyone else had stared in shock, Sonny took Pauline outside, bawling her head off, while her mother sat down and said, 'Sorry, Father, but she deserved that,' then burst into tears herself.

That had all been smoothed over, but now her mother was working herself into another tizz. Sometimes Allie wished her mother drank, because this would be a good time for her to relax with a nice brandy or a gin, but the closest she ever got was a sweet sherry on very special occasions, which this definitely wasn't.

'Well, you might have to wear the grey,' Allie said. 'The shops are all shut till Wednesday morning. You won't have time to buy anything new. Have you got a black hat and gloves?'

'Yes, but that's not what I need. I need a black dress!'

Allie pulled out a black frock. 'Is this the one that doesn't fit any more?'

Colleen nodded. 'It's too tight round the middle and across the bust.'

'Can you let it out?' Allie inspected the seams.

'I already have.'

Allie put the dress back. 'I think you should just wear the grey. It's very smart.'

'I *can't*, Allison. People will talk!'

'It's Nan's funeral, Mum, not a fashion event. We're saying goodbye to her. It doesn't matter what colour your dress is.'

'It does!' Colleen wrenched the wardrobe door out of Allie's hand and slammed it, then stamped out of the room.

Allie was pretty sure there was a large dollop of guilt swirling through her mother's grief because Nan had died alone. She felt utterly awful about that too. And to atone for not being there Colleen wanted the funeral to be perfect, which was impossible because how do you make the last rites and burial of someone you love dearly 'perfect'?

*

Pauline swivelled in the pew to watch the coffin as it was carried into the church. She knew it was heavy because she'd been allowed to help carry it out last night after the vigil, when there'd only been family and a few close friends. She wasn't allowed to help carry it in today, though — her mother said it wasn't the done thing for women to be pallbearers. She'd been surprised at the great weight of it, but had assumed it was the wood, not Nan, because she'd weighed hardly anything when she'd died. At the thought of her poor, bony, helpless little body, Pauline felt tears burn her eyes yet again and she blinked madly. She would *not* cry in front of all these people.

Creepy Mr Grimwade the undertaker, in his shiny black suit and top hat, beckoned the pallbearers towards the front of the church, and she thought, you bloody idiot, where else would they take the coffin? He caught her eye and at his dirty look she realised her face had betrayed what she was thinking. Too bad, you disgusting old deathmonger. She hated him because he'd poked and prodded at Nan's body and filled her up with all sorts of strange chemicals, and all because her mother insisted on it. They should have just left Nan alone and buried her as soon as she'd died, in peace. Because that's what she deserved. Peace.

As the coffin was settled on the bier Pauline faced the front again. She was sitting in the front row of the church with the rest of her family. A lot of people had turned up and the place was full, and here she was wearing a boring grey skirt, a navy blue top and flat black shoes. God. She'd dressed this morning in her white capri pants, a new blue gingham shirt that tied at the waist and white wedges — a nice bright and breezy outfit her Nan would have liked — but her mother had gone so mental about it she'd changed. Donna was wearing head to toe navy, Allie was in black and her mother in dark grey. Sonny didn't own a suit but still looked pretty good in dark trou and a sports jacket. Her father did own one, and was wearing it, but it was ancient and shiny and looked like it had come from the Salvation Army and wouldn't do up across his belly. Good old Dad.

Her mother wasn't talking to her anyway, except to tell her off. Last night she'd said she hadn't wanted to go to the vigil, because she'd been terrified the coffin might be open and she'd have to look at Nan's face, all pale and still and empty. Or even worse, painted up like a doll's, which would have been awful. Her mother had accused her of not caring and hadn't even asked why she didn't want to go, so Pauline didn't bother telling her and it had all got a bit horrible until her dad took her aside and asked her could she please go to the vigil just to keep the peace. And he'd promised that the coffin would be closed, and it was, so it hadn't been that bad after all.

Nan was having the full mass, which meant they'd be up and down like yoyos. Pauline sighed. She rarely came to church, and her parents didn't very often, either, but Nan had come every Sunday without fail, so she supposed it was only right that Father Noonan went the whole hog. There'd be prayers and songs, the lot, and it'd take ages.

It did, and by the time they got out to Waikumete Cemetery it had started to rain, though the weather was still warm and the air dense. Grimwades' Funeral Directors had provided a car and driver for the Roberts family, in which Pauline quite enjoyed being chauffeured, though Allie and Sonny went in their truck. The fresh soil around the open grave had been covered with green cloth which the family, being the most bereaved, got to stand on while everyone else, ladies in particular, had to suffer their heels sinking into the turf. Father Noonan performed the final Rite of Committal, and Pauline closed her eyes as down Nan went into her narrow grave. It seemed like such a lonely, muddy, diminished end to such a loving, clever woman. But at least she was next to Granddad Patrick, or what was left of him. Pauline wondered what *was* left of him. Bugger all by now, probably.

Her boyfriend, Butch, who was a member of the Rebels motorcycle club, reckoned that when you died there was nothing left of the real you, that your body was just the packet you came in, so who cared what happened to it? She didn't agree with that. She thought dead bodies should be treated with respect, but kept that to herself because Butch could be a proper shit if you disagreed with him. In fact he was a shit anyway. They hadn't been getting on lately and she suspected he was about to dump her because she wouldn't have sex with him. That was all right. She wouldn't miss his bad temper, crass jokes and really quite bad body odour, but she would miss his beautiful Triumph motorcycle, which had been the main thing that had attracted her to him.

Also, she had her eye on someone else. She didn't think he owned a motorbike but he was so gorgeous she could probably overlook that for the time being. If the Rebels were in town of a night, and they usually were, roaring round making a noise and scaring the crap out of people, they ended up at the White Lady pie cart on Fort Street, like nearly everyone else out and about late, because it was the only place you could get decent coffee, and she'd seen this boy there a few times, hanging round with his mates. Someone said his name was Johnny someone-or-other. He was Maori and she grinned to herself as she imagined taking him home to meet her parents. They hadn't been that thrilled to start with about Allie and Sonny but now they thought Sonny was the ant's pants, but if *she* took a Maori boy home they would no doubt say, oh, no, we're not having another one. But she hadn't got that far yet. She hadn't even spoken to Johnny whatever-his-name-was, but he did know she existed because he'd winked at her once and given her a little wave, right in front of Butch, which had earnt her a slap before Butch had told her she was walking home.

Nan had known all this. She, Pauline, had gone round to her house at least once a week, every week, to chat, and then when Rose had broken her hip she'd visited her in the hospital even more, usually on her way home from work and nearly always on her own. She hadn't felt the need to tell her mother she visited her nan so regularly, because it was special time, just for the two of them. She'd told Rose everything, and Rose never said she was being bad, or wilful, or stupid. She listened, and only gave advice when asked for it, though one time Nan did ask what it was she thought she was looking for. She'd said she didn't know, just like she didn't know why she couldn't behave. Not that she deliberately set out to do wrong things, people just saw them that way. And what *had* she done wrong, really? She was still a virgin, she hadn't broken the law, and she had a job. *She* thought she was doing all right.

But now Nan was gone and there was no one for her to talk to. Her girlfriends were, frankly, too silly; talking to her parents was out of the question, even her father; Donna never took any notice of her; and Allie had her own problems, after losing poor little Hana and everything. She wouldn't want to listen to her little sister whingeing on as well.

And, finally, Pauline did cry.

*

Donna had been at the Green Lane School of Nursing for one week, and already she loved it. She loved the training and lectures and working on the wards at Green Lane Hospital, she loved how busy she was, she loved the uniform, and she loved living in the nurses' home (even though it was quite shabby) with the other trainee nurses. But best of all, and this had really taken her by surprise, she'd met a man she really quite fancied.

His name was Robert Sullivan and he was a doctor — that was all she knew about him so far — and she thought he was the most glamorous thing in his flapping white coat with his stethoscope slung casually around his neck. She'd met him when he'd barrelled round a corner and nearly knocked her flying. Unfortunately she'd been carefully carrying a full bedpan with a paper bag over it and the lot had gone everywhere. She'd sworn quite loudly then gone red in case someone had heard her, and he'd laughed and offered to take her out for a cup of coffee by way of an apology.

Some of the girls on her floor in the nurses' home squealed when she told them she had a date with a doctor. Well, Barbara Bassett and Helen Dawson did, because she'd become friends with them immediately, but Joan Proctor, who was twenty-one and slightly older and therefore, apparently, superior, looked down her nose then went back to her embroidery.

'I don't think we're allowed to fraternise with the doctors.'

'Well, *we* aren't,' Helen said. 'Donna is, so it's none of your business.'

'I hope Matron doesn't find out.'

'She won't if you don't tell her.'

'It *is* against the rules,' Joan insisted, tying off a thread and selecting a different colour.

'But it's still no skin off your nose, is it?' Barbara said. She was curled in a chair, prising the lid off a tin of chocolate macaroon biscuits. 'This was nearly full yesterday! Who's been hogging them?'

Guilty silence.

'I just don't think it's becoming,' Joan said eventually, 'nurses chasing after the doctors, especially trainee nurses. It gives us a bad name.'

'I'm not chasing him,' Donna said. 'He asked me out for coffee.'

'You're just jealous 'cos no one's asked you out,' Helen said.

Joan sniffed. 'I have a boyfriend. In fact, I'm engaged.'

'Really?' Barbara said. 'That's interesting. We nurses are supposed to be single, aren't we?'

Joan flushed, obviously realising she'd just plummeted from her high horse.

'Ha ha, got you,' Helen said.

'Well, all I'm saying is it's against the rules. And you should be careful, Donna.'

'Careful of what?' She was a funny old trout, Joan.

'Of … everything.'

'Oh, never mind being careful,' Barbara said, stuffing the last chocolate macaroon into her mouth. 'We haven't considered the most important question, have we? What are you going to wear?'

*

Donna decided on her floral, flared Horrockses cotton dress (her best and quite stylish) and her only pair of good sandals, red wedges which fortunately matched. She shaved her legs, painted her toenails, spent ages on her make-up, and agreed to let Helen curl her long, fair hair with a hot tong.

Then, sitting in front of the mirror, she said, 'You know, I don't know why I'm doing all this. I'm here to train as a nurse, not get myself a boyfriend. And my nan just died. I shouldn't be going out having fun.'

'Would she want you to stay in and mope?' Helen asked.

'Probably not.'

'There you go then.'

Donna lit a cigarette. 'It's not as if I banged into him on purpose, you know.'

Helen took another lock of Donna's hair and wrapped it around the tong. 'You don't have to justify yourself to me. Is he picking you up here?'

'He said to meet by the gates to the park.'

Briefly silent, Helen worked on Donna's hair. Then she said, 'Really? That's romantic.'

Donna glanced at Helen's reflection in the mirror. She was sure she'd heard a touch of sarcasm. 'I think he was worried about me getting caught going out.'

'Maybe.'

'Well, we're not allowed out during the week, are we?'

'No. You're right, he's probably just being careful.'

'He's got a car, though. We're going into town, to a coffee bar. Pooh, God, is that my hair I can smell burning?'

Helen whipped the tong out of Donna's hair. 'I've nearly finished. It looks lovely at the back. All shiny and ringlety.'

Finally Donna was ready to go. Leaving through the back door of the nurses' home, she walked along Green Lane Road to the entrance to Cornwall Park, where she sat on a stone wall under the trees to wait.

When Robert arrived he was driving the most extraordinary vehicle — nearly as eye-catching as Mr Leonard's car next door to her parents'. This one was a bright red two door convertible, but it was smaller and sort of more rounded off than Mr Leonard's vast American job.

He got out, trotted round and opened the passenger door for her. 'Your chariot awaits, fair princess. Hop in!'

She did, luxuriating in the cream leather seats. 'Is this yours?'

'Like it? It's a Ford Mark I Zephyr.'

'It's lovely! I have to admit I do rather like American cars, though.'

Settling himself back in the driver's seat, Robert said, 'Fords are American cars.'

'Oh. Are they?' God, what an idiot. 'Well, it doesn't look like one.'

'These ones are made by Ford UK, though this one was actually assembled here. In Wellington, I think. Or is it Petone?'

'Really?' Donna hoped he wasn't going to talk about cars all night.

Robert put his down his foot and off they tore, Donna's hair streaming out behind her in the evening air and immediately losing most of its curl.

'I thought we'd go to the Hi Diddle Griddle,' he said. 'Have you been there? On Karangahape Road?'

Donna hadn't, of course, though she'd heard about it. It served American-style food and was *the* place to eat, and was far too expensive for the likes of her. 'No, but I've been meaning to for ages.'

'Great food, you'll love it.'

Donna's heart sank, though not far because her stomach was in the way, full of the rather stodgy tea she'd recently eaten at the nurses' home. How was she going to manage two suppers? He'd said they were only going for coffee. 'Sounds lovely.'

At the Griddle they were lucky to get seats in a red leatherette booth. Donna looked around. The restaurant was long and narrow, and on one wall hung a huge black velvet mural of Hawaiian scenes that glowed in the dim light. Next to that was a waterfall made of giant clam shells, and farther along was a small stage and dance floor. It was all rather … exotic.

'What do you fancy?' Robert asked, indicating the menu.

Donna read, almost fainting at the prices. Two and six just for a cup of coffee? You could get a three-course meal for that in a lot of cafes. A fairly basic meal, true, but it'd be a lot more filling than a coffee.

'I'm thinking about the New York steak,' Robert said. 'Or maybe the Chicken Maryland.'

Donna checked the menu. Ten and six, and fifteen bob respectively. Bloody hell. Choosing the smallest item she could see, Donna said, 'A fruit cup would be lovely, thanks.'

Robert rolled his eyes. 'Don't tell me you're watching your weight. Come on, push the boat out. My treat. What about a Hawaiian steak, or try the lobster tail. Or maybe a pizza. Have you ever had a pizza? You haven't lived till you've had pizza. Or what about a cheeseburger? They're pretty tasty.'

About to ask for a cheese omelette, Donna changed her mind when she saw the price of that was eight and six. For a couple of eggs! 'I think I'd like a cheese toasted sandwich, thank you.' Two shillings and sixpence.

Robert looked vaguely disappointed, but ordered it for her when the waitress came, a steak for himself, and a corkscrew. He retrieved the bottle he'd put on the floor under the table when they'd arrived, and took it out of its anonymous brown paper bag. Donna thought it might be red wine, which she'd never tasted. She'd never had white wine, either. She drank beer, or sherry, or occasionally Pimm's or gin and orange, when she was being flash.

'They don't mind if you drink here,' Robert said, winding in the corkscrew, 'as long as you keep the bottle out of sight. If the cops come in just quickly put your glass on the floor.' He pulled out the cork with a pop and poured her a glass. 'There you go. It's a cabernet sauvignon. A New Zealand one but it's not bad.'

Donna took a sip. It was disgusting, like drinking oily vinegar.

'You don't like it?'

'Oh, no, it's quite nice, isn't it? Quite ... unique.'

'Would you prefer white?'

'No, this is fine, thanks.' Actually, she'd prefer a Coca-Cola. Or a cup of tea.

'I like a good red,' Robert said, swirling his wine around then smelling it like a dog sniffing another dog's bum, 'though I did think twice about bringing this. I need to be a bit careful about raids, being a doctor.'

'Are you a specialist?' Donna asked.

Robert laughed. 'No, I'm a house officer. I've just started my second year.'

Donna looked at him politely. Surely he'd explain if she sat here long enough.

He did. 'Sorry, I keep forgetting you're new at Green Lane. A house officer is at the bottom of the pecking order.'

'I thought that was first year pupil nurses, like me.'

'Well, yes, but I'm talking about doctors. A house officer is a fellow who's completed their medical degree at Otago University, and is now doing practical work at a hospital. Generally we'll do two years as a house officer, then either go off and be a general medical practitioner somewhere, or continue at a hospital as a senior house officer, then a registrar, then train as some sort of specialist or consultant.'

'And which will you do?'

'I'm going to train as a cardiac specialist. Green Lane is the best place in New Zealand for cardiac care, though no doubt I'll do a stint overseas somewhere as well. London, probably.'

'Have you always wanted to be a doctor?'

Robert shrugged. 'My father's a surgeon and my older brother's an orthopaedic specialist at Auckland Hospital. It was sort of inevitable, really. Why, did you always want to be a nurse?'

'Not until quite recently. No one in my family's ever got a professional qualification, before me.' Donna shut up, wondering if she should have said that.

'So you're not looking for a husband, then?'

He said it with a laugh but Donna could tell he meant the question seriously because his smile hadn't quite reached his eyes, and he was watching her intently, waiting for her to answer. She had a terrible urge to tell him she was, just to see what he'd do.

'At the moment I'd rather be studying towards my general nurse's qualification. Plenty of time for everything else later. Much later. I'm only eighteen, after all.'

'I think you'd make someone a lovely wife,' Robert said.

Donna went bright red, and hoped he couldn't see it in the Griddle's dim lighting.

Whether he had or not, he went on, 'You're charming, and you seem rather clever, and you're very pretty. Not like a lot of nurses.'

Startled, she gawped at him. 'Crikey, that's a really unkind thing to say!'

He laughed, possibly at the look on her face. 'Sorry. I didn't mean to be mean—'

'Though you just were. *Really* mean!'

'It's just that I've often wondered whether some girls go into nursing as a way of excusing them from not being able to get husbands.'

'That is so rude!' Donna couldn't tell whether he was having her on or not. 'Girls go into nursing because they want to help people who aren't well! And who says you doctors are all oil paintings?'

'Of course we're not. Well, not all of us.'

Their meals arrived. Robert's steak was quite big but apart from that Donna couldn't see anything that made it look like it came from New York. And her cheese toasted sandwich was just that, though she suspected there was mustard on it somewhere. They talked constantly throughout their meal. Robert didn't put his knife and fork down between mouthfuls, which Donna's mother always said was a bit common, but neither did he speak with his mouth full or chew with his mouth open, which in fact demonstrated good table manners. Personally, Donna had never subscribed to the putting the cutlery down between bites idea — you'd be at the table for hours. And her father talked with his mouth full, burped and sometimes even farted at the table, so she was quite impressed by Robert's display of etiquette. But with a family full of doctors they must all be quite posh. Good manners or not, Robert still managed to clean his plate before she'd waded through half of her toasted sandwich. She really felt like she might burst and the disgusting wine was going straight to her head and also giving her indigestion.

'Fancy a sweet?' Robert asked.

'A lolly?' Donna said. Why would she want a lolly?

'A sweet. Something sweet from the menu,' Robert clarified.

Oh, a pudding. Why not say a pudding? 'No thank you. Honestly, I couldn't eat another thing. I don't even think I can finish this toasted sandwich.'

'You don't eat much, do you?'

'I had a late afternoon tea.'

'You must get good afternoon teas. All we get are milk arrowroots. If we're lucky.'

'It comes from being homely,' Donna said. 'We've plenty of time for baking because we're not out on dates.'

Robert roared with laughter. 'Touché, Nurse, er ... I don't even know your surname.'

'It's Roberts.'

'Very good, Nurse Roberts. And would you like a cup of coffee before I deliver you back to your castle?'

Donna would, though it was so strong she was sure it caused the last of the curl to drop out of her hair. She was rather hoping Robert would drive right up to the nurses' home — surely no one would see her at this late hour — but he dropped her off on the street outside the hospital 'just to be safe'. Which was stupid, she thought, as he'd told her he lived in the resident medical officers' quarters on the top floor of the main hospital building and would be parking in the hospital carpark anyway, but she didn't say anything.

But before she got out of the car he leant across and kissed her, quite lingeringly. 'I had a great time tonight, Donna. Thanks for coming out with me. I'm really hoping we can do this again soon. What do you think?'

Donna didn't hesitate at all. 'I'd really like that, Robert. Thank you.'

'Friday night, then? Does that suit you?'

Donna couldn't be bothered to pretend she had to consult her social diary. 'That would be lovely.'

He smiled and patted her knee. 'Good. I'm pleased.'

*

'Well,' Sid said, 'I can tell you we won't all be retiring in luxury just yet.'

'You already have retired,' Colleen remarked, plonking a plate of scones fresh from the oven on the kitchen table.

'Cheese?' Allie asked, peeking under the tea towel.

'And date,' Colleen said as she carried the teapot across.

'But she had more squirrelled away than I expected,' Sid went on.

Colleen glared at him. 'For God's sake, have some respect. The poor woman's not even cold in her grave.'

'I'm just saying. It's quite impressive, is all.'

'Well, you're not getting your hands on it.'

'I'm sure I'm not. Pass us one of them scones, love. A date one.'

Allie did, and pushed the butter dish after it.

'Has Nan left us some money?' Pauline asked.

'Wait till I've poured the tea, will you?' Colleen snapped. 'And don't be so avaricious.'

Pauline made a face. 'What's that mean?'

'Greedy,' Donna said.

Allie watched her mother taking her time with the tea. She was still angry, and still taking her grief out on everyone else. She wished she'd stop it because it wasn't improving matters. It was going to be one of 'those' family meetings. Her mother was in a mood, though she had a right to be, Pauline was acting up, and Donna seemed as though she had something on her mind too, though she didn't appear unhappy. Quite the opposite, actually.

Colleen finally finished buggering about with the teapot and opened an envelope tucked beneath a place mat. 'As you all know, this is your Nan's will.' Her voice cracked slightly. 'Donna and Pauline, you get one hundred pounds each, but not until you turn twenty-one. And *don't* argue about it.'

'I wasn't going to,' Donna said.

Allie eyed Pauline, who didn't look pleased at all. Just sad.

Colleen looked at Allie. 'And she's left you her house.'

Sonny spluttered out a mouthful of tea.

'Her *house*?' Allie was stunned. 'In Newmarket?'

Sonny apologised and fetched a tea towel.

'Unless she had another one somewhere I don't know about,' Colleen said.

Allie lost her temper. 'Oh, *stop* it, Mum. Stop being such a cow. We all miss her, not just you. You're just making everything worse.'

Shoving her chair back with a horrible squeak, Colleen marched out of the kitchen.

They sat in awkward silence, then Sid said, 'Don't be hard on her, love. She just needs time.'

Donna cut a scone in half and by the time she'd buttered it, Colleen was back.

'I'm sorry. You're right, I'm not helping.' She glanced at the will again. 'Nan wanted you to have her house so you can save on rent and eventually buy a bigger home, something suitable for a family.'

If we ever manage to actually have one, Allie thought bitterly.

'When that happens, the Newmarket house reverts to me.' Colleen eyed Pauline and Donna. 'Then maybe one of you can have it.'

'But it's got an outside dunny,' Donna said.

Sid said, 'It's a free outside dunny, though, isn't it? Never lift a gift horse's tail.'

Sonny and Donna both laughed, and Donna said, 'At least Mr De Valera will be pleased to be back home.'

That was true, Allie thought. And they would save a lot by not paying rent. But Nan's old workers' cottage was a bit of step down from their nice modern flat with its indoor bathroom. 'What do you think?' she asked Sonny.

'I think it's the most generous thing I've ever heard.'

It was, Allie reflected. It was incredibly generous. Trust Rose to think of everyone else, even after she knew she'd be gone. 'What did Nan leave you?' she said to her mother. 'Can I ask?'

'Her personal things, and some things of my father's, and some money. She had more put away than I thought, actually.'

Pauline sat forwards. 'Mum?'

Colleen's eyebrows went up.

'Can I have Nan's cloche hat? Please? The one she always wore?'

'What for?'

'Because ...' Pauline hesitated. 'Well, because she always wore it.'

Colleen reached out and touched her hand. 'Of course you can. But look after it.'

'I will, I promise.'

Allie felt something inside her ease slightly. Perhaps they'd get through this in one piece after all.

Chapter Eight

David had had to go back to work straight after the Christmas break, and had been away now for a week and a half. Ana missed him dreadfully and so did the children. They'd never really been apart on the farm, but now it seemed they were hardly ever together. He came home once a fortnight, or sometimes once a week if he was working within driving distance, but their time together was never enough.

At Christmas she'd wanted to ask him to stay, to look for work that wouldn't take him away, but the Wool Board job paid well, and she didn't want to deprive him of involvement with the sheep farming she knew he loved so dearly. So she'd kept quiet and told him that looking after Jack wasn't really as hard as it might seem, and that she'd made some friends and was settling into life as an Auckland housewife.

But she bloody well wasn't, and she'd hardly met anyone because she'd had neither the time nor the opportunity, and sometimes when Jack was in bed asleep, lying there with his mouth hanging open snoring his head off, she felt like holding a pillow over his face until he stopped breathing, though she'd never admit that to anyone. She swung so wildly between sorrow and sympathy for him, and exasperation and outright anger at his awful behaviour and the fact that *she* was stuck having to manage it, that some days she thought she was losing her own mind. Her only reprieve came when the kids got home from school and they could help watch him, which was so unfair on them, and her spinning and knitting, which soothed her immensely. She could only do that at night, however, when everyone else was asleep, but it was worth it, and as a result her family possibly had the most extensive and beautiful collection of knitwear in Auckland.

Jack's latest quirk, which had appeared recently, was endless walking. In a way it was good because it seemed to tire him out and he was sleeping better, but he had to be watched every second in case he marched right off the property and away down the street. Right now he was walking in big circles on the back lawn, and had been for the past two hours. She had housework to do so she'd made the children sit on the steps and watch him, which they'd grizzled about because they'd wanted to ride their bikes with the neighbourhood kids.

She went out to see if Jack was tiring — perhaps she could get him to have a nap, then the kids could go out.

But no, there he was, still trudging round and round in a great big pointless circle.

'Has he been doing that the whole time?' she asked.

'Sometimes he turns round and goes the other way,' Rowie said. 'And he did a wee in the feijoas.'

God, Ana thought.

'He looks silly,' Peter said. 'He looks like a horse. Giddy-up, Grandpa!'

Ana hauled him up by the arm and smacked him across the back of the legs. 'Don't you be so damn cheeky! He can't help what he's doing.'

As Peter burst into tears Jack bellowed, 'That's it, Mary, belt the little bugger!'

Ana glared at him. Thanks very much, now the whole street knows I hit my children. 'Time's up, Jack. In you come.'

He didn't hear her, or pretended he didn't, and darted up the path at the side of the house. Ana raced through the house, out the front door across the lawn, and met him at the front gate where she grabbed hold of his shirt.

'No you don't,' she said. 'Back inside, please.'

'Let go. I want to go home.'

'You are home,' Ana said. 'Come inside.'

Jack tried to wrench his arm free, and raised his other hand to her. 'Fuck off.'

'Need some help?'

It was Sid. Ana blew out her cheeks with relief. 'Jack fancies a walk. I'd like him to go inside.'

'Looks like he fancies thumping you, and that wouldn't be on, would it?' Sid slowly reached for Jack's raised hand and eased his arm down.

'Who the fuck are you?' Jack demanded.

'Sid, from next door. We've met but you might have forgotten. I'm the same way meself. Memory like a sieve.'

Jack peered at him through suspicious eyes, his body still tense.

'Anyway, I'm after a bit of advice,' Sid went on chattily, 'I'm thinking about buying a horse and I'm told you're the man to talk to. What do you reckon?'

Jack's hands relaxed, his thumbs went into the waistband of his trousers and his shoulders dropped about three inches. 'Well —' he began.

'Not out here, though, eh, it's too bloody hot,' Sid said. 'What about we go inside and yarn over a beer?'

Jack turned and marched towards the house, beckoning over his shoulder.

'You're a clever man, Mr Roberts,' Ana said.

'It's Sid. And you're a bloody saint, Mrs Leonard. I hope you've got beers in.'

'A few. Thank you so much. I thought he was going to get away from me this time.'

'And I thought he was going to belt you one. I was watching him out the window.'

'Oh, I doubt he'd actually *do* it,' Ana said, then looked quickly away in case Sid could see she was lying.

*

On the fourth Sunday in January, Allie and Sonny visited Louise Taylor, Allie's friend and survivor of the Dunbar and Jones fire. They went on the Indian, so Sonny and Rob, Louise's mechanic husband, would have something to stand around on the lawn and talk about while Allie and Louise were inside gossiping. This was according to Sonny, anyway.

Allie and Louise actually didn't do much gossiping as Louise wasn't that sort of woman and never had been, but they did talk a bit about what they were up to, and Allie told Louise about Rose's recent passing. This brought up the deaths of Daisy Farr and Irene Baxter, and of Terry Hewitt and Miss Button and Miss Willow and everyone else who had died in the fire, though the women kept their voices low because Susan, Louise and Rob's five-year-old, was playing on the sitting room floor.

'Do you think about them often?' Allie asked.

Louise thought for a moment. 'I try not to. I've tried to put the whole thing behind me. I think it's for the best, to just move on.'

Allie stared intently at her friend's face, looking for signs she might be hiding something. She wished *she* could just move on.

'You don't have, I don't know, sudden thoughts, or memories, about what happened? Just out of the blue? Or bad dreams?'

Louise looked baffled. 'No. Do you?'

'Oh, no. I was just wondering.'

'Yes you do, Mummy,' Susan piped up. 'Sometimes you shout out, at night, and Daddy comes to tell me you've had a bad dream and I should go back to sleep.'

'Why don't you go and see what Daddy's doing, sweetheart?' Louise suggested.

Allie said, 'Uncle Sonny might take you for a tiny ride on his motorbike.'

'Like hell he will,' Louise said. 'Go on, off you go.'

Susan tore out of the room, making loud brrrmmm noises.

Scowling, Louise added, 'Thanks a lot. Now you've turned her into a Widgie.'

'Sorry. Um, *have* you had bad dreams?'

After a long moment of silence, Louise sighed. 'A few. Probably more than a few. Why, have you?'

Allie nodded.

'Then why did you say you hadn't?' Louise asked.

'Why did you?'

They looked at each other and laughed.

Louise said, 'I don't know. It's just not something I want to harp on about.'

'I know. It's been two years — you'd think it'd be behind us now.'

'It *is* behind me. I'm not responsible for what happens in my dreams.'

Allie wondered who was then. How easy to say not my dreams, not my problem to worry about. But her dreams came during waking hours as well as at night, and weren't so easy to brush aside, not when they dragged you down like a full set of winter clothes pulled a drowning man beneath the waves. Should she tell Louise about everything else? The terrifying smell of smoke when there was no fire, and the constant grinding dread, and the awful, hollow lack of joy in her life?

The rumbling growl of the Indian brought them both to their feet.

Peeking out the sitting room window Louise exclaimed, 'He bloody well is taking her for a ride!' She shoved open the window. 'Rob Taylor, you larrikin, get her off that motorbike!'

Rob waved back gaily.

They went outside and watched as Sonny rode a short distance up the street at a very moderate speed then back again with Susan perched on the seat behind him, her arms wrapped tightly around his waist and the most enormous grin on her shining face.

'More!' she shrieked as the Indian came to a stop. 'More!'

'Probably not today, love,' Sonny said. 'I don't think your mum's too happy.'

'Bloody nice motorcycle,' Rob said to Louise. 'I'm thinking of getting one. What do you think?'

'I think you should bloody well grow up. You're a married man. Married men don't tear about on motorbikes. You've got responsibilities.'

Allie looked at Louise with genuine fondness and thought that's typical of you, always practical, always down to earth, always a tiny bit judgmental, and decided she'd keep the rest of her worries to herself.

Laughing, Sonny said, '*I'm* a married man.'

'Yes, but you don't have a child, or a business to run,' Louise retorted, then, mortified, clapped her hand over her mouth. 'I'm so sorry, that was so tactless of me. I just meant that Rob —' She shut up, perhaps before she made it worse.

Allie felt sorry for Louise's discomfort. If people mentioned Hana now it was in the past tense. They'd all moved on. But for her and Sonny she still existed, in their hearts if nowhere else, so to them she hadn't really gone at all. If another baby ever came along they'd have two children — the new one and their memories of Hana.

Sonny touched Louise's arm very briefly. 'It's all right, I know what you meant.'

Rob swung Susan off the back of the Indian. 'Was that fun?'

'We went so *fast*!' she burst out. 'We were *flying*!'

Allie slid onto the bike's seat behind Sonny. 'I forgot to say, Lou, if you want to come to the Smith and Caughey fashion parade on Friday I can get you a free ticket.'

'What time?'

'Starts at five.'

'Lovely. Thanks! I'll see if Mum can babysit.'

February 1956

For weeks now Kathleen and Rosemary Lawson had been practising for their debut as fashion models. In the formal lounge Kathleen had pushed the furniture back and, with string, marked out a catwalk on the carpet, and she and Rosemary had walked its length hand in hand, turning slowly and gracefully at the end again and again, until their moves were polished, poised and perfect. Because Kathleen didn't know exactly what they'd be modelling in the parade, they practised in day outfits, formal outfits, ensembles with coats, beachwear (though not swimming costumes — Kathleen drew the line at appearing in public in a swimming costume), and evening wear. Rosemary turned out to be rather good at it, turning so that her skirt flicked out and slipping out of her coat as though she were born to it, while Evie applauded enthusiastically. Geoffrey, and Jonathan when he was at home, ignored them completely, but not so Terence, who desperately wanted to join in.

In fact, Kathleen was grateful that Jonathan was away much of the time, as Terence repeatedly insisted on draping himself in a lace tablecloth and following her and Rosemary up and down the string catwalk, prancing along, twirling with enthusiastic abandon and thoroughly enjoying himself. When she told him to stop it and go away, he'd shout that it simply wasn't fair. Why couldn't he be allowed in the parade? Eventually she would have to order, or drag, him up to his room, which was a chore as he really was getting too big to haul about.

Now there were only two days to go until the event and Kathleen was beginning to feel a little nervous. She was sure she and Rosemary would be well-received by the audience, but it didn't pay to be too brash — one never knew when something out of one's control might occur. Further, her mother and father were arriving from Hawke's Bay on Friday morning and would be attending the fashion parade that evening, which was also upsetting her equilibrium. She got on with her parents reasonably well these days but would rather have spent Friday getting ready for her public appearance than settling them into the house. And she'd *much* rather have spent tonight reading in bed with a face-pack on than going out to a drinks party.

She finished her gin and tonic — admittedly, mostly gin — blotted her crimson lips with a tissue, secured a diamante clip in her hair, eyed herself critically in her dressing table mirror, then went downstairs to tell Jonathan she was ready.

'You look very nice, Mrs Lawson,' Evie said.

Kathleen hesitated only very slightly before replying, 'Thank you.' You could never tell with Evie, who, though unfailingly polite and helpful, said everything with the slightest smirk, which made her feel the girl was laughing at her, though she had no idea why. 'Where is Mr Lawson?'

'In his study.'

And so he was — Kathleen could smell the whiskey from the doorway. She sighed. Vodka martini was Jonathan's morning and early afternoon tipple; whiskey was his 'night on the tiles' drink.

'Are you ready?' she asked.

'I am.'

'Did you say good night to the children?'

'Couldn't find Terence, but I did the other two.'

Terence hadn't been in bed when Kathleen had gone to tuck them in, either. She'd assumed he was in the loo.

'Shall we go, then?' Kathleen said, pulling on her gloves. 'I hope you're not too drunk to drive.'

'Don't be ridiculous.'

As Jonathan put on his hat in the foyer mirror and Kathleen fidgeted, Terence called down to them from the top of the stairs, 'Look at me, Mum and Dad.'

They did.

He waved at them. 'See, I look just like a girl. I *can* be in the fashion parade!'

Kathleen stared in shock. Terence was wearing one of her pale pink satin slips over his vest and a pair of Rosemary's long white, lace-trimmed socks, and was teetering in a pair of her own suede heels. But most bizarre of all was his face, to which he'd applied far too much rouge and a slash of red lipstick. There was also a large pink bow attached to his blonde curls.

'Oh my *God*!' Jonathan sounded horrified. He launched himself up the stairs two at a time, and hit Terence so hard across the side of the head he knocked him right off his feet. 'That is *disgusting*! Wash that shit off your face and get out of those clothes *right now*!' He bent down and snatched the bow out of Terence's hair. '*Now*! Do you hear me? Then get to bloody bed! Christ! *Evie!*' he roared as he came downstairs again.

She appeared, looking startled.

'Get upstairs and sort that boy out,' Jonathan ordered. Then he marched past Kathleen and out the front door.

After a moment, appalled and utterly bewildered by what Terence had done, and at Jonathan's reaction, she followed him.

They said nothing on the way to the soiree, held at a private address, travelling in the car in stony silence. Predictably, Jonathan drank too much but, as always, managed to be the life of the party. Well done you, Kathleen thought bitterly — exuberant, charming and witty, and nothing like you are at home. And tomorrow you'll be fine, no hangover or anything, whereas when she drank to excess, which she had to admit, if only to herself, was occurring more and more frequently, she suffered appalling headaches and nausea the next morning and had to pretend she had a migraine because she'd done most of her drinking in secret.

She thought he was too drunk to drive home and wanted to telephone for a taxi, but Jonathan told her not to be stupid, he was fine, and needed the car first thing tomorrow anyway. So after doing a complicated manoeuvre involving backing across the host's front lawn and into a bird bath, they drove off, and again lapsed into silence. Kathleen desperately wanted to say something about Terence but all Jonathan's bonhomie had left him now they weren't in company and his face was like thunder. And he was *very* drunk.

Once home they went straight upstairs. Jonathan undressed, leaving his clothes on the floor, and collapsed into bed while Kathleen sat at her dressing table and wiped off her make-up. Still he said nothing, and after a few minutes she heard him snoring. She lit a cigarette and sat smoking, thinking about how he'd be flying down south for the next couple of days, leaving her to try and get to the bottom of what on earth was wrong with Terence, and what a bastard he was for it.

Finally she changed into her nightgown and got into bed. But she couldn't sleep. Then she thought she heard someone banging on a door downstairs, but decided that perhaps she was actually drifting off and imagining it because now it sounded like some sort of drumming. But when Jonathan grunted, rolled over and breathed alcohol fumes in her face she knew she was still awake, and she could still hear the noise. She got out of bed and went out onto the landing. The thumping was louder out here.

She padded cautiously to the top of the stairway. A light had been left on in the kitchen so it wasn't completely dark downstairs, but she couldn't see anything amiss in the wide reception area below her. And then she heard a strangled choking sound, and suddenly saw it — a sheet tautly knotted around the balustrade, about a third of the way down the stairs.

She let out a squawk of utter horror and tore down to the reception area to the body jerking and kicking at the end of the makeshift rope. It was Terence, his feet drumming against the wall beneath the stairs, his hands jammed between his throat and the noose he'd made of the sheet, his face swelling, his pyjama pants slid part way down his legs.

'*Jonathan!*' Kathleen shrieked as she grabbed Terence's knees and tried to lift him. '*Jonathan!*'

But it wasn't Jonathan who came, it was Evie, roused immediately and hurtling out of her downstairs bedroom.

'What ... *Shit!*'

Kathleen barely noticed her language. 'Get a knife, Evie, quick! *Jonathan!*'

Evie darted into the kitchen, and was back a moment later with a boning knife and raced up the stairs, her breasts bouncing beneath her flimsy pyjama top. She hacked at the sheet and Terence's body fell; Kathleen caught him and wrenched the noose away from his neck, then laid him on the floor. Coughing and spluttering he stared up at her through bloodshot eyes, then turned his head slightly and heaved up a little vomit. Kathleen sat him up quickly so he wouldn't swallow it, and patted him firmly on the back. She felt as terrible as he looked. Why on earth had he done it? How had he even thought of it, at his age?

'Mum, what's happened?'

Oh God, it was Geoffrey, hanging over the balustrade. 'Nothing, dear. Would you please go and wake up your father and tell him we need him.'

'What's the matter with Terence?'

'He's had a slight accident.'

'But what's happened?'

'Just go and get your father!' Kathleen snapped. 'And make sure Rosemary's door's shut. I don't want her out here.'

By the time Jonathan finally appeared, Terence had vomited again but had managed half a glass of water, and Kathleen had examined his neck. He had angry red 'rope' burns on his throat and quite deep scratches where he'd scrabbled to release the pressure of the sheet.

She looked at his tear-stained face in complete confusion. 'Why, Terence? What did you think you were doing?'

'I don't *know*,' he rasped.

'Did he hang himself?' Geoffrey asked.

'Shush,' Kathleen said.

Staring down at them, Jonathan shook his head. 'For God's sake, boy, what is *wrong* with you?'

Terence started to cry again.

'What do you think could have happened if I hadn't heard you banging?' Kathleen asked, her arm around him. 'You might really have choked to death. Where would you be then?'

'Dead,' Terence said.

'Yes, very, and we'd be heartbroken. It's not a game, you know. It's a very, very serious thing to do.'

'I suppose we'd better take him to the hospital,' Jonathan muttered. 'I'll get dressed.'

'No!' Kathleen exclaimed. She hesitated. 'No, I think he's probably all right. I'll take him to the doctor's tomorrow just in case.'

The hospital was far too public and she didn't want people knowing their business, especially this sort of business. They'd never live it down.

'Well, while you're there, get an appointment for him with a psychiatrist,' Jonathan ordered.

Stunned, Kathleen said, 'A psychiatrist? Why does he need a psychiatrist? He's only nine years old.'

'Because obviously something's not bloody well right, is it? This rigmarole can't go on, all these tantrums and the dressing up and now this. He needs sorting out.'

'He needs his father to pay some attention to him, that's all.'

'Would anyone like a cup of tea?' Evie asked quickly. 'And the children might like cocoa.'

It was then that Kathleen suddenly realised she couldn't take Terence to the doctor tomorrow because she wanted to buy new outfits for her and Rosemary to wear to the fashion parade, and also to find out from Miss Weaver at Smith and Caughey what they'd actually be modelling. Evie would have to take him.

*

Polly lit a cigarette, inhaled deeply and blew twin jets of smoke out through her nostrils. She was in the Mocambo Coffee Lounge on Swanson Street waiting for her friend, but she was nearly always late no matter the occasion so she was thinking about ordering coffee. But then Evie came breezing through the door and Polly had to take it all back as she waved her over. 'You're on time.'

'I know,' Evie said, collapsing onto a cane chair. 'Nearly wasn't, though. I had to take Terry to the doctor then put him on the bus back to school.'

'What's wrong with him?'

'Tell you in a minute. I'm gasping for caffeine.' Evie waved to the waitress, who approached with her order pad at the ready. 'A pot do us?'

Polly nodded.

'Pot of coffee, thanks.'

When the waitress had gone, Evie said as she lit a cigarette, 'You'll never guess what he did.'

'Terry?'

'Mmm.' Evie flapped out her match. 'He only hung himself. Last night.'

'Really? That's a bit … dramatic. Obviously it didn't work, or you'd have been at the funeral parlour this morning, not the doctor's.'

'True. I'm not sure he meant it to work. But I still nearly shat myself.'

'How did he do it?'

'Off the stairs with a couple of sheets.'

'Why?'

Evie blew out her cheeks. 'Christ knows, but he got a hiding from Jonathan last night for dressing up in Kathleen's clothes. Might have been that. He's a bloody bully, Jonathan. Nice-looking one, though.'

Polly knew all about the goings-on in the Lawson household. Evie bitched about her job all the time. 'I've got a cousin who wears women's clothes. And make-up. Everyone just lets him get on with it.'

'It's a bit different, though, when you're only nine years old and from a snotty rich Remuera family. God, they're a strange lot.'

'If you don't like nannying for them, leave.'

Polly didn't know what Evie was doing working as a nanny,

anyway. She was as clever as anything and had passed her University Entrance exams, though hadn't gone on to university, which Polly really didn't understand. Why would you not go to university if you could? She'd had to leave school when she was fifteen because her father had told her she had to go to work. She hadn't even been *allowed* to try for School Certificate. So Evie could have had her pick of jobs, but instead she was looking after some rich people's spoilt kids. And she was very striking-looking with a curvy figure, lovely pale skin and gleaming chestnut hair she wore in an old-fashioned bob with a fringe, like someone from the 1930s. Polly liked her, a lot, but she didn't share much about herself. But then Polly didn't share much about *her*self, either. Sometimes she thought Evie was just marking time with her life, and at other times it seemed she had a plan, though who knew what that might be. She supposed that if Evie wanted her to know, she'd tell her, and so far she hadn't.

'I think I might, soon,' Evie said.

'Did it upset you, what Terry did?'

'It gave me a fright, but no, it didn't upset me, though I do feel sorry for him. He gets a hard time from his parents for being different. Personally I don't care if he wants to be the fairy on top of the Christmas tree, but they can't stomach the idea. Especially his father.'

'But to behave the way he does when he's only nine. It's a bit odd, isn't it?'

'Not really. I think some people just know early on who they are. And he can be difficult but he's not a bad boy. Actually he can be really sweet. He picked me some flowers the other day. And they're all a bit odd, those kids. I blame their parents.' Evie sat back as the waitress brought the coffee. 'They're the ones causing the trouble. They're downright abusive sometimes, if you ask me. If any of those kids turn out to be axe murderers, it'll be their fault.'

'Well, I'm glad he's not my kid,' Polly said.

'How is Gina?'

'She's good. Look, I'm walking in the Smith and Caughey fashion parade tomorrow afternoon. I can probably get you in if you want to come.'

'Already going. Kathleen and Rosemary are modelling mother and daughter outfits. God knows how they managed that. I'm helping them dress.'

That was a surprise, Polly thought. Someone must owe someone a favour. 'Really? Who's babysitting Terry and the other boy, then?'

'Their father. He's refusing to go and watch. Says it's beneath him. And beneath Kathleen and Rosemary.'

'It's not beneath me. I get quite good money for modelling.'

'Better than at Flora's?'

'No. Nothing pays better than Flora's.'

'Hmm,' Evie said thoughtfully as she poured them both coffee.

*

Pauline was working late because of the fashion parade. Usually she finished at four o'clock, even on late night, but today had been frantic because they'd had their usual customers through the tearoom, plus they'd had to get everything ready for the ladies coming for the parade. That meant that all the plates, cutlery, tea and coffee pots had to be cleaned in time for the start of the event, the tables dressed in fresh linen, and extra cakes, sandwiches, scones and savouries prepared. Her legs felt like they were nearly falling off by afternoon smoko, and she knew she wouldn't be getting out the door till probably at least seven. Still, it was exciting and time was whizzing past, not like on a normal day when usually she was dying of boredom, putting endless cream cakes on plates and teapots on trays. She was quite looking forward to seeing all the new clothes, too, and especially the models. Allie said they were really glamorous. She and her mate Peggy and the Helena Rubinstein girls were doing the make-up, which Pauline really wanted to see but knew she wouldn't because she was too busy cutting the crusts off bloody club sandwiches.

The parade started at five and already women were piling into The Cedar Room, jostling and elbowing one another but pretending they weren't to get the best tables near the slightly elevated runway down the middle of the room. From the recesses of the kitchen Pauline stared in amazement. Most of them were dressed as though they thought they were actually *in* the fashion parade, and it seemed the older they were, the more they'd tarted themselves up. She saw feather boas, fox fur stoles with the poor little heads still on, huge hats that would block everyone's views, pheasant feathers that could take your eye out, tiny waists, towering heels, and skirts that were full and stiff enough to shift chairs. No one *she* knew wore clothes like that, but then, she supposed, she didn't mix in the same circles as these sorts of people. She couldn't see these ladies hanging out with the Rebels motorcycle club.

She spotted Allie heading towards her, and waved.

'Can you bring us something to eat and some tea? Enough for four?' Allie asked. 'We're not going to have time for a break. We're flat out. Just sandwiches will do.'

'I'll have to check with Mrs Bitch,' Pauline said, indicating her boss, Mrs Fitch.

'I will,' Allie said, and did. 'She said yes. Quick as you can, love. Thanks.'

Delighted at the prospect of meeting real live fashion models after all, Pauline arranged a tray and made her way around to the area where they were getting ready. Allie was working on Polly, Sonny's stunningly beautiful sister, whom Pauline had met a few times but didn't really know well. She wore a silky robe and her feet were bare, and a cigarette smouldered nearby in an ashtray. Her eyes were closed as Allie applied black liner to her upper lids and she looked as though she was almost asleep.

'Thanks, love,' Allie said as Pauline set down the tray.

Polly's eyes opened. 'Hi, Pauline.'

'Hi.'

Polly reached into her handbag, retrieved a bottle and knocked back a slug.

Pauline gasped, thrilled. 'Is that booze?'

'Want some?'

'No, she does not,' Allie said. 'Behave.'

Pauline glanced furtively about. 'I don't think we're supposed to drink on the premises.'

'She knows that,' Allie said.

Spotting a woman sitting nearby watching them with a very sour look on her face, Pauline said, 'I think that woman just saw you, the one with the little girl. Who's she?'

'That's Mrs Lawson,' Allie replied. 'She and her daughter are modelling mother and daughter outfits. I'm doing them next.' She bent and applied a perfect sweep of lipstick to Polly's full lips, blotted and repeated. 'There, you're done. Don't smudge when you're getting dressed. Pauline, why don't you go and see what Peg's doing?'

With immense regret, because really the only model she'd managed to talk to was one she already knew, Pauline said, 'I'd better get back to work.'

Allie said, 'See you later, then. Mrs Lawson, would you like to take a seat?'

Chapter Nine

Kathleen Lawson had barely settled herself before she said, 'Did I see that girl who was sitting here just before me, the dark-skinned one, take a drink from a bottle?'

Allie sighed inwardly. 'I'm not sure. Did you?'

'It was right in front of you. Surely you saw it too. Was it alcohol?'

'I really don't know, Mrs Lawson.'

'Who is she, do you know?'

'She's one of the models.'

'Well, yes, I gathered *that*. What's her name?'

Allie felt a spike of irritation. 'Why?'

'Because I've a good mind to report her to Mr Holmes, the store manager.'

Oh, and you don't come into the shop stinking of booze? Allie thought. 'Why would you want to do that?'

'Because … it's in their best interests not to drink, isn't it? It's not good for them.'

'Sorry, I'm not sure who you mean?'

'Well, Maoris, of course,' Kathleen said, sounding very tetchy. 'And please stop asking *me* questions. *I* haven't done anything wrong.'

More than a little tetchy herself now, Allie said, 'Actually, she's my sister-in-law.'

'Who is?'

'That model, the Maori girl you're accusing of drinking.'

A longish silence followed, broken only by Rosemary Lawson humming to herself as she played with a tiny doll, oblivious to the drama surrounding her.

Then, staring straight ahead, a hand to her throat, Kathleen said, 'I didn't know you were married to a Maori.'

Allie risked a glance at Peggy, who rolled her eyes.

Another silence, which Allie ended this time. 'Shall we get on with your make-up?'

She'd managed to apply foundation, powder, eyeshadow and rouge and had just discreetly spat into the cake of mascara before Kathleen asked, 'How long have you been married?'

'Not long. About eighteen months.'

'And is he employed?'

'Yes, he's em*ployed*.' Allie hadn't meant to emphasise the last syllable, but it came out anyway.

'Really? What does he do?'

'He's a delivery man for Smith and Caughey. He drives a truck.'

'And is that why you work, dear?'

'Not really,' Allie said. 'Both my younger sisters work. Our parents raised us to be industrious.'

'Of course. They must be quite, well, broad-minded, your parents.'

'Not really,' Allie said again. 'Dad's a dyed-in-the-wool union man on an invalid's benefit and Mum's a semi-lapsed Catholic who has a fit if her nets are hanging crooked.'

'And they're quite happy with ... your choice of husband?'

'Yes. My husband's family weren't that thrilled with him marrying a Pakeha girl, though.'

Kathleen looked up at Allie in absolute shock. 'What?'

Allie nearly laughed, enjoying herself now. 'His mother didn't want him to marry me.'

'Why on earth not?'

'She didn't think I'd fit into the Maori way of life.'

'Oh, rubbish. There isn't a Maori way of life. They either have to fit in with us or … I don't know, disappear.'

Allie rubbed the tiny brush along the mascara cake. 'Could you please sit still with your eyes wide open?' She expertly coated Kathleen's lashes, making them look twice as lush, then asked, 'Do you know what outfits you're modelling yet?'

'Rather charming sleeveless dresses in black and white gingham with large white daisies with red centres randomly placed around the bottom of the skirts. The bodices are fitted and the skirts are quite flared.'

'Shoe colour?'

'Red to match the daisies.'

'I'll do a red lip, then.'

When she'd finished Kathleen, Allie fluffed a bit of powder and rouge over Rosemary's face, applied a pink lip, and sent them both on to the clothing department girls.

'God, she's a piece of bloody work,' Peggy said. 'Disappear? How bloody rude and stupid can you be? Weren't you insulted?'

'She's just ignorant.'

'Don't stick up for her. She was *rude*. She thinks you can do better. It was written all over her pasty, Pakeha face.'

Allie laughed. 'You've got a Pakeha face.'

'Shows what you know. My nannie's Nga Puhi.'

'Really? You never said.'

'You never asked.'

'I'm a bit worried she might dob Polly in,' Allie said.

'Well, you know, it might not do Polly any harm to get dobbed in. It isn't actually that clever to be drinking on the job.'

'I know, but if she loses her modelling job that'll affect her pay, and she gives a fair bit of that to her mother, for Gina.'

'Oh, grow up. You've *told* me where she gets her money, and it's not just from waitressing and modelling, is it? Stop being such a softie.'

Stubbornly, Allie said, 'She's family and you look out for family.'

Peggy sighed. 'I suppose you do, don't you?'

*

Polly stood just beyond the double doors to the tearoom, waiting to go in and glide down the runway in her first gown. In front of her, awaiting their turn in matching outfits, were the woman and child she'd seen in make-up. They weren't professional walkers, she could tell that, but they weren't bad-looking. The little girl in particular was quite sweet.

Then the woman turned to her and said abruptly, 'I saw you drinking alcohol earlier, you know. From the bottle.'

Polly stared at her. 'So?'

'I've a good mind to report you to the store manager.'

'Off you go, then.'

'What's your name?'

'Polly Manaia. What's yours?'

'Mrs Jonathan Lawson.'

Polly leant closer. 'Funny, you don't *look* like a Jonathan. Or, actually, maybe you do.'

The woman flapped her hand in front of her face. 'I can smell the alcohol on your breath even now.'

'I thought that was *your* breath. Gin and tonics for afternoon tea, was it?'

Mrs Lawson's face went red under her foundation. 'Don't be so damned rude.'

'You said it to me.'

'Well, I'll *definitely* be speaking to Mr Holmes now. He's a personal friend, you know.'

Polly heard Miss Weaver, who was compering the parade, announce from the tearoom the mother and daughter outfits. Resisting the temptation to keep her mouth shut, she said, 'You're on.'

'It's not a challenge,' Mrs Lawson said. 'I'm simply doing my civic duty.'

'No, it's your turn on the runway.'

'Oh!' Mrs Lawson grabbed her daughter's hand and hauled her into the tearoom.

Polly smirked after them and wondered if she had time for a quick smoke. She didn't because they were back again in about two minutes, flushed with the triumph of what surely had to be their first modelling job. They'd rushed it, though, or the bitch of a mother had, because they should have taken at least four minutes to go up and down the runway and do the turn-and-hold twice. The woman ignored her on her way past, and Polly was happy with that.

She made her own entrance to a round of enthusiastic applause, as she was well-known as a Smith and Caughey model, and was halfway down the runway when she spotted him. He was sitting with presumably his wife, whom she'd (unsurprisingly) never met, and he was staring directly at her. She looked away, calculating how long it had been since he'd last visited Flora's. Years. Some time in mid-1952, in fact. Yes, she was sure of it.

He didn't look much older, though he was definitely an old man. Somewhere in his sixties, if she remembered rightly. He still looked rich. His family owned a big sheep station in Hawke's Bay, she knew that, and he used to be a banker, then he was an orchardist, then he retired and didn't have to come to Auckland twice a year to talk to the Apple and Pear Board or the Fruit Platter or whatever it was, and he stopped coming to see her. So what was he doing at a Smith and Caughey fashion parade? She wondered if she'd see him later at Flora's.

She swayed along the runway a second time, turned, paused and sent a devastating smile in James Murdoch's direction.

*

By the time all the dishes were washed, dried and stacked away and the table linen was readied to be sent to the drycleaners over the weekend, Pauline didn't actually finish work till nine o'clock. Butch was going to be in a shitty liver because she'd told him she'd meet him at eight outside Currie's Milk Bar. They'd probably left there by now but it wouldn't be hard to find them, their motorbikes made such a racket. She changed in the staff toilets into denim jeans and a shirt tied at the waist, let her hair down and stuffed her uniform into a duffel bag, and tore out, having told Allie earlier she was getting a ride home with someone, which wasn't actually true.

By the time she finally caught up with the Rebels they were making a nuisance of themselves outside Somervell's, intimidating people trying to walk past them on the footpath.

'Where've you been?' Butch demanded as he slouched on the seat of his Triumph, legs spread and the heels of his scuffed motorcycle boots balanced on the ground.

'At work. Things took longer than I expected. Then I was looking for you.'

Butch grunted. 'When you say you're gunna be somewhere, bloody be there. I don't wait for anyone.'

'Well, I'm here now.'

'You're not riding with me. You've bloody pissed me off.'

Pauline was quite relieved. It was a hot night and Butch was surrounded by a fog of body odour. 'OK, I'll ride with Mack.'

'No holding onto him, just the sissy bar,' Butch ordered as he kicked his motorbike into life.

Oh, grow up, Pauline thought as she swung her leg over the back of Mack's Bonneville and wriggled herself into a comfortable position on the seat.

They all roared away up Queen Street and Pauline forgot herself, let go of the sissy bar and grabbed Mack's jacket as he leant his motorbike to turn onto Karangahape Road. As she did she saw Butch giving her the evil eye and knew there'd be even more trouble. They blatted along K' Road, turned onto Ponsonby Road then roared down College Hill Road onto Victoria Street, back onto Queen, then headed for the White Lady pie cart on Fort Street, where they parked, angling their motorcycles into the gutter and scattering the crowd waiting for orders.

Butch dismounted, marched up to Pauline and shoved her off Mack's Bonneville. She landed in a heap on the road.

'Hoi!' Mack said, but that was all he did.

Pauline stood up and brushed her gritty hands on her jeans. She'd had enough of this. 'You're a bloody big bully, Butch Brocklebank,' she shouted, fighting the urge to giggle even though she was so angry. It was really tricky getting all those b-sounds out.

'And you're a bitch and you're dropped,' Butch retaliated.

'Really? Well, fuck you.'

Butch looked aghast. 'What did you just say?'

'Fuck you. And d'you know something? You stink. You really need a bath.'

Someone near the White Lady clapped, but Pauline couldn't afford to shift her gaze from Butch to see who it was. God knew what he might do to her next.

He eyed her for several long moments, his oily quiff leaking Brylcreem in the evening heat, then stalked back to his Triumph. 'Come on, we're going,' he announced to the rest of the Rebels.

There was general grumbling, as the lads (and laddesses) had been looking forward to curried sausages or a pie and a percolated coffee, but they followed orders, mounted up and roared off after him.

'Good riddance, arsehole,' Pauline muttered, swinging her duffel bag over her now bruised shoulder.

'Are you all right?'

It was that boy she'd noticed before, the good-looking Maori bloke. 'Yeah, I'm OK. Thanks.' Pause. 'Was that you clapping?'

He nodded. They both giggled.

'What a bastard,' the boy said. 'I saw him push you over. I was going to come and help you, but I didn't want the shit beaten out of me.'

More giggles.

'What's your name?' Pauline asked.

'Johnny. Johnny Apanui. What's yours?'

'Pauline Roberts.'

'Pauline. That's pretty. Do you want a coffee? Or something to eat?'

'A coffee would be nice.'

'The curried sausages are good. They put hard-boiled eggs and raisins in.'

'I know. Just coffee would be good, thanks,' Pauline said, thinking about curry breath.

In front of the pie cart a trio of trannies pounced on them, none under six and a half feet tall in their high heels and wigs.

'*Sweetie!* We saw what happened, didn't we, girls?' one said, looking at the others for corroboration. Outraged agreement all round. '*What* a brute! You can do without that! You're well shot of him, dear.' She poked Johnny in the chest. '*This* one's *much* nicer. You can't go wrong with a nice bit of chocolate log. Once you try it you'll never go back.'

At first Pauline didn't understand, then felt her face flame when she did. To her immense relief the trannies' order was called and they crowded the counter, fussing around gathering mash for their pies, and sauce, and cucumber and onions, and bread and butter, then clattered away down the street in a cloud of glitter and feathers.

'That was embarrassing,' she said.

'It was, quite,' Johnny agreed. 'Funny, though.'

Pauline thought how nice it was to be with someone who saw the funny side of things. Bloody Butch never laughed, unless it was at someone's else's misfortune. Good riddance to really smelly rubbish. Actually ... She leant very slightly closer to Johnny and breathed in through her nose. He smelt like Brylcreem of course, and ... was it Old Spice? But underneath there was a hint of something not entirely pleasant. Not something you'd expect a person to smell like, but a sharp, sort of acrid whiff.

Dismayed, Johnny said, 'You can smell it, can't you?'

Embarrassed (yet again), Pauline said, 'Well, I can sort of notice something. Your aftershave's nice, though.'

'I work at the Destructor. The stink gets into everything. Doesn't matter how much I wash, I still stink. I bloody hate it.'

'The stink or the job?'

'Both.' Johnny ordered two coffees. 'I'm looking for something else.'

'Anything in particular?'

'Don't care as long as it pays well and doesn't make me pong. Do you work?'

'The Cedar Room at Smith and Caughey. It's pretty boring. I'm waiting till I'm twenty-one and old enough to be a stewardess for TEAL.'

'How old are you now?'

'Seventeen.'

Johnny looked relieved. 'You look younger.'

Pauline didn't know whether that was good or bad. Bad, probably. She'd thought she looked older than seventeen. 'How old are you?'

'Eighteen. Were you going out with that bloke from the Rebels?'

Pauline suddenly felt ashamed to admit that she had. 'Not for long. And only because I liked his motorbike. It's a Triumph Tiger T110.'

Johnny whistled. 'Nice. I'm buying one as soon as I've got the dough together, except I'm looking at an Indian.'

'My brother-in-law's got an Indian.'

'Yeah? Who does he ride with?'

'No one. My sister.'

'He's not with a club?'

Pauline grinned. 'Only Ngati Whatua.'

Johnny grinned back. 'We're Ngati Kahungunu. Whole family came up last year to make our fortune in the big smoke. 'Cept for Alice, my littlest sister. She's still back home.'

'And have you? Made your fortune?'

'Nope. Do you want to go out somewhere?'

'Tonight?'

Johnny nodded.

Pauline looked at his handsome face, clever brown eyes and his lovely white teeth, and hesitated. She'd not bathed since the morning, it had been a hectic day and she wasn't feeling particularly fresh. With Butch it wouldn't have mattered, but now it did. 'Thanks, but I should really get home. It's been a long day.'

'Tomorrow night, then?' Johnny persisted. 'There's a new band on at the MCC.'

'The ... Oh, the Maori Community Centre?'

'Yeah. The music's usually pretty good and there's plenty of dancing. Rock and roll and swing, not old people's stuff.'

'That would be lovely, thank you.'

Johnny made a face. ''Cept I haven't got any wheels. But I can get the tram or bus and come and meet you. Where do you live?'

'Orakei.'

'Jeez. Way over there?' Then he shrugged. 'Never mind. Be an adventure, eh?'

Especially if you knock on the door and Mum or Dad opens it, Pauline thought. 'Do you know Orakei at all?'

'I've been to Mission Bay. That's somewhere near Orakei, isn't it?'

'More or less. You'd have to catch, ah, where do you live?'

'Ponsonby.'

'You'd have to catch either the Ponsonby tram into town to the railway station, then a bus along the waterfront across to Coates Ave at Orakei, or a couple of trams from Ponsonby to Newmarket along Remuera Road and Victoria Ave, then a bus across to Orakei that way.'

'Isn't there a tram that goes the whole way?' Johnny looked a bit confused.

'No, worse luck.'

'At home we just got on a horse and rode everywhere.'

'Mmm,' Pauline said, trying not to laugh. He was so cute.

'See, this is why I need a motorbike.'

'You could take me home tonight and then you'd know what to do.'

Johnny's face lit up. 'See, I was right! The first time I saw you I said to myself, that girl's not just really pretty, I bet she's brainy as well, even if she is hanging round with a cave man.'

Feeling ridiculously flattered and happy, Pauline slipped her arm through Johnny's as they took their coffees and wandered off down Fort Street.

*

Polly watched James's rear view as he washed himself at the hand basin. His pale buttocks were a little saggy and he was fairly solid around the middle, but overall he was certainly still handsome and distinguished-looking, and not in bad nick for a white man of sixty-seven. He'd reminded her of his age before he'd even taken off his clothes, making excuses in advance, she suspected, of what she'd expected would be a lacklustre root. Which happened quite a lot, and she'd always found it odd, because it was her that was supposed to be providing the pleasurable experience, not the customer. As it turned out James Murdoch could still manage quite well in the sack. Not that she cared as long as he, along with all her other customers, paid up.

She lay on the bed, naked and smoking a cigarette, as he splashed away getting rid of all traces of her before he went back to his wife. She took a deep, calming breath because she was actually quite nervous. She hadn't thought she would be, but she was. If she didn't do it now she probably never would.

'So what brings you to Auckland?'

'Lucy wanted to do some shopping,' James said over his shoulder. 'And we both wanted to see Kathleen and Jonathan's new house. They were down just before Christmas and Kathleen made such a to-do over what a palace it is we thought we'd come and see it for ourselves.'

Polly recalled that Lucy was his wife's name. 'Who's Kathleen again?'

'Our daughter.' James reached for a towel. 'She was in that fashion event last night, with our granddaughter. That's why we were there. Obviously. I wouldn't go to something like that otherwise.'

'Your daughter's Mrs Lawson?' That was a bit of a shock.

'You know her? God, you're not friends, are you?'

'Well, that's not very likely, is it?' Polly said.

Bloody Kathleen Lawson had pissed her off and she made an effort to keep the anger out of her voice. It made things easier, though. She sat up, pulled on her pants and hooked herself into her bra, and watched while James fussed about getting dressed.

First a pair of pristinely white Y-fronts, into which he tucked a matching sleeveless vest, followed by a white shirt, charcoal trousers, black socks and shoes, a blue and grey-checked blazer, and a dark tie. He'd always been a smart dresser. Then he combed his greying hair in the mirror and, once satisfied, turned and said, 'That was delightful, Polly. How much do I owe you? I trust your tariff hasn't risen too much since I was last here?'

She told him and he happily handed over the fee, forty percent of which, of course, Flora would get. 'There's something I need to talk to you about, James.'

'What's that?' he said, looking round for his hat.

'You mentioned the last time you were here.'

James spotted his hat on a chair near the door. 'Mmm?'

'Well, you left me with something a little unexpected.'

James froze. 'Not ... not an infection of some sort, I hope? Because I certainly wouldn't have given it to you.'

'No. Something a bit more permanent.'

Polly watched as James's face went as white as milk.

'Not ... a pregnancy?'

Polly nodded.

James looked utterly dumbfounded. Then he blustered, 'How do you know I was responsible? You must go with dozens of men.'

'I do, but at the time you were the only one who insisted on not using a Durex.'

James sat down on his hat. 'I never use those things. I thought you were taking care of all that. You're the one providing the service.'

Polly shrugged. 'Something went wrong.'

'What did you do about it?'

'I had her. She's just turned three.'

James was silent for quite a long time. 'Well, what do you want me to do about it? I already have a family. Including grandchildren, I might add.'

'She'd appreciate some financial assistance. You're her father. You've got plenty of money.'

'Oh, so that's what this is about, is it?'

'More or less.'

'Well, you won't get a penny out of me.' James stood and retrieved his flattened hat. 'I shouldn't have expected anything less from a prostitute.'

'No, you shouldn't have,' Polly said. 'But maybe Lucy would like to contribute something towards your daughter's upkeep.'

'You bitch.'

'I'm just thinking about my child's welfare.'

'You're thinking about lining your own pockets,' James barked.

No, I'm not, Polly thought. I'm really not.

James opened his wallet again. 'How much do you want?'

'Nothing now. I'd like you to send a cheque for fifty pounds to the Queen Street branch of the Bank of New Zealand, to be deposited in the account of Gina Manaia. You were a banker; you'll know all about how to do that.'

'Why don't I just give you fifty pounds now?'

'Because I want you to do it every month.'

'Every month! That's six hundred pounds a year!'

'That's right.'

'This is extortion!'

Polly didn't respond.

He glared at her, then wrenched open the door and marched out, leaving her sitting on the bed.

She lit another cigarette. She didn't feel as victorious as she thought she might, but she'd achieved what she wanted — more money and therefore more security for Gina. Well, if things went to plan she had.

*

Dr Hill's private rooms were very nice, and Kathleen was extremely grateful she and Terence didn't have to see him at a public hospital. The address was a grand old house on Princes Street that had been beautifully decorated with old-style furniture, the sort really wealthy people had, and which made her feel at home. The doctor himself was quite grand, with greying hair and a beard, tortoiseshell spectacles and a calm demeanour that inspired confidence. His fee was outrageous, though. She hoped it would be worth it.

She spoke to him first without Terence, which she thought was a good idea. He'd moved from behind his desk to sit in a chair opposite her and crossed his legs (revealing a pair of rather loud pink and green argyle socks), while she'd told him about the fashion parade business and the awful incident on the night of the drinks party.

'And how would you describe your son, in general?' he asked.

'I'd say he's a fairly normal little boy.'

Dr Hill's eyebrows went up. 'Who dresses in your clothes and has tried to hang himself?'

'Well, apart from that, yes.'

'Prone to tantrums or histrionics?'

'Well, sometimes.'

'Does he prefer to get his own way?'

Kathleen sighed. 'Yes, but doesn't every little boy?'

'Not necessarily. Would you say he is sensitive?'

'Concerning some things, but he can be quite tough too.'

'Mmm.' Dr Hill wrote something on his notepad. 'And are things harmonious in the home?'

'Oh yes. My husband, Captain Jonathan Lawson — he flies for NAC, you know, and is ex-RAF — is away a lot, but apart from that, we're very happy.'

'And does Terence miss his father when he's away?'

'I think he does, yes.'

'Are all your children at school?'

'Terence and Geoffrey, my seven-year-old boy, are. Private, of course. Rosemary will be starting later this year.'

'And do you work, Mrs Lawson?'

Kathleen gave a gay little laugh. 'Hardly. I don't need to, and of course I'm too busy with my charity work.'

'So you have full responsibility for looking after the children?'

'Well, no, I have a nanny.'

Up went Dr Hill's eyebrows again. Kathleen was starting to resent them.

'And what are her duties?'

What's that got to do with anything? Kathleen thought. 'She manages the children in the mornings and after school, and in the evenings, and does a lot of the meal preparation.'

'She lives in?'

'Yes, but she gets a lot of time off. And when she's not there of course *I* look after the children and cook.' Kathleen laughed again. 'I'm not *completely* incapable.'

'I'm sure you're not.' Dr Hill flipped his notepad shut. 'Thank you for that, Mrs Lawson. I think I'd like to talk to Terence now.'

'Shall I fetch him?'

'Yes please.'

Kathleen brought Terence in. Dr Hill hadn't moved from his seat and she wondered where she would sit if Terence took the vacant chair.

The doctor said, 'Hello, Terence. I'm Dr Hill. Please, have a seat.'

Terence sat.

Dr Hill said, 'Thank you, Mrs Lawson.'

It dawned on Kathleen that he was dismissing her. 'Oh, no, I really think I should stay with Terence. He is only nine, after all.'

'I realise that, Mrs Lawson. We shouldn't be too long.'

A prickle of dismay crept up Kathleen's spine. What might Terence tell him? He could be such a little liar. She stared at her son for a moment, then patted his cheek and left the room, fumbling in her purse for her cigarettes.

*

'So,' Dr Hill said, 'is it Terence, Terry or something else?'

'Terry. I hate Terence. I get bashed at school for being called Terence.'

'Do you? That must be hard going.' The doctor tapped his nose with his pen. 'Tell me, if you could choose any name in the world, what might it be?'

'Theresa.'

'Really? Why's that?'

'It's pretty.'

'It is, very pretty. It's a girl's name, though, isn't it?'

'So?'

'Well, you're a boy.'

Terence just shrugged.

'What would your mother and father do if you told them you wanted to be called Theresa?'

'Dad would belt me.'

'Would he? Does he do that quite a lot?'

'Sometimes. Mostly when he's been drinking.'

'And is that often?'

Terence kicked his heel against the leg of his chair. 'Only when he's at home. He says he doesn't drink when he's flying his plane.'

Thank Christ for that, Dr Hill thought. 'And what would your mother do if you told her you wanted to be called Theresa?'

'Tell me to stop it, or to go to my room. Or pretend she didn't hear me or go off and have one of *her* special drinks.'

Dr Hill was silent for a moment. 'Terry, do you *like* your mother and father?'

'Sometimes.'

'Do you feel that they like you?'

Another shrug. 'They like Rosemary better.'

'Is that why you wore your mother's clothes? To be more like Rosemary?'

'No. I just like them. They feel nice.'

'Were you envious of Rosemary when she was chosen to be in the fashion parade with your mother?'

A nod. 'It wasn't fair. I'm just as pretty as Rosemary. We even have the same hair.'

'Mmm.' Dr Hill took a minute to write some notes.

'Are we finished?' Terence asked.

'No, not yet. I'd like to talk about your accident.' The doctor eyed Terence for some sort of reaction, but there wasn't one. Perhaps he'd deliberately erased his memory of such a traumatic event.

Terence stared back at him, clearly puzzled.

'Your attempt to hang yourself,' Dr Hill prompted.

'Oh, that.'

'Do you know why you did it?'

Yet another shrug.

Dr Hill said nothing, and this time let the silence stretch on and on. Terence looked all round the room, then out the window, then finally said, 'They were ignoring me.'

'Your parents?'

Terence nodded. 'And Dad hit me when I put on Mum's things.'

'So you thought you'd punish them?'

Terence nodded again, then said, 'No. I don't know. I just felt like I was going to blow up if I didn't do something. So I did it.'

'And you didn't think about the effect it would have on your parents or your brother and sister?'

'Not really.'

'Do you like Rosemary and Geoffrey?'

'Not really. Rosemary's a bitch.'

Blinking, Dr Hill sat back, stared at Terence for a moment, then made some more notes. 'That's a very harsh thing to say. And believe.'

'Well, maybe not a bitch but she's a bit precious. She's Mum's favourite.'

'Why do you think that might be?'

Terence shrugged. 'Probably because she's a girl.'

'Do you resent Rosemary appearing to be your mother's favourite?'

Another shrug.

'Is there no one in your household you do really like?' Dr Hill asked.

'Evie's all right.'

'Who's Evie?'

'Our nanny.'

'Tell me why you like her.'

'Because she's like a proper girl.' Terence made a woman's curves in the air with his hands. 'I want to be like her when I grow up.'

'And that's the only reason?'

'Well, also she doesn't tell me off, and she listens to me.'

'What do you say to her that she listens to?'

'I tell her I want to be a girl.'

'And what does she say to that?'

'She says I'll be what I'll be. But if I tell Rosemary what I want she laughs, and Geoffrey bashes me even though he's smaller than me, and so does Dad, and Mum just ignores me.'

'Have you ever said anything about wanting to be a girl to anyone at school?'

'No.'

'Hmmm.' Dr Hill was really quite taken aback. He'd seen this in his practice before, of course, males suffering under the illusion that they were women born into the wrong biological bodies. There were certain treatments available — electro-convulsive therapy, and in extreme cases lobotomy, which could be applied with varying degrees of success — but he'd never seen it manifest in a patient so young. It was extraordinary, really. 'The thing is, Terry, you obviously are a boy. Your mother says you have all the physical characteristics one would expect of a male child. Do you play sports?'

'Sports?'

'Yes, rugby or cricket or anything like that?'

'No, I hate sports.'

'Well, what do you enjoy?'

'I like arts and crafts, and dancing.'

Dr Hill suppressed a sigh. Mrs Lawson might have kept a negligently light hand on her son's emotional development, but she'd still managed to indulge him. 'I suggest you forget about the dancing classes and go in for some sort of sport. I recommend rugby in the winter, and something like cricket or swimming, or even rowing, in the summer. Very bracing, rowing.'

'I don't go to dancing classes. I'm not *allowed*.'

Thank God for that, the doctor thought. 'Well, try a sport. You'll thank me for it.'

'I doubt it.'

Dr Hill narrowed his eyes — cheeky little article, though he really was rather bright and quick off the mark for a nine-year-old. 'I think that will probably do for today, don't you?'

'Do I have to come back?'

'Do you want to?'

'No.'

'Well, we'll see. I'll discuss that with your mother.'

As Terence stood Dr Hill offered his hand, but Terence walked straight past and out the door.

Chapter Ten

March 1956

Donna crept up the stairs of the nurses' home, shoes in hand, keeping close to the wall, trying to avoid the risers that creaked. She was pretty sure no one had seen her come in because it was so late, but you never knew who might still be up, wandering round like a ghost, making a cup of tea or pinching the biscuits.

In her room she turned on the light, dumped her shoes and handbag on a chair and sat on the bed. It had been another exciting night. They'd had sex again — the fifth time now — this time in Cornwall Park, which had been very nervous-making. He hadn't had the car because it was having work done on it so they'd caught a taxi to and from town, and there'd been nowhere else to go. His rooms were out of bounds to nurses and she couldn't bring him back here, and with the car out of commission the park had been it. She glanced in the mirror. Oh God, she *did* have leaves in her hair.

She undressed, blushing as she saw the state of her pants. There was a drying, whitish crust in them, the result of her and Robert's love-making. Though she wasn't ashamed of what they were doing because they were in love, she was definitely ashamed of her pants, and hastily shoved them to the bottom of her laundry basket. She was safe, though, thank God. Almost literally, she thought, which made her smile.

The night Robert had mentioned he was off to church the next morning had been quite funny. She'd asked him what religion he was and he'd said, 'Catholic,' and she'd said, 'Oh, so am I!' and he'd said, 'Is that so? Well, that should make things easier.' And she'd said, 'What do you mean?' but all he would say was, 'Wait and see,' which had been rather mysterious at the time.

It turned out he'd been referring to the rhythm method, which she'd never heard of. It had been after the first time she let him have sex with her, during which he'd used a condom, but he said he really didn't like them and explained to her about the rhythm method, which he much preferred. Apparently all Catholics used it and it was pretty well foolproof. You just didn't have sex on days twelve to eighteen after the first day of your period, because these were a woman's fertile days. All the others were infertile days and a woman couldn't get pregnant on them. It seemed a very easy way to avoid falling for a baby, so she couldn't imagine why all those Catholic families had so many kids. But her mother had only had three, and Nan, a *staunch* Catholic, had only had one. So it must work.

It had all been quite embarrassing, though, Robert talking about monthlies. But she supposed he was used to it, being a doctor. Also, at the back of her mind, she'd been half hoping his comment about them both being Catholic making things easier might have something to do with getting married. Her private embarrassment when it was only to do with sex had been a bit of a shock, and she'd been angry at herself for it. But then she told herself off for feeling that way because maybe she wasn't being premature: they really were getting on very well and going out at least twice a week and having lots of fun, and now that they were having sex the next logical step surely would be an engagement. But did she want to give up her nurse training? She wasn't at all sure she did. She was thoroughly enjoying it and couldn't see herself as a housewife, not yet anyway, not even after landing herself a doctor.

*

The alterations to Rose's cottage on Almorah Road were almost finished, which meant Allie and Sonny could move in. Sid and his mate, Bill, and one of *his* mates had done the work, using some of the money Rose had left Colleen. The changes were fairly basic, but Colleen had decided they were necessary as no one should have to bathe in the kitchen or sit in an outside loo in the depths of winter, though Rose had happily done both for decades. So now there was a bathroom with a proper bath and an indoor toilet, and the extra loo outside.

'I wish we had an extra lav,' Colleen said.

'There's only three of you now,' Allie said. 'Why do you need two toilets?'

'You and Donna moving out hasn't changed your father's bowel habits, you know.'

Allie laughed.

'I'll send him round here if you're not careful,' Colleen threatened. 'Where do you want this linen?'

'In the bedroom next to the kitchen, I think. Ta.'

'I take it you won't be setting your bed up in the bay window?'

'Er, no.'

'You could, you know,' Sid said, puffing along the hallway, carrying one end of a bedhead. 'You could sell tickets.'

Sonny, on the other end, laughed, but Colleen tutted. 'Trust you to cheapen everything, Sid Roberts.'

'Said in jest, my love, said in jest.' Sid grimaced. 'Flaming hell, this thing weighs a ton. Where do you two lovebirds want it?'

'Bedroom right behind you, thanks, Dad.'

'Toot!' Pauline warned, ducking past Sonny and her father with a box in her arms. 'Coming through!'

'What's in that one?' Allie asked.

'Allie!' Pauline exclaimed. 'You're terrible!'

'What?'

'It's Mr De Valera!'

Allie's hand flew to her mouth. 'Shit! I left him in the truck!'

'*You'll* be a great mum, you will,' Pauline said, setting the box on the ground. 'Where's the kids? Oh, I left them on the tram.' She opened the top of the box and out jumped Dev, looking most displeased.

Allie ignored the comment.

'Pauline,' Colleen scolded. 'Don't be so thoughtless.'

'Oh, she knows what I mean,' Pauline grumbled.

Sniffing cautiously around the boxes and piles of stuff in the sitting room, Mr De Valera wandered off down the hall, stopping for a good stare at Sonny and Sid wrestling with the bed frame in the bedroom, then headed for the kitchen.

'I think he knows he's home,' Allie said.

'Have you got some food for him?' Pauline asked. 'I suppose that's in the truck too, sitting in the sun, going off.'

'No, I was going to pop down the shops.'

'Give us some money, I'll go,' Pauline offered, her hand out. 'What else do you need?'

Allie made a short list.

'You'll have to get yourself a refrigerator,' Colleen said.

'Why? We got by without one a quarter of a mile away at Crowhurst Street.'

'But you're in your own home now.'

Allie couldn't quite see the logic behind her mother's thinking. 'And a packet of tea,' she said to Pauline. 'Choysa.'

Colleen said, 'You'll be able to afford it now you're not paying rent.'

Ah, so that was it. In that case, Allie thought, now that they were made of money, why not get an electric washing machine, an electric oven, a vacuum cleaner, an electric cake mixer, a petrol-driven lawnmower, brand new lounge and bedroom suites, and a car as well?

When Pauline had trotted off Sonny appeared, wiping his hands on his trousers. 'Your sister seems happy these days.'

'Pauline?'

Sonny nodded.

'I suspect there's a new boy on the scene,' Colleen said, though she didn't sound too pleased about it.

Allie was surprised. Pauline hadn't said anything to her about a new boyfriend. But then she hadn't spent much time with her little sister lately. She really should. 'Really? What happened to the one with the motorbike? The Bodgie?'

'Who cares?' Sid said, sitting down on a box and wiping his brow with his handkerchief. 'God, a man could do with a beer.'

'Not till we've finished everything here,' Colleen said. 'I gather she broke up with the Bodgie, and thank God for that. I think she's had this new one a few weeks.'

'Have you met him?' Allie asked.

'No.'

'Has she talked about him?'

'Not as such.'

'Then how do you know he exists?'

'I can *tell*, Alison,' Colleen said. 'She is my daughter, you know. I can tell when something's going on with her, and usually what it is.'

Oh, you cannot, Allie thought. You never could with me. You might love us very much, but you've never been psychic.

'He's a young Maori lad,' Sid said.

They all stared at him.

'Nice-looking boy,' he went on. 'I saw him waiting for her one night, by the bus stop. She gave him a kiss and they hopped on the next bus and off they went.'

'You never told me that!' Colleen accused. 'When was this? Flaming hell, Sid, why don't you tell me these things?'

Allie knew why. Her father hadn't been bothered at all when she'd brought Sonny home but it had upset her mother, who'd been convinced that if Allie married him she'd be dooming herself to a life of condemnation and nasty comments. Which, to be honest, had, in fact, turned out to be true to a degree, but it wasn't something that particularly worried her any more. Her father probably hadn't wanted her mother to start fretting about the same thing all over again, especially while she was still grieving for Nan.

'Sorry, love,' Sid said. 'Slipped me mind.'

Colleen sighed. 'Well, at least if they were getting on the bus that means he doesn't own a motorcycle.'

'There's nothing wrong with motorcycles, Mum,' Allie said.

'You say that, but I think you'll find it quite difficult to transport your babies on one,' Colleen said, clearly forgetting that Sonny also owned a truck.

Allie didn't answer. Why did her family keep making comments about babies, today especially? Her period had been ten days late and with each passing day she'd allowed her hopes to creep higher and higher, until last night when she'd gone to the loo and found blood on her pants. The disappointment had been like a physical punch in the stomach.

'Will you be wanting to paint in here?' Sid asked. 'The hall needs doing but you could probably leave this a bit longer.'

Allie eyed the shiny, nicotine-coloured walls, stained by her grandfather's cigarettes. 'No, I think we'll do everywhere.'

'We've got a nice lot of pink left over from a job,' Sid said. 'You can have that if you like.'

'Thanks, Dad, but we'll probably pick something.'

'You could go with wallpaper,' Colleen suggested. 'There's some lovely modern patterns coming out these days.'

'You won't know the place when you two have finished with it,' Sid said. 'It'll be like a new home. How many couples your age can say they own a new home?'

'Not many,' Allie replied, 'and not us. This is family property, not ours.'

'It is for now, love,' Colleen said, 'so enjoy it.'

*

Wiki was a small woman, this was her sixth pregnancy, and she was over six months along. Despite the heat in Auckland Hospital's noisy and busy kitchen she'd been wearing a heavy, baggy cardigan over her apron to try and hide her condition, but when she was called into the office of Mr Price, the supervisor, one morning she knew very well what she was about to hear.

'Sit down, Mrs Irwin,' Mr Price said.

He was still wearing the hairnet they all wore for food hygiene reasons, and looked a fool, in Wiki's opinion. She sat, taking care to let the folds of her cardigan fall discreetly over her bump just in case … of what? — he really hadn't noticed she was hapu and was about to tell her she'd been promoted? Don't be stupid, woman. He mucked about for a minute, tidying his pencils and bits and pieces. Wiki realised he was embarrassed. Good job. She kept her mouth shut, determined not to help him out.

Eventually he said, 'It's been brought to my notice that you … that you're …' He cleared his throat, then went bright red. 'I've been informed that you may be expecting. Is this correct?'

Wiki sighed. Here it was, then. 'That's right, I am.'

'Ah.' Mr Price looked relieved, as though he'd thought he was going to have to argue with her about it. 'Well, you know the rules, Mrs Irwin. We can't employ women in your condition. You should have informed us sooner. I'm afraid we'll have to let you go.'

'Will there be a job here for me after the baby comes?'

Mr Price looked vaguely scandalised. 'Won't you want to stay at home and look after it?'

'That's what my older girls are for. I need to earn money to pay the bills.'

'Well, I … Well, we'll certainly keep your details on file, Mrs Irwin.'

That's a no, Wiki thought, heaving herself out of the chair and not caring now if she looked like a cast sheep.

'Thank you for your service, Mrs Irwin,' Mr Price said.

'Yep,' Wiki said over her shoulder.

*

Kathleen had thoroughly enjoyed her turn as a model for Smith and Caughey, at which she thought she'd been extremely successful. Everyone had said so. She'd made a point of going into the store at least twice a week since the fashion parade, to say hello to Miss Weaver and to speak with any customers who might recognise her. Several had, she was sure, though none had approached her. Intimidated, perhaps, or possibly they simply didn't want to intrude on her time.

She'd not spoken to the girl, Allison, on the Elizabeth Arden counter recently, however, partly because she hadn't needed any cosmetics but more as a result of the unpleasantness over the Maori model who'd been drinking at the fashion parade. But today she would. She, Kathleen, hadn't reported the Maori girl to Mr Holmes, but the incident had been festering away in her mind for weeks, not so much due to the alcohol involved but because of the revelation that Allison was married to a Maori. She couldn't really believe it. Allison was so, well, blonde and pale-skinned and obviously of British stock, and so pleasant and politely spoken — unlike that other creature on the Elizabeth Arden counter, whatever her name was. Why would a girl like Allison marry a Maori when she could have any man she liked? Well, any working-class man, that is. It wasn't right and it made her uncomfortable just thinking about it, which was irritating as she'd been thinking about it a lot. Girls like Allison, she'd decided, needed to be saved from themselves before they ruined their lives. Hopefully it wasn't too late.

She was pleased to see as she swept through the Beauty Hall that Allison was by herself on the Elizabeth Arden counter.

'Good morning, dear. Where's your charming friend?'

'Good morning, Mrs Lawson. Peggy's on her tea break. How can I help you?'

Mmm, a bit sharp, Kathleen thought. Must still be on her high horse. 'Let's clear the air, shall we, Allison? I apologise for my outburst before the fashion parade. I was a little anxious, for both myself and for Rosemary. First time nerves, you could say. Please forgive me. Also, I did *not* follow through with my threat to inform Mr Holmes of your sister-in-law's, er, activities. Just so you know. Am I forgiven?'

Allison smiled ruefully. 'Thank you, Mrs Lawson. I apologise, too. We really are very busy during those events and, well —'

Kathleen raised a gloved hand. 'Say no more and let's forget it, shall we?'

'Please. No Rosemary today? Has she started school?'

'Not until June. She's at a birthday party.'

'And the boys? How are they?'

'Oh, they're marvellous. They're back at school, of course.'

And thank God, Kathleen thought. Geoffrey had been fine — he always was — but Terence had been hell since his 'accident'. He'd been to see the psychiatrist, Dr Hill, three more times, then announced he didn't want to go any more. When asked why not, he'd replied, 'Because I don't like him,' and any suggestion that he *had* to go had been met with such antipathy that both she and Jonathan had acquiesced and let him be. A report, however, had arrived in the post from the doctor, recommending a course of action designed to 'masculinise' Terence's behaviour, so he'd been signed up for summer athletics, rowing and cricket at school, been precluded from taking art and French this year, and Kathleen had enrolled him at the local branch of Boy Scouts. Since returning to school he'd done nothing but moan about not being able to do art, which seemed to Kathleen to be particularly petty, and complain about all the sports, but most of all he hated Boy Scouts, which he said was like being in the army. How would a nine-year-old know what being in the army was like? Geoffrey, on the other hand, who'd also joined, absolutely loved the Scouts. But having Terence at school and listening to him moan about it just in the evenings was far preferable, Kathleen thought, to having him home during the holidays, behaving oddly, irritating his father and threatening to cause embarrassment in public.

'Your house must seem quiet without them,' Alison said.

'Yes, I suppose it does. Rosemary and the nanny are usually in, though. Anyway, enough about my family. How are *you*?'

'Me?'

Kathleen thought Allison looked rather startled to be asked. 'Yes, you. What's been happening in your life?'

'Oh. Well. We've, um, we've just moved into a new house.'

Kathleen clapped her gloved hands together. 'Ooh, lovely. Brand new?'

'Well, no. It was my nan's house. She died at Christmas and—'

'Oh, I'm so sorry, Allison. I wasn't aware of that. Please accept my condolences.'

'Yes, thank you, it was a bit of a shock, though she hadn't been well.'

'How awful for you, especially at Christmas.'

'Yes. She'd had a good innings, though.'

Allison dropped her eyes and winced slightly, as though she immediately regretted what she'd just said. Kathleen thought she probably did. People often felt foolish when they came out with vacuous platitudes.

'A tragedy all the same,' Kathleen said. 'So, where in town is your new home?'

'Newmarket, a few streets off Broadway.'

'Sounds lovely,' Kathleen lied. She didn't go to Newmarket often and when she had she'd gained the distinct impression it was a working-class area.

'It's just a worker's cottage but Nan kept it nice.'

Definitely working-class. 'And she left it to you? That was generous.'

'To my mother, but my husband and I have the use of it till we can afford something of our own.'

'And it has all the modern conveniences?'

Allison laughed. 'Hardly. We just finished adding an inside bathroom and loo.'

Kathleen barely suppressed a shudder. 'An electric oven?'

'No, coal range.'

'Refrigerator?'

'No again. My mother's been on at me to get one, though.'

'Electric washing machine?' But Kathleen could see the answer in Allison's amused expression. 'My *dear*, how do you *manage*? Especially when both of you are so busy working.'

'We're used to managing.'

'Are you paying rent or a mortgage?'

There was a short silence and Kathleen wondered if she might have pushed it a bit far.

Then Allison said, 'Neither.'

'Well, there you go, dear. Buy yourself some convenience!'

'We're saving. For our own house.'

Kathleen picked an invisible speck off her lapel. 'But you know what they say, a woman's work is never done. Surely you deserve a treat.' She gave Allison a wide, bright smile. 'I'm sure your husband knows how to treat his wife. Mine certainly does. And if he doesn't, drop some hints. Take him window shopping. In fact, drag him right into the shop and show him what you want.'

'Well ...'

'Well what?' Allison's colleague demanded as she approached, the heels of her pumps clattering on the shiny floor tiles.

Damn, Kathleen thought. 'I was just telling Allison she deserves some modern conveniences in her life.'

'Don't we all? She also deserves a tea break. Go on, love, off you go.'

Allison went, leaving Kathleen warily eyeing the girl. She really was a hard-boiled piece of work.

'Sorry, I seem to have forgotten your name,' she said.

'It's Peggy, Peggy Mitchell, and if you don't mind me saying so, Allie doesn't need your advice.'

Kathleen's hand fluttered to her chest. 'Well, that's rather rude, I must say.'

'And so are you, poking your nose in. Leave her alone. Who do you think you are, the queen?'

'You can't speak to me like that, I'm a customer!'

'I can and I just did.'

'Then I'm reporting you to Mr Holmes.'

'That's not very original. You said that at the fashion parade. But go on, see if I care.'

'Right then, I will!'

The cheek of the bloody girl! Kathleen marched straight to the lifts and jabbed the button for the floor of Mr Holmes's office. She'd show her!

*

All the way home in the taxi Kathleen could hardly keep the smirk off her face. George Holmes had been suitably appalled and apologetic regarding Peggy Mitchell's insolent behaviour, and she was fairly sure the girl would lose her job by the end of the day. How satisfying.

Also, Rosemary and Evie would still be at the birthday party, and Jonathan, who wasn't flying until tomorrow, was at some meeting until this afternoon, so she would have the house to herself for a few lovely, quiet hours. She thought she might just lie on the sofa, read her new book and have a couple of gin and tonics until everyone converged again and shattered her peace.

The taxi driver pulled up outside the house and she paid him and walked down the garden path as he drove off. Jonathan's car was in the driveway but he'd taxied into town earlier, which probably meant he'd arrive home blind drunk. Not that that had stopped him driving before, of course. She unlocked the front door, stepped onto the long carpet extending from the foyer into the reception hall, closed the door behind her and took off her gloves. Then she heard it, a rhythmic thumping and moaning that took her straight back to the night Terence tried to hang himself. Filled with sharp, glassy fear she hurried, almost ran, into the hall, but there was nothing — no one — hanging from the stair rail. But still the thumping went on, even louder now. She moved closer to Evie's bedroom and that's where she saw them — Evie and her husband joined together, thrusting and sweating, over the bed.

Evie was fully dressed and wearing her suspender belt, stockings and shoes, but her skirt was up around her waist and her knickers were on the floor, and Jonathan's trousers and pants were in a heap at his ankles. Evie was bent over the end of her bed, one foot on the floor and the other knee on the mattress, facedown with her round backside in the air, her arms outstretched and her fists bunching the bedspread while Jonathan, his teeth bared, gripped her hips and rammed into her from behind. *She* was doing the moaning while the bedhead banged against the wall, making the thumping sound.

The sight was so awful — so unexpected and *brutal* — Kathleen thought she might be sick. She opened her mouth to say something but nothing came out. She tried again.

'Stop it. Stop that!'

Then when Jonathan turned his head to her and she saw the heavy glazed look of pleasure in his eyes, a monstrous wave of anger hit her.

'You bastard! You utter *bastard*!'

She launched herself into the room at him and he disconnected audibly from Evie, deflating rapidly as he snatched at his trousers. Kathleen took a swipe at his face with her fingernails but he batted her away.

'Get off me, you idiot,' he cried out.

'You pig,' Kathleen screeched. 'You absolute bloody *pig*!' She looked around for Evie, who'd scrambled to the other side of the bed. 'Get out! Get out of my house right now!'

Jonathan took her by the arm and jerked her out into the hall.

Kathleen wrenched herself from his grip. 'Don't you touch me!'

'Let her pack her things. Then she can go.'

'Don't you tell me what to do! This is *my* house!'

'It's mine. Settle down. Go upstairs till she's gone.'

Shaking now with rage and shock, Kathleen cried, 'I *won't*! She'll steal something.'

'She will not. Go on.'

Another almighty surge of rage swept through Kathleen and she swung at Jonathan again and this time he wasn't expecting it, her fist connecting with his jaw. She thought it probably didn't hurt him much but it clearly gave him a fright and he hit back, punching her in the side of the head. Her hat flew off, she saw stars and staggered against the wall. More than anything she wanted to let herself slide to the floor and sit there, knees drawn up, her hands over her head until everything was quiet again, but she couldn't allow herself that luxury.

Instead she picked up her hat and said stiffly, and loudly so Evie would hear, 'I will be in the parlour. Please make sure Evelyn doesn't take anything that isn't hers.'

In her bedroom, Evie finished jamming her belongings into a suitcase, collected her knickers from the floor, stuffed them into her handbag and joined Jonathan in the hallway.

'I'll be going, then. You owe me half a week's pay.'

Jonathan dug around in his trouser pockets and brought out some cash. 'Will that do?'

Watching from the parlour doorway, and hating herself for doing it, Kathleen forced herself to refrain from rushing over and counting the money. The idea of Evie getting more than she was due rankled horribly.

Evie took the money and slipped it into her skirt pocket. 'Oh, my toilet things. They're upstairs.'

'Go with her,' Kathleen said to Jonathan.

'I will not.'

'Then I will.'

'No you won't.'

As Evie trotted upstairs, Kathleen fumed in silence until she returned a few minutes later with her toilet bag. She squeezed it into her suitcase, then, without saying another word, opened the front door and was gone.

'Good riddance,' Kathleen said. 'I always knew that girl was a slut.'

*

Polly's flatmate shouted up the stairs, 'Polly! There's someone here to see you!'

Polly sat up, swung her legs over the side of the bed and stretched. She'd been dozing, having not got home from work at Flora's until that morning. Unfortunately she found it difficult to sleep during the day, so when she worked nights, which was frequently, she sometimes resorted to tranquillisers to knock herself out, though these always made her feel terrible when she woke up. At other times she just drank when she got home, which helped her nod off, but she never stayed asleep long with just alcohol.

She went to the door and shouted back, 'Who is it?'

'Your friend Evie.'

What's she doing here at this hour? Polly wondered as she glanced in her dressing table mirror. She looked a mess and decided she didn't care. She trudged downstairs, avoiding the dodgy loose ones. In fact the whole three-storey, seven-bedroom Ligaro Place house was dodgy. It had obviously once been beautifully grand but had been badly neglected over the years and was very slowly sliding downhill. But, nestled beneath Grafton Bridge, it still had an excellent view of the gully, and Blandford Park and the harbour, and was handy for Newmarket, town and the trams, and the rent was dirt cheap, so no one was complaining.

'Not working today?' Polly asked as she encountered Evie in the foyer. Then she spotted her suitcase. 'What's happened?'

'I got caught rooting Jonathan Lawson,' Evie said matter-of-factly.

'By his wife?'

'Mmm.'

'Messy.'

'It was a bit. She kicked me out. But that's all right, it was time to go anyway.'

'What will you do?'

'I'm off to Sydney. I've had it with this town.'

'Really?' Polly thought Sydney sounded quite tempting.

'But I can't go for a few days. I've got a friend on the *Monowai* and he can sneak me on board but the ship doesn't leave till Friday. Can I stay here till then?'

'"Course you can.'

'I'll give you some money for food and that.'

'Don't be stupid,' Polly said, but Evie had already pulled a small wad of notes from her handbag. With them came a pair of clip-on earrings set with stunningly blue, pea-sized stones, which slipped out of the notes and bounced onto the floor.

Polly raised an eyebrow. 'Did Jonathan give you those?'

Evie smirked as she retrieved the sparkling earrings. 'Not as such. Kathleen did, though she probably doesn't know it yet.'

'Are they real?'

'Of course they're real. Who steals costume jewellery?'

*

Ana Leonard was extremely grateful that the children had settled into a new year at school where, for much of the day, they didn't have to worry about being around Jack. They still thought some of his 'antics' were funny but at the same time they'd become deeply wary of him. None of them liked being alone with him any more, so she made sure that never happened. He frightened them. He'd gone from being their lovable grandfather to a smelly, grizzled old man who didn't recognise them and whose behaviour was very often unpredictable and violent. She thought it was terribly unfair that they should have to live in a house riddled with tension, anger, and, frequently, fear, but David still refused to even take Jack to a doctor, never mind consider committing him to a mental hospital. This alone really got on her wick as David was hardly ever home, so didn't have to shoulder the burden of looking after his father and putting up with his behaviour. And it wasn't that she really wanted Jack locked away in an asylum herself. She loved him — or, at least, she loved the man he'd been. She just wanted ... Well, she didn't really know what she wanted. Help? A rest? A miracle?

David was home this weekend, and was out the back with Jack planting seedlings, as he thought his father might enjoy growing vegetables. She didn't have the heart to tell him that Jack probably didn't know the difference between one vegetable and another these days, or even that vegetables were something you grew and then ate, and that he certainly didn't have the attention span to tend a garden by himself.

Through the kitchen window she watched them come plodding up the lawn, then disappear as they climbed the back steps.

Then, from the back door, David said, sounding really quite dismayed, 'Jack's shat himself.'

Ana thought, I've told you about that often enough. And you were here when he did it at Christmas. Have you forgotten? 'Well, you'll have to sort him out. I'm in the middle of making scones.'

'I don't know what to do.'

'*Don't* let him sit down, it'll squash everywhere, get clean underpants, a singlet and trousers from his room, take him into the bathroom, get him undressed, clean him up, sit him on the toilet to make sure he's finished, then put him in the clean clothes. Then scrape off his dirty underpants, rinse anything else that's dirty, then soak the lot in the tub with a bit of borax.'

David looked disgusted. Jack just looked vacant.

'And don't let him get his hands in it,' Ana added.

'For fuck's sake,' David muttered, leading his father off towards the bathroom.

Rowie appeared, sniffing. 'Has Grandpa done a poo?'

Ana nodded. 'Open the windows, will you?'

'Is Dad cleaning him up?'

'Yes.'

'That's a first.'

'Don't be cheeky,' Ana replied, though she had to agree.

Eventually Jack was tidied up, the scones were baked and the Leonard family gathered at the kitchen table for afternoon tea. Ana sliced and buttered a scone for Jack and poured him a cup of tea. He then proceeded to make an almighty mess by trying to dunk his scone into his cup. It got stuck and in frustration Jack bashed the cup down on the saucer and broke both. Peter laughed; Jack struck out as quick as lightning and whacked him hard across the jaw, knocking him right off his chair.

'Hoi!' David shouted, and before Ana had even risen from her seat on her way to the boy he was out of his and had hauled his father to his feet and had one very strong hand around his throat. 'Don't you *ever* touch my kids, d'you hear? *Never!*'

Jack took a swing at David but lost his balance and staggered backwards like a drunk, not stopping till he hit the wall. He stood there shaking violently, then wiped his mouth with the back of his hand. 'You wait till I tell my son! You just wait!'

'Get to your room,' David ordered. 'Now!'

Ana realised that amid the shock of the fight and the noise of Peter and Jo crying he might not remember where it was. She handed Peter to his father, took Jack's arm — but warily, in case he hit out at her — and led him down the hall, ushered him into his room and closed the door behind him.

In the kitchen David was back in his seat. Peter was sitting on his knee, a scone in his hand, his sobs subsiding to snotty hiccups.

'That's it,' David said flatly. 'He has to go.'

Ana stared at him. 'But you said—'

David cut her off. 'I know what I said, but we can't have him attacking the kids.'

'He's had a go at hitting Mum too,' Rowie said.

'Has he?' David asked Ana.

'Well, yes, but I'm not Peter. I'm not a little boy.'

David held her gaze. 'No, but you're my wife and ... and I'm sorry.'

The relief Ana felt was *immense* and unbidden tears pricked her eyelids. To hide them she turned to the bench for more scones, though there were still plenty on the table.

'He'll have to go away somewhere,' David said. He sagged back in his chair. 'Christ, I don't even know where to start.'

'The doctor will know.'

'What doctor? We don't have one, do we?'

Ana sat down. That was a point — no one had been sick since they'd moved to Auckland so she hadn't bothered to enrol with a doctor. She'd ask Colleen next door to recommend someone. But did Jack actually need to see a general practitioner? Or could you just roll up to the nearest mental hospital and leave your loony loved one outside the gate to be taken in with the milk? Like David, she had no idea.

And now that the time had suddenly come to send Jack away, she felt guilty. It wasn't a vague, mild guilt she could push to the back of her mind and ignore, either, it was a burning in her throat and a horribly tight chest and she could tell by the look on David's face he felt it too.

'This is mean,' Rowie said, 'but I'm glad he's going. I'm scared of him.'

'So am I,' Jo agreed.

'Me too,' Peter said.

David slid Peter onto the floor. 'Well, that does it, then, doesn't it?'

Chapter Eleven

April 1956

Auckland Mental Hospital was a sizeable and very imposing-looking complex, so much so that Ana and David almost changed their minds as they drove through the gate. Did they really want to leave Jack at an institution that wouldn't seem out of place in a Charles Dickens novel? The shitty weather wasn't helping as an early autumn squall drove rain and leaves across the Chevrolet's windscreen. Two long double-storey brick wings flanked a central three-storey building that was obviously the entrance. Behind this main building were many others, the rambling compound situated on farmland between Point Chevalier and Mount Albert. The immediate grounds surrounding the hospital were well kept, with flower beds and large trees, and Ana thought the place might look rather nice on a warm summer's day.

David parked near the entrance and they all got out, David opening the boot for his father's suitcase.

'Bloody flash house,' Jack said, gazing up at the top storey of the entrance building.

Ana couldn't look him in the face. He obviously didn't know where they were, or what they were doing here. He'd had a quiet morning, had behaved when she'd helped him dress in his good trousers, sports coat and hat, but hadn't responded when the kids had said goodbye, or when Jo had cried. In fact his mood had been quite good. When she'd asked if he'd done a number two, he'd replied no, he'd done a number six — his idea of a joke. He'd had no sense of where they were taking him in the car, which had been very sad because it wasn't as if she and David hadn't told him. They had, several times during the week, as gently as they could, but it just hadn't seemed to mean anything to him. He'd even watched her sew name tags onto every item of clothing he'd be taking with him, and had never once asked why.

Now, David said, 'It's not a house, it's a hospital.'

'Who're we visiting?'

Ana thought her heart might break. Taking Jack's arm and feeling like the worst sort of shit imaginable, she said, 'Come on, let's go in, shall we?'

David went first. Inside he found a nurse and they were soon on their way to a ward, walking what felt to Ana like miles along a corridor behind another nurse wearing a white uniform, white stockings and shoes, and whose backside was enormous. Surely if you traipse up and down these corridors all day your bum shouldn't have a chance to get that big? she thought, knowing she was being unkind but blaming it on feeling upset.

The corridor itself was fairly grim. The walls were painted a bilious green colour, though the paint was scratched and scuffed, and the lighting was harsh, emphasising every defect in the flooring and on the walls. The air smelt vaguely unpleasant, disinfectant not quite masking odours of boiled green vegetables, urine and the faint whiff of shit. In fact, Ana thought, the place seemed the very embodiment of everything that had worried them about sending Jack to an institution.

Finally they arrived at the ward where Jack would in all likelihood spend the rest of his life, a thought which submerged Ana in a fresh tidal wave of guilt. It was as bleak as the corridor. The floor was covered with faded grey-and-blue patterned linoleum, the beds — all sixteen — were metal-framed and separated only by flimsy curtains on rails, currently tied back, and the bedside tables were scuffed wooden affairs each accompanied by a tall, narrow cupboard. But at least there were several big windows that let in plenty of light, and a vase of fresh flowers on the nurse's desk just inside the door.

'New patient for you,' their guide boomed to the young nurse sitting there. 'Mr John Leonard.'

'Jack Leonard,' David corrected.

'That's right,' Nurse Big Backside agreed, and lumbered off.

'Where the fuck are we?' Jack said, a look of panic beginning to cross his face.

'It's all right, Jack,' Ana said, patting his arm.

'Good morning, I'm Sister Simpson,' the girl said, apparently ignoring Jack's language. 'Do you have Mr Leonard's medical notes?'

'Er, no,' David said. 'What notes?'

'We have a letter from a doctor.' Ana retrieved it from her handbag. 'Dr Jarvis? We saw him ten days ago? He said he'd be getting in touch with the hospital. He told us to bring Jack in today.'

Sister Simpson read the letter. 'And you're Ana and David Leonard?'

David nodded. 'He's my father. Ana's my wife.'

'Hang on a tick.' Looking vaguely cross, Nurse Simpson ferreted around on her desk, moving piles of brown folders and pieces of paper, then said, 'Here it is. Sorry. Yes, he's been referred with senile dementia, is that right?'

'Well, that's what the doctor said,' David replied.

'And you can't manage him at home?'

Ana said, 'We've had him at home for over two years and—'

'He's hitting the kids,' David interrupted. 'We can't have him there any more.'

Sister Simpson's hand came up. 'I understand completely. It's quite a common problem. More common than you'd think.' She gave Jack a big smile. 'Well, let's get you settled, shall we, Mr Leonard?'

Ana wondered how on earth a girl — though Sister Simpson was probably in her mid-twenties — who was only five feet two and slight to go with it managed to boss around grown men. What if they turned violent? She'd barely been able to manage Jack and she was fit and no wisp of a thing. But Sister Simpson must be capable, if she was in charge of a ward.

As the nurse led Jack to a vacant bed, Ana said, 'Do you mind if I ask, what do you do if they get aggressive?'

'Well, we have medication to settle them. And if things get out of hand I can call for assistance,' Sister Simpson replied, then she frowned slightly. 'Someone *usually* turns up to help.'

'Um, I should tell you,' Ana added, her voice low now, 'sometimes he wets his pants. And soils them.'

'Oh, that's not a problem here,' Sister Simpson said cheerfully. 'We put them in nappies.'

David looked appalled.

Astounded, Ana asked, 'Do they make nappies that big?' Why hadn't she thought of that?

'We have them made 'specially. Would you like to get into your pyjamas, Mr Leonard?'

'No.'

'You'll be more comfortable.'

Jack was getting that look on his face. Ana could see trouble coming.

'It's not bedtime,' he mumbled.

'Is that all he'll do here, lie in bed?' David asked.

'Oh, no. Well, it depends on his behaviour, really. He'll have a few days in bed while he's assessed and his medications are sorted out, then after that he'll be able to visit the lounge and the recreation room, and maybe even walk in the gardens. Supervised, of course.'

David waved a hand at the half-dozen or so other patients lying in bed. 'Good. I don't want him ending up like these sad sacks.'

'David!' Ana was mortified.

'Well, I don't.'

'Come on, Mr Leonard, let's get you into your pyjamas, shall we?' Sister Simpson said, removing Jack's hat.

'Get your hands off me!' he barked, swatting at her.

Deftly dodging him, she said, 'Now, now, that's enough of that. You want to behave for your family, don't you?'

'I haven't got any family.'

'Well, then, who's this?' Sister Simpson asked.

'Fucked if I know.'

Sister Simpson pulled the curtains around the bed. 'I think it might be best if you left for today, if you don't mind. He seems a little confused at the moment. He probably just needs time to settle.'

'We'll see you soon, Dad,' David said. His voice sounded tight.

Ana could barely speak herself. 'Goodbye, Jack. We love you.'

Jack didn't even look at them.

*

Robert Sullivan had taken Donna out to just about every venue in Auckland a girl could want to try. They'd been to the Hi Diddle Griddle twice more, where she'd finally been brave enough to order the lobster tails, the California, La Corvette, and the Gourmet, which was extremely snooty. They went to the pictures (the cinema, as Robert insisted on calling it), and dancing at the Oriental Ballroom on Symonds Street, the Orange on Newton Road, Saint Septs on Khyber Pass, and the Peter Pan on Queen Street. She'd been bursting to go to the Jive Centre at the Trades Hall in Hobson Street where everyone was doing rock and roll, but Robert refused, preferring the other venues where that was banned and there was no chance of 'mature' dancers cutting a more sedate rug getting bumped or rammed by boisterous youngsters, which was a pity. She thought ramming and bumping and swinging each other about sounded like fun. Pauline went to the Maori Community Centre with her new boy all the time and said rock and roll was a real hoot. But Robert was a doctor and couldn't be seen letting his hair down in public, she supposed.

And they went on picnics and for walks in parks and to the beach, but mostly they had sex — in Robert's car, in the bushes, and once in the cloakroom at the Orange. It had been an exhilarating and somewhat fervid romance, and the talk of the nurses' home, even though Robert had asked her to keep their affair under her hat. Well, her hat hadn't been big enough and while she hadn't shared the most intimate details with Helen and Barbara, she'd told them everything else and somehow, after a few weeks, everyone knew.

And now, three months into their liaison, her monthlies were late. She'd missed twice. The first month she hadn't bled she'd attributed to being so busy rushing round like a blue-arsed fly between ward work and lectures and going out with Robert, but now that she'd missed two periods she was worried.

Flopping down on Helen's bed one evening she asked, 'Do you know any girls who've had babies?'

Helen gave her a funny look. 'Only about a thousand.'

'No, I mean personally, right from when they, you know, fell pregnant.'

'My sister's had two. Why?'

'How did she find out for sure?'

Helen put aside her magazine. 'Oh, Donna, you're *not*, are you?'

There was such dismay and sympathy in Helen's voice that Donna felt insulted. 'Don't say it like that,' she snapped. 'And I don't know, not for sure. That's why I'm asking.'

'You'll have to go to the doctor and have a frog test.'

Donna nodded knowingly, though she was utterly baffled. After a moment she said, 'Helen?'

'What?'

'What's a frog test?'

Helen rolled her eyes. 'God, Donna. It's the test for pregnancy.

You give the doctor some wee, he injects a frog with it and if the frog lays eggs or makes sperm, then you're officially expecting.'

Donna had never heard of it. 'Well, I can't go to our family doctor.'

'See if someone at the hospital will do it.'

'And then what? Resign from nurse training when Matron finds out? I can't risk that.'

'Then go to a doctor in town. Have you told Robert?'

'Not yet. I thought I'd find out for sure first.'

'Good idea,' Helen said. 'No point scaring the life out of him before you have to.'

Donna frowned. 'Why would it scare the life out of him?'

'It's him who's got you pregnant, isn't it? The least he can do is offer to marry you.'

'It won't be the *least* he can do. I expect he'll probably want to. If I really am expecting, that is.'

Helen said nothing.

'Don't you think?' Donna prompted.

'I think you deserve a really decent husband, that's what I think.'

Donna thought that was a bit of an odd thing to say, but let it go. She was too tired to make sense of it. And anyway, Helen was always saying mystifying things like that.

The next day, after lectures at the Market Road Preliminary School, she ducked into a doctor's surgery for a casual appointment during which she nervously gave a urine specimen, and her name as Mrs Donna Roberts.

'I didn't know they were letting married women train as nurses these days,' the practice nurse said, staring Donna right in the eye as she handed back the little jar.

'When can I find out the results?' Donna asked. She felt so strange, as though some other person were doing this and she were just watching. Even her voice sounded odd.

'Drop in or telephone in three days. Will you be making this your regular doctors' surgery, *Mrs* Roberts?'

'I don't know. That ... depends.'

The nurse seemed to relent. 'Well, good luck.'

*

The frog laid eggs. Donna cried so hard on the afternoon she found out she had to tell Matron she'd received news of a bereavement, and was sent off Ward Five where she was working to recuperate in her room. On the way she saw Robert exiting Ward Three and tried to avoid him, but it was too late; he called out to her. Quickly wiping her eyes and nose, she reluctantly turned to face him. She wanted to see him but not looking like this.

'What's the matter?' he asked. 'What's happened?'

'I ...' Oh God, she didn't know what to say. Should she tell him now?

Robert put his arm around her. 'Has someone upset you? Tell me.'

His arm felt so nice, so comforting and reassuring. 'I've had some news. I'm ... I'm expecting.'

'You're *pregnant*?' Robert blurted. The word came out really loudly and echoed along the corridor. 'Christ almighty, how did that happen?'

Donna stared at him dumbly.

'I mean, we've been taking precautions,' he went on, lowering his voice. 'I thought you understood what to do.'

'I did, I do. And I was.'

He swept his hair back off his forehead. 'Ah, God. Are you sure?'

His face had gone pale and tiny beads of sweat had popped out on his top lip.

Donna nodded. 'I've had a test. Are you not happy about it?'

'Well, are you?'

'I don't know.'

Robert stood very still for a long moment, staring down at the floor. Then he said, 'Then we'll just have to make the best of it and do what we can, won't we?' He gave her a peck on the cheek. 'Meet me tomorrow night and we'll take it from there, all right? Don't worry, everything will work out.'

Her spirits buoyed somewhat, Donna nodded again. He'd taken charge and if what she thought might happen *did* happen, things would be all right, though some of her plans would have to change. But life never went according to plan, did it?

*

Donna waited for Robert at the entrance to Cornwall Park, prickling with anticipation. Tonight's date could change the whole course of her life. She'd taken some time to get ready, much of which was spent standing sideways in front of her mirror trying to see whether her pregnancy was showing yet. It wasn't, but by her calculations she probably wasn't even three months along yet. Mind you, her calculations concerning her monthly cycle had turned out to be a bit unreliable. She supposed she'd need to go to a doctor soon and work out proper dates and such.

Robert seemed unusually quiet when he picked her up. Or was he nervous?

'I thought we'd just go for coffee. I hope you've had your dinner.'

Donna hadn't. She'd learnt not to have any tea on date nights and was quite hungry.

'I haven't, actually. I'd like to try the Mocambo. It's a coffee lounge but they do dinner as well. I've heard the food's good.'

Robert looked faintly perturbed. 'Apparently it's a bit bohemian. You don't want to go somewhere quieter?'

'What about the White Lady, then? I like a good pie cart.'

Donna wondered why she was being awkward and faintly pushy — she knew Robert didn't like bossy girls. And she knew he especially wasn't keen on girls who'd rather eat a pie than some fancy exotic dish. She'd better watch herself. She could ruin everything.

'No, we'll go to the Mocambo if that's what you want.'

They parked on Swanson Street, and found a table in the coffee lounge. It *was* bohemian, with European posters and paintings of nudes on the walls, and, at this time of night, was busy and noisy with a fug of cigarette smoke you could barely see through. Donna thought Robert didn't look happy, but she loved it. They ordered coffee and while they waited Robert said very little, fiddling with the buttons on his sports coat, apparently getting more nervous as time passed. When their coffee pot arrived he poured them a cup each and gulped his, wincing as he burnt his mouth. Donna ordered a ham and cheese toasted sandwich from the menu.

When he'd recovered from his first-degree burn, Robert said, 'We need to talk.'

Donna nodded, clasping her hands on the tabletop because they were shaking and she didn't want him to see. Here it comes. Would she be engaged to be married by the time they left?

'You're a lovely girl, Donna, you really are, and we've had lots of fun, and the way I see it there's really only one thing for it.' He dipped his hand in his jacket pocket, took out an envelope and slid it across the table.

It definitely wasn't what Donna had been expecting. 'What's in it?'

'Thirty pounds.'

'Why do I want thirty pounds?'

'For an abortion,' Robert said. 'I believe that's the going rate.'

Donna felt as though he'd punched her in the face. 'An abortion?'

Robert leant forwards. 'Look, I'm sorry, but you don't want to be a single mother, do you? I've no intention of getting married, especially not ... Well, I've my career to think of, Donna. You do understand that, don't you? I don't think we should see each other any more. It was only meant to be a bit of fun.'

Donna stared and stared at him. She knew her face had gone white because she actually felt dizzy as the blood drained from her head, then it all rushed back and her cheeks blazed scarlet. He was flicking a bit of money at her to get rid of his little mistake and telling her to bugger off! And my mistake too, she realised dimly. My stupid bloody mistake.

He said something then, but she didn't hear it, the blood was pounding so loudly in her ears. Then he stood, and was gone.

She sat for a while staring down at her coffee cup, and didn't even notice when a waitress brought her toasted sandwich. Eventually she put the envelope in her handbag, then went outside and walked down onto Queen Street to catch a tram out to Green Lane.

*

Pauline and Johnny sat halfway down the tram. It was early Saturday evening and it was packed with blokes exploded out of the pubs after the six o'clock swill and the whole tram reeked of beer.

'But what if they *don't* like me?' Pauline said for about the hundredth time.

'They will, don't worry,' Johnny said patiently.

'But Allie's mother-in-law didn't like her, not at first.'

Johnny grinned his big, white smile. 'We getting married, are we?'

Pauline felt herself go red. 'No! But you know what I mean, because I'm not Maori.'

'My mum and dad don't give a stuff about all that.'

'You sure?'

Johnny made a thinking face. 'Actually, I dunno. I've never asked. But they've never said anything like, look, there goes Wiremu Ngata with that white girl again, we don't approve of that.'

Pauline let out a wobbly sigh. 'I'm shitting myself.'

'Well, don't. You'll be OK.'

They sat in silence after that, holding hands and trying not to be overcome by beer fumes, until they arrived at the stop on

College Hill Road closest to Johnny's street, then walked the rest of the way.

Pauline was a bit shocked by the state of his family's home. Everyone knew Ponsonby wasn't a particularly nice area, but the house looked on the verge of falling down. He led her along a cracked and uneven concrete path to the back of the property, which looked like a tip and had hardly any grass. Someone, though, had planted quite a good veggie garden. There was also an outdoor dunny, and a separate washhouse with no door, in which she could see a copper and a big concrete tub attached to the wall.

'That rubbish isn't ours, it's the owner's,' Johnny said. Pauline thought he sounded embarrassed. 'We asked but he won't take it away. And we had to clean the path with acid, it was so mouldy and filthy. We all kept going arse over tit.'

The back porch was up some rickety steps and on a bit of a lean, but there were two rows of shoes neatly lined up along one wall.

'And your whole family lives here?' Pauline asked.

'Yep, nine of us. We don't wear shoes inside.'

Pauline slipped off her shoes.

Johnny opened the back door and called, 'Mum! Visitors!'

The faces of three boys peered out from what seemed to be a bedroom. One boy chanted, 'Oooh, Johnny's got a girlfriend!'

'Shut up, Sam. These are my brothers, Willie, George and Sam. Hop off, you lot. Mum'll be in the kitchen.'

She was, along with Johnny's sisters, Patricia, Mary and Margaret.

Mrs Apanui, a big, nice-looking lady, gave Pauline a squashy hug. 'Hello, dear, welcome. It's nice to meet you at last. We keep telling Johnny to bring you home. You want to stay for some kai before you go out?'

Pauline looked at Johnny, who said, 'Might as well. Mum's a good cook.'

Tea was pork chops and great bowls of vegetables from the

garden. There wasn't a kitchen table so everyone sat on the floor in the sitting room around a tablecloth.

Pauline liked Mr Apanui too, who asked, 'What does your father do, Pauline?'

'Not much. He was a watersider but got run over when he was a bit shickered coming out of the pub during the strike, and now he's on the sick, but he does the odd job house-painting when he's up to it. Under the table, though.'

Mr Apanui roared with laughter.

Mrs Apanui belted him. 'Stop that, Joshua. It's not funny.'

'It is.'

'We thought it was,' Pauline agreed. 'Well, Mum didn't.'

'Sounds like a bobby-dazzler, your dad.'

'Oh, he is. You should meet him one day.'

'That'd be good.'

'And your mum?' Mrs Apanui asked.

'She works in the tearoom at Mission Bay. She's been there for years. Runs in the family now 'cos I work at The Cedar Room at Smith and Caughey, but one day I'm going to be a stewardess for TEAL.'

'Well, it's good to have ambitions,' Mrs Apanui said, looking pointedly at Johnny.

'What?' Johnny said, reaching for more sweetcorn. 'I've got ambitions.'

'Be nice to know what they are,' Mr Apanui muttered.

'My current ambition is to finish my tea and get to the MCC. Hey, I'm a poet!'

'Honestly, how do you put up with him?' Patricia asked Pauline. Pauline laughed.

After a pudding of jelly and hokey-pokey ice cream, Mrs Apanui wouldn't let Pauline help with the dishes and shooed her and Johnny out the door.

'Go on, off you go and have a good time. And you make sure she gets home all right, Johnny. No sticking her on a tram by herself. You take her all the way home.'

'Yes, Mum.'

'Thanks for tea, it was lovely,' Pauline said.

'You're welcome, dear. Come again any time you like.'

Outside Johnny said, 'Shall we walk down the hill or get the tram? I think I've eaten too much to walk.'

'Me too. Tram,' Pauline said, stifling a burp and lighting a cigarette at the same time, which was quite complicated. 'Smoke?'

Johnny nodded. Pauline gave him the cigarette and lit another, and they crossed into the middle of College Hill Road to wait at the tram stop. They rode down into Victoria Street as far as the Halsey Street intersection, then hopped off and walked to the Maori Community Centre at the intersection with Fanshawe Street. Pauline was quite pleased she'd worn flat shoes, which were best for dancing anyway.

The MCC was a big square ugly building that looked exactly like what it was — an American army warehouse left over from World War II. But, according to Johnny, it was a thriving meeting place for city Maori who came to dance on Friday and Saturday nights and on Sundays after church, and to play sports and attend cultural events and eat boil-up and Maori bread. Tonight they could hear the band from the footpath, and had to fight their way inside because it was jam-packed and already hopping. Johnny dumped his sports coat (no leather allowed at the MCC) on a vacant chair and Pauline set her handbag on top.

She loved it there, and felt a thrill of excitement as she followed Johnny straight onto the dance floor. Why waste time saying hi to friends when the band was pumping out good rock and roll? There'd be time for socialising later.

Johnny grabbed her hand and they swung into the familiar steps — right, left, a step behind, then a spin, and again — and then she was sliding through his legs and barrelling into another couple who skipped out of the way, then turning as he yanked her back to her feet. Soon, once they'd warmed up, she'd be flipping upside down, over his shoulder, spinning out, spinning back, getting dizzy, and never once losing the beat. She loved dancing and there was no one better to dance with than Johnny Apanui. Then the song ended, the guitarist said something funny that made the whole hall laugh, and the band started into a jive number, so off they went again, similar dance steps but twice as fast.

After twenty minutes the band announced a short break and dancers drifted off the dance floor.

Pauline lifted her arm and sniffed her armpit. 'Yuck.'

Johnny laughed. There were large damp patches under his own arms and down the back of his bright blue dress shirt. 'Me too. We'll probably stink by the end of the night.'

They never did, though, Pauline thought. They smelt of sweat, but they never *stank*. And lately they'd smelt of sex, from doing it in the grandstand next to the MCC in Victoria Park. Who knew sex actually had a smell? It was sort of like feijoas. Or was it guavas? Going home afterwards on the bus they'd be sitting there and there'd be this whiff around them, especially if the night was warm, and they'd look at each other and wonder if anyone else on the bus could smell it. It was actually a bit embarrassing, the idea that people might be looking at them and thinking, those two have just done it.

Johnny used French letters, though she couldn't see what was so French about them. He said he got them from his mate at work. They came in a little tin and you could buy them from the chemist, but he reckoned he was buggered if he was going in and asking for them because the chemist asked you a whole lot of questions. What she couldn't work out was, if the stuff that came out of Johnny all went into the French letter, which he threw away afterwards, and not her, why could you still smell what they'd been doing it? Johnny thought maybe having sex changed the smell of their sweat — and they did get pretty sweaty doing it — so perhaps that was it. She was too embarrassed to ask Allie, and Donna wouldn't know, being all prudish and holier than thou now she was a student nurse, and her mother would knock her block off.

Maybe she'd ask one of her girlfriends. When she got round to it.

*

Jonathan crossed to the drinks cabinet and refreshed his brandy. 'I suppose we'd better hire a new nanny.'

'No,' Kathleen said. She was curled on the sofa, nursing her own drink. Well, not exactly nursing — it was her third.

Jonathan added about two drops of bitters to his brandy, swirled his glass, then turned to face her. 'What do you mean, no?'

'No, we're not hiring a new nanny. You'll only end up sleeping with her.'

Sighing heavily, Jonathan said, 'Christ, do you have to bring that up again?'

'It doesn't matter whether I bring it up or not, does it?' Kathleen snapped. 'The fact remains you still did it.'

'Yes, I did, and I've apologised till I'm blue in the face. I really don't know what else you want me to do, Kathleen.'

'I want you not to have done it in the first place!'

'Well, I'm sorry, but I did. And if we're not going to get another nanny, who's going to look after Rosemary and cook the dinners? You?'

'Why not?'

Jonathan laughed. '*You're* the one who insisted you had to have a nanny in the first place! How will you go shopping and out to lunch with your friends with Rosemary trailing along? Being a proper mother and a housewife takes work, you know.'

'I know it bloody well takes work!' Kathleen shouted, because she did know, and she really wasn't sure she could manage it.

It was all very well preparing one Christmas dinner, but Evie had done most of the family's cooking, all the housework, had looked after Rosemary much of the time, and the boys after school. Jonathan was right. If she, Kathleen, had to do all that there'd be no time left to do anything just for her. And she suspected she would hate having to be an ordinary housewife. It wasn't what she wanted out of life at all. But then neither was having a philandering husband, an odd son and women she could really only call acquaintances rather than friends.

But she wasn't leaving Jonathan and neither would she ask, or tell, him to leave. She couldn't anyway: he was right about that too — the house was his. She wouldn't leave him even though she knew that if he was boorish enough to screw Evie in their home, then he was probably screwing other women as well. The stewardesses on his flights, perhaps? Women in cities in which he had stopovers? But then she'd suspected that for some time, hadn't she, but had never permitted the idea to crystallise into something tangible that could really hurt her. Well, now it had, but she couldn't bear the shame of a divorce, and she was too old to start again. So she would continue doing the things that brought her a measure of satisfaction, if not happiness, carry on spending Jonathan's money, and do her best to ignore his infidelities.

Jonathan sighed. 'Look, would you feel better if we hired an older woman? Someone in her sixties perhaps, and more of a housekeeper? I mean, Rosemary will be at school soon anyway. It's time you stopped mollycoddling her. You can't keep her at home forever.'

It was probably the best solution — surely even Jonathan wouldn't try to bed a woman in her sixties — but Kathleen didn't want to agree with him, so she said nothing.

'Why don't you telephone the agency?' he suggested, heading for the door. 'I'll leave it with you, shall I? I've got things to do.'

Kathleen sat on the sofa for a while longer, listening to Rosemary thumping about upstairs. She must be practising her ballet. Then she went to the French doors and looked out into the garden at Jonathan, sitting under a tree on a deck chair, with his booze and his newspaper.

'Bastard,' she whispered.

Chapter Twelve

May 1956

Donna dithered for nearly a month. She'd gone back to the doctor's surgery near Market Road and had been told she was ten weeks pregnant, according to the date of her last period.

Suddenly overwhelmed by panic, she'd blurted, 'I'm not married. What can I do about it?'

And the doctor had stared right at her and said, 'You made your bed, young lady, you lie in it.'

She'd told no one but Helen, who'd said, 'I knew it, you know.'

Startled, Donna had asked, 'What, that I'm pregnant?'

'No, that Slippery Sullivan was bad news.'

'Slippery Sullivan? Who called him that?'

'Most of the registered nurses.'

'You never told me that.'

'You never gave me the chance. You thought the sun shone out of his backside.'

It was true, Donna thought, she had. And now he'd gone, transferred to another hospital a week after he'd told her he wanted nothing to do with her. Matron had been the one to tell her. She'd stopped her in the corridor of Ward Three one day.

'I hope you're not looking for Doctor Sullivan, Nurse Roberts.'

'No, I'm on duty here this morning.'

'Because he's gone to Auckland Hospital. For good.'

'Oh.'

Then Matron, with her heavy legs, formidable bust, homely face and quick, sharp eyes, said, 'And if you want my opinion, which possibly you don't, you're a lot better off without him.'

Donna had opened her mouth, then shut it again.

'Men like Robert Sullivan are ten a penny. We've all known them. Yes, even me. I suggest you do whatever it is you need to do, then get on with the business of learning to be a nurse. You show promise. It would be a shame to waste it.'

Then she'd turned and marched off.

Donna had nearly died of embarrassment. Had Matron known the whole time? And, even worse, did she know about the baby? She'd rushed into the nearest toilet and looked in the mirror but there had been nothing — that she could see — that gave any indication she was expecting.

But still she'd put off making any arrangements, until finally Helen told her that if she left it any longer it could be too late and she'd have to have it.

'But I don't want to have it. I'd have to go away somewhere then give it up.'

'Then get off your bum and do something about it,' Helen said. 'Why won't you? Is it your religion?'

Donna had thought about that and had realised she wasn't enough of a practising Catholic to let that bother her. 'No. I think … I think I'm just scared.'

'Well, which is worse — being scared, or having to chuck in your nurse training? Because I don't think you'd be allowed back after having an illegitimate child, even if you did give it up for adoption.'

'Giving up nurse training would be worse, but you hear all these terrible stories about abortions.'

'Yes, and I know a couple of girls who've had them and they've been fine,' Helen said. 'Just make sure you go to someone reputable.'

'How do I know who's reputable?'

'Well, I don't know. I haven't had one, have I?'

'Can you ask those girls you know?'

'Me? They might think I need one.'

'Say it's for a friend,' Donna suggested.

'Well, obviously. I can try, but not till the weekend. People are careful who they talk to, though, because of, you know, the police.'

Donna nodded. That would be a nightmare — ending up in court being prosecuted for having an abortion. And in the newspapers. 'I'd be very grateful if you would, Helen. I really haven't got a clue where to go. And you're right, I do need to do something, and soon.'

*

The following Sunday night Helen gave Donna a name, an address and a time for the Wednesday evening of the coming week.

'I've made an appointment for you. It's up to you whether you go or not. If you want me to, I'll come with you.'

Donna took the piece of paper and put it in the pocket of her uniform, a uniform that just in the last week seemed to have become slightly more snug across her belly. 'Thanks, Helen. I really do appreciate this. And this person, does she have a good reputation?'

'She was the one who looked after those girls I was telling you about. And it's thirty-five pounds, not thirty. Do you have the extra five?'

Donna nodded. 'And thanks for offering to come with me, but if something goes wrong there's no point you getting in trouble as well, is there?'

Helen's face fell. 'I hadn't thought of that. Are you sure?'

'I'm sure. But thanks.'

The next few days dragged past, especially Wednesday. But finally, after work, Donna caught the tram into town then to

Mount Eden, then walked the last half mile to the address she'd been given. The house was a nice tidy little cottage painted white with lattice-work trim along the top of the verandah, and a brick path leading to the front door. She knocked and waited until a middle-aged woman opened it. Her greying hair had been nicely set and she was wearing a cardigan over her apron.

Donna's stomach roiled with apprehension. 'Mrs Harris?'

'Yes?'

'I think I have an appointment with you. Donna Roberts?'

'Yes, that's right. Come in.'

Donna stepped inside. The house smelt of Dettol or something similar.

'First room on your right,' Mrs Harris said. 'Everything off from the waist down, please, and wait for me on the bed. I'll be in in a minute.'

The room looked like a normal bedroom. Donna didn't know what she'd been expecting but it wasn't this. There were a couple of framed pictures of flowers on the walls, a bookshelf, and a set of drawers on top of which sat half a dozen family photographs — presumably Mrs Harris's relatives. A crocheted lampshade surrounded the ceiling bulb, pink drapes and heavy white nets hung at the window, and a burgundy candlewick bedspread covered the single bed. The only indication that anything medical might occur in the room were the tray on a bedside trolley containing a couple of surgical-looking instruments, and a rubber sheet covering the bottom half of the bed.

Donna undressed as asked and sat down, feeling sick now and listening to the blood pound in her head, wishing she hadn't come. But she'd had to; she'd had no choice.

Mrs Harris returned carrying a steaming bowl of water, into which she dropped a speculum from the tray, and what Donna was pretty sure was a fine gauge steel knitting needle.

'Do you know how far along you are, dear?' she asked.

'I think three months, maybe three and a half?' Donna said.

'Lie down, please. All right, bend your knees, heels against your bottom, legs apart. I'm going to start now so try to relax. You shouldn't feel too much.'

Donna felt something nudge the opening to her vagina and immediately tensed.

'Try to relax, please. This is just the speculum. You know what a speculum is? It opens you up. I need to be able to see what I'm doing.'

Of course she knew what a speculum was. Donna felt it go in and gasped as Mrs Harris released the opening mechanism.

'You *must* relax.'

'Sorry.'

Then the knitting needle came out of the hot water and Donna squeezed her eyes shut. The pain was actually pretty bad and she bit down so hard she felt a piece of back tooth break off, but Mrs Harris seemed to have a deft hand and didn't poke about for too long. Just enough to dislodge and destroy anything growing in there. And then it was finished.

'That's it,' Mrs Harris said, washing her hands in the basin of water. 'You should expect things to start moving in twelve to twenty-four hours. Rest up. If anything goes awry, and I don't expect that it will as I have a very good track record, get medical help but do *not* mention my name. And don't come back here. Do you understand?'

Donna nodded as she struggled to sit up.

'Good girl. I'll make you a cup of tea to drink while you get dressed.'

I don't want tea, I just want to go home, Donna thought. She took her time putting on her clothes. She had to — her belly felt as though someone had jumped on it. Mrs Harris brought the tea, along with four squares of Cadbury's Dairy Milk chocolate, melting against the cup.

'Eat the chocolate, dear,' Mrs Harris said. 'Sugar's good for shock, and you've had one. It's not easy, sometimes, being a woman.'

Donna ate the chocolate, then drank the tea, which must have had at least three teaspoons of sugar stirred into it, and did actually feel a bit better. On the way out she said thank you to Mrs Harris and paid her the thirty-five pounds. Mrs Harris said thank you back, and it was over.

*

Nothing had happened by the next morning and Donna was starting to fear that the abortion hadn't worked. All she had were some vague aches in her lower belly, like a very mild period, and no show at all. She literally broke into a sweat on and off all morning at work worrying about what would happen if she had to have the baby, and the hideous damage that might have been done to it by Mrs Harris's knitting needle.

But by early afternoon the pain was getting worse and she realised, with immense relief, that things were finally moving. She also realised that once again she'd been incredibly stupid and should have gone home. She couldn't have this happen in the middle of a medical institution — everyone would know it was a miscarriage or the effects of an abortion and she'd lose her position anyway.

So at five o'clock she simply walked out and caught the tram into town. By this time she was gritting her teeth against waves of pain, and had had to pinch two sanitary napkins from the hospital as she was bleeding quite heavily. Her first thought had been to go to Allie's house, but there was Hana and now Allie's trouble getting pregnant again, so it would be cruel of her to turn up there. It would have to be her parents and they would be *livid*, especially her mother, but she had nowhere else to go.

As she stood on Customs Street waiting for the bus that would take her across to Orakei she was suddenly overwhelmed by a violent surge of nausea and had to vomit into a rubbish bin outside a shop. No one stopped to help but she got plenty of disgusted looks. She wondered if people thought she were drunk.

Finally the bus came and she got on, hoping she didn't smell of sick, and sat hunched over in a seat, her arms wrapped around her belly, to ease the dragging cramps in her womb.

After a few miles of the bus stopping and starting and jerking her uncomfortably all over the place, a woman in the seat opposite leant across the aisle and said, 'Are you all right, love?'

'Monthlies,' Donna whispered.

'Ooh, I know, they can be a bugger, can't they? You get home and put a hot water bottle on your middle, that'll help.'

Donna nodded her thanks, grateful for her kindness.

At last the bus reached her stop on Coates Avenue and she got off, barely able to stand now. Shuffling along she wondered fearfully what her mother and father were going to say. Her mother would be so disappointed with her. As she walked slowly down the garden path she could smell food frying, and almost threw up again. The back door was open but she knocked anyway.

'It's only me.'

Startled, her mother looked at her from the stove. 'Hello, love. What are you doing home?'

Her father was at the kitchen table, reading the paper as usual, and looked equally taken aback.

'I'm not feeling the best. I thought I'd come home for a bit.'

'Why? What's wrong?' Colleen asked, taking a sizzling frying pan off the element.

It was too much for Donna. She dashed for the sink and vomited again.

'Oh my bloody godfathers,' Sid said.

'It's just a bit of sick, Sid,' Colleen said, patting Donna's shoulder.

'No, the back of her dress, look at it.'

Colleen looked. The skirt of Donna's white uniform was covered in blood. 'Oh my *God*, Donna. What's happened?'

Donna burst into tears, at least partly at the thought of having got off the bus and walked along the road with blood all over the back of her. 'I got into trouble and I ... I had to fix it.'

Colleen went white. 'Oh Lord, not one of those backstreet people?'

'She was *reputable*.'

'Sid, get some towels, now,' Colleen snapped.

She turned off all the elements except one, and set the kettle on it. Sid was back almost immediately. Colleen set a folded towel on a chair and sat Donna down.

'When did this happen?'

'Last night.'

'And how long have you been bleeding?'

'Since after lunch.'

'Are you in pain?'

Donna nodded.

'Well, it won't be far away, then.'

'How do you know?' Sid asked.

'Never you mind. We need to get you out of these clothes, love. Sid, get a nightie and Pauline's robe out of her room.'

'Wait on, I want to know who got our Donna into this mess!'

'No one, Dad,' Donna said. 'Really, he was no one.'

'Not worth it?' Colleen asked.

Donna knew then that things would be all right. 'No, he wasn't.'

'All right, you hold her hand and *I'll* get the nightie,' Colleen said, and marched out of the kitchen.

Donna let her mother lead her into the bathroom, undress her, sponge the blood from her buttocks and thighs, and dress her in Pauline's nightie, a pair of big ugly pants and another sanitary napkin. She felt as though she were five years old again, and she was grateful for it. Her mother and father still loved her, they would look after her, and she was safe.

'Where's Pauline?' she asked.

'Probably out with that boy of hers,' Colleen muttered. 'I'll have to put these in to soak, though we'll be lucky to get all this out.'

'What boy?'

'Oh, she's got a new boyfriend, some Maori lad.'

Sitting on the edge of the bath, Donna doubled over in pain, holding her breath until the spasm passed. 'I didn't know that.'

'Well, you've been busy. Why don't you lie down in your old room?' Colleen handed her a couple of towels. 'Put these under you, just in case. I'll be in in a jiffy.'

Donna shuffled down the hall past Pauline's room, which she'd once shared with her when she and Allie had both lived at home. It looked like a bomb had gone off in it. Her old room, once Allie's, was unnaturally tidy — her mother's work.

She lay the towels over the pink bedspread then eased herself down, wishing that whatever was happening inside her body would hurry up. She didn't know how much longer she could tolerate this pain. Also, if giving birth was anything like this, she definitely wasn't going to be having any babies.

Her mother came in with a hot water bottle. 'This might help. Your father's really upset.'

'I'm sorry, Mum, I really am.'

Colleen sat on the end of the bed, and Donna felt her hand settle on her ankle. 'Why didn't you come to me when you knew you were in trouble?'

'I thought you'd be angry.'

'I am, but not with you.'

'I was really stupid, Mum. I made a really stupid mistake.'

'Shush. We've all made stupid mistakes. It's how we put them right that matters.'

They were silent for a minute, then Donna said, 'You haven't even had your tea.'

'That can wait.'

Donna groaned and curled up around the hot water bottle. 'God, it hurts.'

'That'll be everything coming away.'

'I feel like I need the toilet.'

'That'll be the cramps.'

'No, I really need the loo,' Donna said. 'Help me up?'

Her short trip from the spare room to the toilet off the back porch was a nightmare, convinced as she was with every step she was about to shit herself.

'All right, love?' her father asked as she shuffled through the kitchen, bent at the waist.

'She needs the loo,' Colleen answered for her.

Her mother helped Donna raise her nightie and pull down her pants and napkin, which was soggy with blood, and to sit down.

She wrapped her arms around her middle, opened her legs, leant forwards and groaned, head down, as something slid out of her. There was an audible 'plop' as it landed in the toilet.

Astonished, she said, 'I think that was it.'

'The baby?'

Donna nodded. 'I think so. I thought it was going to be a poo.'

'Sid!' Colleen called, 'bring some more towels.'

'Poor Dad,' Donna said.

And poor me, she thought. And poor, poor little baby. But she was so relieved that her body suddenly felt as though it were filled with air, light and bright and free no matter if there was still pain to come. It was finished. It was done. And it would all be all right.

The towels were handed through the door on the end of a disembodied arm. Donna stood gingerly, wadded a towel between her legs and stepped away from the toilet.

'Don't look,' Colleen warned.

But Donna did. All she could see was a toilet bowl full of blood.

'Come on,' her mother said, taking her arm, 'I'll sort that out. Let's get you to bed, shall we?'

*

Once Donna was taken care of, Colleen returned to the toilet and stood looking down at the bloody mess in the bowl. Then she went back into the kitchen.

Sid was back in his chair at the table. She could see from his reddened eyes that he'd been crying, but she didn't say anything. He didn't like it when he knew he'd been caught weeping.

'I need your help,' she said. 'I don't want to do this by myself.' She opened a drawer and dug through the contents until she found her ladle with the holes in it for straining.

Sid blew his nose mightily. 'What do you need me to do?'

'That's our grandchild in that toilet. I'm not flushing it away like a ... a ruddy dead goldfish. I want to give it a decent burial.' Colleen burst into tears.

Sid went to her and put his arms around her. 'There, there, love. Donna's all right, we'll give the poor scrap a proper little send off, everything will be all right and we'll put it behind us, eh? You'll see. This'll pass. These things always do. We'll manage.'

Colleen nodded against his nice, comfortable, familiar-smelling neck. 'I know. It's just that ... she could have come to me and she didn't.'

'You've had your own worries, love. And they're not kiddies, now, the girls. They're all grown up, even Pauline. They're young women. And she came to you in the end, didn't she?'

'But still. And when I think of the misery she must have gone through finding out she was in trouble and trying to decide what to do all by herself.'

'I know, but that's done, and if our Donna can cope with it so can you.'

'I suppose.'

'Good. Now, what else do we need?'

It took a few minutes more to collect the items Colleen wanted and then they were ready. Fishing around in the toilet bowl with the ladle she lifted out the small mass of tissue that was the placenta. It had tears in it, but was more or less in one piece and was still attached to the tiny, lifeless foetus. She decanted both onto the towel Sid was holding. He gagged.

'Sorry.'

Colleen finally flushed the toilet, which didn't get rid of all the blood.

Then they wrapped the foetus and towel in an Irish linen tablecloth that had belonged to Colleen's mother and carried it in the dark down the garden to a spot under the apple trees. While Sid dug a hole, Colleen held — cradled — it, then they buried it and she said a prayer.

After that they went inside again and Sid sat with Donna while Colleen knelt before the toilet with a brush and a bottle of bleach, scrubbing and scrubbing at the bowl and seat until not a single drop or smear of blood remained.

*

Allie sat in the front room of her rent-free home and looked around at the fresh paint on the walls (warm cream, not pink), and thought about her new bathroom with its shiny porcelain bath and chrome taps, and felt terrible about her miserable mood. She didn't like the house and had been unsettled — even more than usual — since they'd moved in. At first she'd thought it was just the fuss of shifting but it had been nearly two months now and she still felt at odds. Sonny was happy, and Mr De Valera definitely was, but she wasn't.

The nightmares were still coming, filling her nights and now this house too with black smoke, flickering, grasping orange flames and screams of terror. And even after nights when she didn't have the bad dreams she was exhausted because she'd lain awake for hours anticipating them. She would give anything for a proper night's sleep, to wake feeling refreshed and not like a wrung-out dish rag. The other night Sonny had suggested a good-sized whiskey before she went to bed, which she'd tried even though it had nearly burnt a hole in her gullet, but that had made the dreams worse — far more vivid and terrifying — so she was never doing that again.

She'd shouted at him for it too. She'd slept really badly, on and off all night, and in the morning when they were getting ready for work she'd been in a rotten mood and picked a fight, though, at the time, she'd thought he'd started it.

All he'd said was, 'You look tired, love. You've got bags under your eyes.'

And she'd said, 'That's because I didn't get any bloody sleep, thanks to your stupid whiskey idea.'

'You got a bit. I heard you snoring.'

'Hardly any, though. I don't know why you thought whiskey would help. I'm not used to hard liquor like you.'

'Are you saying I'm a pisshead?'

She'd seen then that he'd been trying not to laugh and it had infuriated her. She knew full well he wasn't a pisshead but she'd said, 'Well, you drink enough.'

'Sometimes,' he'd agreed cheerfully.

And that had only made her angrier. It was *so* hard to annoy him. 'And you're bloody useless round the house. I have to do everything and it's not fair.' This wasn't quite true, either, but never mind. 'I have to cook and clean and wash and do the shopping. I'm too tired after work. Why can't we have a refrigerator? Why do we have to live in the stone ages?'

'Because we can't afford one,' he'd said patiently. 'We're saving for a house, remember?'

'But we've got a house,' she'd said, waving her arms around at the bedroom.

'A house of our own, not one lent to us by your mother.'

'Well, that's bloody ungrateful of you.'

'I'm not ungrateful at all. I'm very grateful not to have to pay rent, but we agreed we want to buy our own house.'

'Everyone else has got a refrigerator.'

'No they haven't.'

She'd thoroughly lost her temper then. 'Well, I *bloody well want one*!'

It hadn't been about a refrigerator, she'd known that. It had been about months — years — of poor sleep, and fear and tension, and grief and distress, and wondering if she was losing her mind.

And all Sonny had said was, 'Come on, love, get your things, we'll be late for work.'

He'd gone to the pub this afternoon with his mates because it was Saturday and now, as she sat alone in the house, she wondered if she was going to lose him.

*

Pauline had butterflies. Well, bats, really. She kept looking out the window of the front room for Johnny, though she knew exactly what time he'd be getting off the bus.

'Pauline!' her mother called from the kitchen, 'come and do the cheese sauce!'

'Can't Allie do it?' she shouted back.

'No.'

There were voices, then Allie called, 'I'll do it!'

Pauline sent her sister a silent thank you, then wondered if the bus was late. She checked her watch. No, it wasn't late. She was just having a nervous panic. Then a ghastly thought assaulted her: maybe he wasn't here yet because he'd decided not to come. Maybe he'd decided he didn't want to meet her family after all. Maybe he'd decided she wasn't worth it.

Then he came walking past the Leonards', carrying a bunch of flowers, and she let out a huge breath. She waved at him through the window, tore through the house, down the steps and up the garden path to meet him.

'I thought you might not come.'

He kissed her cheek. 'Why would I not come?'

'I don't know.' Pauline waited for him to give her the flowers, but he didn't. 'You look nice.'

'Ta.'

He did, too. He was wearing smart trousers (pegged, of course), a sports jacket she hadn't seen before, a bright yellow shirt, half a tub of Brylcreem in his hair and a lot of aftershave.

She linked her arm through his. 'Nervous?'

'Shitting myself.'

'Shall we go in?'

Johnny blew out his cheeks and nodded. At the top of the back steps he pecked her on the cheek and said, 'Wish me luck.'

'You won't need luck,' Pauline replied, but he wasn't listening — he was staring over at the neighbours'. 'What?'

'Who lives there? That looks like my auntie hanging out the washing.'

'The Leonards.'

Sonny grinned. 'Hang on a tick.' He trotted back down the steps and over to the fence. 'Hey, Auntie!'

Ana Leonard looked round, spotted him and stared, a damp tea towel in her hands.

Leaping up onto the fence, Sonny swung his legs over and sat there, perfectly balanced. 'It's me, Johnny Apanui.'

'Kura's boy?' Ana looked astounded. 'It is too. What are you doing in this neck of the woods?' She moved over to the fence.

'I'm going out with Pauline.'

Pauline waved; Ana waved back.

'I've been meaning to get in touch with your mother but I don't know where you're living,' Ana said.

Sonny told her. 'And Auntie Wiki's just across the street from us. Mum's been trying to track you down as well.'

'Well, now you can tell her where we are. And everyone's good?'

'Ae. And you?'

'Slowly getting used to the city. The kids like it. They've made friends. Well, I'd better let you go. Mrs Roberts has probably got your tea on the table. Lovely to see you, Johnny.'

'You too, Auntie.' On the steps again with Pauline, Johnny asked, 'Did you hear all that?'

Pauline nodded.

'Fancy that. Mum'll be pleased. She's been trying to track Auntie Ana down for ages.'

Finally they went inside. Pauline introduced her parents and Sonny and Allie, and explained that Donna would have come except she was busy with work. Johnny gave Colleen the flowers, which she said were charming, and everyone rearranged themselves at the table, except for Colleen, who was cooking.

Pauline said, 'Guess what? Johnny's related to Ana Leonard. She's his auntie.'

'*Mrs* Leonard to you,' Colleen said. 'Is that right, Johnny? It's a small world.'

'Well, her and my mother are second cousins, but we call her auntie. Can I give you a hand there, Mrs Roberts?'

Surprised, Colleen said, 'Can you cook?'

'Not really.'

Sid laughed. 'Here, have a beer instead. You *are* old enough to drink?'

'I'm eighteen.'

There was a bit of an embarrassed silence. Then Sid said, 'Got a job?'

'Been working since I was fifteen.'

Sid slid a bottle across the table. 'Then you're old enough for a beer.'

At the bench Colleen scowled.

'So, whereabouts do you work?' Sid asked.

'At the Destructor.'

'Rather you than me,' Sonny said. 'Money must be OK, though?'

'It's all right,' Johnny said. 'I'm looking for something else.'

Sid said, 'Got any interests? Hobbies and the like?'

'Stop interviewing him, Dad,' Pauline protested.

'Just getting to know him. What's wrong with that?'

Johnny shrugged. 'Music. Dancing. Me and Pauline go to the Maori Community Centre a lot.'

'Is that where you've been sneaking off to?' Colleen said to Pauline.

'Motorbikes,' Johnny added. 'But I don't own one.'

Colleen said, 'Well, that's a relief.'

'I've got an Indian,' Sonny remarked.

Johnny nodded. 'Pauline said.'

'I'll take you for a spin one of these days.'

'Cool! Thanks.'

Allie said, 'Pauline said you've got lots of brothers and sisters. Sonny's got dozens too.'

'Well, you know us Maoris,' Johnny said.

Sonny laughed. 'I haven't got *dozens*. I've got ten.'

'I've only got seven. But we live right across the street from my auntie and uncle and they've got five, so there's more or less eleven of us.'

'Seven and five make twelve, don't they?' said Sid the mathematician.

'We left my little sister back home. She's special.'

'And where's home?' Colleen asked.

'Maungakakari, near Napier.'

'What did your family do down there?'

'We were mostly in shearing gangs. We did the Leonards' sheep every year and tons of other farms and stations. Our gang was quite famous round Hawke's Bay. But the wool industry's drying up a bit now so there's not so much work.'

'You would have known Jack Leonard?' Sid said.

Johnny nodded. 'Decent bloke. Really fair.'

'Well, that's a pity,' Pauline said, 'He went troppo. They had to put him in the rat house.'

Colleen glared. '*Pauline!*'

'Well, they did.'

'He's got senile dementia,' Colleen explained to Johnny.

'Shit, has he?' Johnny clapped a hand over his mouth. 'Sorry for the language. That's the old age thing, isn't it?' He twirled his finger next to his temple.

Colleen nodded.

'I didn't know that. I'll have to tell Mum and Dad. That's a shame, eh?'

'So why'd you come to the city?' Sonny asked.

'Thought we could make more money here.'

'And have you?'

Johnny looked down at the table and for a few long seconds Pauline thought he wasn't going to answer. 'To tell the truth there is more money, but everything costs more too. And everything's harder, a lot harder. I never saw signs saying *No Dogs, No Maoris* till I came here. I can't go in a lot of barbershops, I can't sit in the good seats at the pictures, and no matter how hard we try my mum and dad can't rent anything better than a crappy old house in one of the worst streets in Ponsonby. Back home we probably wouldn't put our cow in the house we're living in now. And it isn't even cheap!'

'Welcome to the big smoke, boy,' Sonny said gently.

'You could always go home again if things are tough,' Colleen suggested. Her voice was kind and Pauline was grateful to her for it.

'I think Mum wants to, but Dad thinks we should stay. He wants us kids to grow up in a Pakeha world so we can get on. He says Maoritanga belongs in the past.'

'What do you think?' Sonny asked.

'I just want a motorbike.' Johnny took Pauline's hand and grinned. 'And to go dancing with Pauline. 'Cos nothing else matters then, eh?'

And Pauline smiled back because he was right. Nothing else mattered.

Chapter Thirteen

Hawke's Bay, May 1956

James Murdoch sat on his idling tractor in the middle of a row of apricot trees, staring at nothing in particular. Then he realised what he was — or more accurately, wasn't — doing, put the tractor in gear, drove to the end of the row and headed for the implement shed.

The apricot and peach harvests were well over for the season, the pickers and the fruit itself long gone, and he'd been puttering along tidying up beneath the trees. A late summer storm had come through a couple of days ago, and while the worst of Hawke's Bay's bad weather very rarely reached as far as the hills of Kenmore sheep station, a fair bit of wind had snapped off some of the older branches and hurled them around the extensive orchard that covered the lower slopes of the gentle hill rising behind the homestead. The soil was good and drained well, the land faced the sun and was more or less protected from frost, and for the last twenty years the orchard had paid its way handsomely. James sold some produce to local outlets but most of his fruit — peaches, apricots, plums and cherries — was bought by J Wattie Canneries.

He found the outdoors work, and the process of growing and harvesting, immensely rewarding. He'd once been a banker in Napier and that hadn't suited him at all. He'd come home from the war mentally battered, like most men, but possibly more so due to an incident involving the death of another officer. In fact, he'd shot the man. He, James, had been tried for murder but acquitted, but it had embittered him and he'd taken that bitterness out on his wife, his wider family, and eventually his children. And, seeking release, he'd gambled with money that hadn't been his. God, how he'd gambled. And lost. Basically he'd been a prick, and his arrogance and refusal to listen to advice had drawn him into trouble at the bank and ultimately he'd had to resign. At his wits' end he'd finally taken the time to consider what he really wanted to do with the rest of his life, and that was grow fruit. So he had. With his burdens lifted from his shoulders and his soul soothed he'd changed for the better. But not completely, and now he was facing trouble again.

To date he'd paid Polly one hundred and fifty pounds towards the upkeep of the child she'd said was his. He had no idea whether the child was receiving the money or Polly was simply spending it. All he knew was that it was disappearing from his bank account and that Lucy was bound to notice. Ever since his gambling days, which were long over, she'd checked their accounts for signs of back-sliding, and he didn't blame her. He couldn't easily explain away a deficit of fifty pounds a month, and neither did he want to. He had no idea how long Polly would keep up her demands, but he had no intention of paying her six hundred pounds a year for the rest of his life.

He parked the tractor, had a word with one of his full-time workers, then walked back to the house he and Lucy had built when they'd established the orchard, about half a mile from the Kenmore homestead where, these days, his half-brother, Joseph Deane, and his wife, Erin, lived. He wasn't at all looking forward to making his confession to Lucy. She'd put up with his rotten behaviour for years and deserved to think those times had passed, but here he was, about to shatter her illusions.

At the house he slipped off his boots, leaving them and his hat on the back verandah, and went inside, blinking as his eyes adjusted to the slightly dimmer light.

'Lucy! Where are you?'

'In here!'

He made his way towards the parlour, his socks slipping slightly on the polished floorboards. She was in the armchair nearest the big window, making the most of the light, knitting. Her hair was completely grey now but, in his opinion, she was as beautiful as she'd ever been, and he loved her. He always had, which made the way he treated her inexplicable. What he had to tell her would hurt her very much.

He sat down.

'Any real damage?' she asked.

For a startled moment he thought she'd read his mind. 'What?'

'The orchard, from the storm.'

'Oh. No, just a few broken branches. What are you knitting?'

'A jumper, for Lorraine.'

Lorraine was their granddaughter, Duncan and Claire's child. Lucy had always hoped Duncan and Claire would have more children but they hadn't, so she smothered Lorraine with love. But then she smothered all her grandchildren with love when she got the chance, which wasn't often as she hardly saw Kathleen's children.

James nodded. Finally, he said, 'Lucy, I have something I have to tell you.'

Lucy kept knitting, her eyes on her needles.

'I am so sorry, but about four years ago I was unfaithful to you.'

Tappety-tap-tap went Lucy's needles.

'I went to a brothel during one of my trips to Auckland,' James said. And then he lied. 'Just the once. And I saw the girl I met there at that fashion event Kathleen was in. She was one of the models. She told me she'd had a child and I'm the father.'

The tap-tapping stopped and at last Lucy looked up, her eyes brimming with tears. 'You always were a shit, James Murdoch.'

'I know, and I'm *so* sorry.'

'Then why are you telling me? Why are you *hurting* me?'

James rubbed his face with both hands. 'She's blackmailing me. I've been paying fifty pounds a month and I knew you'd find out sooner or later.'

Lucy hurled her knitting at him. It fell well short. 'You stupid, *stupid* man! Why can't you *think?* Why do you have to be so bloody selfish all the time? What's *wrong* with you?'

James briefly considered trying to defend himself — after all, he hadn't got the girl pregnant on purpose — but kept his mouth shut. What he'd done was actually pretty indefensible.

'And how do you know it's your child?' Lucy went on. 'She must have slept with hundreds of men. How do you know there even *is* a child? Did you see it?'

That shut James up. Briefly. Polly hadn't shown him a photograph: she might have duped him completely. But somehow he didn't think so. She was a prostitute, and obviously also a fashion model and a blackmailer and God only knew what else, but he really didn't think she was a liar. She'd always been honest with him. What you saw of Polly, you got.

'Well, I believed her. Don't ask me why but I did.'

Lucy was silent for almost a minute. Then she asked, 'Is it a boy or a girl?'

'A girl, apparently.'

Lucy stared back at him in silence, her bottom lip caught between her teeth, her eyes bright.

*

Auckland, May 1956

Ted Hollis sat in his car, an unobtrusive green Ford Consul, across the street from Flora's brothel, and ate the last of his homemade cheese and pickle sandwiches. She'd be out soon. He knew this because he'd been in yesterday and asked Flora MacKenzie, with whom he was well acquainted because of his job, for a chat with the Maori girl called Polly, and had been told he'd have to pay like everyone else and she'd be on from eleven o'clock that night till eleven this morning. He didn't fancy paying so he'd asked for Polly's home address and Flora told him to get on his bike, the old bat. He didn't blame her, though. She *was* trying to run a business, albeit an illegal one.

It was ten minutes to eleven now. He took a swallow of his Coca-Cola, wiped his mouth on his handkerchief, shoved the sandwich wrapper into the glove box, lit a smoke and waited.

And twenty minutes later there she was, providing the description James Murdoch had given him over the telephone was accurate, and it should be — apparently he'd screwed her often enough. She was definitely a stunning-looking girl, so he couldn't blame Murdoch. He took a couple of photos through his passenger window, even though the glass might render them a bit blurry.

She took off at a hell of a clip, flustering him. Should he follow her in the car, which admittedly would be a bit obvious, crawling along the road behind her, or tail her on foot? Bugger, he'd have to leave the car here. He grabbed his things, got out, locked up and crossed the street.

By the time he caught up, puffing a bit — she must be bloody fit — she was waiting at a tram stop, having a cigarette. Lucky he wasn't in the car after all. He got on when the tram arrived and sat several seats behind her, jotting the cost of the ticket in his expenses notebook as the tram rattled along the street. They went all the way into town and at Customs Street she hopped off the tram and caught a bus. Again he noted the ticket price, and the route number, aware they must be heading somewhere slightly out of town, or at any rate to some destination the tramlines didn't reach.

While they bumped along, stopping and starting to collect and deposit passengers, he surreptitiously checked the camera in his satchel to make sure there were enough exposures left to get a decent number of photographs. Once on a job he'd followed someone for three hours and when the time had come to photograph the crucial evidence — it had been an 'other woman' situation in a divorce case — he'd discovered he'd run out of film. What a cock-up! But yes, he had plenty today.

By the time they were on Tamaki Drive he had a fair idea where they might be heading. He dreaded traipsing up Kitemoana Street and wished he had the car after all. Then again it might be the only car up there, which meant it would stand out, the occupants of the street being who they were.

He lit a quick cigarette to fortify himself for the walk up the hill, which he suspected would be energetic. Given how quickly she moved she'd probably go up it like a mountain goat and he couldn't afford to lose sight of her.

The bus stopped at Okahu Bay and the girl got off. Yep, he'd been right. He followed her and stood for a moment pretending to admire the view of the massive sewage pipe extending out across the water until she gained twenty yards or so on him. Then he slung his satchel over his shoulder, jammed his hat firmly on his head, and strode off after her.

By the time he reached the top of the hill where the houses were he thought he might pass out, or vomit, but was just in time to see her enter a property. He wrote down the number on the letterbox, then looked around, considering his options. His assignment was to obtain evidence that the girl had a child, and if she did, to get photos of it, close-ups if possible. Today he was just looking for the kid. If there was one, and she lived here, he could come back if necessary and take his time getting decent pictures.

He walked back down the street a few hundred yards and cut across an empty section onto farmland behind the houses, then doubled back so he was just beyond the backyard of the house into which the girl had gone. Finding a handy stand of bushes near the fence he had a pee, then, well concealed, sat down on the grass to attach his telephoto lens to his camera. And then he waited.

Eventually the girl, an older Maori woman, and a little girl came out the back door and down the steps. The little girl looked around three, maybe four, years old. She had a good head of dark hair, was brown-skinned, and did look suspiciously like the girl Polly. Also, she was calling out 'Mummy' to her, which was a bit of a clue. As the two women hung out some washing, the kid wandered around the vegetable garden, singing and pulling up carrots that didn't look ready yet to be picked. The older woman called, 'Gina, leave those alone!' He made a note of the name, then raised his camera and snapped away. He wouldn't know how good the photographs were until he got home and developed them, but he thought they might be good enough for James and Lucy Murdoch. If they weren't, he could always come back.

He'd also need to follow the girl Polly to wherever she lived as the Murdochs wanted her home address, but he'd do that another day. He was too knackered and anyway he thought he'd be pushing his luck if he shadowed her back down the hill. He'd have to tail her from the brothel again, but that was all right. The more he could add to his bill, the better.

*

Kura Apanui flushed the loo, exited the stall and washed her hands thoroughly with the special soap the hospital provided in all the staff cloakrooms. She wasn't supposed to be in there using the toilet at any time other than lunch break or morning or afternoon tea, when access was supervised, but she'd been absolutely bursting. There'd been a spate of thefts from lockers so no one was allowed in the cloakroom except under the beady eye of Mrs Shand, Mr Price's right-hand woman, but honestly, she'd been so close to wetting her pants.

Back in the kitchen Mrs Shand gave her a hard look, but Kura ignored it and went back to stacking clean cups and saucers onto the tea trolley. She was a cow, Betty Shand, and it was common knowledge she favoured the Pakeha staff in the kitchen over the Maori and Pacific Island women, but Kura did her best to keep her head down and out of her way. It was worse too now Wiki had gone, but she was friends with some of the other women so she didn't feel too lonely. And there were always her patients on the wards: she still really enjoyed talking to them and brightening their day with a biscuit, a cup of tea and a cheery word. She filled two large teapots with tea leaves and boiling water, and headed off to do her first round.

When she came back about an hour later Mrs Shand marched up to her. 'Mr Price wants to see you in his office.'

'Now?'

'Yes, now.'

A prickle of foreboding rippled along Kura's arms and legs. Someone had dobbed her in for using the toilet when she wasn't supposed to — Betty Shand herself, probably.

Mr Price's door was open.

'Come in, Mrs Apanui. Close the door behind you. Have a seat.'

Kura sat.

'I've been told you used the Kitchen Staff's cloakroom earlier today, unsupervised. Is that correct?'

Kura nodded.

'Are you aware that another theft occurred this morning?'

Kura's stomach plummeted. 'No.'

'Someone removed twelve pounds from Miss Duffy's purse, which was in her handbag in her locker. Do you know anything about that?'

'No.'

'Are you sure?'

'Yes! I'm not a thief!'

'Well, I've asked Mrs Shand to search your belongings.'

A tide of shame surged through Kura and she felt her face blaze red. 'You could have just asked me! I would have shown you.'

A knock came at the door and Betty Shand stepped in with Kura's handbag and coat.

'Well?' Mr Price asked.

'I found fourteen pounds in Mrs Apanui's purse.'

'That's my rent money!' Kura said. 'I have to pay it on the way home from work.'

'How do we know you didn't steal it?' Betty Shand said.

'How do you know I did?'

'Well, you know what you people are like.'

'Here, now—' Mr Price began, waving his hands about.

Kura stood. 'No, I don't know, but I know what *you* people are like.'

'Ladies, some decorum, *please*,' Mr Price urged. 'Look, Mrs Apanui, I'm sorry but I'm going to have to let you go. This morning's events give a very unfortunate impression, which I can't ignore. I really am sorry.'

'Fine,' Kura declared. 'I wouldn't keep working here if you paid me.'

Smirking, Betty Shand said, 'And I expect you to return your uniform, washed *properly* and ironed.'

Kura thought, all right, you asked for this. She whipped off her cardigan, quickly undid the buttons of her smock, slipped out of it and, ignoring Mr Price's horrified protestations, threw it at Mrs Shand. '*You* bloody well wash and iron it. I don't work here any more.'

Then, putting her cardigan back on and grabbing her coat and handbag, she marched out of the office and through the kitchen, her head held high. It wasn't until she got outside that she started to cry big, hot tears of shame and anger, and also decided she should probably put her coat on over her slip so people wouldn't stare. On the other hand so what if they did? She couldn't feel any more shamed than she already was.

A thief? She'd never stolen anything in her entire life.

*

'Quick, hide,' Peggy said. 'Duck down behind the counter.'

'Why?' Allie asked. Then she spotted Kathleen Lawson. 'Oh, don't be so mean. She's all right.'

'She's not, she's poisonous.'

'Hello, Mrs Lawson!' Allie called.

Kathleen waved and made a beeline for the Elizabeth Arden counter. 'Good morning, Allie.' Ignoring Peggy she checked her fancy watch. 'Or should I say good afternoon, given that it's twelve o'clock.' Her face lit up. 'I've just had the most marvellous idea. Why don't we go out for lunch?'

'No thanks, Mrs L,' Peggy said. 'I had a big fat meat pie at smoko. I'm full.'

Kathleen gave her a dagger-sharp look. 'I wasn't speaking to you.'

'I can't I'm afraid,' Allie said, feeling acutely embarrassed. 'I only have forty-five minutes.'

Kathleen appeared to think for a moment. 'Well, why don't we grab a bite to eat in The Cedar Room upstairs? That will save us looking for a restaurant or a cafe.'

Allie felt herself going red. That would be even worse. 'I don't think we're allowed to mix with our customers socially, especially not, you know, in the store.'

'Why on earth not?' Kathleen asked. 'Besides I'm very good friends with George Holmes and I'm sure he won't mind. Really, you'll enjoy yourself. My shout.'

Allie struggled to recall who George Holmes might be, then realised Kathleen meant Mr Holmes, Smith and Caughey's manager. 'Well, if you think it'll be all right.'

'Of course it will.'

Allie glanced at Peggy, who eyed her back impassively, but Allie could tell she didn't approve. But, really, Peggy wasn't her keeper. 'All right. Thank you. Can I meet you there? I just need to get my bag on the way.'

When Allie arrived at The Cedar Room, Kathleen waved to her from a table next to a window. Sitting down, Allie felt quite pleased to be sharing a table with the most stylish woman in the room. She wondered what the other women having lunch might be thinking.

She said, 'I've never eaten in here before. Well, just sandwiches when we're doing a show.'

'Haven't you?' Kathleen sounded amazed. 'Why ever not?'

Because it's too expensive. 'I usually bring my own lunch to work.'

'It's rather modern in terms of decor, isn't it?'

Allie hadn't thought about it. 'It is, yes.'

Kathleen opened a menu. 'What would you like? Something hot or would you prefer something a little less substantial? I'm thinking of a salad, myself. And perhaps a Cona coffee. I adore Cona.'

Allie had a quick look. 'I think I'd like a club sandwich, thank you. And a cup of tea, please.'

'You don't drink coffee?'

'I'd rather have tea during the day.'

Kathleen ordered, then said, 'While we're waiting I thought you might like to look at these.' From her bag she took a small sheaf of brochures and handed them to Allie.

'Er, thank you.' A bit mystified, she shuffled through them. They were for Kelvinator and Frigidaire refrigerators, a Shacklock electric oven, a Kelvinator fully automatic washing machine and matching clothes dryer, and a Sunbeam Mixmaster electric cake mixer.

'For your new home!' Kathleen said brightly. 'I know you're short of time today but perhaps next time we could go to Farmers and have a look at their range. I know they're not exactly a luxury store, but they do have a marvellous appliance department.'

Now Allie really was uncomfortable. Squashing recollections of the tantrum she'd thrown in front of Sonny about wanting a refrigerator, she said, 'But I can't afford to buy anything like this. We're saving.'

'Well, that's the thing, Allison. You see, at Farmers you can arrange a hire-purchase agreement. All you need to do is pay a small deposit, commit to weekly payments, and you can have anything you like right then and there!'

Allie knew all about hire-purchase. Her parents had never bought anything on the never-never because they disapproved of it, and she knew Sonny wouldn't agree to it, either. He said hire-purchase was for idiots because in the long run, due to fees and interest payments on the principal, you ended up forking out twice as much. 'Aren't there interest payments, though?'

'Well, I expect there might be a little bit of interest in there somewhere, but surely it's worth it to have all these lovely modern appliances? Think of the time and effort you'll save around the house!'

Allie decided she could get away with being a bit cheeky. 'Do you have any hire-purchase agreements?'

'Do *I*?' Kathleen gave a little tinkling laugh. 'Well, hardly. I don't need hire purchase. I always pay cash no matter what I buy.'

'I think we'd rather pay cash too. I know Sonny would.'

When the waitress arrived with their meals Allie saw it was Pauline, but her sister didn't acknowledge her so Allie kept quiet herself.

'But you can't pay cash, can you?' Kathleen went on. 'And you'll never be in a position to, married to someone like your husband.'

Allie started to interrupt but Kathleen flicked up a manicured and be-ringed hand.

'No, please, let me speak, Allison. It's time someone did.' She leant aside as Pauline placed her pot of Cona on the table. 'He may well be charming and good-looking, but everyone knows that Maori men, and women for that matter, do not generally make responsible employees, therefore they're unable to earn a decent amount of money and get on in life. It's a fact. So as long as you're shackled to him you'll never have the things you want. That you *deserve*.'

'That's not true.'

'I'm afraid it is, Allison.'

'You don't even know my husband.'

Pauline set down Allie's club sandwich with a clatter and strode off.

'What a damned rude waitress,' Kathleen remarked. 'I've a good mind to report her. I don't need to know your husband, Allison; I know what people like him are like. I should. I have a great pile of them on one side of my family, I'm sorry to say.'

Allie didn't want her sandwich any more, and neither did she want to be sitting here with Kathleen Lawson. 'Is this why you invited me to lunch? To tell me my husband's useless?'

'No, not at all.'

'Because that's what you've just done.'

Kathleen pulled off her gloves, picked up a fork and stabbed a piece of cucumber out of her salad. 'Well, I'm sorry if I've upset you, but I thought it needed saying. Anyway, you didn't let me finish.'

Allie knew she should get up and go, but she didn't. She waited.

'I was *going* to say you need to be firm with your husband. If you want something you need to make that clear. I'm firm with my husband, and I don't want for anything. I have a lovely home, plenty of money, three beautiful happy children, and a *very* attentive husband, and it's because I'm firm about what I want. You should take a leaf out of my book, that's all I'm saying. If you want a refrigerator, you make him buy you one.'

'I don't think he'd appreciate me throwing my weight around,' Allie said. Though when she had, he'd accepted it with his usual patience and good humour.

Sometimes she thought she didn't deserve Sonny. So why was she sitting here listening to Mrs Lawson run him down? Because Kathleen Lawson was glamorous and sophisticated and she thought a bit of that might rub off on her? But she wasn't Mrs Lawson, not by a long shot. Really, she didn't understand half of what was going on in her own head any more.

'I'm not saying that, I'm saying be firm.' Kathleen reached across the table and patted Allie's hand. 'I'm just trying to help, dear.'

*

Allie, Donna and Pauline sat in a tearoom on Karangahape Road eating cream cakes. It was well past seven o'clock on a Friday evening, and raining, but the street was still busy because of late-night shopping. It was the first time since the previous year they'd managed to spend time together, just the three of them, they were all that busy now.

'How're your insides?' Allie asked Donna. 'Back to normal?'

'Not really. It's been a month now and there's been nothing. I expect it'll take a while.'

'I can't believe how dumb you were, getting caught,' Pauline said.

'Neither can I,' Donna agreed.

'And you've heard nothing from the bloke?' Allie asked.

Donna shook her head. 'Not likely to, either. And I'm happy with that. Let's just say I've learnt a good lesson.'

Allie picked a sponge wing off her butterfly cake. 'Which is?'

'Don't trust men.'

'That's a bit harsh.'

'All right then: only trust men on my terms.'

'I trust my man,' Pauline said.

Allie said, 'Your man's a boy.'

'No, he's definitely a man.'

'You be careful,' Allie warned, pointing a finger at Pauline.

'Don't worry. *We're* not dumb.'

'So you *are* sleeping with him?' Donna asked.

'Yes. So?'

'God, Pauline, I hope you know what you're doing.'

''Course.'

'Well, I thought I did too, and I'm supposed to be a student nurse.'

'Well, that says more about you than me, doesn't it?' Pauline said. 'Anyway, don't worry about it. We're good.'

'You know, it's not really fair, is it?' Allie said. 'I'd love another baby and you had to get rid of one.' She glanced at Donna to gauge her response.

'I know, and I'm sorry. It isn't fair.'

'Sonny and I would have taken it.'

Donna looked guilty, and sad. 'I wouldn't have been able to carry on with my training if I'd had it. I was selfish, I know. I'm sorry.'

'Anyway, she's not a baby factory,' Pauline said, and took a huge bite out of a cream horn, scattering pastry everywhere.

Allie checked her watch. 'What time's our appointment?'

Donna said, 'Eight o'clock. Eat up.'

'Wait on,' Pauline said, her voice muffled by pastry. 'This is yum.'

They were off to have their cards read by a woman recommended by a student nurse friend of Donna's. Apparently she was spot on with her predictions.

Allie shovelled down the rest of her butterfly cake, then they walked along Karangahape Road, getting wet trying to share one umbrella, towards Hopetoun Street and the address Donna had been given.

Pauline said, 'What's her name, this woman?'

'Arabella Fortune,' Donna replied, avoiding a puddle.

'Sounds made up to me. Fortune sounds dodgy, 'specially with her being a fortune-teller. And nobody gets called Arabella these days.'

Allie said, 'She might be ninety years old.'

'True,' Pauline agreed. 'What do you want to find out?'

Whether I'll ever have another baby, and if I'm really going mad, Allie thought. 'I don't know. Just what the future holds for me, I suppose. What about you?'

'If I'll marry Johnny.'

'Really? I didn't realise it was that serious. Don't you think you're a bit young for marriage?'

'It is that serious, and no, I'm not too young. I love him and he loves me.'

'Don't be ridiculous,' Donna said. 'You're only seventeen.'

'Allie wasn't much older when she married Sonny.'

'I was almost twenty-one. That's a *bit* older.'

'Anyway I didn't say I wanted to marry him tomorrow,' Pauline said.

'What do you want to know?' Allie asked Donna.

Pauline said, 'You want to know if you'll get married, don't you?'

'I bloody well do not! Haven't you listened to anything I've said? Christ, you can be annoying.'

'I try.'

'Well?' Allie prompted.

'I don't know,' Donna said. 'Same as you, I suppose. Whatever the cards say.'

Pauline said, 'They'd better say something good. A quid a pop's a hell of a lot to find out we're going to die or something.'

'I don't think she'd tell us if the cards said that,' Allie remarked.

Pauline snorted. 'It's probably all made up anyway.'

Donna turned on her sister. 'Do you *have* to be so contrary?'

'I'm not being contrary. You're just hearing everything I say contrarily.' Pauline frowned. 'Is that a word?'

Allie had just about had enough. 'Stop it, you two. Leave her alone, Donna, and Pauline, stop being a bitch.'

They walked along in silence until Donna said, 'I think this is it.'

They were outside a small, ordinary-looking house set close to the street. On closer inspection a hand-painted sign next to the front door read *Arabella Fortune: Scrying, and Tarot Cards Read; Futures Revealed.* Once they'd crowded onto the little verandah out of the rain, Donna knocked.

The door was answered by possibly the most striking woman Allie had ever seen. Probably not even thirty, she was pretty, with very long hair so starkly blonde it was white. Even her eyebrows and lashes were white, her skin really was as pale as alabaster, and her eyes were an extremely faded blue. But most remarkable, and shocking, were the red, green, blue and black tattoos that completely covered her upper arms to her elbows, and, below her skirt, the top half of her calves. Allie had never seen tattoos on a woman, ever.

No one said anything. Allie realised they must look idiotic standing there with their mouths open, so she said, 'Hello, are you Arabella Fortune? We have an appointment.'

Arabella Fortune looked amused. 'Donna? Yes, come in.'

'No, she's Donna. I'm Allie. This is Pauline.'

Arabella ushered them inside and seated them at a round table in what appeared to be her sitting room, which looked perfectly normal except for the stuffed animals. There were a white ferret, a domestic cat, a rabbit, a small fox, a squirrel, and several birds including one Allie thought might be a raven. They were quite bizarre and she tried not to look at them.

'We're a bit wet, sorry,' she said.

'Well, it is raining,' Arabella remarked.

'We thought you'd be older,' Donna said, then looked embarrassed.

'A lot of people say that. Now, are you happy with the Major Arcana, or would you prefer the Minor Arcana as well?'

Allie, Donna and Pauline stared at her dumbly.

'Have you not had a reading before?' Arabella asked.

Donna said no.

'Well, the twenty-two Major Arcana cards represent the significant issues in the querent's life. Querent means seeker. That's you. The Minor Arcana offer a more nuanced reading of those issues. There are fifty-six cards in the Minor Arcana, so it's an extra pound if you want those. And I'd prefer you to pay up front, if you don't mind.'

'Just the major ones, I think,' Allie said. Donna and Pauline agreed.

After the money had been handed over, Arabella asked, 'Do you have any questions?'

Pauline said, 'Is your whole body tattooed?'

'Pauline! Don't be so rude!' Donna admonished.

Arabella confirmed, 'Yes, I'm fully tattooed.'

'Did it hurt?'

'It did. And it takes years, if you're thinking about it. I meant do you have any questions about the reading?'

No one did so Arabella began by producing a pack of tarot cards wrapped in a piece of bright red silk from a wooden box. The colours on the cards were fading and their edges had softened, and they looked extremely well handled.

'Can't you afford a new set?' Pauline asked.

Donna rolled her eyes. Allie looked at Arabella for signs of offence taken but didn't see any.

'I prefer these. They've been handed down though my family for generations. They were originally owned by my great-great-great-grandmother, Serafina Fortune.'

Allie thought they definitely looked that old.

'Can all the women in your family read the cards?' Donna asked.

Arabella nodded. 'And in my family there is only a female line. We never marry though we've each given birth to a daughter. Never sons. Just one daughter.'

'Where's yours?' Pauline asked.

'Asleep next door. You're quite rude, aren't you?'

Suitably put in her place, Pauline said, 'Sorry.'

'You never marry?' Allie said, amazed. 'None of you have, right back to your great-whatever grandmother?'

'That's right. And before her too, I believe.'

'Can I ask why not?'

'Fortune women don't need husbands. We have our men, but we don't need husbands.'

Allie didn't know whether to believe her or not. It sounded quite a lot like a made-up story to enhance Arabella Fortune's professional reputation — or maybe to excuse an illegitimate baby. But who cared, it didn't matter anyway.

Donna opened her mouth and Allie just knew she was going to say something like 'I agree to not needing a husband', so she kicked her under the table. Donna gave her a dirty look, but there was no sense in giving Arabella Fortune free clues when they'd paid her a pound each to divine their futures.

'Who would like to go first?' Arabella asked.

Donna volunteered, so Arabella gave her the cards to shuffle and cut, then laid seven in a pattern on the white lace tablecloth.

She studied them for quite a while, her white hands splayed on either side of the spread, then said, 'You're going to war.'

Frowning, Donna said, 'Well, that's not right. Do I look like a soldier? And there won't be any more wars. We'll all just be blown to smithereens by an atomic bomb.'

'What about South Korea?' Allie said. 'That was a war.'

'Also, I'm a nurse. I'm planning on specialising in paediatrics.'

Arabella shrugged. 'I'm just telling you what the cards are saying. You have the Tower and the Chariot. In unison that usually means war.'

'Will she get married?' Pauline asked.

Donna said furiously, 'Shut up.'

'Do you want an answer to that?' Arabella asked.

Hesitating only briefly, Donna nodded. Arabella had her shuffle and cut the cards again, then laid them out.

'The answer is probably no. Probably. You will, however, come to know many men, and you'll have a very rewarding and fulfilling life, perhaps more so than if you did marry. You'll travel. You'll become highly respected in your field. You won't regret a recent decision you made, for to have gone down any other path would have altered these positive aspects of your future.'

At this Donna tensed, and Allie was fairly sure she knew what she was thinking.

Arabella looked at Donna. 'But, you know, something

momentous might occur and completely change the course of your future. You might meet your Prince Charming after all.'

'I doubt it,' Donna said.

Arabella gathered the cards. 'Who's next?'

'Allie,' Pauline said.

Shuffle, cut, spread, intense concentration from Arabella, nervous throat-clearing from Allie.

'You'll change your job in the near future,' Arabella declared, 'to something quite different for you. Something involving women.'

Allie wasn't very impressed — she already had a job involving women.

Arabella drummed her fingers on the table. 'There's something a little dark here. Do you want to know about it?'

'I don't know,' Allie said. 'How bad is it?'

'Well, it's not death or a horrible illness,' Arabella said bluntly. 'You've had a death already. A child? Your child?'

Swallowing, Allie nodded.

'This is something else. You have the Moon and the Devil cards in your spread.'

Pauline and Donna both gasped.

Allie stared, goosepimples creeping up her arms. 'The Devil? That *must* be bad, surely?'

'Yes and no. The Devil indicates entrapment. It doesn't necessarily foretell doom, only the need for care. You've been warned now, so it's up to you to avoid the trap.'

'But what trap?' Allie said, her voice rising. 'I don't know what you mean!'

'Well, I don't know, do I?' Arabella replied. 'I'm just reading the cards.' She tapped the Moon card. 'This one means that something in your life isn't what it seems and you'll have to rely on your intuition to see past the dishonesty.'

'But I don't know what you're talking about!'

'Could it be related to this, the High Priestess?' Arabella indicated a third card. 'A significant woman in your life? Your mother, maybe? An aunt or grandmother? Someone who has undue influence over you?'

'Both our grandmothers are dead, and I can't see it being Mum. She doesn't really influence me much at all these days.'

'What about Sonny's mum?' Donna suggested.

'I wouldn't think so. She isn't dishonest.'

Pauline said, 'What about that hoity-toity cow you had lunch with the other day?'

'Mrs Lawson?' Allie said. 'No, she wouldn't …' She trailed off.

'I thought she was a right bitch, going on about Sonny like that. You should have stuck up for him.'

'I did!'

'Well, I didn't hear you.'

'Can we get back to the reading?' Arabella asked benignly. 'Do you have any particular questions?'

Forgetting that she'd kicked Donna for almost doing something similar, Allie blurted, 'I want to know if—'

Arabella cut her off. 'Don't say it, just think it.'

Allie shuffled and cut the cards again and Arabella laid them out.

'You will,' she said eventually, 'but not until after you've changed your job and attended to this matter of being trapped. And also the shadow hanging over you.'

'She'll what, though?' Donna asked. 'And what shadow?' She looked at Allie.

Allie grinned. 'I *will* have a baby. That's what you mean, isn't it?'

Arabella nodded, tapping the Empress card.

'But what shadow?' Donna persisted.

'Your sister knows all about it, but not why it's haunting her,' Arabella said.

'How do you know we're sisters?' Pauline demanded.

'You look alike, you bicker like sisters and it sounds like you had the same grandmothers. You don't have to be psychic to work that out.' To Allie, Arabella said, 'I can tell you the genesis of your misery.'

From the card box she took another pack, unwrapped them and gave them to Allie to shuffle and cut.

'This is the Minor Arcana. Take the top card off the cut and tell me what it is.'

Allie did. 'The Ace of Wands.'

'The root of fire,' Arabella said. 'Fire. Does that have any meaning for you?'

And instantly Allie was back on the third floor of Dunbar and Jones and there were smoke and flames, and wind and tremendous noise everywhere, and Irene was burning and screaming and she'd just slammed the door on her, and the air was so *hot* and there was no way out.

Across the table Arabella had gone rigid and broken out in a sweat, and as Allie cried out in fear she did too, throwing up the same arm to ward off some unseen threat.

Pauline shook her sister. 'Allie! *Allie!*'

And then Allie was back with them, and Arabella was wiping her own white, white face with a handkerchief.

'The Dunbar and Jones fire,' she said, and it wasn't a question.

Allie nodded. 'I have terrible dreams sometimes.'

'You didn't tell us that,' Donna said.

'It's more than that, though, isn't it?' Arabella asked.

Reluctantly, Allie nodded. 'Sometimes I think I'm ... well, I don't know what I think.'

'No, you're not going mad,' Arabella said, 'but you do need to do something about it. You need to heal.'

'But Allie, that was two years ago,' Donna said. 'I thought you'd put all that behind you?'

Pauline said, 'God, Donna, you're going to make a rubbish nurse. Nobody ever puts their friends burning to death behind them.'

Donna bristled. 'Well, I don't see you helping her.'

'I don't know what to do!' Pauline exclaimed. 'Why don't *you* help?'

'*I* don't know what to do, either!'

Allie looked back as they gazed at her, their faces taut with misery.

Then Pauline said, 'Nan knew some of it, didn't she?'

Allie nodded. 'But now she's gone, too.'

They all sat in silence for a long moment, then Arabella slowly gathered the cards and offered them to Pauline.

Pauline's cards included the Empress, the Tower, the Hermit, the Wheel of Fortune and Death.

'Well, I think I can probably say it's all here in one spread,' Arabella said. 'You'll also have at least one child '

'Not if I can help it,' Pauline interrupted.

Ignoring her, Arabella continued, 'In the near future.'

Pauline snorted.

'You'll suffer tragedy too.' Arabella looked up. 'I'm sorry, but I don't pull my punches. You've also got the Tower. That can mean unforeseen, tragic and traumatic events. The Death card, though, while that can sometimes predict actual death, it more often symbolises a permanent and significant change in your life.'

Pauline looked sceptical.

Arabella went on. 'But you also have the Hermit and the Wheel of Fortune, which are both good. The Hermit suggests you're in need of time to examine your life. You might find this time while on a journey away from home, or simply by being alone. Either way you will need to make some decisions. And the Wheel, which is the destiny card, represents a new beginning, and is mostly positive.'

No one said anything for nearly a minute, until it became clear that Arabella had finished her readings.

Donna broke the silence. 'Well, none of that sounded very cheery, did it?'

'Mine was all right,' Allie said. 'I'm having a baby.'

'Under a black shadow, though.'

Allie thought that was a bitchy thing for Donna to say, and wondered if she was upset because her cards said she wouldn't be having children.

Arabella collected the tarot cards, folded them in their silk wrapping and put them away. 'Thank you, ladies. Feel free to make another appointment whenever you like.'

Allie didn't think they'd be back, but Pauline surprised her by asking, 'Do you just read the cards, or are you a medium as well?'

There was another silence, this one quite uncomfortable, before Arabella said, 'Why do you ask?'

'Do you do seances?'

'I have done,' Arabella said cautiously. 'I'd rather not.'

'Thank you!' Allie said brightly, before Pauline could suggest something awful like trying to contact Nan.

Outside, Pauline complained, 'Well, that was a waste of a quid.'

'Then why did you ask her about seances?' Allie asked.

'I don't know. It just popped into my head.'

'Well, I'm not going off to fight in some bloody war, that's for sure,' Donna declared. 'Were you all right in there, Allie, when she said about the fire? I thought you were going to have a fit. Your face went all funny and you threw your arm out.'

'So did that Arabella,' Pauline said. 'Did you notice? It was ... weird.'

'I'm fine,' Allie said.

'You should say when it's bothering you. The fire, I mean.'

'I will,' Allie lied.

Chapter Fourteen

June 1956

Allie had had another bad night. This time she'd apparently leapt out of bed, scaring the life out of Mr De Valera who'd been curled up next to her, and tried to drag Sonny out as well, shouting that his hair was on fire, all while she was still asleep. Sonny had woken her, calmed her, fetched her cigarettes, made her a cup of tea, and told her she was going to see the doctor whether she liked it or not, because something was definitely not right.

She knew something wasn't right, she just didn't know how to fix it — and a doctor wouldn't either. And this morning Sonny had gone off on his motorbike without saying where, or when he'd be back, and she was terrified she'd ruined his sleep once too often and he might have gone for good. Or at least a good while because he was sick and tired of her.

She sat on the back steps for ages, smoking and drinking tea and watching Dev stalk cabbage butterflies in her nan's gone-to-seed vegetable garden, knowing she had washing to do and floors and the bathroom to clean, and not giving a toss. She didn't have the energy. If Sonny had gone there was no reason to do anything any more.

Eventually she became aware of a horn tooting out on the street and thought, oh shut up, will you? But it didn't so she got up to go and give the rowdy bugger a piece of her mind. Halfway round the house, though, the noise stopped, but not before she'd seen a truck parked right outside her sitting room window. The back of the truck was open and two men were rolling a large, gleaming white refrigerator down a ramp. One of them was Sonny. He grinned hugely when he spotted her.

'What's that?' she said, though she could see very well what it was.

'It's a present for you.'

'You bought a refrigerator?'

'Well, you wanted one, didn't you?'

'But it's Saturday. The shops are shut.' Hating herself for thinking it, she wondered if it had been pinched.

'Got contacts, you know.' Sonny tapped his nose. 'Bert opened the warehouse for me. It's from Farmers.' He and Bert righted the refrigerator on the dolly.

'How did you pay for it?' Allie asked.

'Sold the Indian.'

'Oh Sonny, *no*!' Allie suddenly felt as though her chest had filled with concrete and she could scarcely breathe. She turned and ran down the path, through the back door and into the bedroom, where she lay on the bed listening to the thumping and swearing as the men manhandled the refrigerator up the steps and into the kitchen. Then she heard the truck drive off.

Sonny came in and sat on the end of the bed. 'I thought you'd be pleased.'

'But the Indian! You loved it, and so did I!'

Shrugging, Sonny said, 'I know. But we can get another one later. I thought you needed cheering up.'

Allie burst into tears. It must have ripped his heart out selling the motorbike. And what for? So the milk didn't go off? To stop her tantrums? And she hadn't even really wanted a refrigerator. Not really. God, she was stupid. And gullible.

'I do like it, thank you very much,' she said stiffly, though she suspected she'd never really care for it, no matter how handy it proved to be. 'But I do wish you hadn't sold the motorbike.'

Sonny took her hand and helped her off the bed. 'Come on, let's go and put some things in it, shall we? Can you put veggies in? What about beer? Yeah, let's put my DB in it! DB's much better cold.'

'And Dev's meat,' Allie said, following him down the hallway, trying to get into the spirit of things.

'He might not eat it if it's cold. It might hurt his teeth.'

'Well, too bad for him,' Allie said, opening the meat safe. 'Here, put these sausages in.'

'Bread?' Sonny suggested. 'Can you put bread in?'

'Mum doesn't. She says it goes hard and yuck.'

When they'd finished loading the refrigerator and had put water in the ice cube tray in the little ice box, they stood back and looked into it.

Sonny said, 'It doesn't feel very cold, does it?'

'I think we have to shut the door and let it cool down.'

'Right.' Sonny closed the door.

Allie kissed him on the cheek. 'Thank you. I *am* pleased. Really.'

*

After lunch Sonny went to the pub to have a few beers with an army mate he'd served with in South Korea, and Allie thought about going to visit her mother but decided she didn't have the energy. Instead she gave the bathroom and floors a bit of a clean, then lay on the sofa in the sitting room and read. The book — a play, actually — was called *Cat On a Hot Tin Roof* and was really good. Peg had lent it to her. Peg lent her lots of books, which had surprised her at first because she'd thought Peg was probably the sort of girl who'd prefer *True Romance* magazine, but she didn't, she liked quite intellectual books. This one was intellectual and bitchy *and* full of sexual tension.

So she was surprised when Sonny came home that it was five o'clock and she'd been lounging around reading with Dev draped across her legs for nearly three hours. And he wasn't alone.

'This is Don Allen, my army mate. Don, this is my wife, Allie.'

Don inclined his head. 'Hello, Allie. Nice to meet you.'

Mr De Valera hissed at him.

'You too, Don.' Allie thought she could have done with a bit of warning. She was dressed in sloppy old clothes, her hair was scraped back in a ponytail, her feet were bare, and her face was completely without make-up.

'I've brought Don home for tea. That's all right, isn't it?'

Allie tried to remember how many sausages she had. 'Yes, lovely. I'll get started now.'

Sonny followed her into the kitchen and got some beers out of the refrigerator. 'Ah, nice and cold. Hope you don't mind me bringing him home, love. He's just passing through and I haven't seen him for ages.'

Allie didn't mind. Lucky she'd cleaned the bathroom.

To eat they sat at the kitchen table, where Don, who was, Allie decided, a very nice bloke, entertained them with funny stories about working at Patea freezing works down in Taranaki.

'You two ever get sick of the big smoke you should move down there,' he said. 'Bloody nice country.'

Sonny shook his head. 'Nah, I'm Ngati Whatua, man. I can't leave here. And Allie's whanau are from here too. Might come for a visit, though. Sounds nice.'

After the main — sausage casserole (to make the sausages go further) — Allie served tea, and Afghan biscuits she'd made during the week. As she poured she became aware of a change of atmosphere at the table and glanced briefly at Sonny. What was going on?

'Um, Allie,' Don said. 'Do you mind if I talk about something personal?'

Alarmed, Allie wondered, Personal to who?

'Sonny said you were in that department store fire a couple of years ago?'

Conscious that the cup was rattling badly in its saucer, she passed Sonny his tea. 'Yes. I was.'

'That must have been pretty bloody terrible.'

Allie just nodded, not trusting her voice.

'Sonny said some of your mates died.'

Another nod.

Don blew on his tea then took a really noisy slurp, and Sonny laughed, which broke the tension a little. 'Have you ever heard of a thing called battle exhaustion?' Don asked.

Mystified, Allie said no.

'It used to be called shellshock.'

Well, yes, she'd heard of *that*. The poor old man up the road had it, and was rumoured to only come out of his house on Anzac Day, his nerves were so fragile.

'Lots of soldiers have it,' Sonny said. 'Some never get over it.'

'True, eh,' Don said. 'Quite a few of the fellas down my way suffer from it, on and off, and there's a few completely off their rockers. Just didn't come home the same, from the big wars and from Korea. But apparently you don't have to be a soldier to get it. It can happen to anyone who's had something really stink happen to them, like, say, being in a really bad fire.'

Allie took her teaspoon out of her tea and touched it to the chocolate icing on her biscuit, melting it. After a moment she asked, 'What happens to people with battle exhaustion? How do they know they've got it? You said they go off their rockers?'

'Well, not all of them. From what they say — and to be honest they don't talk about it much, mostly only in the RSA or the pub after a few beers — it sounds like they have a lot of nightmares about being in combat, or something terrible they've seen, or mates getting killed and things like that. They reckon sometimes the nightmares happen in the daytime too, though I'm not sure how that works. Like a vision, I suppose. And they feel blue a lot, and angry, and nervy, like something bad's going to happen all the time. They can't keep their minds on anything and don't give a shit about life. And they drink. Bloody hell, do they drink.' Don reached for a biscuit. 'Do you drink much?'

'Not really.'

'Does any of the rest of it sound like you? Because Sonny was telling me about your nightmares and I thought, shit, that sounds like battle exhaustion.'

Allie unstuck the teaspoon from her biscuit. 'If it is, how would you ... how would I get better from it?'

Don sat back in his chair. 'Well, this is the stink bit. I don't know many who have.'

'But you know some, though, eh?' Sonny asked.

'A few. You'd think the government would do something to help other than paying them a piddly war pension, but no. It's sign up and fight for your country, and if you come home fucked — 'scuse me, Allie — too flaming bad. But yeah, a few seem to have got on top of it.'

'Well, how?' Allie almost snapped.

'You're working in another big store now, eh?'

Allie said to Sonny, 'Did you spend the *whole* afternoon talking about me?'

'No, we talked about old mates as well. Not that you're not my mate.'

'Crikey, you don't hear a fella say that about his wife too often,' Don remarked.

'Why do you want to know where I'm working?' Allie asked.

''Cos being in another big store's probably reminding you of the one that burnt down. Every time you walk in there you'll be getting a bad memory. You should get a job somewhere else, somewhere completely different. And you should talk about the fire. Have you?'

'No. Who would I talk to?'

Don nodded at Sonny. 'Your man. Other people who were there. Your family.'

'Sonny doesn't want to hear about it.'

'How do you know I don't?' Sonny said.

'And the people who were there just want to put it behind them,' Allie said.

'How do you know they're not all feeling the same way you do?' Don said. 'Have you asked them?'

'No. It's just something ... I mean, I don't even see a lot of them now.'

'Well, change your job, start talking about the fire, and have a good stiff drink at night to help you sleep. But just one before bed, don't keep going all night and the next day. You don't want to turn into an alkie, eh?'

Scowling, Allie said, 'I tried that. I had a whiskey before bed once and the nightmares were worse. I'm never doing that again.'

Don laughed. 'Everyone's nightmares are worse when they drink whiskey. Try something else. I dunno. Brandy? Gin?'

'It can't be that easy, though,' Allie said, 'or everyone would be getting better.'

Don took a biscuit. 'These look nice. I don't think it is that easy. I'm not really sure why some fellas come right and some don't, but I think, I *think*, the ones who get better are the ones who find something to do that's got nothing at all to do with what fucked them up. Whoops, sorry. You know? They fill their lives with other things, good things and busy things, so there's no room left for the bad stuff. Those are the fellas who seem to be doing OK.'

Allie nodded, because it did sort of make sense. She knew, though, that it would be a lot easier to talk about than to actually do.

Sonny said, 'You can leave work now if you like, and be a lady of leisure while you look for something else. We can afford it. There's money left over from the Indian.'

It was very tempting, Allie thought. No more panicking every time she walked through the staff entrance of Smith and Caughey, no more breaking into a sweat whenever a customer walked by smoking, no more obsessively checking rubbish bins in the staff and customer toilets for fag ends that might not quite have been extinguished. But what would she do instead? All she knew was how to sell dresses and make-up. She had no experience with anything else. But then neither, she supposed, did plenty of other women who managed to get jobs.

'Did he tell you what he did?' she asked Don.

'He did and I can tell you which one I'd rather have.' Don thought for a second. 'Mind you, those cold beers were bloody nice.'

*

Two days later, on the Monday morning, Allie said to Peggy, 'I'm handing in my notice today.'

Peggy, who was applying her make-up at the counter though she'd been told several times not to by the Head of Cosmetics, said, 'Really? Why?'

'I came back to work too early after Hana died, and I'm still having trouble with my feelings about the fire.'

'Really? Right-oh — it makes sense, I suppose. Dunno what I'd be feeling if all that had happened to me. Just being in the fire would have been bad enough, but you lost so many friends. And then to lose Hana, and now your Nan. I don't think I'd have come back to work after any of those things. I'm not sure I *could* have. So good on you – you need some time off. Take care of *yourself*. Read some good books, sleep in, eat chocolate, plant a flower garden, concentrate on getting pregnant. You know, whatever makes you feel better! I'll miss you, though.'

'I'll miss you too. You've been great.'

Peggy blotted her lips and put the lipstick back with the testers. 'You too.'

Allie hesitated, then said, 'I'll tell you who I won't miss.'

'Who's that?'

'Kathleen Lawson. What a bitch.'

'Well, sweetie,' Peggy said, 'you live and learn.'

*

Hawke's Bay, June 1956

James Murdoch opened the buff-coloured envelope and slid out the photographs, letter and itemised account.

'Bloody hell,' he said when he saw what Ted Hollis had charged.

Then he went through the photos. They were in colour, which explained some of Hollis's exorbitant fee, but certainly not all of it. There were some just of Polly, a lot of a little girl playing in a backyard, including close-ups, and some with Polly and an older woman, and a few of two houses — one a state house and the other a rundown two-storey affair — including the letterboxes. James didn't think *they* needed to be in colour. He had a good mind not to pay Hollis's full invoice.

The child was pretty and, he had to admit, looked like both Drew and Kathleen had at that age, except her skin and hair colour were darker. Kathleen and Drew had both been fair, and this child was obviously her mother's daughter, but the similarity was there. His heart sank.

'Show me,' Lucy said eagerly.

Suppressing a sigh, James passed the photos across the lunch table. Ever since he'd confessed his infidelity (and its disastrous outcome) to her, she'd been brooding about it and, he'd suspected — rightly, as it turned out — scheming. Kathleen and Jonathan had three children and, though they didn't often see them, Lucy conceded three was probably a sufficient contribution. And then there were Duncan and Claire, who had Lorraine. Lucy, who believed in big extended families, didn't think one child from them, making a total of four grandchildren, was enough. Privately James wondered if Lucy's yearning for lots of grandchildren was a misplaced response to the loss of Drew, their poor, lost, younger son. Like his older brother, and James himself, Drew had gone to war, and though he'd eventually come home he'd been a ghost of the young man who'd left. He'd spent years as a Japanese prisoner of war — an experience James couldn't even imagine and one Drew had certainly never spoken about — and in the end he'd succumbed to whatever horrors had haunted him and taken his own life. It had been a bitter, bitter blow, and a tragedy the family had never quite overcome. Perhaps understandably, Lucy had grieved terribly after Drew's death, and still did, and James wondered if it might have turned her mind a little. Something had, because it seemed Lucy's latest plan to augment the number of Murdoch grandchildren pivoted on Duncan and Claire adopting James's love child.

When she'd first suggested it, he'd said, 'Lucy, you can't just move people around like chess pieces. Anyway, the child has a mother.'

'But she's a prostitute. If that little girl *is* yours I don't want a Murdoch child brought up by someone morally bankrupt enough to sell her sexual favours.'

James chose not to point out that she was married to someone morally bankrupt enough to purchase someone's sexual favours. 'And what about Duncan and Claire? Do they want another child? Have you asked them?'

'Not in so many words. But Claire has women's problems and I know she would have had more children if she could.'

'Well, I think you're getting dangerously close to meddling.'

'I'm not meddling! There's a little girl out there, James, *your* little girl, who needs a decent home and upbringing, and we can make sure she gets it. That woman Polly doesn't really want her. She was using her to gouge you for money, and God only knows where that's been going. Alcohol? Fancy clothes? Her boyfriend?'

At least that had stopped, James had thought with relief. He'd gone into town the day after he'd made his confession and ceased the order for payment.

Now, in silence, Lucy studied the photographs intently, making two piles as she worked through them, one depicting the child alone, and the remainder, which she handed back to James. 'I don't need to see those.'

James agreed. He probably wouldn't want to look at photographs of someone Lucy had illicitly slept with either.

'What's her name?' Lucy asked.

For an awful moment James thought she meant Polly, then realised she was referring to the little girl. He thought he knew her name, from Polly's instructions regarding the blackmail payments, and Ted Hollis's letter confirmed it.

'Gina.'

'That's a bit common,' Lucy said.

'It's just a name. I think it's quite nice.'

Lucy went back to staring at the photos. 'She does look awfully like our children when they were little. She has exactly the same chin Kathleen had, and see here? She has Drew's eyes. And Duncan's. I bet if I could see her ears they'd be the same too, but she has such lovely thick hair. I bet she has Murdoch ears.' She looked up beseechingly. 'We have to rescue her, James, we really do. Please?'

And James, who already felt as guilty as hell for cheating on her, didn't say no.

*

Auckland, June 1956

Kura and Wiki had been knitting like mad. Wiki had already made enough for three babies since she'd been let go from the hospital in March, but now that Kura was also out of work they'd made so much they could have opened a stall at the market. They knitted obsessively: very fine gowns and leggings and rompers, cardigans and jumpers, and hats and booties and mittens and wraps, and two full sets for the sleeping basket consisting of mattress covers, blankets and quilts. Every day something new was finished and added to the lovingly folded pile, and Henare asked Wiki if she was giving birth to a rugby team. Wiki said she bloody well hoped not.

Then one day Joshua and Henare had a talk, and told Kura

and Wiki that neither family could afford to buy any more wool and the knitting had to stop. And when it did Wiki and Kura looked at everything they'd made and realised that things probably had got a bit out of hand. It was funny in a way but not really, because neither understood what had driven them so persistently to do it. Kura's daughter Patricia said they'd been doing 'angry knitting', but Kura didn't know what she meant, and didn't ask her to explain in case she heard something she didn't care to know about. In the end Wiki chose what she wanted to keep from the pile and Kura took the rest to a shop on Ponsonby Road that sold craft items on commission. A week later Wiki had woken up early with a dragging pain in her lower back and knew things were moving along, but didn't tell anyone. In April she'd reluctantly been to see a doctor because she'd had a bit of bleeding, which had turned out to be nothing much, and he'd made arrangements for her to go to the women's hospital at Cornwall Park to give birth. But she didn't want to. She'd had all her other babies at home: why shouldn't she have this one at home, too? Henare had told her she'd be much better off in a modern city hospital where they had all the flash machines and proper doctors and nurses, but she disagreed. Kura could help her. Kura had pushed out eight babies and she'd had five — what they didn't know about childbirth between them didn't matter. But Henare went on and on about it, making her wish she'd never told him about the women's hospital in the first place, so in the end she'd said yes, she would go.

And now the baby was coming so she shut up about it until the little kids had gone to school and Henare and the big kids, Rena and now Vicki, had left for work. Then she gathered together the bits and pieces she'd need to deliver the baby, and got on with clearing the breakfast things, doing the dishes and making the beds, taking her time and resting when she needed to. At about eleven o'clock she went across the street to let Kura know what was happening, but she wasn't home. That was OK — she knew she wouldn't be far away.

Then she hung out some washing that hadn't dried properly the day before; you couldn't leave it on the line overnight because it got nicked. After that she had a rest and made herself a bit of lunch. It was only a slice of bread and a bowl of veggie soup with a few ham bones thrown in, but she felt she needed something in her belly, even if it would all come back up later when the baby was on its way out. Then the cramps started in earnest so she walked — up and down the hallway, into the front room, out the back round their little yard, and back along the hallway again. Her waters broke when she was lumbering up the back steps.

Yvonne and Eddie came home a little after three. Not Charlie, though, but then he always loitered.

Wiki said to Eddie, 'Run across the road, love, and tell your auntie the baby's coming.'

Eyes big, Eddie shot off.

Yvonne looked thrilled. 'Right now?'

'Soon.'

Kura appeared within minutes, standing in the doorway, her hands on her bulky hips, looking cross. 'I thought you were supposed to be having this one at the women's hospital?'

'Too late now.'

'Bloody hell, girl.'

Wiki flapped a hand at her. 'I'll be all right.'

'Will you? You're no spring chicken these days.'

''Scuse me.' Wiki pointed at her belly. 'If I was that old I wouldn't be like this, would I?'

Looking exasperated, Kura said, 'Ah, never mind. How far along?'

'Waters have broken and I've been having the cramps since about midday. Say another two or three hours?'

'Your babies always did come quick.' Kura took off her cardigan. 'You got everything ready?'

'I've put newspapers down on the bed and there's towels and flannels in there, and the baby's things.'

'Got a bowl? You know you always spew.'

'Yep.'

'Scissors for the cord?'

'Yep.'

'Done a tiko?'

'Ae.'

'Boiled plenty of water?'

Wiki said, 'Yvonne, put on a pot of water, will you, there's a good girl. Use the boil-up pot.' She made a slightly pained face and eased herself on her chair. 'I need to walk again in a minute. I hope it's arrived by the time Henare gets home.'

''Cos he'll be angry you didn't go to the hospital?'

'Mmm. I don't need him in my ear.'

'Mind you, how did he think you were going to get there?' Kura said. 'On the tram in the middle of your cramps? In a taxi you've got no money for?'

'Oh, I don't know. Come on, let's go for a walk outside.'

They walked up and down, up and down the footpath outside the house till it was time for Wiki to take to her bed. Charlie had come home a while ago and by this time Rena and Vicki were home from work. Kura dashed across the street to check on her kids and to ask her eldest girls to prepare enough tea for both families, as Wiki definitely wouldn't be cooking and Rena and Vicki would also be busy. Henare, Joshua and Johnny, she knew, wouldn't be home till after six o'clock closing. She didn't know what pub they went to, and didn't really care as long as Joshua only bought a jug and they all came home in one piece.

Wiki was pacing around the little bedroom she shared with Henare, then she knelt on the mattress, put her head down and rocked. 'I'm going back to that doctor and getting my tubes tied as soon as I can after this.'

'Have you got any spare sheets?' Kura asked. 'I'll put one down over these papers.'

Wiki shook her head.

Kura said to Charlie, peeking in the door, 'Run across the road, love, and tell Patricia to bring over my spare set of sheets. They're in the hot water cupboard. Good boy.'

'They'll get all mucky,' Wiki warned.

'Ae, but you can't have this baby on yesterday's news like it's two shillings of fish and chips.'

They both laughed.

Wiki said, 'I came over to your place this morning but you weren't home. Did you go for a job?'

'A job? Oh, no, I went to that shop where I took that knitting we did? On Ponsonby Road? And do you know, they sold the lot and we've made twenty-three pounds!'

Kura helped Wiki change into a nightie, the sheets arrived, and Kura spread one over the newspapers. By now it was a little past six o'clock. Wiki had stopping moving restlessly about and was lying on her side on the bed, her hair stuck sweatily to her face, panting and grimacing in pain, but bearing up in silence.

Wiki heard Henare walk past the bedroom window, whistling. A minute later he was at the bedroom door.

He stared for a moment, then said, 'Why aren't you at the hospital?'

'Fuck off,' Wiki grunted.

Very wisely, he did.

'I'll be back in a tick,' Kura said to Wiki.

Wiki nodded, not really listening, focused almost completely now on what her body was doing.

When Kura returned, she said, 'He's out the back, having a smoke. I told him to go over home for a feed but he wants to stay here till the baby comes.'

'I don't want him in here,' Wiki said. She was on her knees again. Rena was pulling her damp hair back in a ponytail.

Kura said, 'Not much chance of that.'

Wiki felt her stomach contract — her actual stomach, not her womb.

'Bowl!'

Kura shoved a mixing bowl under her face and she vomited her lunch into it. She definitely knew the baby was on its way out now. She always threw up just before her babies arrived. 'Can you have a look?'

Kura handed the bowl to Vicki, bent down behind Wiki and lifted her nightie. 'I can just see the head. Lots of hair! Rena, go and get some of that boiled water.'

Wiki straightened her arms and spread her legs, then gave an intense, sustained push and the baby's head emerged, its little face all purple and screwed up.

'Good girl, head's out,' Kura said. 'Keep going.'

Wiki rested for a few moments then gave another ferocious push, her face turning the colour of watermelon, and the baby slid out in a squelch of blood and fluid into Kura's waiting hands. He wasn't making any noise so she hung him upside down by the ankles and lightly smacked his tiny bum, which made him wail.

'It's another boy, Mum,' Vicki said. 'You've got the full set now. Aren't you clever?'

'Can we call him Vincent?' Yvonne asked.

'No,' Wiki said, turning onto her back.

Kura wiped the muck off the baby's face, wrapped him in one of his many new blankets and laid him on her chest. 'Will Henare want to cut the cord?'

'I don't know. Ask him.'

Vicki ran out to get her father. He came in, grinning. 'Another boy?' Turning back the blanket he peeked at the baby. 'Jeez, he's nice, eh? You're good at this, girl.'

'This is the last bloody one, and I mean it,' Wiki said vehemently.

'Do you want to cut the cord?' Kura asked.

When Henare said yes, Kura washed the scissors in the bowl of hot water and handed them over. She put a hairclip on the umbilical cord to stop it bleeding everywhere, then, wincing slightly, Henare dissected it.

'What do you want to call him?' Wiki asked.

'Dunno yet.'

'Well, think about it. Why don't you go and get some tea? You too, girls. You were a big help.'

Off they all went.

Wiki made a pained face.

'Afterbirth?' Kura asked.

Wiki nodded.

'Do you want a massage?'

'No. I can feel it coming.'

The afterbirth was expelled about twenty minutes later. Kura inspected it carefully to make sure it was in one piece.

'Is it all there?' Wiki asked.

'Ae. It's not going to last till you get a chance to go home, though.'

'I know that.'

Wiki had been thinking about this, and it was upsetting her. The whenua of her five other children were all buried beneath a pohutukawa tree on their marae at Maungakakari, near those of Kura's kids, and all the babies born to the hapu, and she dearly wanted the afterbirth of this one to be buried there too. It was where it belonged because Maungakakari would always be where the child would belong. But it would rot long before they could get it there. They had no car they could race down to Hawke's Bay in, and no fancy refrigerator with an ice box.

'We could cure it,' Kura suggested.

'Smoke it?'

'No, salt-boil it, then dry it in the oven, like meat. Then you can just put it away till you can get home.'

'You know, Kura Apanui, you're not just a pretty face, are you?'

Kura grinned. 'I'm not a pretty face at all, but I'm practical.'

*

Kathleen Lawson left the jewellery shop on Queen Street feeling quite satisfied, knowing that the solid gold bangle she'd just purchased with one of Jonathan's cheques would hurt his pocket, if nothing else. She was still deeply aggrieved by his behaviour with that tramp Evelyn and hadn't forgiven him — she never would — but things between them had reverted to more or less their normal bland and uncommunicative state. Rosemary had now started school so Mrs Wright, the new woman they'd hired, had less to do, but they'd kept her on for housekeeping duties, cooking, and to manage the children in the afternoons. She was ancient, well into her sixties, and wore a strange, squashed little felt hat all day long, but she was a good cook and household manager, didn't take any nonsense from the children, not even Terence, and Kathleen was grateful for her.

Rosemary was enjoying school, and Geoffrey was, as always, doing well, but Terence still hadn't really settled. In fact, she'd been called to his school to discuss an incident the week before. Jonathan, of course, had been away, so she'd had to go alone. It seemed that Terence had been beaten up by a group of boys. At home she'd noticed he'd had a bruise on his face, but he'd told her he'd fallen over, so the beating had been complete news to her when she'd met with the school headmaster and Terence's house teacher.

She'd asked him in the headmaster's office, 'But why would they pick on you for no reason? You must have done something to annoy them.'

And Terence had said, 'I *didn't*. They just all ganged up and started hitting me.'

'But you must have done *something*.'

'I *didn't*!'

'But didn't they even say anything?'

Terence had mumbled something.

'What?' Kathleen had said.

'They said I walk funny.'

'You *walk* funny?' Kathleen had looked at the headmaster, bewildered. She'd felt extremely embarrassed, and even more so at what the man had said next.

'There is also the matter of Terence's hair. We feel it is a trifle too long and, pardon me for being blunt, also somewhat feminine in appearance. We suggest you take Terence to a barber. Very soon, in fact, as his current hairstyle is breaking school rules. As for the incident regarding the fight, and by all accounts Terence is not blameless as he fought back somewhat viciously, we will take no more action, given his, er, recent illness.'

Kathleen had almost died of shame at that — a spoken reference to the hanging accident. They'd had to inform the school about it because the bruises on Terence's throat hadn't faded for weeks, and he'd also needed time off school for his appointments with Dr Hill. There had been no avoiding it.

Then the headmaster had addressed Terence directly. 'But I do expect you to pull up your socks, young man. There is much to be said for individualism, but there comes a point when eccentricity simply becomes irritating and an embarrassment to others. Do you understand what I'm saying?'

Terence had nodded, but Kathleen had doubted he'd even been listening. He seemed hardly to listen to anyone these days. She'd dumped the job of Terence's haircut onto Jonathan, who was home last Friday and had taken him into town that night to the barber. She was grateful for that, as she couldn't bear to see his beautiful golden curls cut off, or witness his distress. He was very proud of his hair. He'd come home with an aggressive short back and sides and a splotchy red face from crying, and with Jonathan in a foul mood because Terence had put on such a performance in the barber's chair. Terence had been weeping on and off ever since, and had been really quite subdued, shutting himself in his room and apparently brooding.

Kathleen walked up Queen Street, looking in shop windows, stopping outside a furrier and eyeing a hip-length jacket. American musquash, probably. Very nice. She didn't have a short fur jacket, only a calf-length one Jonathan had bought her in England. Should she go in and try it on, perhaps even buy it? That would teach him to dally with other women. No it wouldn't, but it would make her feel better.

But would it? Already the thrill of the new gold bangle in her handbag had worn off. She hadn't even bothered to put it on her wrist. She thought of something more satisfying to do and walked on towards Smith and Caughey.

*

Peggy Mitchell stifled a sigh as she explained yet again to Marian, the new girl, how to store the lipsticks in the drawer beneath the counter. Marian was very pretty but there did seem to be a fair bit of wind whistling between her ears.

'If you don't keep all the same colours together, you'll think we've run out when we might not have, see? Then we'll re-order and end up with too many. Also, it'll take you ages to find what you want if they're not all in the same place, or they're not there at all. Systems, Marian, that's what you need to be thinking. Systems.'

'But it's just make-up.'

'No, it's the key to a woman's happiness. Don't you read what is says on the packaging?'

'Should I?'

Peggy sighed out loud this time. 'Probably not. Oh, good.'

'What?'

'Here comes someone I don't like.'

Marian looked confused but Peggy ignored her and turned to face Kathleen Lawson, who she could see determinedly approaching down the middle of the Beauty Hall, gussied up like a Christmas dinner as usual in a tan coat with fur trim, black shoes and gloves, and a little black hat with net edging.

'Good afternoon,' Kathleen said coldly.

'Good afternoon, Mrs Lawson,' Peggy replied with a lovely big smile. She was going to enjoy this.

'Who's this?' Kathleen asked, indicating Marian.

'Our new Elizabeth Arden sales girl.'

'Why? Where's Allison?'

Peggy made a mildly concerned face. 'Oh, didn't you know? Allie doesn't work here any more. She left a little while ago.'

Kathleen Lawson looked alarmed. 'She's left Smith and Caughey altogether?'

'Yes, that's right. She's one hundred per cent not here at all.'

Kathleen narrowed her eyes.

Peggy gave her another of her special smiles.

'Do you know where she went?' Kathleen asked.

Peggy was tempted to say out the door, but decided that was probably too cheeky, even for her. 'No, I've no idea.'

'She doesn't have a job somewhere else?'

'Really, Mrs Lawson, I don't know.'

Peggy knew Allie wasn't in a hurry to find a new job and was probably at home, but she wasn't telling Kathleen Lawson that. It was none of her bloody business.

'You're not being very helpful, you know,' Kathleen said.

'Sorry,' Peggy said insincerely.

'Could you give me her home address?'

Peggy said, 'We're not allowed to give out personal information about staff.'

'But she's not staff now, is she?'

'She was, though, wasn't she?'

'What about just her telephone number?' Kathleen asked.

'She's not on the phone. Why don't I tell Allie next time I see her you'd like to get in touch, then she can get in touch with you?' Peggy suggested, thinking that would probably be when hell froze over. 'I have your details here in our customer file.'

'Oh, look, if that's the best you can do.' Kathleen opened her handbag and took out a card. 'Give her this. It has my address and telephone number on it. You really have been most unhelpful.'

'Thank you!' Peggy said. 'Enjoy the rest of your afternoon!'

When Kathleen had gone she shoved the card in a drawer. She wouldn't even bother telling Allie that Kathleen Lawson had been looking for her.

*

Ana had already tried her cousin Kura's house but there had been no one home, so she crossed the street and knocked on the back door of the house opposite. After a moment she heard footsteps inside and the door opened.

'Ana!' Kura said, a wide smile lighting up her face. 'Come in, come in!'

They hugged. 'Oh good, I have got the right house,' Ana said, stepping into the narrow hallway. 'I wasn't sure. I went across the road and there was no one home. How are you?'

'Me? I'm good. I'm helping Wiki with the baby. You know she just had another little boy?'

Ana nodded, and held up the flowers she was carrying. 'Your Johnny said. He's going out with my neighbours' girl. He told you we met over the fence? He gave me your address.'

'Ae, Pauline. Nice girl.'

'Who is it?' came a disembodied voice from the front of the house.

'Our Ana, from home,' Kura called back.

Wiki appeared a moment later, carrying a very new baby. 'Kia ora, Ana. Long time, no see.'

Embracing Wiki, Ana said, 'I know, I've been meaning to visit for ages, but you know. These are for you,' she added, giving Wiki the flowers then having a good look at the baby. 'Isn't he *gorgeous*! What's his name?'

'Vincent Rawiri.'

'You must be thrilled.'

'Sort of.'

'Not planned?' Ana asked.

Wiki snorted. 'None of mine were planned. He'll be my last.' She looked down at him fondly. 'He is lovely, though. Anyway, come and sit down, tell us what you've been up to.'

While Kura made tea, Wiki and Ana sat in the front room and Ana had a very satisfying cuddle with Vincent. He was dressed head to toe in beautifully hand-knitted clothing and wrapped in several knitted blankets, and so he should be, Ana thought, because it was bloody freezing in Wiki's front room. She hadn't even taken her coat off, it was that cold. There was no heating and she could see condensation running down the inside of the windows and the dark shadows of mould creeping up from skirting boards.

Delving in her bag for a parcel, she said, 'I did a quick bit of knitting when Johnny mentioned you were expecting soon, but I can see he's probably got everything he needs. You always did knit well.'

Wiki opened the package to find two little white gowns with matching cardigans. 'Thank you, Ana. These are lovely. But me and Kura did do quite a lot of knitting. We had to sell some of it, actually, we had that much.'

'Did you?'

'Ae, it was easy. Sold really quickly.'

Ana thought that was really interesting. 'Whereabouts?'

'In a little shop on Ponsonby Road.'

Kura came in with the tea on a tray. Wiki said, 'No cake, sorry. The kids have eaten it all.'

Judging by the state of the house, Ana suspected there was very rarely cake in the Irwin home — or the Apanui household. She should have thought, and brought something along herself.

'I'm watching my figure anyway. So, you're not working at the moment, Kura?'

'I was,' Kura said. 'We were both in the kitchens at Auckland Hospital, then Wiki got the boot when she started to show and I left not long after.'

Ana caught a quick glance between Kura and Wiki, but didn't ask what it meant. If they wanted her to know, they'd tell her. 'I haven't worked at all in Auckland. I've been looking after Jack, but he's in the hospital now.'

'Ae, we heard he was sick,' Wiki said. 'That's no good, eh?'

'Where is he?' Kura asked. 'That Kingseat?'

'No, Auckland Mental Hospital, over by Point Chevalier?'

'They're all bad, those mental places. Full of kehua. What did you put him in there for?'

'He belted Peter, and I couldn't cope with him.'

'You should have said. Me and Wiki would have helped.'

'I know.'

'Is he coming home?' Wiki asked.

Ana sighed. 'I don't know.'

'Poor old Jack,' Kura said.

'Least you've got your days and nights back,' Wiki said, ever the pragmatist. 'Remember when Henare's Auntie Tuku went a-roro, Kura? What a nightmare.'

'Ooh, it was, eh?'

'So you can get a job, now, if you want one,' Wiki said to Ana.

'If I can find one, you mean,' Ana said.

'Well, I can't find a decent job,' Kura said. 'There's the factories but the pay's nothing to write home about, unless you do the long shifts. I'd have to be away early and home late, and who'd look after my youngest ones? My big girls are all out at work now.'

Ana said, 'I don't fancy working in a factory, but unfortunately I can't do anything particularly useful. Probably not much call for mustering, sorting fleeces and fixing fences here in the middle of Auckland.'

Wiki and Kura cackled with laughter, giving Vincent a fright. Wiki lifted him onto her shoulder. 'I'd like a job I can do at home. Then I could look after this one at the same time.'

Kura said, 'Pity no one will pay us for our knitting.'

'They did, though, eh? How much did we get again?' Wiki said.

'Twenty-three quid between us?' Kura replied. 'I can't really see me feeding and clothing my lot on eleven and a bit pounds a week, can you?'

'Wiki was telling me about that,' Ana said.

'Ae, we took some to a shop that sells crafts and clothing and the like,' Kura said. 'It was just baby clothes and blankets.' She giggled. 'Me and Wiki got a bit carried away before Vincent came. Got told off for it too. Now we can't afford to buy the wool. We've been unravelling things the kids can't fit any more.'

'What else do you reckon you can knit?' Ana asked.

'Anything, I suppose,' Wiki said. 'All sorts of baby things. And we've done cardigans and jumpers for us and for the whanau, and vests and hats, and gloves and shawls. I've done a few women's jackets. You did a dress once for Patricia, didn't you?' she said to Kura. 'Pity we can't knit groceries or a car.'

Ana said, 'Well, I can knit just about anything.' She thought for a moment, the excitement of an idea beginning to rise within her. 'Tell you what, can I come back one day soon, and we can talk about this some more? And I might bring Pauline's sister, Allie, with me.'

'Be lovely,' Kura said. 'For morning tea?'

'That'd be nice,' Wiki agreed, 'but why would we be having a meeting about knitting?'

Ana grinned. 'Because I've thought of a way we might all be able to make some money.'

Chapter Fifteen

Kura and Wiki had half-guessed Ana's idea, and Kura couldn't resist going up to the shop on Ponsonby Road. It was a little place packed with all sorts of things produced by people hoping to make a few pounds, like tatted doilies and embroidered tablecloths and pot mitts and aprons, and pyjama bags and dolls' clothes and people clothes and little bits of woodwork, and it was run by a big Samoan lady called Mrs Siosifa who wore bright shapeless dresses and a flower in her hair.

'Morning, dear!' Mrs Siosifa called as Kura went in.

'Morning. How are you?'

'Oh, pretty good. You?'

'Not bad.'

'That's nothing to complain about then! Now, what can I do for you?'

'You know those baby things I brought in a few weeks ago, some little knitted outfits and a few blankets?'

'Ioe, they went really well. Got snapped up straight away.'

'Well, would you take more?'

'Crikey, yes. 'Specially in white or cream.'

'Ae? Why's that?'

'Well, it was the Island ladies that bought everything. We like our babies to look pretty in church, you know, and we only wear white or cream to church. Also the ladies like to shop here 'cos everyone knows that everything's made by brown hands.'

Kura looked around. 'Is it?'

'Ioe. So you won't see a white person shopping in here. They might think they'll catch, what's your word for them?' Mrs Siosifa scratched her head vigorously, dislodging her flower.

'Kutus?'

'That's it. Kutus from the wool or the fabric, or something worse.'

'Well, that's ... rude.'

Mrs Siosifa shrugged and tucked her flower back behind her ear. 'It's the way it is, though, eh? Those white women don't want anything made by Maoris or Islanders touching their babies. Or them, either.'

'But not *all* of them?'

'The ones with money to spend.'

'How do you know?'

'Because they come in, ask who's made all this, I tell them and they walk out again. I should lie, eh, but I can't because I'm a church-going woman. But yes, I'll take as many baby clothes and blankets as you can make, especially those fancy ones you did last time.'

Mrs Siosifa reached under the counter and offered Kura a paper bag containing homemade biscuits. Kura took one and bit into it before she was out the door, but didn't really taste it. She was too busy thinking.

*

'Right,' Wiki said, adjusting Vincent on her breast, 'can we start this meeting?'

Ana had introduced Allie (calling her Mrs Allie Manaia) as Pauline's big sister and experienced in sales, which made Allie blush, and explained that she was also in the market for work. She was welcomed immediately then had to spend several minutes fielding questions about Sonny's general genealogy — the usual.

'Wait on, I've forgotten the lamingtons.' Kura jumped up and dashed into the kitchen.

Raising her eyebrows at Allie, Ana said, 'Lamingtons? We *are* spoilt.'

When Kura returned it was with a plate of cakes loaded with cream, which she set on a tablecloth on the floor next to the fresh scones, jam, more cream, a teapot and cups and saucers.

'You've over-whipped that cream,' Wiki observed.

'I have not. It's just right. You always under-whip it.' Kura handed out plates. 'Help yourselves, girls. Sorry we haven't got a table. Tea for everyone?'

Ana saw that Allie, bless her, was refraining from looking too pointedly at the state of Kura's front room. It was a horrible little house — as bad as Wiki's — and should probably be condemned, but her cousin had done what she could with it, and there wasn't a speck of dirt to be seen. There wasn't much furniture, either, which was why she was sitting on a beer crate topped with a cushion. She felt awful for her relatives having to live in accommodation like this, especially when she knew that the houses they'd left in Hawke's Bay were so much more comfortable. They weren't flash, but they were well built and homely and everyone had their own space and enough of it. She wondered why they didn't just pack it in and go home.

Wiki said, 'Bit of a dump, eh? Like mine.'

Uncomfortable, Ana replied, 'I've seen worse.'

'Bet *you* wouldn't live in it,' Kura said. 'We wouldn't either if we could get something better.'

'Honestly, if things are so bad,' Ana said, 'why don't you just go home?'

'I'd like to, but it's for the kids.' Kura looked at Wiki. 'Eh?'

Wiki agreed. 'There's not much for them at home any more. Or for us. You know that. The kids're better off in the city, where they can get jobs, make a bit of money and learn to get on.'

'Learn to be Pakeha, you mean?' Ana asked.

Kura said, 'Not really, 'cos they're not Pakeha, they're Maori.'

'Because that's what'll happen to them, you know,' Ana went on. 'They'll still be brown but they'll forget what it is to be Maori. They'll forget all about who they are.'

'Well, have you?' Wiki said. 'You're three-quarters Pakeha and you haven't.'

'And there's the Maori Community Centre,' Kura added. 'They do things the Maori way there.'

'Rubbish,' Wiki said. 'Rock and roll and jive isn't the Maori way.'

Kura said, 'But singing and dancing is, and they have big feeds with puha and fish heads and Maori bread, and kowhaiwhai on the walls just like in a wharenui. No booze, either. Johnny goes all the time and so do my big girls. Do you go, Allie?'

'No, actually, we've never gone.'

'Suppose you don't need to, eh? Your man already has his marae and all that.'

'Have you been?' Ana asked her cousins.

Kura looked at Wiki and they burst out laughing. 'Can't see Joshua throwing me over his shoulder in the jive, can you? It's more for the young ones.'

Wiki said, 'I've seen you doing the jive, Kura Apanui. But they do have some good steel guitar bands at the MCC. That's more for the oldies.'

'You can do a nice waltz or a quickstep to the steel guitar,' Kura said. 'But Joshua doesn't dance.'

'Neither does Henare.'

And neither would David, Ana thought, so there would be no point to them going, though it sounded like fun.

When everyone had tea and something on their plates, Wiki said, 'Now we can't have a meeting 'cos we're eating.'

'Well, talk with your mouth full,' Kura suggested. 'Has that baby finished his kai? Shall I take him so you can drink your tea?'

Wiki tidied herself, handed Vincent — now happily nodding off — to his auntie, and bit into a scone. 'Not bad. Could have done with a few more minutes in the oven.'

'I'll put you in the oven,' Kura muttered.

'You've always made a good scone,' Ana said. 'Jack loved them.'

'David coming right?' Kura asked.

'Yes and no.'

Wiki said, 'What about the kids?'

Ana sighed. 'Well, they were frightened of him so it's a bit of a relief having him gone, to be honest. But I think they miss the old Jack.'

Kura raised her eyebrows. 'And you?'

'Oh, you know me.'

'Soldiering on,' Kura said. 'You're just like your dad, eh?'

'I'm not as stubborn as he is.'

Kura and Wiki both laughed.

Ana sipped her tea, washing bits of coconut out of her teeth. 'Anyway, knitting. I've been thinking. That shop you took your baby things to, do you think they'd be happy to sell more?'

Kura said, 'Ae, I've already asked.'

'Did you sell them on commission?'

Kura nodded. 'But she didn't take that much. I forget what the percentage was.'

'Well, why don't we set up a little knitting circle and see what we can make selling our things in shops like that? If there's one shop keen to take good quality hand-knitted clothing there'll be others. In fact, why not go for gold and try the babywear shops? Hell, why not the department stores?'

'Excuse me,' Allie said, 'I'm sorry if I sound negative, and I don't mean to, but doesn't everyone knit? Why would people buy knitted things when they can just get the wool and make them at home?'

'Hang on a minute.' Wiki rummaged through a bag at her feet, then passed Allie a pale blue, long-sleeved baby gown, jacket, bonnet, mittens and booties. The pattern matched throughout and was so fine and intricate the set looked as though it were made of lace.

'You knitted *this*?' Allie said, holding the gown up to the light.

Wiki nodded. 'Size eighteen needles, single ply merino.'

'God, this makes my knitting look like a potato sack.'

'A potato sack can come in handy, though,' Kura said.

'And all of your knitting's like this?' Allie asked. 'You know, this is as nice as anything we had at Smith and Caughey. Or Dunbar and Jones.'

'Not all of it,' Kura said. 'Just the best stuff. It takes a while to make something like this. Two days, maybe?'

'The little gown?'

'No, the whole set.'

'Well, we wouldn't want to concentrate completely on garments of that quality anyway,' Ana said, 'though we could certainly put a good price on them. It wouldn't be commercially viable.'

Wiki and Kura looked at her. Wiki said, 'Get you and your big words.'

'Well, I do know a little bit about business,' Ana said. 'From the farm.'

Kura said, 'Explain?'

'She means if we spend all our time making beautiful things like this,' Allie said, 'and charging a moderately high price, we still won't make much money because we won't have the time to make a lot of other items we can sell at a lower price. You have to get the balance right between quantity and quality.'

'Ha, I knew you'd be useful!' Ana said. 'You can be our retail consultant, as well as knit our potato sacks.'

Kura put a lamington on her plate. 'This is all lovely, but we can't knit anything if we can't afford to pay for the wool. And we can't.'

'That's the other part of my idea,' Ana said. 'It's too early for raw wool from this year's clip, or I'd suggest getting a bale sent up from home, but why don't we buy a bale, or even just a half-bale, from a wool store up here? Wiri's probably our best bet.'

Allie, Wiki and Kura stared at her.

'What? We can dye it all sorts of colours and spin it into any yarn we want. Can any of you spin?'

More blank looks.

'Well, I can, and I know how to dye wool as well.'

'Don't you need all sorts of special gear for that?' Allie asked.

Ana shook her head. 'Just a copper, a fire, water, your dyeing agents, somewhere to hang the wool to dry and a bit of elbow grease.'

'We've got plenty of that,' Kura said.

'Wiri's still not that close,' Allie said. 'How would we get the bale here?'

'On the train.'

'That's true,' Kura said. 'Joshua's on the railways. He could make sure it gets off all right when it arrives.'

'And we could borrow Sonny's truck to bring it home,' Allie said.

'Can you drive it?' Ana asked.

'No, but I've been meaning to learn.'

Ana laughed. 'I can. I drove the farm truck, and the tractor.'

'Where would we do all this?' Kura asked. 'In the washhouse?'

'Best to do the dyeing outside, if we're doing a biggish batch. It can stink a bit.'

'Might as well do it here, then,' Wiki said. 'It always stinks in this part of town.'

'But we can knit anywhere,' Ana added. 'You're all more than welcome at our house, you know that.'

'It sounds like a lot of work,' Allie said. 'Especially for you, Mrs Leonard, if you're going to be doing all the spinning. Not that I mind working hard.'

'*I* mind you calling me Mrs Leonard, Allie. It makes me feel old. It's Ana, please.'

'Ae,' Kura said. 'And I'm Kura and she's Wiki.'

'Thank you very much,' Allie said. 'And I wasn't meaning to sound rude or lazy, but if we spend too much time making our garments from scratch, we won't be able to make enough. That's assuming we can find a successful market for them.'

'You *are* a clever girl, aren't you?' Ana remarked. 'But I have thought of that. Right now we can't afford to buy yarn, so we'll process our own wool, do a really good job of it and make some beautiful clothes. Are we agreed we'll start with baby things?' Nods all round. 'Good, because they're fairly quick because they're so small.'

'Blankets aren't,' Kura said.

'But they're not complicated, are they?'

'No. I can do a pretty one in a day and a half.'

'Then, when we've built up a bit of money, *that's* when we start buying yarn ready for knitting,' Ana said. 'It means the money goes straight back into the business rather than our pockets, so no one will be any better off for a while, but we probably won't be worse off, either. It's just whether everyone can hang on long enough till we start to benefit financially. And if we do, it'll be lovely because we'll be running our own business. Think of that!'

'I like the sound of that,' Wiki said.

Kura stood to hand a sleeping Vincent back to her, then changed her mind. 'Do you want a hold?' she asked Allie.

'Ooh, yes please,' Allie said, and settled the baby in the crook of her elbow.

'What if one of us *has* to get a job?' Kura asked as she sat down again. 'It'd be nice to have our own business, but we've still got kids to feed and rent to pay.'

'Then you take the job,' Ana said. 'You could still knit for the business outside of work hours.'

Kura beamed. 'Ae, I could, eh? Rather be right in the middle of it, though. Knitting and gossiping and drinking tea. That's not work, that's fun!'

*

James and Lucy Murdoch got out of the taxi and James paid the driver. Too late, James wondered as it drove off whether he should have asked the man to wait.

'Not a very nice part of town.' Lucy observed.

James agreed. 'It does look a little run down.'

They'd stayed the past two nights with Kathleen, Jonathan and the children, telling them James was in Auckland on business. Lucy had wanted to tell them the real reason for their visit but there was obviously something going on between Kathleen and Jonathan, so they'd decided to tell them later. Kathleen hadn't seemed happy at all and Jonathan had been hitting the booze even harder than usual. Lucy said she'd given their daughter plenty of opportunities to talk about what might be bothering her, but nothing had been forthcoming. She'd always been like that, though, Kathleen, close-mouthed about her problems. There was a new housekeeper-cum-nanny too, an older woman called Mrs Wright. James wondered where the last one had gone, the attractive young one, but hadn't asked. Perhaps that had something to do with the frosty atmosphere in the house.

And now he was about to talk to Polly about her daughter. Their daughter. If Polly was at home, that was.

'Would you mind waiting out here on the footpath while I speak with her?' he asked Lucy.

'Yes, I would. This has as much to do with me as it does anyone else.'

James had thought she might say that. Stifling a sigh, he knocked on the door, noting it could do with a bit of paint. Some girl he didn't recognise answered.

'Good morning. I'd like to talk to Polly, if I may.'

'Wait on,' the girl said, then bellowed up the stairs, '*Polly! Door!*'

Eventually Polly appeared, wearing calf-length jeans, a short-sleeved top and nothing on her feet. She stopped when she saw him. 'What are you doing here?'

'I'd like to speak to you about Gina.'

'You're behind in your payments.'

James felt Lucy step past him, and his heart sank.

'No he isn't,' she said brusquely, 'because he won't be making any more. I'm James's wife, by the way.'

The expression on Polly's face didn't change. 'I know who you are. I saw you at Smith and Caughey's.'

'We have a proposition for you.'

Oh Lucy, do shut up, James thought, fearing she'd charge in heavy-handed and ruin everything.

'Do you mind if we sit down?' he asked.

'Suit yourself,' Polly said, and sat on the stairs.

'No, I mean somewhere more amenable to conversation.'

'There's the front room.' Polly waved at a doorway on James's left.

He went into what had once been quite a grand room but was now very tired, and equipped with mismatched furniture. Lucy sat next to him on a dusty old sofa while Polly curled into an armchair opposite.

'Well?' she said.

'I've told Mrs Murdoch about our liaison,' James said, praying that Polly would be decent enough not to mention that there had been far more than one. 'And the child.'

Polly's dark eyes narrowed slightly, but all she said was, 'If you're going to call your wife Mrs Murdoch, then you can call me Miss Manaia.'

Lucy said, 'Oh, for God's sake. I'm Lucy, you're Polly and he's James, all right? We're here to talk about Gina, not to play silly games.'

'Gina? What about her?'

James felt his face heat up. He did feel quite embarrassed about this part of it. 'Well, I, er, I employed a private investigator to collect some information. Photographs, mainly. We wanted to see what the child looks like. He photographed her, and you, while you were at an address on ...' Forgetting the name, he had to check his papers. 'Kitemoana Street.'

'You bastard! That's my mother's house! You had me followed?'

'Yes, we did,' Lucy said. 'I, *we* wanted to know if the child really is James's.'

'And you think you can tell that from a couple of pictures?'

'They're very good close-up photographs, in colour, and Gina looks like our children when they were little,' Lucy said. '*Just* like them.'

'And you *told* me she's mine,' James said.

'I did,' Polly said.

'So,' Lucy went on, 'we'd like to make you an offer.'

Polly regarded them in silence.

Now that they'd reached this point James's heart was thumping in his chest and he felt faintly ill. This was such an enormous thing, almost preposterous. Lucy looked at him and he held her gaze, willing her to ask the question, because now the time had come he didn't think he could.

Lucy turned to Polly and said, 'Our family would like to adopt Gina.'

Polly still said nothing.

'My son, who is an RAF hero, and his wife, a nurse, are quite well off. They only have one child and they'd desperately like another but are unable to have more. Gina *is* James's daughter, after all, and Duncan and Claire would raise her as their own. She'd grow up in a lovely home with two parents, go to the best schools, have everything she needs and wants, and access to the best opportunities when she gets older. And yes, I know, she's part Maori, but that's never been an issue in our family. Our family tree is quite diverse.' She paused for a moment. 'And, of course, we'd compensate you for the loss of your daughter. Handsomely. Very handsomely, in fact.'

Polly was looking down at her fingernails. 'She doesn't live with me. She lives with my mother.'

'But surely she'll see it would be best for Gina?'

'No. She won't see that.'

'Perhaps we could compensate your mother as well?' James suggested.

Polly said, 'She'd be disgusted if you offered her money.'

'But she's your daughter,' Lucy said. 'It's your decision, isn't it, what happens to her?'

'Yes, it is. It is my decision.'

Polly was staring at the floor now. James watched her. He hadn't expected this level of vacillation; based on how she'd used the child to blackmail him, he'd thought she'd jump at the chance to offload her for a decent profit. Perhaps he'd misjudged her.

'The best of everything, Polly,' Lucy repeated. 'She'll grow up in a moneyed Hawke's Bay family, very well educated and with every opportunity she could hope for. And you'll receive three thousand pounds for your trouble.'

James nearly fainted. Three thousand pounds! That wasn't the figure they'd talked about! He glared at Lucy but she deliberately refused to look his way.

'Your son and daughter-in-law,' Polly said. 'How old is their other kid?'

'She's ten. Her name is Lorraine and she's a delightful child. I know for a fact she'd adore a little sister.'

'And they have a nice house?'

'It's charming. Fairly new, on the hill, built after the earthquake. Very modern.'

'And they've got plenty of money?'

'Oh, yes. Duncan is a part owner of a local shipping company, and of course he has shares in Kenmore, James's family's sheep station.'

'All right,' Polly said.

James blinked. He looked at Lucy again, who looked rather satisfied, not shocked at all, as though her plan were the height of common sense.

He said, 'Pardon?'

'I said all right, you can have her. But you'll have to just take her, without my mother knowing. And I want the money in cash.'

James thought that sounded more like the Polly he thought he knew.

'Oh, no, we're not kidnapping her,' he said. 'You'll have to bring her to us. It will be kinder that way too.'

Polly sat for a moment, thinking. 'Then this is what'll have to happen.'

*

Awhi was folding washing, making nice neat piles on the kitchen table.

'I'm taking Gina down to Mission Bay,' Polly said.

'What for?' Awhi asked, not looking up.

'An ice cream.'

'Not really ice cream weather, is it? It's the middle of winter.'

'*Ice cream!*' Gina shouted.

'Go and get your shoes and a jumper,' Polly told her.

Gina shot off.

When she came back, her shoes on the right feet but her jumper on backwards, Polly said, 'Give Nannie a kiss goodbye.'

Gina gave Awhi a light peck on the cheek.

'No, a better one than that,' Polly said.

Climbing onto Awhi's lap, Gina gave her nannie a big hug and a smoochie kiss.

'Ooh, that was nice,' Awhi said.

Hopping down, Gina grabbed Polly's hand. 'Come on, come *on*! Ice cream!'

They walked together across Michael Joseph Savage Park, the strong winds nearly knocking them off their feet and making them laugh, then down the other side to Mission Bay. At the tearoom Polly said hello to Sonny's mother-in-law, bought a hokey-pokey ice cream in a cone for Gina and a cup of tea for herself, then they sat at a table so Gina didn't drip her ice cream everywhere and she could have a smoke. When she checked her watch her hands were shaking.

At a quarter to two they went outside, crossed the road to the reserve and she pushed Gina on the swings for a while. Then the taxi pulled up. She lifted Gina off the swing, took her by the hand and led her to the kerb. The back door of the taxi swung open. James and Lucy Murdoch sat inside. Between them rested an enormous plush teddy bear with a pink bow around its neck.

Polly got down on one knee, held Gina by the arms and looked into her face. 'Gina, love, I want you to go with these people, all right? The lady's called Lucy and the man's called James.'

Lucy leant out of the taxi. 'Hello, dear!'

Gina stared at Lucy, bewildered.

'Look at me, Gina,' Polly said. 'They live in a lovely place with lovely people and you'll have everything you ever wanted.'

'But I don't want to.'

'I'm sorry, sweetie, you have to.'

'Can you come?' Gina asked.

'I can't, love. I have to stay here.'

'Can Nannie?'

'No.' Polly lifted Gina into the taxi. 'You be a good girl, now.'

Gina started to bawl.

James said to the taxi driver, 'She's never come to stay with us on her own before. She's a bit upset, I think.'

Lucy surreptitiously handed Polly a fat envelope and said under her breath, 'Please don't contact us after this. She's better off making a clean break.'

Nodding her agreement, Polly closed the door and stepped back as the taxi drove off. She waited until it had disappeared up the road before she let herself cry.

Then she headed for the nearest pub.

*

Awhi waited and waited, but when Polly and Gina still weren't home by four o'clock — Gina's teatime — she knew something wasn't right and decided she had to get to the Mission Bay tearoom before it closed. She rushed out of the house (and rushed back in to take off her apron and swap her slippers for street shoes), then charged across the park, ignoring shouts of 'Go, Nanna!' from some rude youths on bicycles. The tearoom was on the verge of closing when she marched in, her breath ragged and her hair escaping from its long plait.

Colleen Roberts was at the till, cashing up. 'Mrs Manaia, you look out of sorts.'

'I am. I'm looking for my daughter, Polly — you know, the one that models? And my mokopuna, Gina. My granddaughter. Have they been in here this afternoon?'

Mrs Roberts nodded. 'About one o'clock, a quarter past one, something like that? Then I think they went across the road to the swings and slides. Wait on, I'll ask if anyone else saw them.'

Awhi waited nervously, her heart refusing to slow down, as Colleen Roberts went out the back. When she returned she said, 'Apparently a taxi came not long after that and the little girl got in but not your Polly. And then the taxi drove off.'

Awhi thought she might faint clean away. Oh, Polly, Polly, you evil girl, what have you done?

'Are you all right, Mrs Manaia?'

Realising she was holding on to the countertop for dear life, Awhi took a deep, shaky breath and nodded. 'Yes, thank you, Mrs Roberts. Thank you for your help.'

She turned on legs that felt like Edmonds jelly and lurched out of the tearoom to the taxi stand outside. Although there was a taxi there, she belatedly realised she hadn't brought her purse. She wouldn't have been able to afford a taxi anyway. She started to cry, dabbing at her eyes with the hem of her cardigan.

Then Mrs Roberts was beside her. 'Do you need some money?'

'I have to get into town to talk to Sonny. He'll still be at work. I'm not on the telephone at home.'

'I'm so sorry,' Mrs Roberts said, 'but we can't use the telephone at my work for personal calls. Here, take this.'

Awhi felt something pushed into her hand: a five-pound note. 'Oh, no, I couldn't!'

'Go on, go and see your boy. A bus will take forever.'

Awhi got into the back of the taxi, then realised she didn't know what to do next. She'd never been in one by herself.

Mrs Roberts told the driver, 'Smith and Caughey in the city, service entrance at the back, please, where the delivery vans load up, and hurry, it's an emergency.'

And they were off, Awhi gripping her five pounds and trying not to slide all over the seat as the driver wove through the traffic and jumped on and off the brake. In fact, he was so reckless she tapped him on the shoulder and said, 'Hey, mister, it's not *that* much of an emergency. Slow down, eh?'

The trip seemed to take no time at all and soon the driver skidded to a halt in a narrow little lane behind Smith and Caughey. 'This here do you, missus?'

Awhi wasn't sure as she didn't know where to find Sonny, but Colleen Roberts had sounded like she did. 'Yes, thank you.'

The driver told her the tariff. Awhi had no idea whether she was being cheated, but she paid it and was given change.

'Hope everything works out,' the driver said before he tore off.

Awhi stopped the first person she saw. 'I'm looking for Sonny Manaia. He drives delivery trucks here. Where would I find him?'

'Dunno, missus,' the man said. 'If he's not out on a delivery he's probably getting one ready to go.' He looked at his watch. 'Or maybe not. It might be a bit late. You could ask at the despatch office.'

'Mum? What are you doing here?'

And there was Sonny wearing an ugly grey cotton coat with *Smith and Caughey* embroidered on the chest pocket.

'That *wicked* bloody sister of yours,' Awhi burst out, anger rising up to mingle with her fear now she didn't have to manage this all on her own. 'Gina's missing. Allie's mother saw her getting into a taxi at Mission Bay, but without Polly, and—'

'What? Mum, slow down. Stop. What are you talking about?'

Awhi took a deep breath to calm herself. 'Polly took Gina to Mission Bay this afternoon at about one for an ice cream. They didn't come back. At four o'clock I went down there. Allie's mother said she saw ... No, someone at the tearoom saw Gina get into a taxi and go off, but Polly didn't go with her.'

'Well, where's Polly now?'

'I don't know. I haven't seen her since they left to go to Mission Bay.'

'And Colleen's sure Polly didn't get in the taxi as well? Because they could have gone somewhere together.'

'The person who saw it said it was only Gina. Something's wrong, Sonny, I know it is! Polly's done something terrible!'

'How do you know that?'

'I can feel it, that's how!'

'Stop panicking, Mum. There's probably a good explanation for everything.'

'There won't be, and I'm not panicking!' Awhi *was* panicking and she knew it.

Sonny put his arm around her. 'Wait a few minutes till I knock off, then we'll go round to Polly's and see if she's there. OK?'

But Polly wasn't at her house at Ligaro Place, and Sonny said he didn't know which restaurants she waitressed at on which nights. Awhi had the feeling there was something else he wasn't telling her, and she waited and waited on the ride in his truck back to Kitemoana Street, but he never said it.

Finally, *she* said, 'There's something you're not telling me about Polly, isn't there?'

'Could be, but I don't think it'd have anything to do with Gina, so it's not worth talking about.'

'Tell me anyway.'

'No. Really, it's not worth it.'

Awhi gave up, because when Sonny said no, he meant it.

Gina wasn't back home when they got in, and Awhi burst into tears again. The house felt empty and dead without her little granddaughter, as if she'd just died.

Sonny made her a cup of tea and an egg on toast, which she couldn't eat, then went next door and asked the neighbour to come and sit with her.

'I'll have a look around for Polly tonight, Mum, and if I can't find her I might take the day off tomorrow. Don't worry. She won't be far away. Neither of them will be. It'll be OK.'

'It won't,' Awhi said, dread pulling down the corners of her mouth. 'That girl's done something, and I know it won't.'

*

Sonny did take the next day off, phoning his boss at Smith and Caughey from a telephone box and saying he was sick. Then he and Allie drove over to St Mary's Bay to the brothel at Ring Terrace, about which he'd been so reluctant to tell Awhi.

'Do you want to come in?' he asked Allie.

'No thanks, I'll wait out here. Have you been here before?'

Sonny laughed at the miserable look on her face. 'Don't be a twit. Half the city knows about Flora's. Doesn't mean I've been here.' He kissed her on the cheek. 'Hopefully she's in. If not we'll have to keep looking.'

'What if she's, you know, busy.'

'Then we'll wait till she isn't.'

Inside, the place was really quite flash — far nicer than Sonny had expected. He'd thought it would be sleazy, but it wasn't. He was standing in the hallway feeling a twerp when a woman barrelled out of a doorway with her hand out, giving him a hell of a fright. She was quite old, fat, dressed in something that looked like a sleeping bag, smelt of booze, and was surrounded by darting little dogs.

'Good morning, dear, how can we help you?'

Sonny decided this must be Flora MacKenzie. She surely couldn't be one of the girls. 'Morning. I'm looking for Polly Manaia.'

'I'm sorry, dear, but she's not working today.'

'No, I don't want ... I just want to talk to her.'

'You'll still have to pay.'

'I don't think so. I'm her brother.'

Flora frowned, then bent and picked up a dog. 'Is Polly in trouble?'

'Why do you say that?'

'A private investigator was asking after her a few weeks ago. A month, perhaps? He wanted to talk to her as well. *And* he wanted her home address. Naturally I sent him away with a flea in his ear. My girls are entitled to their privacy, and I told him so. Nasty little man.'

'Did you get his name?'

'I didn't need to. It was Ted Hollis. He's often loitering across the street trying to take photographs of my customers as they leave. Stupid man doesn't realise we have a back door.'

'Did you tell Polly he'd been around?'

Flora shook her head. 'I didn't think it was worth worrying her about.'

'And when did Polly last come to work?'

'Let's see, that would be three days ago? But you'd know your sister. She comes and goes as she pleases. *Is* she in trouble?'

'I don't know yet. Thanks for your help, Mrs MacKenzie.'

'It's Miss MacKenzie, and you're welcome.'

Back in the truck Sonny said, 'She's not there, but we need to find a private investigator called Ted Hollis.'

'A private — Why?'

'Because he was asking after her and I want to know why.'

'God, who's that?' Allie asked, looking out the window.

It was Flora MacKenzie, sailing across the street, her odd garment flapping around her. She tapped on the glass.

Allie opened the window.

Flora passed in a piece of notepaper. 'Here's Ted Hollis's phone number and business address, if you want to speak to him, though I don't know if you'll get much out of him. I looked it up in the telephone book.'

Another round of thanks and Sonny and Allie were heading back towards the city and Wellesley Street. Ted Hollis had an office on the first floor of quite an old building. The lift and its brass cage doors rattled so alarmingly that they wished they'd used the stairs, and the corridor leading to Hollis's office was dimly lit, laid with dull, scuffed linoleum, and deathly quiet.

'I usually expect clients to make an appointment before coming in, you know,' Ted Hollis said as they sat down, even though he'd opened his door barely a second after they'd knocked.

Sonny looked around. The office was small, and contained a desk with a telephone, a metal filing cabinet on which sat a wilting peace lily, and a wall calendar for 1955. Also, the room smelt like sardines. It didn't look like he could afford to be choosy about his customers, or when they came in.

'Anyway, you're here now. What can I do for you?'

'You've been asking questions about my sister,' Sonny began.

'Well, that depends on who your sister is,' Ted Hollis said.

What a smartarse, Sonny thought. 'Polly Manaia. She works at Flora MacKenzie's brothel. You were there not long ago. I want to know why.'

'You'd have to ask her. Why does any girl work in a brothel?'

Sonny wondered if Hollis *wanted* his face punched in. He leant forwards. 'Why were you asking about her? Who was paying you?'

Ted Hollis sat back in his seat, making it creak. 'Normally discretion is my middle name but, as it happens, that particular client's on my shit list. Pardon me, missus. He stiffed me on my bill. Says I overcharged him, which I can assure you I did not.'

He made a steeple of his fingers and put the tips to his mouth, as though he were contemplating a decision, though Sonny suspected he'd already made up his mind.

'Yes, I will,' Hollis said. 'I'll give you that information because that client doesn't deserve respect. He's not an honest man.'

Sonny waited. Beside him he could feel Allie tense.

'His name is James Murdoch. Apparently he's the father of your sister's child.'

Allie gasped.

Sonny felt equally stunned. 'So who the hell is he?'

Ted Hollis shrugged. 'I never met him, though I talked to him on the telephone. An older bloke, I think. Married. Well-to-do. From Hawke's Bay. Owns an orchard or something.'

'And what did he hire you for?'

'To provide him with photographs of the little girl.'

'What the hell for?'

'I gather he and his wife wanted to adopt her.'

Sonny and Allie gaped at each other.

'And was Polly in on this?' Sonny asked.

'No idea.'

'Can you give us this Murdoch's contact details? Because they're missing, you know, Polly and her daughter.'

'No. That would be going too far,' Ted Hollis said. 'I've got scruples, you know.'

*

'Sorry to interrupt,' Sonny said when Ana came to the door. 'Oh, are you on your way out?'

'I was just off to visit Jack but I can catch the next bus.'

'We can come back,' Allie said.

'No, really, it's all right.' Ana put her handbag on the kitchen bench. 'Come in. How can I help? Would you like tea?'

Sonny said, 'No thanks, we won't keep you. It was just something you said quite a while ago, about your family down the coast.'

'Sit down,' Ana urged.

'Thanks. You said you were related to some Murdochs in Hawke's Bay.'

Ana nodded. 'Which ones do you want to know about?'

'Just their names would be good,' Allie said, 'if we're not being too nosy.'

'Of your living relatives. The Pakeha ones,' Sonny added.

'Well, it's a bit of a complicated story. After my grandmother, Tamar Deane, had an illegitimate child, who I think I told you is my father, she married Andrew Murdoch and had James, Thomas, Keely and Ian, except Ian died during the war. The first one, that is, though he did leave an illegitimate child of his own.'

Sonny asked, 'So James Murdoch would be your …?'

'My uncle. His kids, my cousins, are Duncan, Kathleen and Drew, but we lost Drew after the second war. Duncan was in the RAF and was badly burnt but he's all right now. I'm not really in touch with Kathleen. Or rather, she's not in touch with me and I'm fine with that. And then there are Auntie Keely's children, and Uncle Ian's boy, who's really Billy's son, my brother who died overseas, not to mention Uncle Thomas and his wife, but they don't have any children. Do you mind if I ask what your interest is?'

Allie fiddled with the brass buttons on her coat cuff.

Sonny said, 'Ah.'

Blushing, Allie said, 'This is really difficult to say.'

'As difficult as chasing your naked father-in-law round the back lawn in front of the neighbours?' Ana asked.

That was a point, Sonny thought. 'My sister Polly sometimes works as a prostitute.' He checked Ana's face for a reaction — nothing. 'And she has a little girl. She's three years old. Gina. We've just learnt that a James Murdoch from Hawke's Bay, an older man who owns an orchard, is the father. Apparently he and his wife wanted to adopt Gina, and now she's missing, and we can't find Polly, either.'

Ana was silent for a moment. Then she said, 'What a bizarre situation. I wouldn't be surprised if it was Uncle James. He always was a ratbag. And poor Auntie Lucy's never been quite right since Drew died.'

'So we were wondering if you could tell us how to find your uncle. If they do have Gina we'd like her back.'

'I really don't think he would have just taken her. Uncle James has done a few dodgy things in his time but he'd never kidnap a child.'

'I'm sure he didn't.' Then, for the first time, Sonny said it out loud. 'But I wouldn't put it past my sister to sell one.'

*

Ana got off the tram near the hospital's front gate and trudged down the long driveway towards the entrance. It was bitingly cold today and she was glad she'd worn her heavy winter coat and a beret. In her bag she had a hat and scarf she'd knitted for Jack, which she thought he might appreciate. Though who knew, with him?

It wasn't much warmer inside the hospital, though she knew the radiators in the corridors were going because she could smell them. It smelt like someone had draped dusty, dead mice over the fins and was slowly toasting them. Everyone she encountered seemed to have colds and bright red noses, and was sneezing and coughing and not bothering to cover their mouths. No wonder they were all sick.

Jack wasn't in his ward, and when she asked the sister on duty, an older woman today, where he was, she said she didn't know. Ana sat down by his bed to wait, and that's when she noticed the damp, dark yellow stain on his sheets. Revolted, she didn't even need to sniff to know it was old urine. His bedding had never been this bad before. His water pitcher was empty and his teeth were sitting dried out in the bottom of a plastic cup. On opening his locker she saw that the clothes jammed inside weren't even his. She caught the eye of the man in the bed next to Jack's, who bared his teeth at her. Quickly, she looked away.

Finally, she stomped over to the nurses' station and demanded, 'Look, you must know where he is. You're supposed to be in charge of him.'

'Well, he might be in the lounge, or outside in the garden. We don't watch them every hour of the day, you know.'

'Don't you?' Ana said. 'You should. At home I *had* to, otherwise he got into terrible trouble.'

'Look, dear, this is a mental hospital. The place is full of people like your, er ...?'

'My father-in-law.'

'Yes, and we just can't do that here. There aren't enough of us. Try the lounge or the garden. Or maybe the rec room. Or the lavs? He can't get out, you know.'

I bet he bloody could, Ana thought. '*You* look in the lavs. And he won't be in the garden, will he, not on a day like this. Where's the other nurse gone? Sister Simpson, the nice young one?'

'She left. Got married, I think.'

Ana made her way to the patient lounge, which, as usual, stank of wee and cabbage. Why, she wondered, did hospitals always reek of cabbage? Didn't they cook anything else? Half a dozen men sat in the room, apparently listening to something on a radiogram from the New Zealand Broadcasting Service. Or perhaps they were just staring into space. At first she didn't see Jack but then she spotted him, slouched in a chair near the window. Even though it was late morning he was still wearing his pyjamas, dressing gown, socks and one slipper, he hadn't been shaved for several days, and his hair was unruly. As she approached she saw the remains of food crusted around his sunken mouth, and splodges of something on his pyjama jacket. And he smelt rank. She wondered when he'd last had a wash. Appalled, she felt like crying.

He looked dazed and lethargic, but when he saw her a little light sparked in his eyes and he said, 'Mary?'

'It's me, Jack, Ana.'

'I don't like it here, Mary. Take me home. I want to go back to the farm.'

A huge pain swelled in the back of Ana's throat and she couldn't swallow. She'd visited Jack weekly on Wednesdays for the past three months, and with David on weekends, and he'd barely said a word to either of them. Not civil, sensible words, at any rate. This was the first time in ages he'd said something that contained echoes of his old self, and it hurt badly.

She tried and tried to swallow, and finally some spit went down. 'Wait here, Jack. I'll be back in a second.'

Hurrying back to his ward she grabbed his teeth from the bedside table and shoved them in her pocket, then looked around for his other slipper, found it, then returned to the lounge.

'Come on, Jack, let's go,' she said, jamming his foot into the slipper.

'Where are we going?'

'Back to the farm.'

'I don't like it here.'

'I know.'

He lurched down the corridor beside her, tripping and banging into the wall. His balance seemed shot and Ana wondered what sort of medicine he'd been given. At the hospital entrance she put his new hat on him, wound the scarf round his neck, and tied his dressing gown belt securely. Then, her arm through his, they walked off the hospital grounds and out to Point Chevalier Road where they caught the next tram into the city.

People stared, and no one sat near them on the tram, probably because of the way Jack looked and smelt, but Ana steadfastly ignored it all. At one point Jack wept, so she held his hand until he stopped. In the city they changed to a bus, attracting even more stares, and rode to Orakei. She looked out the window, wondering how taking him home would affect the children, and her. She'd made such plans — the wool was due to arrive from Wiri soon. She supposed she could appeal to Sid from next door to help keep an eye on Jack while she was busy, but that was a lot to ask from a neighbour, even good-natured Sid.

When they got home, she ran a bath and washed Jack from head to toe like a child, dried him, dressed him in a pair of David's pyjamas, and put him to bed in his old bedroom, where he fell asleep immediately. Then she threw his old pyjamas and things into the incinerator in the back garden and burnt the lot. When the kids came home from school she'd go down to the telephone box, phone the hospital and tell them she'd taken Jack home.

Stuff them.

Chapter Sixteen

July 1956

Sonny's boss said, 'Where's your overall? Come on, hurry up, we've got loads to shift today.'

'Actually I've only come in to ask for a few days off,' Sonny said. 'I've got some urgent family business I need to sort out.'

'Not one of your week-long bloody funerals? You just had a sick day.'

'No, but it's important.'

'Well, so are Smith and Caughey's deliveries. You bloody Maoris have got no idea what commitment to the job means, have you?'

Sonny, who'd only ever taken one sick day (yesterday) and statutory holidays since he'd started at Smith and Caughey, said, 'I probably only need four days. I don't mind taking the time off without pay.'

'No. I can't spare you.'

'Well, I have to take it.'

'If you do you're fired.'

Sonny didn't hesitate long. 'Then I'm fired.'

Before they left for Hawke's Bay — in Sonny's truck, which they really weren't confident would last the distance — Allie and Sonny went round to Polly's house one last time, and got a bit of a shock when she actually answered the front door. She tried to slam it shut again but Sonny shoved his foot in the way and barged in.

'Where's Gina?' he demanded.

'I don't know.'

Sonny grabbed her wrist and twisted it. 'You do so. Jesus, Polly, you're bloody unbelievable sometimes. Your own daughter!'

'Leave me alone!'

'Please, Polly,' Allie begged. 'How much did they pay you, because we'll have to give it back when we go and get her.'

Polly looked both enraged and disconcerted. 'Don't interfere! Leave her. She's better off where she is.'

Sonny said, 'Like hell! You're bloody mad.'

'How much?' Allie persisted.

'I didn't get paid anything,' Polly insisted.

'Bullshit, you didn't,' Sonny said.

Allie felt her belly knot up even more. If Polly wouldn't tell them they'd have no idea about how much money they'd need. All they'd been able to scrape together was four hundred and seventy-five pounds. It was all they and Awhi had. Maybe the Murdochs hadn't paid Polly anything, but Allie didn't think so, and that upset her because she liked Polly.

'Is she with James and Lucy Murdoch?' she asked.

'No,' Polly said. 'Now get out of my house.'

'She is and we know she is,' Sonny said. 'For Christ's sake, stop lying.'

'I'm *not*.'

Sonny let go of Polly and pushed her, just a little bit. 'I don't understand why you've done this, Polly. I can't think why *any* mother would do it. You've just about ruined Mum. What's wrong with you? Really, what's *wrong* with you?'

And then Polly looked at her brother with such venom that Allie nearly shivered. 'You've got no idea, have you? No bloody idea.'

'No. I haven't.'

'Well, then you can fuck off.'

So Allie and Sonny did.

*

When Sonny and Allie had gone, Polly went upstairs to her room, sat on her bed, lit a cigarette and poured a glass of brandy. She was shaking badly. He *didn't* have any idea and she was never going to tell him.

She desperately hoped they wouldn't bring Gina back. If they did they'd ruin her chances of ever having a decent life.

And *she* hadn't been paid any money. The three thousand pounds the Murdochs had given her was in Gina's bank account, waiting just in case Gina might need it one day.

She smoked and drank, and decided her time in Auckland was probably up.

*

Also before they left Auckland, Allie and Sonny paid a quick visit to Awhi. She remained distraught to the point that Sonny's sisters, Ruth and Hine, and Hine's three little kids, were staying at the house to keep her company.

'We finally caught up with Polly,' Sonny said.

Awhi, who knew by now the story and background of what had happened to Gina, clapped her hands over her ears. 'Do not speak that she-devil's name in my house.'

Sonny gently pulled his mother's hands away from her head. She was fifty-five but at the moment she looked twenty years older, her eyes sunken with grief and her skin seemingly wrinkled overnight.

'I have to say it, Mum. She says she wasn't paid any money for Gina—'

Awhi interrupted with a rude noise. 'That harlot would sell her own nannie.'

'Stop that, Mum,' Hine said. 'Saying nasty things will only make you feel horrible yourself.'

'She is a harlot,' Awhi said.

Hine and Sonny exchanged a weary glance over their mother's head. The revelation that Polly worked in a brothel had hit Awhi very hard and, along with everything else, was coming out of her as anger.

'Anyway, she says she wasn't paid,' Sonny repeated.

'So why did she give away my Gina?' Awhi demanded. 'She's not some bit of clothing you don't want any more!'

'I'm not sticking up for Polly, but she did give Gina to her father,' Sonny said, deciding not to tell his mother that Polly had said Gina wasn't with James Murdoch.

'She doesn't even know that man *is* Gina's father! Blimmin' thousands of men could be Gina's father. Millions!'

Ruth pointed out, 'If it was millions, Mum, we wouldn't have seen Polly in …' she counted on her fingers '… 1952 at all. She'd have been too busy.'

Awhi looked at her. 'What?'

'It's not funny, Ruth,' Sonny said.

'I know. I'm just saying.'

'And you told her you're going down to bring her back?' Awhi asked.

Sonny nodded.

'And what did she say?'

'She told us not to interfere.'

'Not to interfere? Not to interfere? That witch has no right to give orders about Gina. She's an unfit mother and she's proved that. As far as I'm concerned she'll never be welcome in this house again, even when Gina comes back.' Awhi's mouth formed a grim, straight line, then she said, 'In fact, from now on she's dead to me. I never want to see her or hear about her again.'

*

The road trip to Napier was slow, requiring many stops to prevent the truck from over-heating, and took two days. But then, neither Allie nor Sonny had jobs now and the neighbour was feeding Mr De Valera, so they had the time. They stopped at Putaruru on the first night, making the second day a very long slog, and ate pies and cream buns from bakeries along the way, and talked and talked. Allie talked about the friends she'd lost in the Dunbar and Jones fire and how she couldn't understand why they'd died and she hadn't; Sonny talked (for the first time to Allie) about similar experiences he'd had fighting in South Korea; they talked about how they'd have to hurry up and find jobs when they got home as the money left over from the Indian wasn't going to go far, especially if they had to give it to the Murdochs; and they talked about why on earth Polly had given Gina away.

'I can't believe she did it just for the money, if there actually was any,' Allie said. 'I mean, I know she's a hard nut, but no mother sells their own little girl. She loves Gina.'

'In her own way,' Sonny agreed, squinting into the cracked side mirror. 'Come on, pass if you're going to pass.'

A car tore recklessly past, pulled in front of the truck then slowed down again to forty miles per hour — on a fifty mile per hour open road.

'Arsehole,' Sonny muttered. 'I don't think it was for money, either. I think it was for Gina. Maybe she really does think being rich and all that's better for kids than being with family who love them. Doesn't matter: she shouldn't have done it. She shouldn't have hurt Mum like that, and she shouldn't have ripped Gina away from everything. Poor little thing must be terrified.'

'I know. What time do you think we'll get there?'

'Bloody never, at this rate.'

'Did you believe Polly when she said James Murdoch doesn't have Gina?'

'I don't know. I don't know if I believe anything Polly says any more. But he must be pretty old if he's got grandkids. Would he want to be raising a young child at that age?'

292 Deborah Challinor

'Maybe it's his wife who wanted her. Ana did suggest she's a bit, you know.'

'Batty? I hope not,' Sonny said. 'Have you got the piece of paper Ana gave us with the son's address? And the auntie's? They're both in Napier, aren't they?'

Allie checked. Yes, it was tucked safely in her handbag.

'Maybe we should ask at the son's house first,' Sonny suggested. 'See if he knows anything. We won't have time to go all the way out to this sheep station tonight by the time we get there.'

'Where will we stay?'

'I don't know. We'll find somewhere.'

'It'll need to be somewhere reasonable if we've got Gina.'

Sonny squeezed her hand. 'I know. Don't worry. It'll be all right.'

By the time they arrived in Napier it was past teatime and dark. They drove around with their map looking for Duncan Murdoch's address. Finally they found it, a house on the hill overlooking the township and out to sea, not that they could see the ocean because the night was cloudy. Allie could smell it, though, the salt riding inland on the cool wind. The house looked modern and quite flash, with a well-laid-out garden. They parked on the street and looked at each other.

'Are *you* worried?' Allie asked.

'A bit.'

'Me too.'

Sonny kissed her cheek. 'Come on then.'

It was Allie who knocked on the door. They heard footsteps inside, a light came on in the porch, a blurred figured appeared behind the etched glass door, then a woman opened it. She was maybe in her late thirties, pretty and pleasant-looking with dark hair and a freckled nose.

'Hello?'

'Evening,' Sonny said. 'Is this Duncan Murdoch's house?'

The woman looked worried now. 'Yes, Duncan's my husband. I'm Claire Murdoch.'

'Well, we're sorry to barge in. You don't know us, but my name's Sonny Manaia and this is my wife, Allie. We're looking for a little girl called Gina.'

Claire Murdoch's demeanour changed completely. 'Oh, thank *God* you've come. She's *so* upset. Please, come in.' She stepped aside and ushered them inside, shouting, 'Duncan! Gina's family are here!'

A man appeared, carrying Gina. The moment she saw them she burst into tears and stretched out her arms, crying, 'Allie, Allie! Sonny!'

Allie ran to her and snatched her up, cuddling her close and rocking her and telling her everything would be all right. She noted the little girl was wearing a new flannelette nightie, a new chenille dressing gown and fluffy slippers, and that her hair was clean and brushed and she smelt of soap.

'The poor little thing,' the man said. 'She's been beside herself.' He offered a hand to Sonny. 'I'm Duncan Murdoch.'

Sonny shook. 'Sonny Manaia, Gina's uncle. This is my wife, Allie.'

Allie nodded over Gina's head.

'God, what a mess,' Duncan Murdoch said, sweeping a long fringe back off his brow.

Allie couldn't help looking at his scars. The skin on much of his face was knotted and shiny, one eye was almost closed, his nose was oddly foreshortened, and his lips looked vaguely like small, raw sausages. If she squinted he nearly looked normal, but if she stared blatantly, he didn't. There was also a mass of scarring beneath his chin, and his hands had that same shiny skin on them.

'Burns,' Duncan Murdoch said brusquely. 'I was in the RAF.'

'Sorry for staring.'

Duncan shrugged. 'Everyone does.'

'We're so sorry about your niece,' Claire Murdoch said. 'We had no idea Duncan's mother and father were planning ... what they did. They just turned up with Gina the other day, told us she's James's child, and that we're to raise her as our own. It's absurd.'

'It's damn well absurd, all right,' Duncan said. 'It's my mother's doing, the barmy old woman.'

'She is not barmy, Duncan,' Claire said, 'she's troubled. But we don't want another child. We already have one whom we love very much, and who is *very* upset by all of this. Not that Gina isn't a lovely little girl, she is. But she's not ours.'

Gina reached for Sonny, who took her. 'How's my best Gina-ballerina?'

'OK,' Gina whispered.

'Shall we take you home to Nannie tomorrow?'

Gina nodded, sighed, and rested her head against Sonny's neck.

'What were you told about her?' Sonny asked.

Duncan said, 'That my father met her mother, your sister I suppose, a few years ago and Gina was the result. And that when my father recently discovered this he told my mother, who wanted Gina raised in this family.'

'Why?' Sonny asked.

Claire looked embarrassed, though it was impossible to read Duncan's expression. 'I suppose because they thought they could give her a better life.'

'Than my sister the prostitute could?' Sonny said.

'Something like that, yes,' Duncan agreed. 'Sorry.'

'My mother was raising Gina, not my sister,' Sonny said. 'My mother's a very fine, upstanding woman. She's been shattered by this.'

'Then why did she let Gina go?' Claire asked.

'She didn't,' Sonny said. 'My sister took her without her knowledge and gave her to your in-laws.'

'She didn't exactly *give* her to them,' Duncan said. 'I'm sorry to say it seems that money changed hands.'

Allie blurted, 'How much?'

'I believe something in the order of three thousand pounds.'

Dismayed, Allie glanced at Sonny, saw the terrible hurt in his eyes and almost couldn't bear it. She knew he'd privately been hoping Polly hadn't taken any money, and now he knew without doubt she had. How bloody awful for him.

Sonny blew out his cheeks. 'God. Well, we can't pay it back. We just don't have it.'

'I don't see why you should,' Duncan said. 'That's between my parents and your sister, isn't it? And frankly, if my mother and father have been graceless enough to actually purchase a child, then they deserve to lose their money.'

Allie noted that Duncan and Claire weren't making any unpleasant comments about Polly selling Gina. How kind they were.

A girl appeared then, about ten years old. She hung back behind her father, who drew her forwards, a hand on her shoulder. Her hair was the same bright bronze as his, tied in a long plait down her back, and she had her mother's pretty features.

'This is our daughter, Lorraine,' Duncan said. 'Lorraine, this is Mr and Mrs Manaia, Gina's aunt and uncle. They've come to take her home.'

The girl's face lit up in a smile. 'Tonight?'

'Lorraine,' Claire said, a hint of warning in her voice. 'I'm sorry, but she hasn't adjusted to having another child in the house.'

I'm not surprised, Allie thought. 'It's a bit late tonight. We'll be driving back tomorrow, though.'

'Well, we'd better be off,' Sonny said. 'Thanks very much for being so understanding.'

'Where are you staying?' Claire asked.

'Don't know yet. We only just got into town.'

'Look, why don't you stay here?' Duncan suggested. 'You can have the room Gina's sleeping in. It'll be less disruptive for her, and you can get away first thing in the morning.'

Allie felt a little prickle of unease. What if it was a trick? What if James and Lucy Murdoch turned up later tonight or in the morning? What if Duncan Murdoch got in touch with a lawyer or something?

'It's not a trick,' Claire said.

Allie blinked at her, dismayed that her thoughts were so transparent.

'We feel awful this has happened,' Claire went on. 'She was foisted on us, lovely little thing that she is, just to fulfil some need that my mother-in-law has, and it's been a disaster. She's been desperately unhappy and we couldn't even take her back to Auckland because Duncan's parents wouldn't tell us where she lives, and Gina doesn't know her address.'

'She did tell us Kitty Street, but we couldn't find that on a street map,' Duncan said. 'My Uncle Thomas is a lawyer, well, he's retired now, and he was going to try and track down where she'd come from if we couldn't force it out of my parents, but obviously we don't need to do that now.'

Claire lowered her voice to a whisper, 'So as you can see we really don't want her,' then raised it again, 'but I mean that in the nicest possible way. God, this is so awkward. Duncan, your *bloody* parents!'

'Are Gran and Grandpa in trouble?' Lorraine asked.

'They most certainly are,' Duncan said.

'So you're welcome to stay, if you'd like to,' Claire said.

Allie and Sonny exchanged a glance. They were both exhausted from tension and the very long drive, and Gina had fallen asleep in Sonny's arms.

'Thank you,' Allie said.

*

Everyone awoke early in the Murdoch household. Duncan was due at work, Lorraine was off to school, and the Manaias had to hit the road. After a huge breakfast, Sonny loaded their overnight things into the truck along with a bag of clothing and bits and pieces Claire had bought for Gina. Allie offered to pay for them but

Claire waved her off, saying she'd enjoyed shopping for a little girl again. Then Sonny put Gina on the seat between himself and Allie, turned the key and was rewarded with an ominously flat 'click'.

'Shit. The battery's gone flat.'

Sonny and Allie both got out again. The Murdochs, waiting to wave goodbye, came over.

'Trouble?' Duncan asked.

'Flat battery,' Sonny said.

'You hop in, we'll push.'

While Allie, Claire and Duncan went to the back of the truck, Sonny turned the ignition on, pulled out the choke, put the gearstick into second, his foot on the clutch and yelled, 'OK, ready!'

At first a snail could have passed them but then they picked up speed, the truck crested the top of the hill and sailed down, Sonny let out the clutch, the truck lurched (making Gina laugh), the engine rotated and fired, Sonny pushed the clutch back in and revved the accelerator like mad. When the engine was running more or less smoothly he turned around and drove back up the hill to collect Allie.

'Thanks, mate, thanks, Claire,' he said to the Murdochs. 'Come and see us if you're ever in Auckland.'

'Ditto next time you're back this way,' Duncan said.

Then Sonny waved out the window and they roared off in a cloud of grey smoke.

*

Awhi wept and wept when Sonny carried Gina into the kitchen at Kitemoana Street, falling on the child, cuddling her and covering her with kisses.

'Is she all right?' she wailed. 'Have they hurt her?'

'She's fine, Mum. They were nice people,' Sonny said.

But Awhi couldn't, or wouldn't, hear him, taking off Gina's cardigan and removing her dress.

'Mum, stop that. She was very well treated. They were really decent.'

'People who buy babies are never decent!'

Sonny took Gina off his mother, making the little girl cry, and gave her to Allie to dress again.

'Look, Mum, settle down. You're upsetting her. Just calm down and listen. And you two—' this to Hine and Ruth '—stop standing there gawking like the two ugly sisters. Put the kettle on.'

'No need to be rude!' Ruth said.

'She wasn't with James and Lucy Murdoch; she was with their son, Duncan, and his wife and daughter. They looked after her really well and bought her new clothes and fed her properly and everything. They didn't do anything wrong at all.'

Awhi blew her nose loudly. 'Except for stealing her.'

'They had nothing to do with that. That was Duncan's mother and father. Apparently his mother's a bit cracked.'

'Like your sister.'

Sonny sighed. 'Yes, like Polly.'

'Your sister's a blimmin' *lunatic*. She's *evil*.'

'Stop saying that, Mum,' Ruth said, fetching cups and saucers while Hine set the teapot on the table.

Gina had stopped crying now and was wriggling to be put down.

'Give her back to me,' Awhi demanded.

'Only if you stop inspecting her,' Sonny said. 'She's fine.'

Allie put Gina down and she immediately pulled on her trouser leg. 'Outside! Swings!'

'No, love, it's raining.'

So Gina climbed onto Awhi's lap and this time her nannie just cuddled her.

'So why did the son have her if the old people took her?' Hine asked.

'Apparently they wanted her raised in the family because James Murdoch is her father, but I'm guessing they're a bit old and that's why they gave her to Duncan,' Sonny said. 'At least, James Murdoch's *supposed* to be her father.'

'I always wondered who her father was,' Ruth said.

Hine said, 'What do you mean, *supposed* to be?'

'Well, she didn't look anything like Duncan Murdoch.'

Allie stared at her husband. He must be *very* tired. 'Sonny, he was completely covered in scars. How could you tell what he looked like?'

'No, I mean his hair and the colour of his skin where he hadn't been burnt. And the shape of his head. And Lorraine as well. Gina's nothing like them.'

'But she'd be a mix of Polly and a Pakeha man, so, well ... Oh, I don't know.'

'But Gina's dark,' Sonny said flatly. 'I don't see much Pakeha in her at all.'

Nobody said anything for a minute, then Gina let out a whistly snore.

'She's tired out,' Awhi said, standing carefully to avoid waking the little girl. 'I'm putting her to bed.' At the doorway she turned and said quietly, 'Thank you. Thank you for bringing her back to me.'

Allie and Sonny headed for home.

On the way Sonny said, 'Bugger it, I'm going to tell Polly we brought Gina back.'

They detoured to Ligaro Place, parked the truck and knocked on the door. It was answered by a girl wearing black trousers and a baggy black jumper.

Sonny asked, 'Is Polly in?'

'Polly's gone.'

'What do you mean?'

'Moved out, a few days ago.'

'For good?'

'I suppose. All her stuff's gone.'

'D'you know where she went?'

The girl shrugged. 'Who knows, with Polly?'

Part Three

Chapter Seventeen

August 1956

Jack Leonard's gratitude towards Ana for bringing him home from the hospital hadn't lasted long. It couldn't, because he was unable to remember he'd even been there. In fact, he didn't know where home was, either. When he'd woken after his long sleep the day she'd brought him back, Ana had asked, 'Do you know where you are?' and he'd replied, 'No. Do you know where *you* are?' So he was back to his normal, shitty self. Anna had sighed but her conscience felt eased. At least at home he'd be fed well and kept relatively clean. She did wish she had a supply of the adult nappies that nice Sister Simpson had talked about, but perhaps they'd been a tall story anyway, as Jack certainly hadn't been wearing them the day she'd brought him home. Anyhow, she'd worked out how to make them herself, out of sanitary napkins wrapped in flannels pinned into his underpants. As long as she could get the pants on him without him noticing the pads he was fine. If he spotted them, though, he fiddled and fiddled until the pins popped open and poked him somewhere painful. They weren't perfect but they certainly helped contain the mess.

When David had come home in the weekend she thought he might have been cross at what she'd done, but he wasn't. Instead, after tea on the Friday night, he'd sat the whole family down at the kitchen table — except for Jack, who was walking up and down the hall — and said, 'Well, what are we going to do?'

'What we were doing before, I suppose,' Ana had replied.

And David had said, 'No, that isn't fair on anyone. I've been thinking. I'm getting a bit fed up watching blokes shear when I can't do it myself.'

Ana had been quite shocked. It was the first time she'd ever heard him speak negatively about his handicap. The kids had been taken aback too; she could tell by the looks on their faces.

'So I think I might ask the board if they can give me a job here in Auckland. A normal nine to five spot, where I come home at the end of every day.'

The kids had all started jumping up and down and cheering. Ana had thought she might start to cry. In the hallway Jack plodded up and down, up and down.

'Wait on, wait on,' David had said, laughing and raising his hand. 'It'll probably mean less money. Can we live with that?'

'We can sell our bikes,' Rowie had suggested. 'They might be worth something.'

Jo had said, 'I'm not selling mine.'

That had made Ana want to laugh.

Then David had said to her, 'And I can be home to help with Jack. Would that be a good idea?'

Ana had thought that would be a bloody good idea, and so it had proved. Jack no longer recognised his son, but he did appear to understand that David was bigger than he was, and these days stronger despite having only one arm, and as a result his aggressive behaviour was easier to manage. Now, when Sid from next door came over, it was usually for a cup of tea, a smoke and a natter, though he still came in handy when David was at work.

The children were much happier too, knowing they only had to help babysit their grandfather for a few hours until their father came home. As a result their fear of him had diminished a little and the house was happier all round. True, money was tight as David did have to accept a significant pay cut to take a position at the Wool Board's offices in town (and he hadn't said so outright but Ana suspected he really wasn't happy with the job), but the compensations of having him home every night far outweighed the inconvenience of always having to buy the discounted products at the grocer. Also, she still wasn't sure what to do with Jack when the knitting circle's wool arrived, but she'd worry about that when the time came.

But still, Ana wondered how long they'd be able to care for Jack. On one of her visits to the hospital Sister Simpson had told her, very kindly, that in the not too distant future Jack would become bedridden, forget how to eat and probably die of pneumonia or blood clots. He'd definitely have to go back to the hospital if that happened. But surely, if it did, he'd be completely off with the fairies anyway and wouldn't know anything about it? She hadn't mentioned Sister Simpson's comments to David, but it was obvious to everyone that Jack was going downhill. Perhaps the only person who didn't know it was Jack himself.

*

But Jack does know. In a place deep in his brain where small clusters of cells still now and then function in an orderly fashion, he knows. He can never articulate the fact, but, in occasional flashes of perception that come like distant lightning, he knows that something terrible has gone wrong with his mind, and that his body is failing too.

It's a shock, this knowledge, and it frightens him and disturbs his happy existence on the farm where he belongs with his horses and his dogs and his beloved wife, Mary. People he doesn't know intrude and demand things of him, and things aren't where they should be and the world is strange, and he just wants to be left alone to bring the sheep down and muck out the horses. But sometimes his mind plays tricks and he can't trust it, and his arms and legs and insides won't do what he tells them, and none

of that's any use to a man who works on the land. He's like a
good dog too injured to work any more, and you don't let them
suffer. You put them down.

So one day he climbs a fence and starts walking. He crosses
a stretch of grass then randomly follows some streets until he
comes out onto a much bigger area where there are no houses.
The grass there is nice on his feet, which are getting sore because
he's come out in just his socks. Looking down across a long
grassy bit he sees the sea at the far end. It looks grey, like silver
that needs a polish, and there're waves farther out. He's very, very
tired now but he sets off again, not stopping when he reaches a
road. Something makes a loud honking noise but he keeps going.

The sand on the beach slips and squeaks beneath his feet and
there are little rocks everywhere. It's hard to walk on them and
he stumbles. At the water's edge he takes off his ragged socks
and leaves them on the wet sand.

Then he wades into the cold, winter water and strikes out for
the golden hills.

*

All the Apanuis and Irwins came to Jack's funeral, including little
Vincent, now eight weeks old and wrapped tightly in a blanket.
It was cold out today. Kura and Wiki arrived at the church in
their black tangi clothes with greenery tucked into their hats,
their men suited and hatted, and the younger family members in
their Sunday best.

Ana was delighted to see them and there was quite a bit of
crying in memory of Jack, and for Hawke's Bay, which they all
missed.

Colleen, Sid and Pauline Roberts had also come, as had Allie
Manaia, who apologised for Sonny's absence — apparently he'd
just started a new job. A good handful of David's friends and
colleagues had come from the Wool Board too, which was nice,
and, to Ana's surprise, Sister Shirley Simpson was also here.

As Ana sat in the church looking at Jack's coffin, not really listening to the minister drone through the service, she wondered, as she had since they'd learnt Jack had died, whether it was her fault. If she hadn't brought him home from the hospital, if she hadn't been in the washhouse rinsing his shitty pyjama trousers, if she'd bloody well tied him to the kitchen table, would he still be alive? David hadn't blamed her and, knowing him as she did, she suspected he never would. Nobody at all was blaming her. She almost wished they would. And was it awful of her to feel, beneath her genuine sadness and guilt, an element of relief? Yes, she and her family had been released from their burden, but so had Jack. His life had ended horribly, not in the waters of Okahu Bay, a death she fervently hoped had been quick, but in a long, drawn-out shambles of confusion, fear and indignity. It had been so cruel and undeserved, especially for a man who had been so competent and self-contained and respected for most of his life.

Thank God my parents are still fit, she thought as she opened a hymnal to 'The Lord Is My Shepherd' and pretended to sing. Her father was in his mid-seventies and her mother ten years younger, but her father was still belting around Kenmore on his artificial leg, as fit and as hale as a man in his fifties. He wasn't, though, she reminded herself, and that worried her. Her parents weren't here today because it was lambing time, and she missed them both and hadn't seen them in ages, and ... She shut her mouth. Why didn't they just go home? Suddenly excited she glanced at David sitting beside her but he was frowning and staring down at his hymnal not even bothering to pretend to sing.

Then she remembered the awful argument they'd had after Jack messed up the lease on the farm and they knew they'd lost it, and the excitement faded a little. She'd wanted to ask her father to hire David at Kenmore, but David wouldn't let her because he'd been so embarrassed by their predicament. He'd thought it would be charity and had gone mad at her for wanting to interfere, and accused her of not believing he could provide for his family, which hadn't been true at all. She'd only been trying to help. David was a damn good sheep farmer and her father would have been pleased to have him on the station, and had said so on several occasions, but no, David got on his high horse and stayed on it. And then he'd been offered the job with the Wool Board and they'd all had to uproot themselves and come to Auckland.

But he was stuck pushing papers around in an office now, so would he still feel the same way about working at Kenmore? Probably. Ana sighed. There were the kids to think about too. They'd made so many friends at school, which they loved, and along the street. Would it be fair to return them to the backblocks of Hawke's Bay and correspondence school and a limited social life? Perhaps she'd leave it for a while until everything settled down, and then raise the subject. Things would be different now, anyway, with Jack gone.

She realised everyone was rising, and quickly stood. It wasn't that she didn't care about Jack's funeral service, but the minister had never met him and was churning out the usual trite remarks, and as far as she was concerned the man who'd drowned in Okahu Bay wasn't the Jack she'd known. That man had left them some time ago and she'd been grieving ever since. This bit was just a formality.

As Jack's coffin was carried from the church, the Apanui and Irwin men, young and not so young, performed a noisy and rousing haka, which made David blot his eyes with a handkerchief. Ana was extremely proud of her relatives, and proud of Jack for eliciting such an honour.

While David was shaking hands with various folk, Ana caught up with Sister Simpson. 'Hello. I believe you have a new surname?'

'Yes, I'm Mrs Hunt now.'

'Well, congratulations, and thank you very much for coming. Jack would have appreciated you being here. I think he liked you.'

Shirley Hunt laughed. 'Oh, I don't know if Jack liked anyone, but I quite liked him. He was a character. I suspect he was a fine man before he fell ill.'

'He was. He really was. We'll miss—' Ana stopped, flustered. 'Well, we miss the old Jack.'

'I expect you do. He's one I certainly miss from the mental hospital. I'm working at Middlemore now.'

'Oh. I was given the impression you'd stopped work,' Ana said.

'Only at the mental hospital. I hated it there. It was an awful place.'

'It was, wasn't it?'

Shirley hesitated, then asked, 'I read in the paper that Jack drowned. May I ask, do you think he did it deliberately?'

'Do *you* think he did?'

'Well, I didn't look after him for long, but I wouldn't have thought he'd be capable of it. I wouldn't have thought he'd have known how ill he was, to want to, you know, put an end to it. It's so hard to tell.'

'So he might just have got it into his head to go for a swim, and got into difficulties?' Ana asked.

'Honestly, Mrs Leonard, I really don't know.'

'I was only in the washhouse for a few minutes. I don't even know if he wandered out the front gate or hopped over the fence or ...' Ana tailed off. 'I should have been watching him.'

Shirley put a hand on Ana's arm. 'You can't watch them all the time. You just can't. We never could at the hospital and that was our job.'

'But still—'

'But still nothing. You did your best. You cared for him and you cared about him. You couldn't have done more than that. And now it's finished and you and your family have lives to get on with.'

Ana was relieved. And impressed. 'How can you be so wise at your age?'

'I'm not wise,' Shirley said. 'I'm hard, and that's why I had to leave the mental hospital.'

Ana didn't know what to say.

'Anyway, I must go or I'll be late for work,' Shirley went on. 'Nice to see you again, Mrs Leonard.'

'Yes, you too. Thanks for coming.'

Shirley waved as she walked off.

'Who's that?' Kura asked, settling a hand on Ana's shoulder.

'One of Jack's nurses from the hospital. She's lovely. Works at Middlemore now.'

Wiki drifted over, and soon a group of women had congregated. Outside the church Jack's coffin lay in the back of the hearse. Ana wondered what the undertaker was waiting for. Jack was bound for the crematorium, a final destination many, she knew, would think unconventional, but if they did decide to go back to Hawke's Bay they wanted to be able to take Jack's remains with them. It was, they were sure, where he'd rather be.

The men had also gathered in a group, smoking or standing round with their hands in their pockets. Ana could do with a rare cigarette herself but none of the other women were smoking; nice women just didn't, not out in public. She also spotted one of Kura's younger boys surreptitiously sticking his used chewing gum to the tyre of the hearse, the little bugger, and marched over.

'You get that off right now, Sam Apanui.'

He looked at her, his eyes innocently big. 'It tastes yuck. I didn't know where else to put it.'

'I don't care. Get it off.'

Reluctantly, Sam gouged the gum out of the tyre's treads and stuck it in his pocket. Giving him a look, Ana returned to the women.

Kura said, 'Oh, I forgot to say, Joshua says our wool's arrived and we have to hurry up and collect it. And it's a half-bale. That what you ordered?'

Ana nodded. A full bale of wool would be far more than they needed.

She, Kura, Allie and Wiki looked at one another.

'Hell,' Allie said. 'I'd better learn to drive, then.'

*

Sonny wasn't sure if he liked his new job, but the money was much better than his wage had been at Smith and Caughey, so he was sticking with it.

He tried not to look down. That was the worst part. If he didn't look down he was OK. He supposed he'd get used to it but for now he'd focus on keeping his head up and looking out across the harbour or over at the city, or at what he was supposed to be doing, which was driving rivets into steel.

He was working on the northern anchorage at Northcote Point of the new bridge across Waitemata Harbour, and wasn't really that high up, but he'd never been that good with heights, though he'd lied and said he was when he'd applied for the job because he'd heard the money was great. It was bloody cold and windy too: his ears had nearly frozen off during the first few days so he'd bought himself one of those hats with the flaps like the ones they'd worn in South Korea. He wasn't a steelworker either, but he had an army mate on site who'd vouched for him, and the work wasn't that complicated, just physically demanding, so he was doing all right. And the job would go for years as the bridge wouldn't be finished till 1959, though he wasn't sure what would happen when they got right up and out over the water. He hoped he might have conquered his fear of heights by then.

So apart from having a job that made him nearly shit his pants every time he looked down, things were good. The money was coming in again, and plenty of it, and Allie seemed a lot better since she'd chucked her job at Smith and Caughey. Even her bad dreams seemed to be going away — she'd only had two lately, two which had woken her up, anyway. She hadn't found another job, except for this knitting circle thing she was doing, which wasn't really a job, but that didn't matter much at the

moment. Gina appeared to have forgotten all about her trip to
Napier, which, Sonny thought, was an indication that nothing
awful had happened to her there except homesickness.

He and Allie had received a letter from Duncan and Claire
Murdoch the other day, which he'd thought was very nice of
them. It had said:

Dear Allie and Sonny,
We hope your journey home went well and that Gina is
happily settled back with her grandmother. This is just
a note to let you know what happened after you left. As
you can imagine, my mother and father were somewhat
surprised to learn Gina had gone back to Auckland.
Actually, I don't think my father was too upset as I
suspect he'd always been a little uncomfortable with the
idea of adding Gina to our family, and also separating
her from her mother (though I'm surmising here), but my
mother certainly was. She demanded that my father and
I come to Auckland to retrieve Gina, but obviously we
said no.

Anyway, regarding the matter of the money paid to
your sister, I think what I said to you when you were
in Napier stands. My parents have been fools and I can
more or less guarantee they won't be pursuing your sister
for repayment, to avoid the affair being made public.
My father could probably bear the embarrassment as,
unfortunately, he's no stranger to shame, but my mother
certainly couldn't, not now at her age.

So I think we can consider the whole business over
and done with. We're very sorry it happened in the first
place, and we hope that everything is back to normal at
your end. It was very nice to meet you, Allie and Sonny,
and thank you for your understanding and patience.

Kind regards,
Duncan and Claire Murdoch

So that was that. He couldn't tell Polly because nobody knew where she was. He thought she was probably wise not to show her face for quite a while. He didn't even know if she knew Gina was back in Auckland. Awhi still wouldn't speak her name.

And there he was, travelling to and from the north shore every day on the Devonport ferry for work, with a tram ride from Newmarket to the wharf both ways as well, so that by the time he got home he was so knackered he could hardly eat his tea and collapse on the sofa, but it was worth it. Another five or six months of this and he'd be able to buy another motorcycle. And if Allie did find a job they really would be quids in.

He hammered in another rivet, his feet hooked under a steel girder to keep him balanced as he bashed the tail end. There were two more jobs coming up in his crew and he thought young Johnny Apanui might be good for one of them. Then he wouldn't have to work at the Destructor any longer and go round smelling like a rubbish bin. He'd have a talk to him at some stage.

*

Donna Roberts was very happy. Her nurse training was going well and she'd put the nightmare of Dr Slippery Sullivan behind her. There had been no more boyfriends since and she hadn't even looked at a man in a white coat unless he'd been giving instructions at the hospital. Of Robert Sullivan himself there'd been no sign, and for that she'd been grateful. Her friendships with Helen and Barbara had become stronger, and even grumpy old Joan had turned out to be not such a bad old stick. She knew Donna had had a failed love affair (mortifyingly, it seemed that everyone on Donna's floor of the nursing home knew), but instead of saying I told you so, Joan had said, 'Bad luck, old thing. Why don't you join a club? I met my fellow at badminton.' Which had been kind of her, Donna thought, but she was buggered if she was going to leap around playing badminton just to meet a bloke.

When she looked back on everything that had happened with Robert, she wondered what on earth had got into her. She'd run around after him, made herself available for him, had done stupid things just to please him, and put up with all sorts of pompous rubbish from him. He'd been an arrogant, self-serving big-noter, and she'd thought he was the cat's meow! When she told Helen and Barbara some of the things he'd said and done, they'd laughed and laughed, and so had she.

The only thing she didn't talk much about was the abortion. That was too personal. She was glad she'd had it, and *so* grateful to her mother and father for helping her and not chastising her for it, but it was something she wouldn't ever want to have to do again. And the way to avoid that was to not get involved with men. Simple.

The abortion had also raised another small dilemma for her. She'd been planning on specialising in paediatrics but really, how could she do that now, after she'd been directly responsible for aborting her own child? To care for babies and children after having taken such deliberate measures to destroy her own baby was surely the height of hypocrisy. So now she thought she might focus on general nursing when she'd finished her initial training, or perhaps look at specialising as a theatre nurse. With general you got a bit of most things anyway.

So, yes, she was happy. She'd learnt a valuable lesson and she liked to think — hoped — she was a lot smarter now. She went out with her girlfriends for coffee and sometimes a meal, they had midnight feasts at the nurses' home, and now and then they went to the pictures, but that was it for her social life and she was content with that. She went home more to see her parents and Pauline, and to visit Allie and Sonny. Earlier in the year, when she'd been busy going out with Robert, she'd hardly seen them at all. Perhaps if she had, she might not have got into such trouble. Someone, Allie perhaps, or more likely Pauline, who always called a spade a spade, might have told her what a twerp

Robert really was and that she was making a fool of herself. But would she have listened? Probably not.

She was making up for it now though, and she'd realised, to her dismay, that by not spending time with her family she'd been cheating them and, even worse, hurting them. She was the first Roberts to go on to any sort of education beyond high school and they were so proud of her, her parents in particular, and she'd been so full of herself she hadn't even bothered to share any of it with them. She did now, though, sometimes too much, especially at the tea table, according to her mother, who said things like, 'Thank you, dear, I don't think we need to know what an anal fistula is.'

Tonight she was telling them about a young mother and child.

'I was on the children's ward today changing a baby's nappy, and I said to the mother, "I know you, don't I?" And it turned out she had him at the Bethany home at Grey Lynn, where I did work experience last year.'

'An unmarried mother?' Colleen asked, spearing a carrot.

'They all are at Bethany, Mum. I quite liked her. Anyway, the baby's really sick and had to be brought up from Waikato Hospital. He sleeps too much, has fits, vomits for no apparent reason and has trouble breathing. And there're bruises all over him. Poor little thing. He's only eight months old.'

'What's wrong with him?' Pauline asked.

'The doctors aren't completely sure,' Donna said, 'but the police came and talked to the mother today.'

Pauline said, 'Talked to her about what?'

'Whether she had anything to do with the state he's in, I suppose.'

'You mean *she* belted him?'

'It does happen, you know,' Colleen said. 'On occasion I could easily have thumped the daylights out of you girls when you were little. You in particular, Pauline. You just never settled.'

'You didn't, though,' Sid said. 'You yelled at me instead.'

Colleen nodded. 'That's right, I did too.'

'So did the police arrest her?' Pauline asked.

'No, they just went away again.'

'Do you think she hit him?' Colleen asked.

Donna said, 'I don't know. I hope not. But I remember before the baby was born the mother was planning on putting it up for adoption, but changed her mind after she had him. Matron was quite angry about it and said she'd be sorry, and something about heaping one misery on top of another.'

'What's that supposed to mean?' Pauline asked.

'I don't know. Anyway she took the baby home with her. She was only about sixteen.'

'Maybe the first misery was getting in trouble and the second one was keeping the baby,' Pauline suggested.

'Or she might have been, you know …' Sid waved his fork vaguely '… got at.'

Donna could see her dad didn't want to say 'raped'.

'This is a fun conversation, isn't it?' Pauline said.

'No, it is not,' Colleen said and got up from the table. 'Does anyone want more potatoes? There's plenty left.'

Pauline announced, 'If I had a baby I wouldn't belt it.'

From the bench Colleen said, 'If you had a baby, young lady, you'd have a husband to help you with it. If you're going to keep a child, then you make damn sure you hold on to its father too.'

Donna scoffed, 'Husbands don't help with babies. Did Dad?'

'I'll have you know I changed Allie's nappy,' Sid declared.

'Once,' Colleen said, 'and you nearly threw up from the smell and had to go to the pub afterwards to recover.' She paused. 'Though I admit you did spend a lot of time playing with them and you didn't mind pushing them in the pram or the pushchair. A lot of husbands wouldn't even do that back then. They won't do it now.'

Pauline asked, 'So what will happen to the sick baby?'

'I don't know,' Donna said. 'He's too ill to go home.'

'Well, what will happen to the mother?'

'I don't know that, either.'

Chapter Eighteen

September 1956

After a fair bit of stalling, gear-graunching, bunny-hopping and embarrassed giggling, Allie managed to drive the truck, with Kura in the passenger seat, to the railway station down near the docks — unfortunately right in the middle of town — and convince some nice railway workers to load their half-bale of wool onto the back. They took it to Kura's, where they rolled it off and around to the back of the house. And lucky it *wasn't* a full bale too, the women realised when they cut the stitching holding the jute closed, as wool went everywhere. Fortunately, since they'd bought it from a storage facility, it had already been scoured, so it wasn't stinky and full of lanolin and dirt and sheep shit, and didn't need washing.

Then came the dyeing, which Ana decided to do before the spinning. The wool had washed out to a nice pale cream, so they chose to leave some of it undyed, and picked dyes for the remainder — light blue, pale pink, lemon and mint. Ana showed the others how to form the wool into rovings, or long tufts, then, when that was done, she got everything ready at Kura's house. They'd be doing quite big batches so they bought an old copper for three pounds from a second-hand dealer and set it up over a fire pit in Kura's backyard. To save money, they hauled some of the abandoned lumber over from Wiki's place and chopped it up for firewood. Ana had never dyed such a lot of wool at once and hoped she was getting the quantities right, holding her breath as she added the dye dissolved in water to the steaming copper and then, one at a time, the dampened rovings.

Gingerly she began to stir with a long wooden dowel.

'Well, the stick's going blue,' Allie said.

'So's the wool, see?' Kura noted. 'Can I have a stir?'

Ana handed her the dowel. 'Gently, though, or it'll get tangled up.'

Kura stirred with utmost concentration while Ana used a pair of fire tongs to pull a couple of pieces of wood off the fire. If it got too hot and the water boiled, the wool would turn to felt.

The four women stood around the copper, staring into its depths, mesmerised.

Wiki laughed. 'We're like those witches in that play. What's it called?'

'*Macbeth*?' Allie said.

A voice came over the fence. 'Hoi! What have you got in that pot?'

Wiki muttered, 'Your nosy neighbour again.'

Kura called out, 'The last person who asked us that.'

Snorting with muffled laughter, the women elbowed one another.

There were no further comments from the neighbour.

After fifteen minutes Ana added a decent measure of white vinegar to 'set' the dye. Then, when the water was almost clear, they lifted the dripping rovings — now an attractive pale shade of blue — out of the copper and laid them on sheets provided by Ana (Jack's and a bit stained), and rolled them up to get most of the water out. It looked like it might rain, which was annoying, so they hung the newly coloured wool all around Kura's front room and along the hallway walls to dry.

A couple of days later, David drove Ana over to collect the wool, which they laid carefully in the boot of the car. Kura plied David with cake and in return he took all the Apanui offspring for a ride in the Chevrolet, which they loved. When they got back, the Irwin kids were lined up on the footpath, so off he went again.

On the way home he said to Ana, 'That house of Kura and Joshua's is disgusting. Can't they find anything better?'

'No, and I told you why. And Wiki and Henare's place is just as bad. I've been over there.'

'How bloody depressing. They're hard up at the moment too, aren't they?'

'They are while Wiki and Kura aren't working.'

'What if we gave them a bit of money?'

'Well, that would be nice,' Ana said, 'but have we got any spare?'

David thought for a moment. 'Not really.'

'And I don't think Joshua and Henare would be happy about it. Or Kura and Wiki for that matter. They'd see it as charity.'

'But it wouldn't be. They're your relatives. Family helping family isn't charity.'

Ana looked at David sideways. 'Do you mean like you working at Kenmore wouldn't be charity, it'd just be family helping us out?'

David stared straight ahead. 'That's different and you know it.'

'How is it different?'

'I'm used to being my own man. I ran that farm of my father's more or less by myself. I couldn't work for anyone else.'

Ana could see that the moment the words were out of his mouth he knew he'd said something idiotic. Should she say it, or leave him his dignity?

'But you *are* working for someone else.'

Red in the face now, David said, 'Yes, and I got that job myself. You didn't have to go crawling to your father begging for it.'

'My father would *love* to have you at Kenmore, David. He's said it often enough.'

'Not to me, he hasn't.'

Ana thought, God, you stubborn bastard. But she didn't want to argue and there was only one way to stop it.

'No, maybe not. Look, I'm sorry I brought it up. It wasn't where I was heading with the conversation at all.'

David was silent for several ill-humoured minutes, then he said, 'Well, where were you heading?'

'I was going to say I really hope the knitting business works out, because then they'll have something they'll have worked for and built up themselves. They, or rather *we*, will be self-employed. Surely that'll be better than working for someone else in a horrible factory somewhere.'

'You'll have to make a fair bit of money to pay a reasonable wage to all four of you. It's no good if you keep on doing it for nothing. It's just a hobby then and you'll still be in the same boat as when you started, financially.'

'I know that.'

'So how are you going to make sure you make money?'

'Well, we'll have to knit something first, won't we,' Ana said, 'and see who wants to buy it? Or rather, sell it.'

*

It was lunchtime and Marian was on her break. Peggy waved as Pauline Roberts wandered towards the Elizabeth Arden counter — come for one of her occasional chats, probably.

'Hi,' Pauline said. 'How's things?'

'Good. And yourself?'

'OK. How's the new girl?' Pauline asked.

Peggy said, 'Thick as two short planks, but she's a sweetie.'

'Allie says you're welcome to visit any time.'

'That's nice of her. I really should get off my arse and do that. No baby news yet?' Peggy knew how desperate Allie was to have another baby. She'd talked about it often enough.

'Not as far as I know,' Pauline said, 'and I expect she'd have told me.'

'She'd have told everyone. What about the job hunting?'

'No job either, but it doesn't really matter now Sonny's working on the bridge. He's making *tons* of money.'

Peggy's pencilled eyebrows went up. 'Tons? Maybe I should get a job doing that.'

'Johnny's going to. He's seeing the boss next week. Sonny's fixed it for him. Allie is doing something, though.'

'What's that?'

'She's joined a knitting circle.'

Peggy said, 'Crikey, that sounds exciting.'

'They're going to knit stuff to sell and have a proper business and all that.'

'Really?' Peggy took a good, hard look at Pauline. 'How are things going with Johnny?'

'Good. We're still going strong. Going to the MCC most weekends and all that. It's great. He's lovely.'

'Well, you be careful.'

'I'm always careful.'

Peggy thought, hmm. 'Are you well?'

'Yeah, why?'

'You look tired.' Peggy reached into a drawer and grabbed a couple of lipsticks and eyeshadows. 'These are discontinued shades. Do you want them? There's nothing wrong with them.'

'Yes, please. Thanks!'

'The plum might be a bit dark for you, but the two lighter shades will work and so will the eyeshadows. Just don't put them on with a trowel, like I do. You're too young and pretty for that.'

'Thanks, Peggy. Well, better go. Got to get some smokes before I go back to work.'

'Bye, then. Say hi to your sister. Tell her to eat lots of seaweed. It's supposed to increase fertility.'

'Seaweed?'

Peggy shrugged. 'I read it in a magazine somewhere.'

'I will. Bye.'

As Pauline walked off, Peggy thought, Poor Allie. First Donna accidentally gets pregnant, which Allie had told her all about, and now — maybe her little sister too?

*

Awhi and Gina went out to the letterbox, which they did together every day. Sometimes there was something interesting and sometimes there wasn't. Once, Gina had reached in and felt around and a huge big spider had come out sitting on an envelope, and she'd run shrieking and laughing down the path. But usually there were just bills, or, more often, nothing at all.

But today there was a letter. Awhi looked at the post mark: Sydney. She had a few relatives living in Sydney, and some in Melbourne and Brisbane, but they never wrote to her.

They took the letter inside and Awhi sat at the kitchen table to open it. When she saw the handwriting she almost threw it straight in the bin, but she couldn't help herself; she had to read it.

> *Dear Mum,*
> *I know you probably don't want to read this, but I'm writing to say I'm sorry for taking Gina off you. I did it for her. It's in her best interests.*
> *I don't want her to grow up like I did. She deserves everything she can get.*
> *I'm happy where I am. I've got a job and I'm making good money.*
> *Your daughter,*
> *Polly*

There was no date, and no address.

'Who wrote it, Nan?' Gina asked.

'No one, love,' Awhi said, and put the letter in the bin. The stupid girl didn't even know Sonny had gone and rescued Gina and brought her back home.

But later that day Awhi dug though the rubbish and found

From the Ashes 323

the letter, brushed off the potato peelings, and put it in the top drawer of her dressing table.

*

Ana sat at her spinning wheel in her front room, wondering how much longer she'd be able to keep going. She'd been spinning more or less constantly for six days, and her left wrist was so sore from twisting the wool she couldn't even lift the kettle or her pots. But most of the wool was now yarn and she was going to finish it if it killed her. David said she had shearers' wrist, something shearers got after using hand clippers for days on end, but she didn't think so. She wasn't shearing sheep, for a start. She just needed a rest. But the yarn was lovely — nice and soft and a beautiful colour. She'd leave it as single ply as it was for delicate, quality garments, but when — if — they started to make cardigans and jumpers for adults, and if they still couldn't afford to buy wool, she'd spin at least double ply.

And while she was doing this, she knew Kura and Wiki were beavering away, knitting dear little baby outfits with the undyed wool, which she'd already spun.

She heard a knock at the back door, started to rise, then, 'It's only me, Colleen!'

'Come in, I'm in the front room!'

Colleen appeared. 'Good Lord, spinning. You're clever. I can knit but I have to say spinning's beyond me.'

'My mother taught me,' Ana explained.

'Is this for that knitting circle Allie's been talking about?'

Ana said yes. 'She's a clever girl, your Allie. I think she might have quite a good head for business.'

Colleen looked vaguely surprised. 'Really? We've never seen her use it.'

'She's had a lot of experience in the retail trade. Some of that's bound to rub off, don't you think?'

'Maybe. To us she's always just been a shop girl.'

'The same way you just heat up sausage rolls?'

'No,' Colleen said rather sharply. 'I balance the till at the end of every day and I'm in charge of ordering inventory twice a week.'

'Sorry, Colleen, I didn't mean to be rude. But do you see my point?'

'Well, yes, I suppose I do. I'm not sure how she's going to use this business head knitting babies' booties, though.'

'She might not end up knitting. She might liaise between the company and our markets.'

'Oh yes?'

Ana didn't think she sounded convinced.

'Well, at least it's keeping her occupied,' Colleen added. 'Would you like me to put the kettle on? You look like you could do with a cup of tea.'

'Oh, I'd love one. Thanks, Colleen.'

'David still at work?' Colleen asked when she returned.

'He doesn't usually get home until about six. Any sign of my children on the back lawn?'

'I didn't see them.'

'Little swine. They said they were going up the street on their bikes for half an hour about two hours ago.'

'They'll be all right.'

Colleen sat and watched Ana for a while. 'That looks like it could be very ... what's the word?'

'Calming? Therapeutic?'

'That's it. It looks very soothing working those pedals and the wool. As if you can do it without thinking and just let your mind relax and wander.'

'That's exactly what it's like, except I've done a bit much of it lately and my wrist hurts.'

'Sounds like a sprain. You could put a poultice on it. My mother always made a good one for sprains and sore muscles. I'll bring the recipe over if you like. Sid's probably got everything you'll need in his garden, though you might need to buy the almond oil. In fact, why don't I make one up for you?'

'I'd really appreciate that, Colleen. Thank you very much.'

Colleen made the tea and brought it in. 'Actually, I did have a small favour to ask.'

Ana raised her eyebrows over her cup, inviting her to go on.

'Well, it's this Johnny lad our Pauline's going out with. You're related to the family, aren't you?'

'He's my nephew, more or less.'

'Well,' Colleen said, 'he's a very nice lad and we've had him round to tea a few times, and Sid and I both like him, but he and Pauline seem to be getting very serious.'

'Serious in what way?'

'Pauline's only seventeen and she seems very keen on him, and he's only just nineteen. At that age you should be going out with a crowd, not just one person. It worries me. I was wondering if his mother's said anything to you.'

'What about?'

'What she feels about the pair of them.'

'I think she's just happy he's staying out of trouble.'

Colleen looked alarmed. 'Why? Is he a troublemaker?'

'No. But a young man in the city, especially a young Maori man, well, you know, sometimes they do end up going astray. I think Kura worries about that.'

'Do you think he will go astray?'

'Not at all,' Ana said, though she had no idea. Johnny had a cheeky streak that could well get him into trouble one day. And he was a bit of a daredevil.

'What are they like, his family?' Colleen asked. 'I mean, I'm sure they're decent people.'

'They are, they've very decent. Hardworking and honest. But they don't have much money, and to be truthful I'm not sure Auckland is the best place for them.' Ana stopped, thinking she might be saying too much. 'But they're here and they're making the best of it. Why don't you go and have a talk to Kura yourself if you're worried about things?'

Colleen looked horrified. 'Oh, I couldn't do that. What would I say?'

'That you don't want your daughter getting pregnant and having to marry her son. That would be a start, wouldn't it?'

Her face scarlet now, Colleen didn't know where to look. 'I never said that.'

'But that's what you're worried about, isn't it?'

Colleen let out a huge sigh. 'What's *really* worrying me is she'll get pregnant and *want* to marry him. She says they're in love and do you know what? I think they are. I'm not too old to remember what young love looks like.'

'Would that be such a bad thing? Allie and Sonny seem to have a good marriage. They can work, you know, mixed race marriages. Look at me and David.'

'But Allie and Sonny were older when they married, and Sonny, well, he's a very decent man, isn't he? And I didn't approve of that either, at first.'

'How do you know Johnny's not a very decent man?'

'But he's *not* a man, is he? He's a boy. He's only nineteen. And Pauline's still a child.'

'They're growing up a lot quicker these days.'

'Would you let your girl marry at seventeen?'

'No.'

'Well, there you go.'

Ana put down her cup. 'That was a lovely cup of tea. Well, don't worry, I don't think Kura and Joshua would want Johnny to marry at nineteen, either. But I do think Kura's quite fond of Pauline.'

'That's the thing, though, isn't it? They might have to marry if they're not careful.'

Anna took up her wool again. 'I suppose you'll just have to trust them.'

'Yes, well, I trusted Donna, and she got into trouble.'

Ana was a bit shocked at that. 'Did she? Really?'

'Earlier this year.'

'During her nurse training?'

Colleen nodded ruefully.

'You'd think a nurse would know about that sort of thing.'

'You would, wouldn't you?'

'Did you never …?'

'What's the point of telling them how to avoid trouble? They'll only ask for it then.'

Ana thought that was possibly the most stupid and futile thing she'd ever heard. 'Obviously she isn't having the baby, or we'd have …'

'No, she had an abortion, and very unpleasant it was too. She had to come home for help.'

'Oh, Colleen, I'm so sorry.'

'Well, better that than being an unmarried mother, I suppose.'

Ana wasn't sure about that. At home, in Hawke's Bay, unmarried mothers and their babies tended to be absorbed into the community fairly comfortably. Among her father's people, anyway.

'Mmm, possibly. You said before you needed a favour. What exactly would you like me to do?'

Looking deeply uncomfortable, Colleen said, 'If you could see your way, could you please talk to Johnny's mother and ask her to talk to Johnny. I just want him to be aware of his responsibilities. I don't want my girl pregnant.'

Ana thought Kura probably didn't want Colleen's girl pregnant, either, and had probably already given poor Johnny an ear bashing. Pauline was an interesting girl, bright and lively, but she was a little bit unpredictable and definitely on the wild side, qualities which no doubt Johnny found attractive, but which Kura might not necessarily want in a daughter-in-law. And, as Colleen rightly said, they were too young, both for marriage and parenthood.

'I can do that, Colleen. I'll have a quiet word the next time I see her.'

Collen seemed to deflate with relief. 'Oh, Ana, thank you. You don't know how much better that makes me feel.'

Chapter Nineteen

It was while they were dyeing the last of the wool, mint this time — without interference from the nosy neighbour — that Allie said, 'If this is going to be a proper business, we need to have a name for it.'

'You know, I hadn't even thought of that,' Ana said.

'Whenever we ordered in clothes at Dunbar and Jones it was always from flash-sounding companies,' Allie went on. 'You know, Liberty or Cole of California or Jacques Fath or Christian Dior. Even the local companies had posh names. And stores have their own house labels too.'

'What about Apanui of Ponsonby?' Kura suggested.

They all had a good laugh at that.

'I thought something-or-other knits might be good,' Allie said.

Wiki said, 'Mana Motuhake Knits?'

'Bit of a mouthful. What does it mean?' And a bit too Maori for white customers, Allie thought, but she didn't want to say that.

'Independence.'

'I like that, though.'

'What about just Mana Knits?' Ana suggested. 'Prestige and integrity.'

'That's good,' Wiki said.

Kura agreed and Allie liked it, so now they had a name for their business.

Ana said, 'We need a headquarters for the business, too, and copies of a letter Allie can give to potential customers outlining what we can do.'

'Me?' Allie said, startled. 'Why am I giving them a letter?'

'Because you'll be going out looking for business.'

'But why me?'

'You're the one with experience in the rag trade,' Ana said.

'I only sold clothes in a department store. I don't know how to go round touting for business.'

'Don't worry, you'll be fine.'

'And you're the one with the white skin and blonde hair,' Kura said.

That stopped Allie in her tracks. 'Well, that shouldn't make a difference.'

'Oh, don't be dumb, girl,' Kura said. ''Course it makes a difference. Look at me and Wiki. Who's going to order clothes off us? Can you see us in Milne and Choyce or Smith and Caughey? Or even Farmers? They'll think we made them crouching in the dirt at some pa somewhere.'

They all looked round at the bare dirt and the landlord's rubbish littering Kura's backyard and giggled.

'Even I'm probably too dark to get away with it,' Ana said. 'Anyway, you know the business. I don't.'

'Then hadn't we better pick a different name?' Allie said.

'No. Everyone will think it means manna from heaven. But we'll know what it really means.'

'Only if they can't spell,' Kura noted.

Wiki said, 'Good, that's all settled.'

'We can use my house as the headquarters if you like,' Allie suggested. 'We've got a spare room. We could keep everything in there.'

'You're not on the phone, are you?' Ana said.

'There wouldn't be much point. We don't know anyone else who is.'

Ana said, 'Well, we can't run a business without a telephone.'

Allie was starting to feel a bit annoyed. First she had to go tramping all over town pestering people, and now she was supposed to have the phone on, just to sell some booties. 'Why don't we wait and see how we get on? If we do manage to sell a few things I'll talk to Sonny about a telephone.'

'I don't mean you have to pay for it,' Ana said. 'The business would pay. But you're probably right, let's see how we go first.'

It took close to another two weeks for all of the wool to be spun and samples knitted in all colours. By then Allie had bought herself a smart suit and some stylish new shoes, the cost of which would be reimbursed when the company coffers were overflowing. On her first day out approaching potential retailers, she carried a small suitcase containing examples of Mana Knits' baby clothing and wraps, and a letter, professionally typed by her friend Louise, outlining the company's raison d'etre (the exact meaning of which they'd had to look up in the *Oxford English Dictionary*), the origin of the wool they'd used, and its hand-crafted qualities. And, of course, contact details for the company for future orders.

She started early on a Wednesday morning, visiting all the children's-wear stores in the central city, and finding quite a degree of success. By two o'clock she had seven small orders, and was wondering whether Kura, Wiki and Ana would be able to knit fast enough to keep up. She was also wondering what had possessed her to buy such high heels as her feet were killing her. At Milne and Choyce, the first department store she tried, she went straight to the shoe department and bought a more sensible pair, sighing with relief as she slipped them on and shoved the others into her suitcase. Milne and Choyce placed an order, but just for the wraps, as they'd just received a large shipment of baby clothes, and Rendells placed an order for every style and colour she had. This made her wonder if they were under-pricing their goods as Rendells was, to be frank, at the bottom of the department store pile, and if their buyer thought she was getting a deal, maybe they were slightly missing their mark.

By this time she was exhausted and caught the tram home. Tomorrow she'd tackle John Court, George Court, Smith and Caughey, and Farmers, all department stores, though she wasn't at all looking forward to Miss Weaver on the Fashion floor at Smith and Caughey. She might think she was being an upstart.

At home she changed out of her nice suit and started to get the tea on. She desperately wanted to tell the others her news about the orders, but couldn't unless she visited them personally, and she was too tired to do that. And a telephone wouldn't be much use unless they all had one. But she could, as Ana had predicted, see a time coming when they would need one, if retailers wanted repeat orders.

When Sonny arrived home he ate his tea, had a beer then lay down on the couch, groaning.

'Hard day?' Allie asked.

'Just the wind. It goes right through your bones. Did you sell a million pairs of booties?'

Allie smiled. 'Not quite, but I did take quite a few orders. More than I thought I would.'

'Well, that's good news,' Sonny said, pulling Allie down to sit on his belly. 'Isn't it?'

'It will be if we can keep up with them.'

'That many? You might have to recruit more knitters.'

'We might too. How's Johnny getting on?'

Johnny Apanui had started work with Sonny a week ago.

'Still giving me bloody heart attacks. He walks round on those girders like a flaming monkey in a tree. I keep telling him, bloody well hold on to something! But I suppose some people are good with heights.'

'And some people fall off them,' Allie said. 'Tell him to behave and stop showing off.'

'Do you think I haven't? Little smartarse.'

They were silent for a moment, then Allie said, 'Can we get the telephone put on?'

Sonny pulled her down so she was lying on top of him. 'If you like.'

'You haven't even asked why.'

'That's true.'

'Do you want to know?'

'Dunno who you'll be ringing up. Who do we know who's got a telephone?'

'It's so stores can order more of our clothing. The business will pay for it when we start making money.'

'You can have whatever you want, my love.'

'Can I get it connected myself, do you think, or will you have to do it?'

'Don't know.'

'I'll go into the phone company tomorrow and ask.'

'Good idea,' Sonny said. 'But for now I'd rather do this.'

'What?'

Sonny started unbuttoning her shirt.

*

Pauline and Johnny were having a busy Friday night. First they'd had tea at Johnny's house, and now they were on Karangahape Road looking in jewellery stores at engagement rings. Johnny had asked Pauline to marry him. She'd been utterly delighted (and secretly very relieved), but they were keeping the news to themselves until Johnny could pay for the ring, which wouldn't be far away given the recent increase to his income.

'Do you like this one?' Pauline asked as they leant over a glass case. 'The one with three diamonds in a row?'

'It's sparkly,' Johnny said.

They waited for the sales clerk, or perhaps he was the jeweller himself, to come and help them, but he was leafing through a ledger by the cash register. Johnny knew, however, that he was keeping a close eye on them. They waited some more, then even longer.

Finally Johnny said loudly, 'Hey, 'scuse me, do you work here or are you just standing round?'

Pauline stifled a giggle.

The man closed his ledger and moved around the counter. 'Can I help you, sir?'

'How much is this ring? The one at the front with three diamonds? Is it silver?'

'It's set in platinum,' the man said, 'and the price is four hundred pounds.'

Fucking hell, Johnny thought. 'Do you have anything smaller?'

'Cheaper, you mean?'

'No, I mean smaller.'

'Perhaps sir would like to consider this selection.' The man took a tray of rings from beneath the counter and set them on the glass, so far away from Johnny and Pauline they really had to stretch to see them.

Johnny had a squiz but they just looked like rings to him. 'See anything you like?' he asked Pauline.

'That one's quite nice,' she said pointing to a diamond flanked by two much smaller stones.

'How much is that?' Johnny said.

'Two hundred and forty-five pounds.'

Christ. 'See anything else?'

More minutes went by.

'This one?' Pauline suggested.

It was a single small diamond set in a circle of faceted platinum.

'Price?' Johnny asked.

'Good choice, madam,' the man said. 'That particular model has an illusion setting, which really shows off the diamond, don't you think?'

'What's the price?' Johnny said again.

'One hundred and eighty-nine pounds, sir. Anything less than that and you're only buying diamond chips. Hardly a compliment to your fiancée, is it?'

'Well, it'll do for starters,' Pauline said.

Alarmed, Johnny looked at her. She smiled back tranquilly.

He asked the man, 'Have you got lay-by?'

A big, theatrical sigh. 'We do. I'll work it out.' The salesman scribbled something on a pad. 'Ten pounds deposit and seven pounds, four shillings and sixpence a week over six months.'

'That's nothing,' Pauline said. 'My fiancé's working on the harbour bridge and you how much *they* make. In a year we'll be back to get that ring with the really big diamonds.'

'I'll look forward to that,' the man said as Johnny handed over ten pounds.

Outside he asked, 'What did you say that for? I can hardly bloody afford the ring we're lay-bying.'

'I didn't mean it. I only said it because the stuck-up bugger thought you were cheap and we're rubbish.'

'Me?' Johnny was aghast. 'I'm not cheap. I just haven't made enough money yet. And we're *not* rubbish.'

"Course we aren't.' Pauline tucked an arm though his. 'Come on, let's go down to the MCC.'

The Maori Community Centre was, as usual, packed. There was a new band playing tonight from Rotorua called the Howard Morrison Quartet and the gen was they were pretty good, but first on were Dave Dockery and His Rhythm Pals. By now Sonny and Pauline were very familiar faces at the MCC, and both were grinning like mad at their engagement secret, and it took them a while to extract themselves from friendly greetings, but eventually they made it onto the floor where a space immediately cleared for them. They were dancing so well together now they'd become an attraction themselves. And they made a striking couple; dark-haired, coffee-skinned Johnny with his muscular build and flashing white teeth, and Pauline with her fair skin, tawny hair pulled back in a ponytail, and her shapely little body.

But tonight Pauline seemed to be running out of puff.

'You all right?' Sonny asked as she avoided a move that would have flipped her over his shoulder, and instead danced a sedate turn.

'Just knackered. Long day.'

'D'you want to sit down?'

'After this dance?'

They found a pair of seats and Johnny offered her a drink from his hip flask of whiskey smuggled in inside his jacket. He preferred beer but suitable amounts were hard to sneak in to the MCC under the watchful eyes of the door wardens.

Pauline took a huge gulp, and coughed until her eyes watered. 'Bloody hell, I thought that was beer.'

'Sorry, should have told you.'

She took another smaller sip and gave the flask back. 'Can you get me an orange squash or something?'

By the time he returned Pauline was greeting a friend neither of them had seen for some time.

'Hi, Gloria. Haven't seen you for a while.'

Gloria looked embarrassed. 'I've been away.'

'Yeah? Whereabouts?'

'Napier.'

'Work or visiting?'

Gloria shook her head. 'Neither. I got in trouble.'

Everyone knew what 'in trouble' meant. 'Really? God. You kept that quiet.'

'It's supposed to be a secret.'

'Was it Ihaka's?'

Gloria glanced at Johnny. He knew Ihaka, who hadn't said a dicky bird about getting Gloria up the duff.

'He wouldn't have a bar of it when I told him,' she said. 'I thought we'd get married but he reckoned his mother and father said no. Mine definitely did.'

'Why?'

'I don't know. I just don't think he wanted the responsibility. Had the fun, though.'

'Bastard. Where did you have it?'

'Bethany. Some Pakeha family took the baby.'

'Why didn't someone in your family take it?'

'Too shaming 'cos I'm only sixteen. We're all turning into Pakehas these days, eh?'

Pauline, bursting to tell someone she and Sonny were engaged, realised Gloria wasn't going to be the right person. Perhaps it was best kept a secret after all.

*

'For fuck's sake, will you be careful!' Sonny exclaimed.

'Keep your hair on!' Johnny said, a big grin on his face.

He was sitting on a girder, his legs swinging, not holding on and lighting a cigarette. He was using his beloved Zippo and the wind kept blowing the flame out. It was a bad weather day and Sonny was surprised they were on the job, but they were a little behind schedule and the boss was worried.

Johnny finally got his smoke going, shoved his cigarette packet and the Zippo in his pocket, then stood and walked nonchalantly along the girder to Sonny's perch and sat down again.

'You look a twerp in that hat,' he said, grinning again.

Sonny said, 'Probably, but it saves my ears.'

'I've got cast-iron ears, me.'

'Good for you. Come on, let's get these rivets in.'

Sonny got to work but after a minute he noticed there wasn't any hammering coming from behind him. He turned and saw that Johnny was eating a pie now. For God's sake.

From far below and about twenty yards away, on the very edge of Northcote Point's cliff, the boss bellowed through cupped hands, *'Apanui! Eat on your own time!'*

It was Sonny's turn to laugh. 'That'll teach you.'

Johnny jammed the last third of the pie into his mouth, crumpled the paper bag and dropped it, then gave a cheeky thumbs-up, completely unable to speak. Soon he was bashing and clanging away along with everyone else. Sonny had to admit he was a good, fast worker when he put his mind to it.

Sonny put his head down (focusing on the girder and not the rippling waves below) and got into the swing of it: hammer a rivet in a hole, bash the tail end to secure it, complete the section, shuffle along on his arse, start a new section. So when he heard shouts he was jerked out of his rhythm with a hell of a fright. He looked up, then around at Johnny.

But Johnny wasn't there.

Some of the blokes were scrambling along the girders while others seemed paralysed, staring down at the sea.

And then he saw a handful of men sliding down the less steep side of the cliff, and two already in the water, striking out.

Then he saw the body, floating face down in the ocean.

God, oh God no, please don't let it be Johnny.

He crawled along the girder, scrambled down a ladder, almost falling himself, and scurried along the lower girders till he could jump onto land. Sticky with cold sweat and shaking badly, he raced for the cliff edge and scrabbled, leapt and slid on his arse down to the water's edge, in time to meet the men with the body.

It was Johnny, and when they lifted him out of the sea a piece of the back of his head came away.

'Ah, God.' Sonny shut his eyes, dreadful scenes from South Korea briefly flooding his mind.

Someone vomited. Several men swore.

A voice said, 'Someone go up and get a blanket or something. We'll have to carry him up.'

Sonny opened his eyes, took off his silly flappy hat and put it on Johnny's head to cover the mess.

The boss arrived. 'Ah, shit. Bloody, bugger, shit. He only just started.'

Someone said, 'We're getting a blanket to carry him up.'

'Bugger that,' the boss said. 'We'll take him up in the crane. Hang on.' And off he went to organise it.

'What do we do with that?' a man asked, pointing at the piece of Johnny's skull lying on the sand.

Sonny picked it up and popped it under the hat on Johnny's head.

'Oh, for fuck's sake,' the man said, then gagged.

Sonny ignored him. He'd done similar things during the war. And Johnny might need it for burial: he wasn't sure whether or not Ngati Kahungunu needed all their bits and pieces to pass over.

Christ, what was he going to tell the Apanuis? And Pauline? She thought the sun shone out of Johnny's backside.

Why hadn't the stupid little bugger just held on properly?

*

The boss closed down the site for the rest of the day, and gave Sonny the following day off as well. Probably, Sonny thought, because he was so grateful he'd offered to tell the Apanuis their son was now lying in Auckland Hospital's morgue.

Allie wasn't in when he got home. He thought she was probably at Kura Apanui's or Wiki Irwin's, knitting. They'd been flat out with that lately. He hoped so, anyway — Kura would need her friends. He had a very quick wash, gave Mr De Valera something to eat, then jumped in the truck and drove over to Ponsonby.

He knew where the Apanuis and the Irwins lived as he'd been over to collect Allie often enough, but the closer he got, the sicker he felt. He was dreading doing this but Kura deserved to hear the news from someone she'd at least met. It was a pity Joshua would still be at work. And then there was Pauline. He'd have to take Allie to Smith and Caughey so she could tell her face to face. She was going to be heartbroken.

He parked the truck on the street and walked down the path at the side of Kura's house, wincing as he heard laughter coming from inside. It sounded like they were having a party. He knocked on the back door, but no one heard, they were making that much noise. He knocked again. Still no answer so he went in, past the kitchen and down the hall.

'Oh my *Lord*!' Wiki shrieked, spotting him. 'I thought you were a burglar!'

'Not today,' Sonny said.

There were five women in the room and four roared with laughter. Allie didn't.

She said, 'Why aren't you at work?'

'I need to talk to Mrs Apanui.'

They all fell suddenly silent.

'It's my Johnny, isn't it?' Kura asked, her knitting frozen mid-stitch.

'It might be better if we talked in the kitchen, Auntie,' Sonny said, using the term of respect for older Maori women to try and soften the blow. As if it could.

'These are my friends, dear,' Kura said. 'You can say what you need to in front of them.'

Sonny wished he were anywhere but here, doing this. 'It is Johnny, Auntie. He fell. I'm really sorry, but he was killed.'

'He's dead? My Johnny's dead?'

Sonny nodded.

Kura put the piece she was knitting over her face, stamped her slippered feet like a child having a tantrum and let out a dreadful wail.

The women scattered like ants. One to the kettle, one to Vincent, who'd started bawling at the noise, one to hand round a packet of smokes, Wiki to comfort Kura, and Ana down the street to the telephone box to phone David and ask him to go and tell Joshua at work.

'I'm really sorry,' Sonny muttered, almost to himself.

'You poor thing,' Allie said, putting an arm around his waist.

'We should go and tell Pauline.'

Allie closed her eyes. 'Oh God.'

'Is there anything we can do?' Sonny asked Wiki.

Tears were pouring down Wiki's face. 'No, boy. Thank you for coming to tell us. You're a good boy.'

'He's at Auckland Hospital, at the morgue. He's ... he hit his head. Quite badly.'

Wiki nodded. 'Ae. Thank you.'

Sonny and Allie waited a few minutes more, then quietly left.

In the truck Allie burst into tears. 'Poor Kura. All of them. Pauline said he was the apple of their eye.' She threw her cigarette butt out the window and blew her nose. 'How did he—? How did it happen?'

'I don't know. I didn't even know he'd fallen till I heard shouting and turned round and he wasn't there. He must have banged his head on the way down. It was pretty bad.'

Allie winced. 'His face?'

'The back. His skull. I told him to hold on properly.' Sonny belted the steering wheel, accidentally tooting the horn. 'I fucking well *told* him.'

The driver ahead of them turned and shook his fist. Sonny gave him an angry jab of the fingers.

'It's not your fault,' Allie said. 'You shouldn't think that.'

'No, but I was ...' Sonny rubbed a hand over his face. 'God. Bloody hell.'

They drove the rest of the way into town in silence and parked near Smith and Caughey, went in and up to The Cedar Room. Pauline wasn't behind the counter but Mrs Fitch, her boss, was.

Allie said, 'Hello, Mrs Fitch, can I talk to Pauline, please?'

'She's a bit busy at the moment, Allison. Can it wait?'

'Not really.'

Mrs Fitch looked annoyed. 'Well, as you can see, we're just finishing the lunch run. She hasn't got time to gossip.'

Sonny watched Allie's head lift and her jaw set and thought, Good girl.

'Someone's died. She needs to come home. Will you please go and get her.'

'Oh. I'm so sorry, Allison. In that case …' Mrs Fitch hurried off.

Pauline appeared a minute later and lifted the flap in the counter. 'What's going on? Mrs Fitch said you wanted to talk to me?'

Allie took her arm and looked round for an empty table. 'Come and sit down.'

'Why? I don't want to sit down.'

'Just come and sit.' Allie almost had to shove Pauline onto a chair.

Pauline looked from her to Sonny and back again. 'What?'

Allie took her hand. 'We've got some really bad news, love. Johnny had an accident this morning. We're so sorry, but he's died.'

There was a long, long moment of silence.

Then Pauline said, 'Oh, piss off.'

Sonny had thought this might happen. Young people never thought death could be real. 'It's true, sweetie,' he said gently. 'I was there. He fell off the bridge.'

Pauline stared at him, then said, 'Well, that's just fucking great, isn't it?'

After a moment she put her head down on the table and wept. Allie moved to stand behind her, patting her shoulder and stroking her hair, looking at Sonny in anguish.

People were staring now.

'You take her to the truck. I'll get her things,' Allie suggested.

By the time they got Pauline home she'd stopped crying and was unnaturally silent. All she'd asked on the way was the whereabouts of Johnny now.

Colleen was at work but Sid was home, and he was incredibly sympathetic, as Allie and Sonny had known he would be.

'My poor little honey bun,' he said, giving Pauline a huge hug when they told him. 'Your heart must be breaking, eh? What can we do about that?'

Allie put the kettle on while Sid sat Pauline down at the table and dragged his chair, with a horrendous screeching noise, next to hers and sat with his arm round her shoulders. At his ministrations she burst into tears again, collapsing against him, which made Sid cry too.

Finally, when Pauline seemed cried out, and Sid had blotted his red face with a hanky, Allie served tea.

Pauline took a single sip then pushed her cup away. 'Where will they bury him?' she asked Sonny.

He didn't know but made an educated guess. 'They'll probably take him home, back to Hawke's Bay.'

'Because I want to go to the funeral.'

'It'll be a tangi. Three days,' Sonny said.

Pauline frowned. 'They haven't got a car.'

'Sorry?' Sonny wasn't sure what that had to do with anything.

'How will they get him there?'

'The whanau will come up and collect him, and everyone else.'

'Will they take me?'

'I don't know. You'd have to ask the family, I suppose,' Sonny replied, feeling uncomfortable. She was in a bloody awkward position.

'We were—' Pauline began. But then she stopped.

'We were what?' Allie asked.

'Nothing. It doesn't matter. Nothing matters now.'

*

It wasn't until she and Sonny were in bed, much later than night, that Allie was struck by a monumental realisation: when they'd gone into Smith and Caughey today there'd been no imagined smells of smoke, no illusive flickers of flame, no faint screams in her head from trapped and dying friends, and no crushing sense of dread. And now that she thought about it, she'd barely registered anything like that when she'd been in and out of the big stores with the knitting samples, only fleeting wisps of what had once utterly terrified her, nothing more than ghosts of ghosts.

And now even they'd gone.

Was she so busy now that she didn't have time to be barmy? Was she getting better without even realising it?

*

Pauline went to view Johnny's body two days later. After a post-mortem examination he'd been embalmed ready for his final journey to Maungakakari, and was spending one last night at his family's house.

Sonny and Allie drove Pauline over to Ponsonby, and when Pauline knocked on the back door, Kura's eldest girl Patricia welcomed her with open arms. The house was jammed with people Pauline didn't know but she found Kura, who enveloped her in a squashy hug.

'Our beautiful boy's gone,' she said, her face puffy and her eyes red. 'Come and say goodbye.'

Johnny was in the front room, his coffin set on a pair of sawhorses. On a little table near his head stood a plaster statue of Jesus, a photograph of Johnny grinning in his best clothes, and a vase of freesias. At first Pauline was afraid to look in case his lovely face was disfigured, even though Sonny had told her it hadn't been, but she gritted her teeth and did.

It didn't look like Johnny. The body was far too still and Johnny had always, always been on the go. And the face had unnaturally pink cheeks and lips, like a ventriloquist's doll, and Johnny had always had such lovely, evenly-coloured brown skin. She thought she might have wanted to kiss him, just lightly on the cheek, but now she didn't because his skin looked so waxy and strange. She *hated* bloody undertakers. Instead she just touched the collar of his jacket. She was relieved in a way: because the body didn't look like the real Johnny she could go on thinking he wasn't really dead, even though she knew he was.

At her shoulder Patricia said, 'You're welcome to go across the road to Auntie Wiki's for a feed. I think your sister and her husband are over there.'

Pauline crossed the street and found Sonny. 'Why's the food over here?'

'Well, Johnny's in the other house, isn't he?' Sonny waved at someone he knew. 'Can't have the kai and the body in the same space. It's tapu.'

Pauline wasn't sure what he meant, and didn't want to eat anyway. She went back to the Apanuis' house. There were so many people there — from the family's church, she supposed. Joshua was in the kitchen with Henare and some other men, having a quiet beer and a smoke, and the hallway was crammed. She looked around for Kura again, whom she found weeping on someone's shoulder.

When she was free, Pauline asked, 'Will Johnny be going home to Hawke's Bay for his funeral?'

'That's right, dear. We're leaving in the morning.'

Pauline waited, but nothing else was forthcoming, so she said, 'Is the whole family going down?'

Kura nodded. 'And Wiki's. Our whanau have come up for us.'

'Will it be a big funeral?'

'We're expecting hundreds.' Kura dabbed at her eyes. 'He was a popular boy. My poor baby.'

'Well, I hope you have a nice day.'

'Thank you, dear.'

It was then that Pauline truly realised Kura was far too preoccupied to pay attention to her, and that she wasn't even on the Apanuis' list of priorities, never mind near the top of it.

She went across the street again and told Allie she wanted to go home.

*

A fortnight later all of the Robertses had gathered at Colleen and Sid's for Sunday lunch, as usual a roast with all the extras.

When Pauline was in the loo, Allie asked, 'How is she?'

Colleen stuck out her hand, palm down, and waggled it. 'Some days she mentions him and other days, nothing. I think she's taking it hard. She's barely been out since it happened.' She looked at Sid. 'In fact, I don't think she's been out at all, has she?'

Sid shook his head. 'Well, they did everything together, didn't they? I expect she's lost contact with a few people.'

Everyone shut up as Pauline came back and sat down. 'Are you talking about me?'

'Yes, we're worried,' Colleen said. 'It's time you started going out with your friends again.'

'Why? What's the point?'

'Why? Well, all young people go out, don't they?'

Pauline lit a cigarette. 'I go to work. That's out, isn't it?'

'Put that out, love,' Colleen said. 'I'm just serving lunch.'

While they ate, Donna chatted about her training and some funny — and sad — things that had happened at the hospital; Allie proudly informed everyone that Mana Knits had delivered their first orders; Sonny told an amusing Gina story; Sid wondered aloud whether he should try eggplants in the garden this summer (Donna said, 'What for? They're horrible.'); and no one mentioned Johnny. Pauline didn't say much at all.

When she helped herself to extra roast potatoes, Colleen remarked, 'Do you really need those, love?'

'Yes.'

'Well, not *really*,' Donna said. 'Look, you can hardly do up your shirt.'

Everyone looked. It was true; Pauline's shirt barely met across her bust, leaving a gap between the buttons, and the bottom two over her belly were nowhere near their corresponding buttonholes.

A horrible silence fell across the table.

Donna broke it. 'Oh, you're *not*, are you?'

Pauline sat back. 'All right then, I am.'

'Oh, *Pauline*!' Colleen put her head in her hands. 'For God's *sake*!'

Allie looked at Sonny. Her bloody sisters, getting pregnant at the drop of a hat! Why couldn't she? Sonny squeezed her knee under the table.

'Is it Johnny's?' Donna asked.

''Course it's bloody Johnny's,' Pauline snapped. 'I've never been with anyone else.'

Sid put his hands over his ears.

Colleen slapped his arm. 'Stop that and act your age.'

'I don't want to hear all this!'

'Well, too bad. How far along are you?' she asked Pauline.

'About five months?'

Colleen groaned.

'Too late for an abortion then,' Donna said.

'You'd know,' Pauline muttered.

Colleen said, 'You'll have to have it, then. You'll have to go away somewhere and have it. But you can't keep it.'

'Don't worry, I don't want it.'

Allie looked at her sister, really quite surprised. 'Don't you? But it's Johnny's baby. It's the only thing left of him.'

'For Christ's sake, don't go giving her ideas,' Colleen said.

'I just thought—' Allie began.

But Pauline interrupted her. 'No, it's Johnny I want. I don't want a baby, not without him.'

Sonny said, 'Johnny's mother might take it in.'

Colleen fixed him with a look. He shut up.

'No. Pauline has her future to think about. She'll go away, have the baby, give it up for adoption, then come home and get on with her life.'

'Who made you God?' Sid asked.

Startled, Colleen stared at him. 'What?'

'I said, who made you God? Are you sure that's what she really wants?'

'Is it?' Colleen asked Pauline. 'Is that what you want?'

'It is. I don't want to keep it. But why can't I have it here?'

Allie and Donna mouthed silently to each other, What will people think?

'What will people think?' Colleen said. 'No, I'm sorry, love, you'll have to go away. Plenty of girls have managed before you and plenty will after, I've no doubt. You'll see.'

'I could just stay inside.'

'No, it won't do.'

'You're ashamed, aren't you?' Pauline said.

'I am, a little,' Colleen said. 'And I'm disappointed. And I'm sad for you too. I know what you thought of that lad. If I could have stopped any of this happening, any of it, I would have.'

Surprised, Allie looked at her mother. It had been a very heartfelt and honest thing for her to say.

'She might *have* to stay inside for a little while,' Donna said. 'I don't think the Bethany homes take girls till they're six months along.'

'"She" is the cat's mother,' Colleen admonished. 'Well, why don't you find out? You're the nurse. We'll also need to know which home will take her.'

Pauline got up and went to the toilet again. Allie didn't think she looked particularly pregnant, more like she'd just put on a bit of weight. Did she have her dates wrong?

'Have you seen a doctor?' she asked when she came back.

'About a month ago. He said I was sixteen weeks along.'

Sid looked uncomfortable again and Sonny was staring at his fingernails. Sid said, 'Come and have a squiz at my garden. Got some bloody nice carrots at the moment.'

As the men escaped, Allie said, 'Did you not notice you'd missed your monthlies?'

'Not so much the first one, but after that I did.'

Donna said, 'And you didn't think you might be in trouble?'

'No.'

'Weren't you using anything?'

'French letters.'

'French letters?' Donna repeated. 'No one calls them French letters.'

'Johnny did.'

Allie remarked, 'You don't look very pregnant.'

Pauline shrugged.

'You could probably work for a few more weeks, if you wanted to.'

'Maybe.'

'Will you tell Kura?'

'No. What's the point?'

'Did Johnny know?' Colleen asked.

Pauline shook her head. 'I was saving it. For a surprise.'

Chapter Twenty

It had been a mistake, coming back to work. She should have chucked it in straight after Johnny died. Nothing she could do was right. Mrs Fitch had told her off enough before, but now it felt like she was on her back all the time. She was either too slow, or too messy, or gormless, or smart-mouthed, or rude to customers. Nothing she did could please the old bag and, really, she couldn't see how her behaviour was any different to that of the other girls working at The Cedar Room. And what a stupid name for a tearoom anyway.

Today it was her job to make the asparagus rolls, and the smell of the asparagus was making her want to spew. She had the fresh white bread, all thinly sliced, spread out on the trays and had just finished buttering them — 'Right to the edges so they stick, Pauline!' — and now she was holding her nose and laying two asparagus spears diagonally across each slice.

Then Mrs Fitch appeared at her elbow and said, 'Oh, you're doing it wrong, Pauline. You have to top and tail them so a frond peeps out at each end.'

'Well, did you tell me that?'

'I thought you'd have the brains to work it out.'

Pauline stood very still, holding the tongs and the asparagus bowl. The grief and anger inside her were awful, all bubbling away and getting ready to explode like that big geyser in Rotorua. She put the bowl and tongs down and turned to her boss.

'Do you know what? I don't want to do this any more. You can stick your asparagus rolls. I'm off.'

Mrs Fitch gaped at her.

Pauline took off her apron, dropped it on the bench, and walked out of the kitchen. She kept going all the way to the staffroom to collect her bag and coat, expecting the anger to ease now she'd done something dramatic, but it didn't. It remained, making her ears pound and her heart thump and her breath come too fast. She felt emotionally mutilated and she wanted to hurt someone back. She wanted revenge.

She went down to the Beauty Hall.

'Hi, Peggy.'

'Hi there, Pauline. How are you?'

'OK. Can you do me a favour?'

'What's that?'

'You know that Kathleen Lawson woman Allie was friends with? Do you know where she lives?'

Peggy opened a drawer and, in silence, handed Pauline a card.

She read the name and address on it. 'Ta.'

*

Pauline caught a tram to Remuera, hopped off near Portland Road and walked down to Eastbourne Road. It was certainly a posh area, filled with big old two-storey houses with beautiful gardens and lovely views across the city and the harbour. Obviously only rich people lived here, but then she already knew that. She walked along Eastbourne to number three. Would anyone be home?

She knocked on the front door and stood in the spacious porch, waiting. There was no answer, but it was a big house so she knocked again. Still nothing, so she followed a path around the back, past a clipped lawn and flower beds, peering into windows as she went. All she could see were reflections of herself.

The back lawn was huge, like a park, and full of trees and bench seats and a couple of bird baths. It was nice but it didn't have an amazing vegetable garden like her father's. There was a verandah on the rear of the house and French doors to several rooms. She looked in but still couldn't see anyone. She tried the doors but they were locked. Someone, though, had left a window open, so she climbed up on a garden chair and wriggled through, finding herself in the kitchen on a bench next to a sink, where she crouched, listening for signs someone was home. Nothing, just the ticking and creaking of a big, wooden house.

God, her mother would kill for this kitchen. There were cupboards everywhere, a *huge* refrigerator, a sparkling cooker with four elements and a window in the oven door, an electric cake mixer and two or three other gadgets she couldn't even recognise on the bench. What a spoilt bitch Kathleen Lawson was.

She left the kitchen and explored. She looked into all the rooms on the ground floor, then went upstairs and had a good poke around in what she assumed was the Lawsons' bedroom. She opened the wardrobes and looked at Kathleen's clothes, tried on a few pairs of her shoes, then sat down at her dressing table and fluffed on a dusting of face powder with a big brush. Then, thinking she looked a bit pale — very pale in fact — she added a bit of rouge.

Kathleen's jewellery box was interesting. She had some very flash costume brooches and necklaces and earrings, all big sparkly crystals, and some earrings and rings with smaller stones she thought might be real. Should she pocket them? She thought for a bit then decided no, she wasn't a thief. She did bend the pins on all the brooches so they wouldn't close, though, and broke the clips on the earrings.

She had a wee in the toilet, flushed, washed her hands, then went back downstairs to the front room. Except it wasn't at the front of the house and Kathleen Lawson probably called it the drawing room or the parlour or something just as snobby. It was filled with chairs and sofas, long heavy curtains framed the windows, and a big fireplace took up part of one wall, though it didn't look like it was used much because a vase of dried leaves and flowers sat right in the middle of it.

Pauline looked around. Where should she start? She prowled the room till she spotted a gas heater connected to the wall by a hose and bayonet fitting, tucked tidily between a sofa and a window. Grunting, she shoved the sofa along to give herself some room, then squatted in front of the heater. How did you turn these bloody things on? And then she worked it out. Dragging it towards her she pressed the red button on the side, but nothing happened. She did it again, holding it down for a few seconds. This time she smelt gas, which made her feel sick, but couldn't see any flame. So she pushed repeatedly and suddenly a line of blue flame popped up along the bottom the heater.

She watched it for a while, feeling the air before her heat up. When her face was hot, she turned the heater around and pushed it against the wall. Then, for good measure, she tucked an edge of curtain between the wall and the heater. Satisfied, she retreated to an armchair on the other side of the room and lit a cigarette.

While she watched, the wallpaper above the heater gradually turned brown, and after a while a flap lifted and curled, smoking. At the same time, wisps of smoke began to drift up from the side of the curtain. By the time she saw proper flames she was on to her second cigarette, but still she wanted to stay, worried the fire might go out. She knew she couldn't, however — someone was bound to come home soon. And she did feel relief now, as though somewhere inside her a pressure valve had opened. Her terrible rage had faded and now she just felt ... flat.

She left the house the way she'd come in, thinking that's what you get for being a bitch to my sister, Kathleen Lawson, though she knew at some level that what she'd just done hadn't really been about Allie and Mrs Lawson. But that didn't matter; someone had to pay for what happened to Johnny. Someone had to pay for her unbearable pain. It didn't matter who.

*

October 1956

Allie laughed. 'Staring at it won't make it ring.'

Her mother was sitting on the sofa and every few seconds her gaze would slide towards the telephone, as if she expected it to do something. 'Can I have the number?'

'What for? You can't ring it.'

'I can, from the telephone box down the road.'

'That's true.'

Allie wrote the number on a piece of paper.

'Has anyone phoned you yet?' Colleen asked.

'Yes, and I just about jumped out of my skin when they did. I was sitting where you are, knitting. Honestly, I nearly died.'

'Who was it?'

'A children's-wear shop. They wanted more of the little cardigans and gowns. Oh, and some bonnets too.'

'Already?'

'I know. Good, isn't it?'

'You'll be knitting yourselves silly.'

'We are. Kura's already got another lady from her church helping out.'

Colleen said, 'Why is that cat staring at me?'

Mr De Valera was sitting in the doorway, giving her the evil eye.

'You're in his seat,' Allie pointed out.

'Oh, well, pardon me.'

Dev glared a bit longer, then stalked over to Allie's knitting bag and wedged himself into it, crushing her work in progress and getting fur all over it.

'Get out of there, Dev!'

Mr De Valera turned his head away, making himself cross-eyed by staring steadfastly at the wall.

Colleen eyed the phone again. 'I'm thinking of getting a telephone connected myself.'

'Are you? But who would you ring?'

'You for starters. And your sister. They've got it on at the nurses' home.'

'And you could ring Pauline when she goes away. I'm sure they'll have a telephone at the home. I'll definitely be phoning her.'

'Will we be allowed?' Colleen asked.

'I can't see why not. It's not as if she'll be in prison. And she can phone us.'

'It's such a long way away, isn't it, Wellington?'

Allie said, 'I thought you'd be pleased. Less chance of her being recognised down there.'

Colleen gave her a look. 'You can be very unkind sometimes, Allie.'

'So can you. You're the one who's shrivelled up with the shame of having an unmarried pregnant daughter. You're the one who wants her out of the way till the baby's been dealt with.'

'Because it's the best thing to do.' Colleen pointed a finger. 'You just wait till you have daughters of your own, then see what it's like.'

'I had one, Mum, remember, and I'd *love* another. *I'd* take that baby if everyone wasn't so anxious to get it out of this family.'

'Would you?' Colleen said. Then, 'No, I don't think that would be a good idea, do you? It'd only remind Pauline of Johnny.'

'Maybe. Probably. I don't know.'

Allie and Sonny had talked about taking the baby, and Sonny said he'd be happy to if she was. And she would be, if she could convince herself that Pauline could live with watching her and Johnny's child being raised by someone else. And she doubted Pauline could.

'No, I don't think that would be a good idea,' Colleen said again. She patted Allie's hand. 'Your time will come again, you'll see.'

But when, Allie thought. When?

'Is Pauline all packed?' she asked.

'More or less. I had to buy her a new suitcase. Sid got down our old cases and one smelt like a cat had peed in it, and the lid came right off the other one.'

Allie opened a bag. 'I've got some things for her. A couple of baby outfits and a wrap, which I didn't knit, but I did knit this bed jacket. Can you put them in her case?'

'You can do that when you come round to say goodbye.' Colleen pinched her top lip and was quiet for a moment. 'Allie?'

'Mmm?'

'Do you think we should tell Johnny's mother?'

'Pauline doesn't want us to. She said so, remember?'

Colleen said, 'No, she said, "What's the point?" The point is she's pregnant with Mrs Apanui's grandchild.'

'And yours,' Allie pointed out. 'And it's a bit late to be thinking about that now. Pauline's off the day after tomorrow. Everything's been organised.'

'I know, but just as a matter of courtesy—'

'Mum! Telling a mother her dead son's left a girl pregnant isn't a matter of courtesy! Either we should have done that as soon as we found out, or we don't do it at all. Pauline's giving the baby up anyway. That's what you want, isn't it?'

'Yes. It's what Pauline wants, too.'

'So stop dithering about things.'

'I don't dither!'

'All right, then stop making things harder.'

'I'm not. I just … It's just I keep thinking the baby would be that woman's — our — grandchild.'

'And my niece or nephew. And Donna's. Don't forget that.'

'So it would,' Colleen said sadly, as though she hadn't thought of that.

*

Allie and Sid went with Pauline on the bus to the city railway station, where they waited with her for the mainline express to Wellington. Sid and Colleen hadn't been able to afford a ticket for the Night Limited, which had sleeping and dining cars, but Pauline wasn't worried. The trip would still only take fourteen hours and she didn't care if she had to sleep sitting up. Her belly even now wasn't very big, though she was showing, and she wasn't particularly uncomfortable. She'd never travelled long distance on a train, however, and wondered if she'd sleep at all.

The train was actually at the station but not due to leave for twenty minutes.

'I think I'll get on,' Pauline said.

'You don't want a cup of tea?' Sid asked.

Pauline shook her head. 'I'll only have to go to the loo in half an hour.' She had a terrible thought. 'Is there a toilet on the train?'

'Don't worry, love, there'll be a couple. But be careful when you flush you don't end up on the tracks with it.'

'True?' Pauline eyed her father suspiciously. You never knew when he was pulling your leg.

'And don't get trampled in the rush for your cuppa and pie at the refresh.'

'The what?'

'The refreshment rooms at the train stops. I tell you, it's like a rugby scrum trying to get in and out of them in one piece.'

Pauline thought that sounded a bit farfetched as well. Or at least exaggerated.

'Well, I'm off,' she said, lifting her suitcase.

'I'll carry that,' her dad said, taking it off her.

Allie gave her a kiss and a hug. 'Phone as often as you like. Teatime's probably best. We're nearly always in then. If you have to pay at your end, just say hello and I'll phone you back, all right?'

Pauline nodded, then hugged her father. 'Thanks, Dad.'

'You're welcome, love. Take care.'

'And Dad? Can you tell Mum I'm sorry?'

'I think she knows that, sweetheart.'

'Well, she doesn't act like it.'

'Neither do you.' Sid laughed and brushed Pauline's cheek. 'You're peas in a pod, you and your mother. Maybe that's why you've never really got on.'

Pauline was outraged. What a mean thing to say!

At the train the guard took her case from Sid and stowed it in the baggage van. Then Pauline climbed aboard and found a seat next to a window. She waved at Allie and her father, hoping they'd leave; she didn't want to sit here waving for the next ten minutes. They'd been great, but if she had to go away, and it seemed like that's what everyone wanted her to do, then she just wanted to get on with it.

Her dad gave one last wave and he and Allie walked off. Pauline felt a sharp pang as she watched them go, and then it was just her, on a train bound for Wellington, on her own for the next three months.

*

The Lawson family were also preparing to relocate to Wellington. After the fire in their home, which had burnt out the back half of the house and rendered it uninhabitable, they'd lived in rented accommodation for a month until Jonathan had been able to find something suitable to buy in Khandallah, overlooking Wellington Harbour. He'd had to arrange a loan, but that would be taken care of once the insurance money came through.

Kathleen had had enough of Auckland. Her life there wasn't panning out the way she'd envisaged it might and the fire, she insisted, would give the family the impetus for the fresh start everyone needed.

Geoffrey, however, grumbled that he didn't need a fresh start: he was perfectly happy at his school and with his Auckland friends. Jonathan maintained he didn't really care where they lived, as long as it was near an airport into which NAC flew, which meant Dunedin, Christchurch or Wellington. This disappointed Kathleen, who thought she might like to go home to Napier, but NAC's bigger planes didn't land there and Jonathan wouldn't even consider the idea of piloting the smaller planes or flying for a more provincial airline. Rosemary didn't have a say about the move as she was too young, and no one was really talking to Terence.

Geoffrey rarely spoke to Terence much these days anyway, and Kathleen and Jonathan were privately harbouring a very unpleasant suspicion regarding their eldest son. The police had become involved with the house fire as a window in the kitchen had been found open, but then Mrs Wright had very apologetically admitted she'd left it that way, as she'd been cooking before she'd gone to the shops and the room had needed a bit of an airing. But still, the police thought the fact that the heater had been facing the wall while turned on suspect.

'Are you sure neither you nor your husband didn't inadvertently do that yourselves, perhaps before you retired to bed?' a policeman had asked. 'Perhaps when it was quite late?'

'Of course we didn't,' Kathleen had said. 'It was obvious when the heater was on and when it was off.'

'Hmm.' The policeman had made few scribbles in his notebook. 'Were you and Mr Lawson in the habit of taking alcohol at home in the evenings?'

'Hardly ever. What a question!'

'Because I've spoken with your neighbours on both sides, though I admit not the people across the street as they weren't home at the time of the fire, and no one saw anyone entering or leaving your property.'

'Well, that doesn't mean anything, does it?'

More scribbles. 'Are you aware of anyone who might have been holding a grudge against you? I'm thinking of the open window. Perhaps someone saw it and thought they'd take the opportunity to cause mischief?'

'Not at all. We're a very popular family. My husband is ex-RAF, you know, and a pilot for NAC, and I'm on multiple charitable committees. I was also a model in Smith and Caughey's summer fashion parade.'

'Really.'

Kathleen hadn't much liked the policeman's tone. 'Yes, really. I expect we're the least likely people in Remuera against whom someone might choose to hold a grudge.'

Then the policeman had closed his notebook, said, 'Right, thank you,' and they'd never heard from him again.

But it had set her thinking about who might have had something against her and Jonathan, and the only person she could think of was their own son. He was still livid at them for cutting his hair, and he was, well, he was an unusual boy. And unhappy.

She'd told Jonathan about her suspicions.

'Surely he wouldn't be that much of a shit?' Jonathan said. 'And when would he have done it? It was a school day.'

'He could have ducked into the parlour, switched the heater on and turned it to the wall before he went out the door. It would have only taken him ten seconds.'

'But the house was burning at lunchtime. Surely it wouldn't have taken all morning to catch fire?'

'Well, I don't know, do I? I'm not an arson expert. Perhaps he set the heater on low.'

Jonathan had been silent for a while. Then he'd said, 'I wouldn't put it past him. If a kid can hang himself just because he can't wear a dress in a fashion show, he can set fire to a house. God, the little bastard.'

'But we can't tell anyone,' Kathleen had warned.

'Christ, no,' Jonathan agreed. 'We'd have to say goodbye to the insurance.'

'Shall we talk to him?'

'What the hell for? He'd just deny it.'

'But we don't *know* he did it, do we?' Kathleen said. 'Not for sure.'

'Well, who else was it, if it wasn't him?'

'Have you made any enemies?'

'Me? I doubt it.'

'Not even any ex-girlfriends?'

Jonathan's lip curled. 'I was waiting for you to say that.'

'Well, what do you expect me to say?'

'What about you? You're hardly Miss Congeniality. Have *you* made any enemies?'

'What do you mean I'm not Miss Congeniality?'

'You get on people's wicks, Kathleen. You must have pissed someone off somewhere along the line.'

'No, I most certainly have not.'

Jonathan sighed. 'So if I don't have enemies, and you say you don't, it must have been bloody Terence, mustn't it?'

After a while Kathleen said, 'Do you think he'll get any better when we move?'

'No. Do you?'

'No.'

'Then what are we going to do about him?'

'I don't know.'

'Boarding school?' Jonathan suggested. 'I'm not sure I want the little bugger in the house after this.'

*

Her father had actually been right about the scrum. When the train stopped at Frankton station near Hamilton, there was an almighty stampede of people charging off the carriages and into the refreshment room, elbowing and shoving one another to get in first, then fighting their way out again with a cup of tea and a sandwich or a pie. Honestly, they'd only left Auckland an hour and a half ago. *And* they brought their cups and saucers onto the train — what happened when the next train came and those passengers wanted a cup of tea? Pauline wondered.

She'd brought her own supplies — sandwiches her mother

had made for her, and biscuits, and strawberries from her father's garden, as well as tea in a big Thermos. Which was just as well; she didn't fancy going into battle with everyone else. Her carriage wasn't quite full, but she imagined people would be getting on and off as the train made its way down the main trunk line to Wellington. So far the seat next to her had remained empty, which she'd done her best to encourage by scowling at anyone who looked like they might want to sit in it, but she might just have to put up with a neighbour. It would be all right, she supposed, as long as no one expected her to talk to them.

As the train pulled out of Frankton the door at the end of the carriage opened and a woman came through. Pauline glanced at her and just knew where she'd choose to sit. The woman was even older than her mother and wore a black coat with a fox fur collar with a real fox head, and a black hat with a stupid little bird on it. Pauline leant into the aisle to see if she had her feet stuck up a pair of cats' bums. No, just ordinary shoes. Also, her lipstick was bright, bright red, which didn't suit her powdery pink skin. The woman paused and considered a seat next to a man farther up the carriage, then moved along, looked at another beside a fat lady, flagged that one as well, then spotted the gap next to Pauline.

She sat down heavily, wafting the smell of old lady violets in Pauline's face.

'Hello, dear.'

'Hello.'

'Oh, what a day I've had,' the woman said.

Pauline didn't reply.

'I'm Mrs Evans. What's your name, dear?'

Shut up and go away. 'Pauline.'

'I've been in Hamilton, staying with my sister. I live in Taumarunui. I come up about four times a year, for the shopping. It's so much better in Hamilton. Are you from Hamilton, Pauline?'

'No.'

'Oh? Where are you from, dear?'

'Auckland.'

'Oh, I do love Auckland. It's such a pretty city.'

On and on she went but Pauline stopped listening. Instead she took her sandwiches out of her duffel bag and opened them, hoping like mad her mother had put something really stinky on them like sardines. No, just cheese and pickle. Bugger. She put them away again.

Mrs Evans was saying, 'So anyway, I said to her, I wish I'd bought the pale blue one after all, and she said, but the burgundy really does suit you. But I don't know, I have such a lot that would go with the pale blue. So I'm wondering if they have a postal catalogue. You don't know if they do, do you?'

'Pardon?'

'Milne and Choyce? Have a postal catalogue?'

'I don't shop at Milne and Choyce.'

'Don't you?' Mrs Evans lowered her voice. 'It's just that I thought I'd seen that maternity frock for sale there when I was shopping the other day.'

Pauline thought that was pretty unlikely. Her mother had bought her some new clothes to take to Wellington but they were more likely to have come from Farmers or Rendells than Milne and Choyce.

'Someone bought this for me.'

Mrs Evans frowned. 'Ooh, that was quite a personal gift, wasn't it? In my day we made all our clothes when we were expecting.'

Well, don't bring the subject up if it bothers you, Pauline thought.

'Unless it was your husband,' Mrs Evans said, brightening.

Pauline had been waiting for this, and was looking forward to getting the empty seat back. 'I'm not married. I'm seventeen, I'm pregnant, and I'm on my way to the Bethany Maternity Home in Wellington. And the father's a Maori boy.'

Mrs Evans immediately broke eye contact with her. She

waited for what she clearly thought was a decent interval — two minutes — then picked up her handbag and moved to the seat next to the fat lady. Pauline sighed with relief and spread her stuff across the vacated space.

Not long after, a boy came through the carriage with a basket collecting up the cups and saucers brought on board from the Frankton refreshment room. Presumably they'd go back there from the next station on a north-bound train. Pauline was happy to see it. She didn't like loose ends.

She slouched in her seat and gazed out the window. It all looked the same — paddocks, cows, more paddocks and cows. She wished she'd bought a map so she knew which bits of the country they were passing through. Still, she supposed the train stations would tell her that. She started to relax. The rhythm and sound of the train felt nice and she wondered if she might be able to sleep after all. It was a pleasant, soothing feeling, the gentle rocking of the carriage and the click and clatter of iron wheels rattling over the tracks.

And then the baby moved, which was not a nice feeling because it only reminded her that she was pregnant with Johnny's baby and that Johnny was dead, lying cold and alone in the ground at Maungakakari. There had been a vacancy at the Bethany Home at Napier, but she'd chosen Wellington because she couldn't stand the idea of being that close to Johnny's grave. It would have driven her mental. The baby had started moving about three weeks ago and she knew that would continue now till it was born. Three more months of daily reminders that Johnny had gone. She didn't know how she would cope with it.

By the time the train went through Te Kuiti her backside was numb, the cows had changed to sheep, and there were more hills. She didn't think she'd ever want to live in Te Kuiti — the railway line ran right alongside the main street. But then the railway ran right along the bottom of Auckland's main shopping district too, next to the dirty old wharves, and that didn't seem to stop people going to town, spending money and having a good time.

After Te Kuiti the man sitting in front of her turned and said, 'You want to get out at Taumarunui. It's your last chance for a while for something to eat and drink.'

'I've got food and drink, thanks,' she replied.

'Have you done this trip before?' he asked.

Pauline sighed inwardly. 'No.'

'The Raurimu Spiral's coming up. Very spectacular. Hopefully there'll still be enough light to see it. You'll enjoy that.'

She doubted it. There were no stops between Taumarunui (another stampede into the refreshment rooms) and National Park, but the scenery certainly changed. It was extremely hilly and bush-clad, and at one point the train laboured in a full circle and went through a tunnel to haul itself up a particularly steep hill, which, she realised belatedly, was the Raurimu Spiral. Then it was down the other side and onto a flat, barren plain. When the train stopped again it was at Waiouru station, and it was dark.

She fell asleep after that, but woke some time later bursting to use the toilet. There was a boy in the seat next to her. She hadn't even woken when he'd sat down.

'Excuse me, please.'

He got up to let her out.

She made her way along the carriage to the toilet, went in, locked the door, wiped the seat with paper, and sat down. The relief! Then she washed her hands in the tiny hand basin and let herself out, wiping her hands dry on the front of her dress.

The boy next to her looked about twelve years old. He was reading now, squinting in the dim carriage light. He stood up to let her back in, apparently engrossed in his book.

Pauline wondered if he'd got his book out so he wouldn't have to talk to her. Good for him if he had.

'Hello,' he said as she sat down.

'Hello.'

He said, 'I got on at Feilding.'

Pauline nodded. 'Where are we?'

'Next stop Waikanae, then Paraparaumu, then Wellington.'

'Right.'

The boy went back to his book. Pauline ate the last of her sandwiches, finished her tea, and offered the boy a biscuit, which he accepted.

At Paraparaumu he left the train, and Pauline arrived in Wellington the way she'd started her journey — alone.

*

It was very early in the morning and still dark when Pauline stepped off the train at Wellington station and stood waiting on the platform for the baggage van to be unloaded. A cold, sharp breeze smelling of brine cut through her, and she suspected they must be near the sea. She spotted her suitcase on the growing pile emerging from the baggage van and grabbed it, then looked around for an exit sign. Not seeing one she followed everyone else and found herself walking into one side of rather a grand building, across a marble floor, and out the other to a semi-circular roadway. A row of taxis sat at a rank and she approached the first in line.

The passenger window was down and she said through it, 'Can you take me to Eighteen Kensington Street, please?'

The taxi driver immediately looked at her belly, and then winked. 'Hop in, love.'

Pauline nearly didn't, but she was cold, and tired. She got in.

The driver pulled out, humming to himself. After a while he said, 'In a bit of trouble, are you, love?'

Pauline stayed silent.

The driver turned round, not bothering to watch the road. 'Cat got your tongue?'

Piss off, Pauline thought. 'How far away is Kensington Street?' She wondered if she could walk the distance.

'Down the other end of Willis Street.'

Well, that doesn't mean anything to me. You idiot.

'Kensington Street's the home for unwed mothers, isn't it?' the man went on. 'I've driven a few lasses like you to that address.'

'Good for you.'

'Still, as long as you had fun getting where you are.' The driver paused. 'Did you?'

Pauline wound down the window and stuck her head out. The air was freezing and made her eyes water but at least she couldn't hear him any more.

Finally they arrived. She hauled her suitcase out of the car, went to the driver's window and thrust the tariff at him, money carefully saved by her mother and given to her so she wouldn't have to negotiate tram or bus timetables when she arrived in Wellington and could travel to the home in comfort and safety.

The driver gave her a card. 'That's my contacts. If you feel like a good time while you're here, phone me.'

Pauline handed the card back. 'Do you know what? I wouldn't touch you if you were the last man on earth, you *pig*.'

Then she picked up her case and walked up the driveway.

Chapter Twenty-one

November 1956

Kura Apanui said to Allie, 'How's your Pauline?'

'She's well,' Allie replied carefully, unrolling a bit more wool from the ball.

'We haven't see her since, well, not since our Johnny passed. Tell her not to be a stranger. She's a good girl, your Pauline.'

'I will. I will tell her that.'

Allie felt guilty. Pauline hadn't wanted Kura to know about the baby, so she'd supported her sister's decision. But it was hard to sit there in Kura's front room, knitting away, knowing she'd have a grandchild in eight weeks, a child of Johnny's, and not be able to tell her. She wouldn't, though, because if Pauline was anything she was loyal, and she'd be the same for her.

She'd been roped into knitting because they were so busy, but because they *were* so busy, she didn't really have much time to help with the knitting. She'd delivered the initial orders for baby clothes and blankets herself in Sonny's truck, though she still didn't have a driver's licence, and frequently crashed the truck's elderly gears in places like Queen Street's busiest intersections, but she was definitely getting the hang of it. Several of those orders had been repeated, and now they were receiving requests for lighter, summer baby clothes, which they could certainly make. If things continued to go well, they also had plans to introduce a range of quality, lightweight jumpers and cardigans for women and older children, and were knitting samples of those in quite a wide range of colours. Because of their initial sales, they could afford now to buy processed wool, and as they were purchasing in bulk they could get a discount, which was a bonus. But no matter how quickly Ana, Kura and Wiki knitted it wasn't fast enough, so there were two part-time women on board helping now, both expert knitters. Kura's girls Patricia and Mary were pretty good, but the family couldn't afford for them to leave their factory jobs as Kura wasn't making enough money yet. The business was actually bringing in some cash, and everyone was getting a little bit, but most of it was going back into wool, to pay for Allie's telephone, and other business expenses.

Ana had also had the telephone connected, at her own expense (actually, David's), and so had Colleen. Allie couldn't believe the difference it made to daily life. In just a few weeks it really was hard to even imagine how she'd managed without it. Back then, if she'd wanted to talk to Ana she had either to wait until she saw her next, or make a special trip to visit her. Now, she simply spoke to her on the phone, provided she was at home. Her mother had been even more delighted and had been ringing several times a day — until she'd realised how much it was costing her, after which the calls had dropped off markedly. But Kura and Wiki were still incommunicado, so the plan was to get them connected next, courtesy of the business.

Also, Ana had pointed out that now the business was making a bit of money, it would have to pay tax. Well, that had stopped everyone in their tracks. Tax? On the piddly amount they were getting? So Allie, who didn't want to admit she didn't know much at all about that side of things, had gone to see Louise, who did know because she did the books for her husband, Rob. Apparently, they could all be shareholders in Mana Knits and get paid a dividend once a year, which was no use to anyone, or they could all own the company and pay themselves a salary, or some of them could own it and employ the rest. It didn't matter which option they chose, tax would have to be paid on money generated by the company somewhere down the line. It sounded a bit complicated to Allie, but when she drew it on paper in the form of diagrams it made sense.

Wiki and Kura had understood the concepts quite readily (which had made Allie feel slightly stupid), and after a vote, they'd decided they'd form a proper company owned by Ana, Wiki, Kura and Allie, who would take a salary, and anyone else would be an employee. It was all a bit theoretical, however, given that at the moment there was hardly any money to pay anyone, but the papers had been lodged with the Companies Office, they'd appointed directors, and registered for tax. So they now felt rather important, but still broke.

At one knitting session at her house, Ana had said she thought it was important that if money did start coming in, then what they, as the company's owners, paid themselves shouldn't be more than what their employees were paid.

'Otherwise our women will feel like they might as well be working in some factory. There'll be no sense of ...' She'd trailed off, trying to think of the right word.

'Whakahoa,' Kura had said.

'Fellowship. Yes, that's it.'

'Ae, Maori women running their own business, making plenty of money. I like that,' Wiki had said.

'Except I'm not Maori,' Allie had pointed out.

And Wiki had said, 'You can be our token Pakeha.'

That had got a laugh.

And then Ana had said, quite seriously, 'So should we not hire any more Pakeha women? That's a bit rude, don't you think?'

Kura's reply had been, 'I don't care what colour they are, as long as they're bloody gun at knitting.'

'Wiki?' Ana had asked.

Wiki had taken ages to reply, so long, in fact, that Allie really had thought she was going to say no, she didn't want any Pakeha women in her company. It had been a really unpleasant feeling, waiting for Wiki's verdict.

In the end she'd said, 'I want women who all get along. I want women who've seen a bit of life. I want us to be strong, and happy to help one another. It doesn't matter if we're brown or white or green.'

And Kura had said, 'Don't know where we're going to get the green ones from.'

So now they were a band of four plus two part-timers, who could well become full time, depending on future orders. They might look at other part-timers too. Allie thought perhaps Awhi Manaia might be interested, and maybe even her own mother. They both knitted very well, though all part-timers would need to be carefully coordinated as every single item had to be knitted to a very specific size and pattern.

Now Allie said, 'I've been thinking, we might need to look at a proper delivery van if our orders pick up even more.'

'You mean buy one?' Ana said in alarm. 'We can't afford that.'

'No, I mean contracting a delivery service.'

'What's wrong with the truck?' Wiki asked.

'Well, imagine if Mr Holmes looks out his window and sees me climbing out of Sonny's old bomb and getting all these lovely baby clothes for his posh shop off the back of it. Won't do our reputation much good, will it?'

'Who's Mr Holmes?'

'Smith and Caughey's manager.'

'What's he doing looking out the window when he's supposed to be working?'

Allie started another row of knitting. 'It's a hypothetical situation, Wiki. But I do think we need something better than the truck.'

'You just don't like driving it,' Kura said. 'I've heard you graunching the gears.'

'I think you're probably right, Allie,' Ana said, 'but we'll have to wait. Let's see how we go over the summer, shall we?'

So Allie had to be happy with that as she drove home. She was cheered up when she discovered an envelope from Pauline in the letterbox. She'd been away for six weeks now and had written every week, which had been a bit of a surprise. And not only to her, but to Donna, and to Sid and Colleen as well. Allie hadn't really thought her sister was the letter-writing type.

She went inside, put the kettle on, fed Mr De Valera, flopped onto the sofa and opened the letter.

4 November 1956
Dear Allie and Sonny,
I hope you are well. I am doing all right. I have seven weeks to go and my belly is sticking out quite a long way now. It is getting annoying. I can still see my feet but only just. Lying on my back in bed is uncomfortable so I have to sleep on my side. I am having to do a wee just about every hour, which is also annoying.

I am still getting on quite well with my room mates, Nancy, Alice and Bev, but not with Carol, who is still being a proper cow. I am amazed she managed to get anyone to make her pregnant. What a bitch.

We are still being worked liked slaves here. All morning we are cleaning our rooms, the hallways, the bathrooms, the kitchenette and the lounge. But I refuse to clean the toilets. Why should I stick my hand down a dunny someone else has crapped in? It is disgusting. Matron says I am a stuck-up prima donna, but I have told her I have never done ballet in my life. She has given me extra cleaning duties.

She is such an old bat, Matron McCormack. I think she dislikes all of us, me especially. She is so religious. She tells us we are lucky God has not struck us dead for being so sinful. I told her if God really cared about us he would not have let us get pregnant and she said I'll go to hell for that. Where does she think we are now?

*We still have to do religious instruction every day,
and say prayers at every meal. I do not really mind this,
as it is not that different from church when we were
little. And it helps to pass the time. Other things we have
been doing are knitting, sewing, gossiping, smoking and
reading* True Confession *and Raymond Chandler books,
which we have to hide under our bedding.*

*We have been out a few times to do some shopping,
but we are not all allowed out together as people will
stare. There are fourteen of us unmarried mothers, and
I suppose that would look a bit funny, all lumbering
around like elephants.*

*Anyway, that is it from me for this week. I will write
again next week. Only seven weeks to go and I will be
back to normal. Yay!*

Love, your sister
Pauline

*

Wellington, November 1956

'Look, stop using my hairbrush, will you!' Carol brandished the
item in question in Pauline's direction. 'How many times do I
have to tell you?'

Pauline took a drag on her cigarette and barely looked up
from her magazine. 'And how many times do I have to tell *you*,
I haven't used it?'

'It's got white hairs in it. You're the only one with fair hair in
this room!'

'*Fair*, not white. Maybe someone's been brushing Matron's
cat with it.'

Carol stared at her brush, horrified. 'You *bitch*. I'm telling
Matron.'

'"I'm telling Matron,"' Pauline parroted in a silly voice as
Carol rushed off.

'Did you really?' Nancy asked.

'What?'

'Brush Snowball with her hairbrush?'

'So what if I did?'

Nancy laughed. 'You're such a cow.'

'I do my best. Anyway, she deserves it. She's always trying to get me in trouble.'

'She doesn't need to, though, does she?' Bev said. 'You do that yourself.'

Pauline shrugged. Who cared?

'Come on, let's get this room cleaned up.' Nancy urged. 'Matron'll be in soon.'

Sighing, Pauline stubbed out her smoke and heaved herself off her bed. Only five more weeks and she could stop rolling around like a beached whale. Actually, she was a little smaller than the other girls who were due with Christmas babies, but they'd been told that first babies often didn't arrive on their due dates. Hers was 18 December, but it was possible she'd be late and have a 'Jesus' baby, as the girls called infants born on Christmas Day. She'd always thought that would be really unfair, having your birthday on the same day as Christmas, but she wasn't bothered about her baby. She wouldn't be buying it presents.

She bent over her bed, smoothed and straightened the sheets, tucked them in at the corners with the requisite precision, folded her nightie under the pillow, then pulled up the candlewick bedspread. The bed was an old metal hospital job, with saggy springs on which a foam rubber mattress lay, which was uncomfortable and becoming more so the bigger she got. She also had a bedside table, a wardrobe, and a padded chair. Her suitcase was pushed beneath the bed and her things stored in the wardrobe. The room was reasonably large, fortunately, with big windows, and the bathroom down the hall was cold and white and contained two baths, a row of hand basins and several toilet stalls. Both were in the old part of the maternity home. The private patients — that is, the respectable, married women, whose fees helped cover the costs of the unworthy single women — were accommodated in the newer part of the home, along with the delivery suite and the nursery, but the two groups never mixed. In fact, Pauline had never once even seen a private patient.

Carol returned, announcing triumphantly, 'Well, I told her.'

'Good for you,' Pauline said, before plodding off down the hall to fetch the carpet sweeper.

Catching sight of Matron McCormack she tried to duck behind the open door of the storage cupboard, but was too slow.

'Pauline?'

Pauline shut the door and turned to face her. Matron stood squarely in the middle of the hallway, looking immaculate as usual in her beautifully pressed white uniform with the Salvation Army epaulets, starched white veil, and white stockings and shoes.

'May I remind you that you have an appointment with your social worker this afternoon at two o'clock? In the interview room?'

'I won't forget,' Pauline said, though she had.

'Please tie up your hair and wear something nice.'

'Are those people coming in again?'

'They are, and I would like you to make a good impression.'

Pauline nodded, thinking she could definitely manage that. She opened the storage cupboard again, looking for the carpet sweeper.

Then she heard: 'And Pauline? Please do not groom my cat with your room mate's hairbrush. Snowball doesn't care for it.'

As Matron's footsteps receded, Pauline smiled. She *could* be a right old bitch, Matron, but she had an amazingly good sense of humour sometimes. She dragged the carpet sweeper back to her room, then ran it back and forwards over the aging carpet. It didn't pick up much, threads of cotton and wool defied it completely and it had to be emptied every few minutes, but it was better than nothing. Then she just had the dusting to do, a quick wipe of the windows and sills, and a walk down to the big kitchen with the contents of the room's rubbish bin and ashtrays, and she was finished. Room-cleaning was the easiest of their chores, and the bathroom was the worst, as far as she was concerned.

As she went downstairs, she thought about what she might wear this afternoon. The couple she'd met last week with the social worker had been all right. They'd been married six years but couldn't have a baby and desperately wanted one, and were thinking about adopting hers. Matron had said it was a real opportunity because they knew the baby would be half Maori and didn't mind at all. So she was to be on her very best behaviour and present herself well. She expected that meant no smoking, or putting her feet on the furniture, or swearing. Well, she could refrain from being common for half an hour, she supposed. She'd wear the plain sapphire-blue dress with the short sleeves. She liked that one — it didn't make her boobs look like balloons. And perhaps she'd just put her hair back in a half ponytail. Or would that make her look as though she was twelve? How had she worn it last time? She couldn't remember.

Passing though the kitchen on the way to the big bin out the back she asked the cook, Mrs Riley, 'What's for lunch?'

'None of your business,' Mrs Riley snapped.

Well, it is if I have to eat it, Pauline thought. She didn't like Mrs Riley, who was always in a shitty liver, and hadn't met anyone at the home who did, not even the staff. Sister Atwood said privately they called her Rancid Riley, even though her cooking was quite good, which surprised Pauline because it didn't sound very Salvation Army of them, but it made her laugh.

She bumped into Sister Atwood on the way back upstairs.

'Morning. Early shift this week?'

Frances Atwood was hurriedly tucking her hair under her veil. 'Yes, and I was late to work. The chain came off my bicycle. Matron was *not* happy.'

Pauline couldn't think of anything worse, or sillier, than cycling round Wellington, because it looked very hilly, at least from her bedroom window. She liked Sister Atwood, though, very much, whom she thought was anything but silly. She also wasn't judgmental, or unkind, or prone to bad moods, and she was only in her twenties. She wore the Salvation Army epaulets yet she knew what it was to be a young woman. She went out to dances and the pictures, she had a boyfriend, and she had plans for the future, which she didn't mind chatting about with the girls in the home. And instead of making them feel as though they were missing out they felt included, as though their lives were only on hold, not ruined. It was nice.

'Why don't you just catch a tram or a bus?' Pauline said.

'Cycling's better for you, though I must admit it isn't on really windy days. Oh, while I remember, Matron says she forgot to say, but could you please pop in and see her in her office twenty minutes before your appointment.'

'What for?'

Sister Atwood shook her head. 'I don't know.'

Pauline shrugged. 'Well, here's a message for you. Don't go in the kitchen. Rancid Riley's in a proper mood. She snapped at me just before and I only asked her what's for lunch.'

'Message received.' Sister Atwood saluted. 'Good luck with your interview if I don't see you again before then, which I probably won't. I'll be in the delivery suite.'

Pauline said thanks. She knew Frances Atwood would be busy; one of the girls in the next room had gone into labour in the early hours and been moved across to the new wing before breakfast.

And she wouldn't need luck for her interview this afternoon either. The couple would either take the baby, or they wouldn't. And if they didn't, someone else would.

*

'Sit down, please,' Matron McCormack said.

Pauline did. Matron's little office was as tidy as she was, with everything in it straight, neat and dust-free. On the wall behind her desk were some framed certificates and a photograph of some old bloke in a Salvation Army uniform.

Sitting behind her desk, Matron clasped her hands on her blotter. 'You look very nice, Pauline.'

'Thank you, Matron.'

'Before this meeting shortly, I wanted to have a little word with you about your attitude.'

Pauline tried really hard to suppress a sigh as she thought, here we go, but a tiny bit of it escaped and she saw Matron notice. 'I won't ruin things,' she said. 'I want the baby to be adopted.'

'You won't ruin things on purpose,' Matron said. 'But you really can be quite an angry girl, Pauline. I would be very disappointed if for some reason that anger happened to show itself in front of these prospective adoptive parents. It's entirely possible they may worry that the personality of the mother may manifest in the child, and have second thoughts about the adoption. And that would be a tragedy, wouldn't it?'

Pauline nodded, because it would.

'Have you ever stopped to think about why you have these angry feelings?' Matron asked.

Astounded, Pauline stared at her. Finally, she said, 'Could it be, do you think, because my fiancé was killed, and now this baby's got no father?'

'Yes, I'm sure your boyfriend dying—'

'*Fiancé*,' Pauline interrupted.

'Fiancé, then. I'm sure your fiancé dying has a lot to do with your feelings, but Pauline, that's life.'

'No, it's death.'

Matron shook her head. 'It's life. It's part of the great tapestry that God weaves for us. You must understand that, being Catholic. As Salvationists our theology, of course, is Wesleyan, and as you've seen we don't celebrate the sacraments of holy communion, or of baptism, but the over-arching principles of our teachings aren't dissimilar to Catholicism. God has a plan for us, whether we like it or not. It's up to us how we accept that plan and ultimately use it to promote His message and bring hope and salvation to others. You can bring hope to another

couple by giving them your baby. Don't let your anger derail
your gift to them.' She leant forwards. 'And don't let your anger
at what has happened derail your own life from now on, Pauline.
Accept your loss as God's plan and look for the good in it. It will
be there.'

Pauline was buggered if she knew what that good might be.
Johnny was dead, he wasn't coming back, and that was that.
'I don't have a life now.'

'Of course you do. In a month or two all this will be behind
you and you'll go home, find yourself some work and everything
will go back to normal. Perhaps you'll even meet a nice young
man and start a proper family one day.'

'I was hoping to train as a stewardess for TEAL when I turn
twenty-one,' Pauline said. 'That probably isn't going to happen
now, is it?'

'I really have no idea what the criteria might be for a
Tasman Empire Airways stewardess. I've never even been in an
aeroplane!' Matron said, then laughed as if the very idea were
ludicrous. 'But I can't see why it shouldn't happen. I do know,
however, that *won't* come to pass, and, in fact, I think you'll find
that hardly anything positive at all will happen, if you don't curb
your anger and stop behaving badly.'

'But—'

'No buts, please. I know other people try your patience,
Pauline. They try mine too. You certainly do. But that's no
reason for you to be unkind, or rude, or to stir up trouble. Try
not to pick fights with people.'

'Do you mean Carol?'

'Perhaps.'

'Well, tell her. She's the one who's always moaning and
complaining and telling tales. What a miseryguts.'

'Have you ever considered the possibility that there might be
a reason for her unhappiness?'

'Yes, she got herself in trouble. None of us want to be here,
you know.'

Matron sighed. 'Try and find some serenity, Pauline. You'll feel better if you do, I promise you.' She looked at the watch pinned to her uniform. 'Now, it's time for your appointment. Go in there with your head up and do your best.'

Pauline dashed to the toilet, had a wee, tidied her hair one last time then knocked on the door of the interview room. The social worker, Mrs Nash, let her in.

'Good afternoon, Pauline.'

'Hello, Mrs Nash.'

'You remember Mr and Mrs Webb, don't you?'

Pauline nodded at the couple sitting at the table. 'Hello.'

Mr Webb half stood and did a little bob. Mrs Webb smiled and waggled her fingers. He had on the same sports coat and trousers he wore the previous week, but she was wearing a different dress, a blue spotted number with a white collar and a wide, tightly cinched red belt, and a little white hat. Pauline wondered if her waist would ever be that small again.

She sat in the last vacant seat. No one said anything for a moment, then Mrs Nash and Mrs Webb spoke at the same time. They laughed in that embarrassed way people do when something isn't actually funny, then Mrs Webb gestured at Mrs Nash to go first.

'I was just going to say, Pauline, have you been well?'

'Yes, thanks. Getting bigger, but I feel good.'

'That dress looks lovely on you,' Mrs Webb said. 'The colour suits you.'

'Thank you.'

It was strange, Pauline thought, Mrs Webb was probably only a year or so older than Allie, but thinking of her as 'Mrs Webb' made her seem nearly middle-aged. Mind you, thinking of Allie as 'Mrs Manaia' made Allie seem nearly middle-aged too.

'We've brought you a little something,' Mrs Webb said, handing a parcel across the table. It was wrapped in paper decorated with poodles holding ribbons in their mouths.

Pauline said, 'It's not my birthday.'

'No, it's just a small gift. For here, in the home. Go on, open it.'

Rigid with embarrassment, Pauline unwrapped the present. It was a quilted pink satin bed jacket. 'Oh, lovely. Thank you very much.' She already had the one Allie had knitted for her, which she much preferred. Maybe someone else could use this one.

Mr and Mrs Webb looked at each other and shared a little smile.

Mrs Nash retrieved some forms from her briefcase and set them out on the table. 'We were hoping you might consider signing the papers today, Pauline. How would you feel about that?'

Pauline looked down at the forms. 'To give up the baby?'

'Only if you feel the time is right.'

'It's just that babies are in such short supply,' Mrs Webb blurted. 'We had our name down for two before this and we lost them. We ... well, we really would like this one.'

'How do you mean you lost them?' Pauline was intrigued. Had she accidentally put them out with the rubbish?

Mrs Nash looked annoyed by Mrs Webb's outburst. 'It really was rather unfortunate,' she said. 'The first mother decided at the last minute she didn't want to give up her baby, and the second infant died minutes after it was born.'

'It died?' Pauline said. 'Crikey, that's unfortunate, all right.'

Mrs Nash's eyes narrowed ever so slightly.

'But that's not going to happen here, is it?' Mr Webb said, opening his mouth for the first time. 'You look as healthy as a horse. So if you could just sign the papers?'

'I'm not sure today's the right day after all,' Pauline said. And it wasn't the right day because she was starting to think she might not like the Webbs. She didn't want the baby, but she did want it to go to nice people. 'I'm not due for another five weeks. I'd prefer to leave the papers a bit longer.'

She watched Mrs Nash glare at Mr Webb as though he'd ruined everything. Had he? She wasn't sure yet.

Mrs Nash stood, opened the door and said brusquely, 'Thank

you very much for coming, Mr and Mrs Webb. I'll be in touch in a day or two.'

The Webbs drifted towards the door, looking a bit bewildered. Mrs Webb said, 'But the papers will be signed? We *will* get our baby?'

'Oh, the adoption will go ahead, don't you worry about that. I'll be in touch.'

Mrs Nash shut the door after them, and sat down again. She gave Pauline a long deliberate look, then took off her cat's-eye spectacles and polished the lenses on her handkerchief.

'Well, Pauline, you have come very close to ruining your chances there.'

'Why?'

'They don't have to take a little brown baby, you know. There are white babies available. In fact, there will be white babies available in this home very shortly.'

'I know. But it's true there aren't enough babies to go round, isn't it? If they don't want it someone else will. I just thought they were a bit pushy. Actually, Mrs Nash, I think *you're* a bit pushy.' Whoops, she was back-sliding. Matron would be disappointed.

'Well, dear, I won't tell you what I think of you, because that isn't really relevant. It's my job to match babies with childless married couples, and that is what I intend to do. The Webbs are decent people. If your baby went to them it would receive everything it needs, it would be loved, it would grow up in a stable home, and it would be far better off than it would be if it stayed with you. Frankly, I firmly believe unmarried mothers who keep their babies are selfish. It's a far more responsible thing to do to give up a child than to keep it. Now, I *strongly* suggest you sign these papers in the very near future, before the Webbs decide they can't be bothered with you and look elsewhere.'

'But how do you know they're the right people for the baby?' Pauline said. 'I should have a proper say in where it goes, shouldn't I? It's my baby, after all.'

My baby.

*

A week later Pauline caught sight of Mrs Nash after she'd visited one of the other girls in the home. She stood near the stairs and watched the social worker hurry outside in her sensible shoes, then went after her.

'Mrs Nash! Wait!'

Mrs Nash stopped, looking harassed. 'What is it? I'm in a bit of a rush.'

'I'll sign those papers, if you want. Now.'

The social worker was suddenly all smiles. 'Well, I've certainly got time for that! You won't regret your decision, you know. The Webbs are a lovely couple.'

She took Pauline by the arm and steered her back inside, where they sat down in a pair of chairs in the foyer. Mrs Nash set her briefcase on her knees and ferreted around for the adoption papers she'd filled out for Mr and Mrs Webb, and which they'd already signed. 'Don't tell me they're at the office,' she muttered. 'Oh, no, here they are.' She ran her eyes over each page, then handed both to Pauline. 'Here you go, dear.'

'Where do I sign?'

'Hold on, before you do, you're legally required to read the form.'

Pauline did, most of which she understood. Sort of. It was a bit lawyer-ish in places. Then she took the pen Mrs Nash offered her and signed her name at the bottom. Mrs Nash reclaimed the form, slipped it into her briefcase and snapped the lid closed.

'You've made the right decision, Pauline. For everyone. But may I ask, why didn't you want to sign before?'

'It's not that I didn't *want* to. I just didn't think I needed to. What's the hurry?'

'Well, surely the Webbs are entitled to some assurance? Try to look at it from their point of view.'

'Do you ever try to look at it from our point of view? Us girls?' Pauline asked.

'Of course. No one's ever forced to give up their child.'

Pauline raised one arched eyebrow.

Mrs Nash smiled brightly. 'But fortunately for childless couples, plenty of you choose to.'

Heaving herself to her feet, Pauline said, 'Doesn't mean it's easy, though. Here's your pen back.'

*

Early December 1956

Two weeks previously, Carol's baby had dropped. They'd all noticed, of course. She was still telling everyone she was due on 31 December, nearly a month away.

'She might be early,' Bev remarked, blowing twin jets of smoke out through her nostrils like a dragon.

Nancy agreed. 'She must have her dates wrong. You drop two to four weeks before you give birth and that's a fact.'

'Who told you that?' Pauline asked. She was knitting a little hat, though why, she didn't know. She had half a dozen beautifully knitted and complete baby outfits in the suitcase under her bed.

'Sister Gordon.'

'What does she know?' Pauline said.

'Probably quite a lot, actually. She *is* a maternity nurse.'

Bev said, 'My mother told me you can drop a couple of months before the baby arrives.'

'How many brothers and sisters have you got?' Nancy asked.

'Nine.'

'That might have something to do with it.'

They all giggled.

Everyone looked up as Carol lumbered into the lounge, her hands beneath her enormous belly. She'd been for a physical examination, and looked grumpy and uncomfortable. Backing up to a chair she lowered herself onto it.

'All right?' Bev asked.

'Well, *did* you get your dates wrong?' Nancy asked.

'No.'

'Sometimes it's hard to work it out,' Bev said kindly.

Carol stared at the window for such a long time Pauline thought she wasn't going to answer. She can't have been admiring the view, either — the net curtains were too heavy to see through. 'Not for me it isn't.'

'Why not?' Pauline asked.

Carol sighed and turned back to face them. 'I'm so sick of keeping this a secret. I really am. I only had intercourse once.'

Pauline exchanged a quick glance with the others: God, what shitty luck.

'And I didn't even want that,' Carol said. 'It was revolting. And terrifying.' She lit a cigarette and puffed on it angrily.

A heavy, embarrassed silence descended as the implications of her admission set in.

Then Nancy asked tentatively, 'Did you know the father?'

'I knew who he was, but no, I didn't know him.'

More silence, then Bev said, 'That must have been awful.'

'Did you tell?' Pauline asked.

Carol shook her head.

'Why not?'

'I live in a really small town. Would you have told?'

Pauline knew she probably wouldn't have. And she knew she should apologise to Carol for being mean to her, but she probably wouldn't do that, either. They all had private burdens.

'The baby, then,' Nancy said, indicating Carol's belly. 'How do you feel —?'

'I just want it out,' Carol interrupted. 'Out and gone. It's nothing to do with me.'

Bev asked, 'You've signed papers, haven't you?'

Carol nodded.

'Do the new parents know ... well ... how you got in the family way?'

'I don't know and I don't care. Matron did all the arranging.

I didn't want to talk to them. I still don't. They can just have it.'

They all stared at her. She sounded like she hated her poor little baby. Pauline wondered if maybe she did.

Her own baby dropped over the next few days, and what an odd feeling it was when it had settled, though at least she could breathe better now. Whenever the baby moved she could feel it in her bum and fanny, and also, unfortunately, even more in her bladder. Half her time now was spent in the loo. She already wasted enough time in there as it was, trying to crap, but it didn't matter how many stewed prunes she ate her bowel seemed to have gone on strike. Sister Atwood said the baby was pressing on it, and had given her some senna tea to try. She was supposed to have one small cup at night before bed, but she'd sniffed the leaves in the packet and they smelt so disgusting she hadn't had any yet.

She was moaning and whingeing about feeling bloated to Nancy one afternoon, while Nancy was fiddling around giving her a new hairstyle, when Carol came back from the bathroom saying her waters had broken.

'Shit,' Nancy said, alarmed, 'that's a bit early, isn't it?'

'Three weeks,' Carol said.

Pauline asked, 'Have you told a nurse?'

'No.'

Nancy handed Pauline the comb. 'Well, for God's sake, sit down. I'll go and get someone.'

Pauline lit a smoke and offered it to Carol.

'No, thanks, I feel a bit sick.'

'Are you not having any pains?' Pauline said, smoking the cigarette herself.

'I am, but they're not bad ones.'

'Why didn't you say something?'

Carol shrugged.

Nancy came charging back with Sister Gordon right behind her.

'Nancy says your waters have broken. Is that true?' Sister Gordon demanded.

'I think so.'

'Well, what was it like?'

'Water.'

Sister Gordon looked like she was about to lose her temper, but that wasn't unusual. 'What *colour* was it?'

'A bit pinky.'

'Was there meconium in it?'

'I don't know. What's meconium?'

'Baby's first bowel motion.'

Nancy and Pauline looked at each other and made disgusted faces.

'I don't think so.'

'And this was in the bathroom?'

Carol nodded.

'Did you clean it up?'

'No.'

Sister Gordon helped Carol heave herself out of the chair. 'It's off to the delivery suite for you, I think. And you two can go and sort out the mess in the bathroom.'

'Like hell,' Pauline exclaimed. 'I'm not cleaning up someone else's baby water!'

'You'll do as you're told, young lady!' Sister Gordon said over her shoulder as she led Carol away. Nancy and Pauline stayed where they were.

When Bev appeared a few minutes later, she asked, 'What's going on? I just heard Carol's baby's started.'

'It has,' Pauline told her.

'It's a bit early, isn't it?'

Nancy said, 'That's what I said.'

'We're supposed to be cleaning up the mess she made in the bathroom,' Pauline remarked, lighting another smoke. 'That's where her waters broke.'

'Well, why aren't you?'

'We don't want to.'

Bev snorted. 'Oh, grow up, the pair of you.'

'No one orders me around, 'specially not Grumpy Gordon,' Pauline said.

'Then why don't you do it for Carol, as a favour? How much fun do you think she's having right now? How much fun do you think this whole bloody thing's been for her? Come on, let's get the bucket and mop. It won't take us long.'

Grumbling, Pauline and Nancy got up and they all took turns swishing water and disinfectant around the bathroom floor, pulling the mop through the ringer in the bucket, then drying the floor with rags under their feet. There was no news about Carol and they didn't expect there would be for some time. Apparently first deliveries could take ages. Afternoon tea came and went (malt biscuits), then so did supper (cheese and parsley omelettes), and by bedtime they knew she wouldn't be back that night.

Pauline changed into her nightie and sat on the side of her bed, eyeing her bulbous stomach with distaste. 'I feel disgusting,' she announced.

'You're not *that* big,' Bev said. 'I'm bigger than you and you're due before me.'

'It's not just my belly. I've got hideous stretch marks, my belly button's popped out, my nips have gone all huge and dark, and my arse won't work and it *really* hurts.'

Nancy laughed. 'Your arse does?'

'Mmm.' Pauline felt her face redden. This was so embarrassing. 'I think something might be wrong. It's got these lumpy things on it.'

Bev shrieked. 'You've got piles.'

Giggling like mad, Nancy said, 'You get them from straining on the loo. It's sort of like the inside of your bum's falling out.'

Pauline was *horrified*. 'Will they go away? How do I get rid of them?'

'I think you just have to stop being constipated. And ask Sister Atwood for some pile ointment.'

Immediately, Pauline opened her bedside drawer, got out the little packet of senna tea and made herself a cup in the kitchenette. It really was foul, but she drank a second cup just to make sure.

In bed she tried to read a book, but couldn't focus. Nancy and Bev were also reading, magazines propped against their bellies.

Interrupting them, she asked, 'Have you ever thought you might want to keep your babies?'

Both girls looked at her.

'No,' Bev said. 'What's brought this on?'

'Nothing.'

Nancy said, 'I haven't, either. My parents would kill me if I went back home with a baby. It was shameful enough for them with me having to leave town. *Everyone* knows what that means.'

'Have *you* thought about it?' Bev asked.

'No,' Pauline replied.

'Then why ask?'

'I was just wondering.'

Nancy frowned. 'You've signed the adoption papers anyway, haven't you?'

'Last week,' Pauline said, then looked back at her book. She didn't want to talk any more: she'd asked her question and got her answers.

Chapter Twenty-two

Auckland, December 1956

Three weeks before Christmas Allie and Sonny went round to visit Gina and Awhi. It would be Gina's first Christmas without her mother and Sonny wasn't happy about it. Allie, though, felt a little differently.

'I don't think it matters whether it's Easter or Christmas or St Patrick's Day or whichever holiday to Gina,' she said to Sonny in the truck on the way over. 'When you're little, holidays are just about presents and food. I think she probably misses Polly every day.'

'I don't see why she should. She never *saw* Polly every day.'

'Well, you know what I mean. She must wonder where she is, why she hasn't been to see her.'

'I think Mum's told her she's gone away.'

'That's not very helpful, is it?'

'What's she supposed to tell her? Polly has gone away.'

'I can't believe no one's got a clue where she is.'

'I can,' Sonny said. 'She was always the best at hide and seek when we were kids at Okahu Bay. Once she hid for two days. She was up on the church roof.'

'She's been gone longer than two days, though, this time, hasn't she?'

Sonny said nothing. On Kitemoana Street he parked outside his mother's place. They'd barely hopped out of the truck before Gina came belting round the side of the house, followed closely by Awhi, shouting, 'Come back here, you!'

Poor Awhi, and poor Gina, Allie thought. Awhi hadn't let her granddaughter out of her sight for a second since the Murdoch episode, and the effort was running her ragged. Perhaps she and Sonny could take Gina for a little while, and give Awhi a break.

'Uncle Sonny! Auntie Allie!' Gina shrieked, racing for the gate.

'Hello, sweetheart!' Allie called.

Sonny stepped over the gate and picked her up, swinging her high into the air until her screams reached an ear-piercing pitch. Allie could see Awhi trying not to wince.

'Put her down, Sonny, your mother'll have a stroke.'

'Hello, Mum,' Sonny said, settling Gina on his shoulders, queen of the world.

'Hello, son, Allie.'

Gina grabbed Sonny's ears like handles and kicked solidly at his chest with her little bare heels. 'Giddy-up, horsey!'

Allie suppressed a smile as Sonny, grimacing, bent at the waist, flipped Gina over his head (more screams) and set her on the ground. 'No horsies today. Uncle has to talk to Nannie.'

Undeterred, Gina danced around them, a pixie filled with the energy of five adults.

'I've just put the kettle on,' Awhi said.

As they headed inside Allie noticed she was limping. 'Have you hurt yourself?'

'I blimmin' well slipped going down the back steps chasing that one. It's nothing.'

'Is it your hip?' Sonny asked.

'Probably.'

Allie knew Awhi had had a sore hip on and off for years. 'Have you been to the doctor?'

'The doctor?' Awhi said, astonished. 'I don't go to the doctor.'

Allie laughed. 'You sound just like my nan. She never went to the doctor, either.'

'The one that died?' Awhi asked.

'Mmm.'

'Ae, well.'

Sonny helped his mother up the back steps. Inside, Allie made her sit down while she got the tea things together.

'Have you heard anything from Polly?' Sonny asked.

It was the same question he asked every time they visited.

'No,' Awhi replied.

'Mummy's gone away,' Gina said.

'I know,' Sonny said. 'Where do you think she's gone, Gina-ballerina?'

Gina giggled at his name for her. 'Heaven?'

Allie nearly spilt boiling water on herself. What had Awhi been telling her?

Sonny said, 'Gina, do you know what heaven is?'

'God's house.'

'And what else does heaven mean?'

'You get free lollies when you get there?'

Awhi made a rude noise. 'Ah, it's those idiot kids from next door, filling her head with rubbish.'

'Sweetie, do you know what dead is?' Sonny asked.

'Mmm, no,' Gina replied.

'Well, that's good.'

'Mummy's coming back,' Gina said.

Allie said, 'How do you know that?'

''Cos if she doesn't, I won't see her again,' Gina replied, with perfect logic.

When Awhi shuffled off to the toilet, Allie whispered to Sonny, 'Why don't you suggest we take Gina for a while? Awhi really needs a rest, don't you think?'

Grinning hugely, Sonny said, 'Would you like that?'

'I'd love it. Gina can come to work with me, and if I have to see customers, the Mana ladies can look after her, or I'll bring her here.'

Delighted with this idea, Sonny gave Gina her colouring book and crayons so her ears wouldn't flap, then manoeuvred the conversation in the right direction. Awhi realised fairly quickly what he was suggesting.

'No.'

'You need a break, Mum. She'll be fine with us, and you can see her whenever you like.'

'I can drive the truck now,' Allie pointed out. 'I can bring her over here, or come and pick you up to visit us. Actually, we're thinking about another part-time knitter for our business. If you were interested, you'd see her a lot because she'd be with me.'

Awhi flapped a dismissive hand. 'I don't want to sit around knitting with a lot of nosy old whaeas, listening to all that gossip.'

'Well, you know,' Allie said gently, 'you'd probably be the oldest one there.'

Sonny laughed.

'Shut up, you,' Awhi grumbled.

'We do gossip a bit, though,' Allie admitted.

Awhi asked, 'Would I get paid?'

'Not much to start with, but more and more as time goes on. Fingers crossed, that is.'

'And if you took her for a while, you'd give her back?'

Sonny patted his mother's hand. ''Course we would, Mum. It's just to give you a rest. Just for a few months.'

'I am tired,' Awhi said. 'And nearly all my savings are gone. It's not cheap, looking after a moko.'

'Well, we'd pay for everything for her, wouldn't we?' Allie said to Sonny.

Sonny nodded. 'Do you need some money, Mum?'

'No. I just need …' Awhi sighed heavily. 'All right, you take her. But just for a while, mind. Just till I'm back on my feet again, you hear? That little girl's my responsibility.'

'She's not really, Mum. She's everyone's. She's family.'

Awhi said, 'But she's special.'

Because she's Polly's, Allie thought, and Polly's gone. And you still love her.

*

Wellington, December 1956

Carol gave up her baby as easily as she might offer someone a cigarette. She was born at two-thirty on the morning of 12 December, two weeks and six days early, so a little under-cooked, as Carol herself said. Though Carol never actually saw the baby, as she was taken to Karitane Hospital as soon as she was born. She didn't want to see her, either. Carol stayed on at Bethany for another eight days until her milk dried up, during which time she heard from one of the nurses that the baby was doing well and her new parents were thrilled with her, then she packed her things and went back to Masterton. Bev and Nancy offered to write, but Carol said no thanks, because she probably wouldn't write back.

Pauline went into labour on 17 December.

'Trust you to do it right on time,' Nancy said as Pauline stood looking at a damp patch on her chair in the dining room.

'I thought I was wetting my pants,' Pauline said. 'Yuck, it's still coming out.'

Bev grabbed a tea towel off the servery and handed it to her. Pauline stuck it between her legs.

'Ew, that could have been anywhere,' Nancy said.

Pauline waddled upstairs and lay on her bed. How annoying. It was shepherd's pie for lunch too. Rancid Riley made a really nice shepherd's pie. Bev had gone to fetch Sister Atwood, who soon knocked on the bedroom door.

'Pauline, it's me. Can I come in?'

No other staff member asked permission to enter — they just barged in.

'Course you can.'

Frances Atwood sat on the end of the bed. 'Have your waters broken?'

'Looks like it.'

'Can I have a feel of your belly and a bit of a look? Can you take your knickers off?'

Pauline nodded, wrestled her soggy pants down and dropped them on the floor. Sister Atwood carefully felt her stomach, then had a look up her dress.

'Whoops,' she said after a moment.

'What?'

'How long have you been having contractions?'

'The crampy feelings?'

'Yes.'

Pauline thought. 'I don't know. Since about five this morning?'

'Oh God, Pauline, you twit!' Bev exclaimed.

'And have they been getting stronger?' Sister Atwood asked.

'They have, actually.'

'Because I think I can see the top of baby's head.'

Pauline's heart nearly leapt out of her mouth. 'Am I in proper labour?'

'I'll say you are. Come on, up you get. I'll get the wheelchair.'

Pauline was taken straight to the delivery suite. Matron McCormack hurried in a few minutes later, a theatre gown on over her uniform.

'Well, you're a bobby-dazzler, aren't you?'

Pauline had been given a gown of her own to wear. Matron lifted the hem and inspected her nether regions. 'Yes, definitely on its way. Are the contractions not bothering you?'

'Yes,' Pauline admitted, because they were now her waters had broken.

'Well, don't push yet.' Matron had another look. 'That's a fine collection of haemorrhoids you have there. I suspect they'll be even worse by the time baby's arrived.' She turned to Sister Atwood. 'We won't have time for an enema or to shave the patient. It'll be out before you've found the razor.'

Pauline grimaced. 'Am I supposed to feel like I want to go to the loo?'

'Hopefully it's just the baby pressing on your back passage,' Matron said.

'When can I push?'

'Just wait.'

'I *really* want to push.'

'I said *wait*. We're not quite ready. *You* might not be ready.'

Pauline grabbed her knees, put her chin on her chest and gave a great, grunting shove. Her vagina felt as though it was being stabbed with flaming knives and the pressure in her pelvic area was immense, but she clearly felt the baby's head pop out. Matron darted forwards to support it in her hands. 'Well, you'll have to deliver the rest now, won't you?' she said crossly.

Panting, Pauline closed her eyes. Then, when the next contraction came, she bore down so forcefully everything went red, she saw gently floating stars and blood pounded in her ears. This time she thought the pressure in her pelvis and bum might explode her spine, but the baby stayed stuck. The dreadful cramp passed and she gathered herself, bore down again mightily with the next one, and with a last burning, stabbing rush, it was out.

'Oh look, you've got a little boy,' Sister Atwood said.

'Sister!' Matron snapped at her.

The umbilical cord was cut, the baby dried off, then he was weighed, wrapped and a little blue cap placed on his head.

'Would you like to hold him?' Matron asked.

Pauline opened her mouth to say no, but what came out was, 'Yes.'

Matron placed the small bundle in her arms.

He was a bit purple, but he wasn't all wrinkled and squashed-looking like a little monkey, like some new babies Pauline had seen. He had lots of black hair and huge dark eyes and a lovely nose and the sweetest lips.

And he looked just like Johnny.

*

Pauline said, 'Well, you'll just have to tell them I've changed my mind.'

Something very unexpected had happened to her the moment she'd seen her baby. In an instant he'd gone from being something she'd thought she just couldn't tolerate in her life, to the very essence of what she wanted most. He was a tiny Johnny, a little living, breathing reminder of everything she'd loved in her man, and although this baby would grow up to be someone else, Johnny would be in him. She wasn't giving that away. She loved him already. She was going to be one of those selfish, irresponsible unwed mothers and bloody well keep him.

'I don't think you quite understand, Pauline,' Mrs Nash said. 'It's too late. You've signed the adoption papers, and so have Mr and Mrs Webb. It's all been arranged.'

'Then I'll unsign them. I've changed my mind. I'm keeping him.' Pauline looked at Matron McCormack. 'I can do that, can't I?'

Matron opened her mouth to speak, but Mrs Nash butted in. 'Pauline. Dear. The Webbs have gone to *considerable* expense preparing for the arrival of their new baby. In fact they've furnished an entire nursery, and it's delightful too. I've seen it with my own eyes. They've bought a bassinet, a cot — I know, already! — a lovely suite of white bedroom furniture, a pram, a highchair, and so many clothes and toys! Now, what do you have for the child?'

'Nothing, but—'

'That's right. Also, Mrs Webb has recently resigned from her job specifically to raise their new baby, so that's also a consideration, although Mr Webb, of course, is perfectly able to support the family on his income alone. How will you support yourself and the baby, Pauline?'

Matron had another go. 'Mrs Nash—'

The social worker cut her off again. 'Not to mention the

terrible disappointment the Webbs will feel if they are to be deprived of this child. As I think you'll recall being told, Pauline, if you withhold your baby, this will be the third time they miss out on an adoption.'

Yackety yack yack, Pauline thought.

'Mrs *Nash*!' Matron nearly shouted. 'If you will please allow me to speak.'

Her mouth clamped shut, Mrs Nash finally looked at her.

'Good. Thank you,' Matron said. 'Now, I know that Pauline has entered into a written agreement with the Webbs, but you and I both understand that those agreements are not legal documents. We also know it is recommended that girls who are considering giving up their babies be given at least some time after the birth to reflect on that option. Don't we, Mrs Nash?'

'Well, yes, we do know that. However, and forgive me for stating the obvious, Matron, isn't it your organisation's mission to help find homes for babies born to unwed mothers? Why are you apparently trying to prevent this adoption?'

Eyeing her, Pauline didn't think Mrs Nash gave a shit whether Matron forgave her or not.

'I am not trying to prevent it,' Matron said. 'I am simply requesting that we follow the recommended procedure. If I allowed every baby born in this home to be rushed out to new parents within twelve hours of its birth, I would have to consider myself to be colluding in a practice no better than ... than baby farming.'

Mrs Nash looked aghast. 'Baby farming! Are you accusing me of being a baby farmer?'

'Of course not. And I agree that a child is much better off with two parents, even if those parents are adoptive, and that the unwed mother who gives up her baby is to be admired for her sense of responsibility. But, really, the baby in question was only born last night, and I really would prefer that we abide by the guidelines.'

'When would you release the baby?' Mrs Nash asked.

'Perhaps you could come back at the end of the week?' Matron suggested. 'Baby would have had the benefit of the breast by then too.'

Mrs Nash stood. 'All right, then, Friday. I'll be back then. Good day.'

*

'I heard breastfeeding was supposed to feel nice,' Pauline said, making a pained face. 'It doesn't. It bloody well hurts.'

'Are you doing it right?' Nancy asked.

'How should I know? How can it hurt? He hasn't even got any teeth. Ow!'

Sister Gordon appeared. 'What's the problem?'

'It hurts when he tries to feed,' Pauline said.

'Try him on a bottle. He doesn't need the breast. He's going on Friday, isn't he?'

'Ah, fuck off, you old bat,' Pauline muttered. She was getting sick and tired of people saying that.

'I beg your pardon?'

'She said take off his hat,' Bev said quickly, whipping off the baby's little knitted cap, making him blink in surprise. 'It *is* quite warm in here.'

'Where's Sister Atwood?' Pauline asked. 'She's on today, isn't she?'

'She's busy,' Sister Gordon said. 'I'll make up a bottle. We'll try him on that.'

When she'd gone, Pauline put the baby on her shoulder. 'Nance, can you go and find Sister Atwood for me, please? She'll know what to do.'

'Have you thought of a name yet?' Bev asked.

'Daniel John.'

'I like that. John after his dad?'

Pauline nodded; of course John after his dad.

Nancy returned with Sister Atwood in tow. 'Is he not latching on properly?' she asked. 'That's usually what causes painful feeding.'

'Dunno, but my nips are killing me.'

Sister Atwood took the baby. 'Here, let me show you how to put him on. Oh, isn't he sweet?'

'His name's Daniel John.'

'Oh, that's lovely. Two saints.' Frances Atwood frowned. 'Not that we worship saints in the Salvation Army. We admire them, though.'

She settled Daniel in the crook of Pauline's arm, then showed her how to place her breast against his chin so the nipple went fully into his mouth at the proper angle to allow him to suck efficiently.

'God, that's better!' Pauline exclaimed. After a minute she blurted, 'Daniel and I are leaving tomorrow, at lunchtime. We're going home.'

Bev and Nancy exchanged a nervous glance.

Her gaze still on the baby, Frances said, 'Are you?'

'He's mine and I'm keeping him,' Pauline said. 'I'm not waiting round till Friday for that Mrs Nash to come back.'

Frances asked, 'Will you be up to it? It's only been twenty-four hours.'

'I'll be on the train most of the way. Not much effort involved in that. I just wanted to get the feeding sorted out before we go.'

'It'll take a bit of practice,' Frances warned. 'Especially when your milk comes in properly. How's your bleeding?'

'No worse than my monthlies. How long will that last?'

'A week or so, then you'll get dribs and drabs. How are the cramps?'

'Fine,' Pauline said. 'It's a secret, us leaving.'

'I gathered that.'

'Will you tell Matron?'

'Not if you don't want me to.'

'Why wouldn't you? You're a Salvation Army nurse. Don't you think I should give him up?'

'I think you should do what you think is right, and I really don't think someone else should be making that decision for you. It's not right, putting pressure on girls to give up their babies if they don't want to. That's not doing God's work, that's—' Frances stopped abruptly. 'Anyway, I'm not sure how you're going to sneak out of here with a suitcase *and* a baby.'

'I won't have to sneak. I'm not in prison. I can just walk out.'

'Well, I'm afraid I won't be able to help you,' Frances said. 'It's my day off. Also, I don't think Matron would be very happy with me.'

'That's OK, I didn't expect you to help,' Pauline said, and she didn't.

'How will you get to the train station?'

'I don't know. There'll be a bus or something.'

'Try him on the other breast now,' Frances suggested. 'Have you told your family you're bringing a baby home?'

'No,' Pauline said. 'Not yet.'

*

It was raining the following day. Pauline had an umbrella, but not a raincoat, and she could see out the window how the wind was whipping the trees and bushes in all directions. Her umbrella would be inside out in five minutes.

She took her time with her morning chores, then chose a warm outfit for Daniel, and packed her suitcase before sliding it back under her bed.

Just before lunch she went across to the nursery. Daniel was sleeping but woke when she picked him up out of his plain little crib, and cried until she got him settled again.

'Where are you going with that child? It's not feeding time.'

It was Sister Walsh, who supervised the babies before they left the home.

'I've just come for a cuddle. I'm allowed,' Pauline said. 'He's going on Friday. Matron said I'm allowed to have time with him.'

Sister Walsh said, 'I'm not aware of that arrangement.'

'Well, ask her.' Pauline knew she probably wouldn't — she'd be too busy.

'Fifteen minutes, then. I don't want his routine disrupted.'

'I'll just take him for a little walk in case he cries again.'

Pauline took Daniel back to her room, dressed him quickly in several layers, wrapped him, then put on her outdoor shoes and shoved the last of her things in her suitcase while Bev and Nancy had final cuddles with Daniel.

And then it was goodbye. They'd already swapped addresses so there wasn't much left to say. They hugged, Pauline settled Daniel in her right arm and grabbed her suitcase with her left hand.

'Thanks, girls. Wish me luck.'

'Take care, keep in touch,' Bev said.

Nancy said, 'We'll miss you.'

'I'll miss you, too. Good luck with your babies.'

And then she was walking away, down the stairs, and out the front door, where the wind snatched at her hair and whipped rain into her face and stray leaves around her legs. She thought about her umbrella, but to open it she'd have to put everything, including Daniel, down, so she didn't bother. Instead she held him against her front to protect him and headed down the driveway. By the time she reached the street her hair was stuck to her head and water was running down her face, but she kept going, peering up and down the road in the hope of seeing a bus or tram stop.

A car horn tooted but she ignored it. Daniel was crying now, and her left arm felt as though it was made of lead from the weight of the suitcase and she'd only gone about a hundred yards.

The car tooted again, then a little Morris Minor drove up beside her. The driver's door opened and Frances Atwood jumped out. She ran round and took Pauline's suitcase off her.

'Honestly, you're soaked!' Frances scolded, opening the passenger door. 'Hop in.'

Pauline got in while Frances put the suitcase on the back seat, then started the car and drove off.

'I didn't know you had a car,' Pauline said.

'I don't, it's my boyfriend's.'

'Fancy you driving past just when I came out.'

Frances rolled her eyes. 'I've been waiting for you since eleven o'clock. I'm taking you to the train station.'

Pauline stared at her, then burst into tears.

'Oh, look, I'm sorry, Pauline, I didn't mean to upset you,' Frances said.

Waving the apology away, Pauline checked her pockets for a handkerchief, but gave up and wiped her nose on the edge of Daniel's blanket. 'I'm not upset. It's just … that's really nice of you. Why is he crying?'

'He probably didn't like getting rained on. Put him on the breast. A fed baby is a happy baby.'

Pauline did just that. David latched on straight away, which was a relief. By the time they pulled up outside the train station he'd fallen asleep. Frances held him while Pauline went to the booking counter and bought a ticket with the last of her money for the mainline express to Auckland, which was leaving shortly. A ticket on a 'mixed' train — that is, one that hauled freight as well as passengers — was cheaper, but the trip took longer because there were more stops, but Pauline thought bugger it. She'd just have to starve.

She almost missed the train, though, because she was in the toilets changing her sanitary pad. She rushed out when she heard the boarding announcement over the tannoy, to find Frances standing by the train holding Daniel and looking like she was about to have a fit.

'Hurry up!' she called. 'The doors are closing in a minute!'

Pauline hurried over, feeling her post-baby belly wobble annoyingly, grabbed her suitcase and hurled it onto the train.

A guardsman came trotting up. 'Hang on, that can't go on there. It has to go in the baggage van.'

'Stiff cheese,' Pauline said. She took Daniel from Frances, kissed her cheek and stepped onto the train. 'Thanks for everything. You've been fantastic.'

'I'm glad to have helped. You look after yourself and Daniel,' Frances said. 'Oh, and I've popped a few things in your case, for the trip home.'

A whistle blew, flags waved and the train doors closed. Pauline watched through the window as the platform receded and then Frances was gone, and then it was just her and her baby, on their way home to Auckland.

*

Pauline realised she was probably going to arrive back in Auckland at roughly the same time of day she'd got to Wellington, which had been very early morning. What time did the buses start running, she wondered, because she definitely didn't have enough money for a taxi from the train station to Orakei. She could scratch together enough to ring her mother from a call box, now that she'd joined the twentieth century and had the phone put on, but what would be the point? Her parents didn't own a car. And to ask Sonny and Allie to pick her up would be thoughtless, when they were so desperate for their own baby. She'd rather break the news to them more gently than that. Oh well, she'd worry about getting home when the time came.

And then it occurred to her: She couldn't be so casual about her arrangements any more — she had Daniel to think about now. It wouldn't do to sit around in a bus shelter for two hours until the buses started running, and neither could she wander the streets before dawn waiting for the trams. Daniel needed to be indoors, safe and warm. The responsibility of him made her mouth go dry and her heart thump, but that didn't help with the problem of getting home. It just made it worse.

Once again she'd managed to get a seat by herself, possibly, she thought, because no one wanted to sit next to someone with a baby. A week ago she wouldn't have, either. But he wasn't crying; he was still fast asleep. She loosened his wrap and felt his nappy beneath his knitted pants. Still dry. Good, though she didn't know how long that would last, or where she'd change him when the time came. She didn't fancy doing it in the train toilet. Yuck. And where was she going to put his dirty things? She hadn't thought of that. Perhaps she'd empty her duffle bag and shove everything in there.

Actually, looking at it, there were quite a few things she hadn't thought about. For example, she'd only brought three sanitary pads with her, and she'd already used one. It would be incredibly embarrassing, but at this rate she might arrive in Auckland smelling like a fishmonger's at the end of a long, hot day. Also, she'd have to take Daniel with her when she went to the loo, and she really didn't want him somewhere so germy, not to mention leaving her suitcase unattended. What if someone pinched it? Mind you they couldn't go far, could they? And there was also the matter of having run out money. She knew she'd be dying for at least a cup of tea at some stage. Frances said she needed to drink lots to help her milk come in, and she couldn't if she was skint. But then she couldn't get off the train at the refreshment stops with Daniel anyway, could she? They'd be killed in the crush. God.

By the time the train had passed through Paraparaumu she was bored, so she opened her suitcase to see what Frances had put in there for her, and what she found nearly made her cry again.

There were some home-made corned-beef sandwiches, a packet of barley sugars, a slightly squashed bunch of grapes, a packet of sanitary pads, four new nappies, a small box of tissues, four empty folded paper bags, several *New Zealand Woman's Weekly*s, and an envelope containing a five-pound note.

Saint Frances, Pauline thought, smiling to herself. Saint Frances of Bethany.

When the train stopped at Waikanae, a girl got on and asked if she could take the seat next to Pauline. She was Chinese, and slender with very long, straight hair.

Pauline could see there were no other seats, so she moved her suitcase to the floor and put her feet up on it.

'That's a very sweet baby,' the girl said. 'Is it a boy or a girl?'

'A boy.'

'He looks brand new.'

'He is. He's just over two days old.'

'That *is* new. I'm Lee Bao. Bao's my first name.'

'I'm Pauline Roberts. This is Daniel.'

'Hello, Pauline.'

'Hi, Bao. Is that spelt B-o-w?'

'No, B-a-o. It's my great-great-grandmother's name. She was a pirate.'

'True?' Pauline was impressed. 'I don't know what my great-great-grandmother was. Hungry, probably, from the potato famine. Are you from China?

'No, I'm a New Zealander. I was born here. My people came here to Lawrence in the gold rush. Some stayed and some moved on. I was living in Wellington but I've been visiting family in Waikanae, and now I'm off to live with family in Auckland. Where are you from?'

'Auckland.'

'Have you been away to have your baby?' Bao asked.

Pauline was amazed by her frankness. She decided she quite liked it. 'I have, actually.'

'And you're keeping him?'

Pauline nodded.

'You're very brave. Good on you.' Bao giggled. 'My mother and father would skin me alive if I brought a baby home. But he's so lovely. You must be very proud of him. Does the father not want him?'

'He died.'

'Well, *that* stinks.'

Pauline laughed. 'It does. And it's not really funny. It stinks a lot.'

But, she decided, having Lee Bao as a companion on the way home to Auckland wouldn't stink. She was chatty but not in an annoying way, she was interesting, and she was refreshing. And she seemed *delighted* by Daniel. When she tentatively asked if she could hold him, Pauline was happy to let her, and nipped to the loo while she had the chance. And then when he woke for a feed, Bao held up his blanket to give them some privacy. Breastfeeding on a train would have been awkward enough, but she didn't have a maternity bra, so exposing a breast for Daniel could have been a disaster. The same applied when it came time to change him: behind the blanket curtain they were nice and private and no one could stare at his tiny little bottom, or see that she wasn't very good at pinning nappies yet.

But Bao really came into her own at the refreshment stops. Bloody hell, that girl would be handy at the pie cart, Pauline thought as she watched her shove and barge her way off the train and through the crowd to the front of the queue. A few minutes later she was backing out of the tearoom, elbows tucked in, barking at people to watch out, a cup of tea balanced in each hand, sandwiches and biscuits sticking out of her jacket pockets.

And then they'd share the feast, accompanied by squashed grapes and barley sugars, as Daniel lay across their laps and the train rattled on up through the North Island. They dozed and woke, dozed and woke, until finally the train pulled into the Auckland city terminus down near the docks.

Pauline and Bao gathered up their things and disembarked, and stood on the platform in the cool, pre-dawn air, stretching while Bao waited for her luggage to be unloaded from the baggage van.

'Which way are you heading?' Pauline asked.

'Up to Grey's Avenue.'

'Chinatown?'

Bao nodded. 'My family have a restaurant there. Which way are you going?'

'Over to Orakei.'

Spotting her suitcase, Bao dived in and grabbed it. The crowd of passengers on the platform was starting to thin out now.

The girls hugged and Bao kissed the top of Daniel's head. 'Good luck, Pauline.'

'Thanks, Bao. You too.'

As she walked off Bao suddenly turned and called, 'Keep in touch, if you like. The restaurant's called Mr Lee's.'

Pauline waved. Then she stood, wondering what to do next. She probably had enough left for a taxi home, thanks to Frances, so she walked to the rank up the road and waited. A taxi appeared fairly quickly, so she got in and asked to go to Orakei.

'You're up early,' the driver said. 'Or is it late?'

'Late. Just got off the train from Wellington.'

'Well, let's get you home, then.'

Pauline relaxed. She'd half expected him to say something rude about Daniel. He couldn't have known where they'd come from, but the nasty memory of the Wellington taxi driver was still fresh.

Unfortunately, when the taxi pulled up outside her parents' house, the fare the driver quoted was a little more than the amount of money she had left.

'Wait on,' she said, 'I'll run in and get the rest. Won't be a minute.'

She left her suitcase on the lawn and hurried down the path and up the steps and banged loudly on the back door. Nothing happened for a few minutes but eventually a bleary-eyed Colleen opened it.

'Pauline! What are you doing home!'

'Hi, Mum. This is Daniel, your grandson. Can I have some money for the taxi?'

Chapter Twenty-three

Auckland, December 1956

'He really does look like his father, doesn't he?' Colleen said, gazing down at Daniel.

The baby was nestled in the crook of his grandfather's arm, while Sid drank his morning tea and read the paper out loud to him.

'He does,' Pauline agreed. 'I don't think he's that interested in the news, Dad.'

Colleen said, 'Get off your backside, Sid, and make some toast. Come on, it's my turn to hold him.'

Pauline smiled to herself. They'd been home four hours and so far her mother and father hadn't been able to keep their hands off Daniel. To think how much she'd worried about telling them she wasn't giving him up. Even more to the point, to think about the lectures her mother had given her about how she'd have to! What a lot of agonising for nothing. They'd fallen in love with him, just like she had.

She yawned. 'I need a sleep, and so does Daniel. And we both really need a bath.'

'I'll give him his bath,' Colleen volunteered.

'Don't you have to go to work?'

'I'll phone in and say I'm sick. It's not every day your grandson comes home.'

'Mum?'

'Mmm?'

'I thought you didn't want me to keep him?' Pauline said.

'I didn't, but you have, so things have changed.' Colleen looked at her. 'It won't be easy, you know. People will talk about you.'

Pauline shrugged. 'I don't really care. But you will, won't you?'

'I will, but ...' Her mother looked down at Daniel. 'Well, we've got him to think about now, haven't we?'

'You've changed your tune,' Sid said, setting a plate of singed toast on the table.

'Oh, for God's sake, Sid, throw that out for the birds. Yes, I have changed my tune. And aren't you lucky I'm such an accommodating person?'

'Accommodating?' Sid snorted and put more bread under the grill.

'Mind you, Pauline,' Colleen said, 'you'll have to get a job to buy the baby all the things he'll need, which means you'll have to pay for child-minding, and that'll probably eat up all your pay so you'll end up back where you started. I can't give up work to look after him, you know.'

'I'll look after him,' Sid said.

'You? You're too old to play at being a father.'

'I am not.'

'And you've probably ruined your chances of getting a husband,' Colleen went on. 'Daniel's a lovely little thing, he really is, but what man wants to take on another man's child?'

'I don't want a husband,' Pauline said. 'I only wanted Johnny.'

'Look, love, I know you say that now, but things will change. Time will pass and one day you'll find yourself wishing you had someone to share your life with.'

'I'll have someone to share my life with. Him,' Pauline said, pointing at the baby.

Colleen shook her head. 'Tell me that when he's thirteen and up the street with his friends, and you, me and your father are sitting here playing Chinese Checkers and Snap.'

Pauline had to admit that did sound pretty awful. She'd still only be thirty years old by then. 'Well, I don't know what might happen, do I? I haven't got a crystal ball.'

But Arabella Fortune had tarot cards. Perhaps she should go back and see her. She'd been right about the baby and all that stuff about tragedy.

Sid opened the kitchen window and threw out a second lot of burnt toast. 'You'd better come and do this, Col. I seem to have lost me touch.'

'No, I'm about to bathe the baby.'

'What in? The copper? We haven't got a baby's bath.'

Colleen said, 'We'll have to do it in the basin in the bathroom.'

'Why can't I just put him in the bath with me?' Pauline suggested.

'It's dangerous. You might drop him.'

'Bollocks I will.'

Sid remarked, 'I see they also had classes in social graces at that Bethany.'

'I can feel a shopping expedition coming on,' Colleen said, not unhappily. 'And I must ring Allie and Donna.'

'Taiho,' Sid said. 'Ring Donna if you like, but think on before you talk to Allie. You know how she is about babies.'

Affronted, Colleen replied, 'I know my own daughter. I'll not tread on her toes.'

*

The Mana ladies were knitting at Allie's place today, and had begun arriving at around nine o'clock. All six were now crowded into her front room, as well as some of the stock about to be sent to shops, which had been stored in the spare room currently occupied by Gina, and Gina herself. But at least Mr De Valera was on the outside, perched precariously on the window ledge glaring ferociously in through the net curtains at the women who'd usurped his domain.

Allie had made tea for everyone before they'd started work, and now she had an announcement. Ana knew, but so far no one else did.

She clapped her hands to get attention. 'I've got some really good news to tell you. In terms of our proposed junior and adult lines—'

'Ooh, get you!' Kura said.

Everyone laughed and so did Allie. It *did* sound a bit lah-di-dah.

'OK then, as far as our big kids' and grown-ups' jumpers and cardigans and vests are concerned, we've had confirmed orders from eight specialist stores and four of the department stores, and that's on top of the children's wear.'

The women all cheered and clapped.

Allie grinned, while keeping a surreptitious eye on Gina, who was on her hands and knees and heading towards the back of the sofa. You had to watch her *all* the time; no wonder poor Awhi was exhausted.

'So while that's really good news, and the new range isn't due for delivery till February, it means we're going to be knitting our heads off over Christmas and the summer holidays to get it ready. Sorry, ladies. Is there anyone who can't be available?'

'My kids are at the neighbours' today,' one of the part-timers said, 'but some days I might have to bring them with me. Is that all right?'

Gina's little dark head popped up behind the sofa.

'Why don't we pay someone to look after all the kids?' Wiki suggested.

'You'd have to pay them a small fortune,' Kura said. 'Especially for my lot.'

'Just the little ones,' Wiki said. The bigger ones can look after themselves.'

Suddenly Gina whipped back the net curtain and bellowed 'Boo!' at Mr De Valera. The cat shot off the window sill, several of the women shrieked, more than one cup of tea was spilt, and Vincent started bawling, his little face turning bright red.

'Gina!' Allie exclaimed.

'Pussy got a fright.'

'Christ almighty, so did I.' Kura fanned her face, her hand on her ample chest.

'This is what I mean, eh?' Wiki said. 'Someone who can manage this sort of thing.'

'I don't know who that would be,' Ana mumbled.

The phone rang. Allie, whose heart was still galloping, picked up the handset and stepped into the hallway, stretching the cord.

'Hello, Allie Roberts speaking.'

'Hello, this is Colleen Roberts speaking, your mother.'

Allie rolled her eyes. Her mother always announced herself like this when she rang. 'Hi, Mum.'

'I've got some news, Allie. Pauline's home.'

'She's home *now*? Last time I talked to her she wasn't due back till after Christmas.'

That had been four or five days ago and Pauline had told her she'd have to stay at the maternity home until she'd recovered from giving birth and her milk had dried up.

'She had the baby a couple of days ago,' Colleen said, 'and she's kept him.'

Allie felt suddenly quite dizzy. 'She's *kept* him? She's got him now?'

'I've just given him a bath and they're both asleep in Pauline's room. They arrived on the train this morning. She's called him Daniel John.'

'Well, you've done a bloody great about-face, haven't you?'

'You need to see him, Allie. He really is the sweetest little thing.'

'Does he look like Johnny?'

'The spitting image.'

Oh God, Allie thought, what she going to tell Kura?

*

Allie and Pauline had a bit of a row about it. Allie, of course, thought Daniel was gorgeous, and said so.

She also said, 'It's not easy, Pauline, raising a child by yourself. You need all the help you can get.'

'I know you're only trying to help,' Pauline replied, 'but how would you know? You've never raised a baby on your own.'

'No, I haven't, not on my own. And we only had Hana for four months, and there were two of us, and even that wasn't easy. But I can't see it being any easier with one parent with all the getting up during the night for feeds and the lack of sleep, and the endless washing and trying to get things dry, and never having a minute to yourself. You'll be expecting Mum and Dad to help you, and they're getting too old for all that.'

'You will be too,' Colleen said.

Pauline said, 'No I won't.'

'He'll be waking us up anyway, probably, so we might as well help.'

Allie said, 'The point I'm trying to make is the more people you have to help you with him, the better.'

'So?'

'So why don't you tell Johnny's family about Daniel?'

'No.'

Colleen said, 'I think maybe you should, Pauline.'

'I said no!'

'Why not?' Allie asked.

'Because he's mine.'

'He can still be yours. What's wrong with sharing him a bit with his other grandparents and his aunts and uncles?'

'They'll end up taking him over.'

'No, they won't. Why would they?'

'They will. They're like a great big sponge, that lot. They just ... absorb people.'

Allie said, 'What are you talking about? That's a good thing, isn't it? Kura was very nice to you, wasn't she?'

Pauline looked away. 'Not always.'

'What do you mean?' Colleen demanded. 'When were they not nice to you?'

'Oh *God*, it doesn't matter.'

'It does matter,' Colleen insisted. 'When were they not nice?'

'Well, when Johnny died, if you must know.'

'Why, what happened?' Allie asked.

'Nothing,' Pauline said, sounding about eleven.

'Something must have.'

'They didn't *include* me! They wouldn't take me down to the funeral!'

'But love, they probably had so many other things to think about,' Allie said. 'And the grief. They would have all been heartbroken. I'm sure it wasn't deliberate.'

'*I* was heartbroken too! And I had the baby to think about. All I got told was I had to go away and give him up.'

Allie glanced at her mother, who had the good grace to look guilty.

'So if they couldn't be bothered thinking of me when I needed help,' Pauline said, 'I'm not going to think of them now.'

Allie opened her mouth to speak, but her mother beat her to it. 'That is so childish, Pauline. Call yourself someone fit to raise a baby? All I can say is you're going to have a very lonely and difficult life.'

'I know for a fact Kura would feel *awful* if she knew how upset you were at not going to Johnny's funeral,' Allie said. 'And she'd feel a hundred times worse if she knew you thought it was her fault. She'd *die*.'

Pauline said nothing.

'She thinks you're a lovely girl,' Allie went on. 'She keeps telling me to tell you to visit them, and I've been having to keep on making up excuses about why you can't, because you haven't been here because you've been away having her grandson, but you won't let me tell her that, and you won't tell her yourself because you're so bloody *stubborn and selfish*!'

'Don't call me selfish!'

'Well, you are,' Colleen said. 'It's dreadful to have lost a lover—'

'Not *a* lover! Johnny was the love of my *life*!'

'I know, love, I know,' Colleen soothed. 'But try and imagine what it might be like to lose a child. Imagine what it would be like for you if you loved and adored and raised Daniel for eighteen years, and then he died. I'm sure that won't happen, but that's exactly what's happened to Johnny's mother. You've suffered horribly, but so has Mrs Apanui.'

Allie said, 'You need to tell her, Pauline. Let her have part of Johnny back.'

There was a long, long silence.

Finally, Pauline said, 'I'll think about it.'

*

On the day before Christmas, which was a Monday, Pauline was looking out the window of her mother's front room, patting Daniel's back in the hope that he'd do a decent burp. Her milk was well in now and he was a proper guts, drinking and drinking until his little tummy was quite tight, and then he'd grizzle until he'd let out a good bit of wind. She was sure he'd grown already, though her mother said probably not as babies tended to lose a little weight after they were born. She must get him signed up at Plunket. She must get herself on a diet too. Her own stomach had gone down a lot but the waistband on her capris was definitely snug.

As she patted and soothed Daniel, she saw women arriving next door at Ana Leonard's, including Allie and Kura Apanui.

'Mum,' she called down the hall. 'What's Allie doing next door?'

'They'll be knitting, for the business,' Colleen's voice came back.

Pauline rubbed and patted some more, until finally a satisfyingly resonant burp came out of Daniel, and also, unfortunately, some sick, which landed on her shoulder. She wiped it off with his wrap and went into the kitchen.

'What time are you going to work?' she asked her mother, who was ferreting around in her handbag.

'Soon. Why?'

'I thought I might take Daniel to see Kura. Did you want to come with me?'

'Are you asking me if I will?'

'Um, yes. Please.'

Pauline thought her mother looked pleased. 'Well, I suppose I could catch the next bus. We'll have to go now, though.'

'What's that on your top?' Sid asked.

'Baby spew.'

'Go and put something clean on,' Colleen said crossly. 'Quickly, go on.'

Pauline changed into a clean blouse and together she and Colleen walked over to Ana Leonard's house and round the back.

'Why don't you wait here for a minute and I'll call you?' her mother suggested as they reached the corner of the house.

Pauline shrugged, then spat on a corner of Daniel's wrap and cleaned his face. He smiled at her and she smiled back and kissed his nose. He was *so* advanced for only a week old.

She heard her mother knock on the back door, the door open, then Ana Leonard say, 'Colleen, hello, come in. We're having a knitting session. Your Allie's here, actually.'

Then her mother said, 'To be honest it's Mrs Apanui I've come to see. Is she available?'

'Kura? Wait on, I'll just get her for you.'

Pause, then her mother saying, 'Hello, Mrs Apanui. You might not remember me but I'm Mrs Colleen Roberts, Allie and Pauline's mother? We met briefly at Jack Leonard's funeral.'

'Ae, I do remember, Mrs Roberts. How are you?'

'Good, thank you. And yourself?'

'I'm good, yes.'

Pauline heard her mother say, 'I thought you'd like to know we have something in common.'

'We do?'

Pauline tensed. Here it comes.

Her mother said, 'We're both grandmothers.'

Pauline couldn't see Kura's face, but she could hear the frown in her voice. 'No, I'm not a grandmother.'

Colleen called out, 'Pauline?'

She walked round the side of the house and up the steps, Daniel in her arms. 'Hi, Mrs Apanui. This is Johnny's son, Daniel John.'

Kura stared down at the baby for a long, long moment, then let out a shriek. Poor Daniel's eyes nearly popped out of his head, his arms flew out and he started to cry. A thunder of rapid footsteps sounded inside the house and the porch filled up with women, all peering over Kura's shoulder.

Keening now, she clapped her hands over her mouth. 'Is it really? Is it really my Johnny's boy?'

'It is,' Pauline said, 'and he's a week old. Would you like a hold?'

Kura nodded dumbly and gathered the baby in her arms, tears pouring down her face. 'Oh, he looks just like him. The eyes, the ears, the little nose. Wiki, look, he does, doesn't he? It's Johnny all over again.'

Wiki Irwin nodded, dabbing at her eyes with a hanky.

Cuddling Daniel to her bosom, Kura said, 'You're a good girl, Pauline. We've missed you. We've been wondering where you were. And you know? This is the best Christmas present we've ever had.'

*

January 1957

The inside of St Michael's church was definitely cooler than it was outdoors, where it was sweltering, but the temperature still wasn't particularly comfortable. Allie could feel sweat beading on her upper lip and trickling down her sides. Poor Sonny looked like he could do with ten iced beers — his face was shiny and he kept dabbing at his forehead with a handkerchief. She knew he was dying to take off his jacket, but wouldn't because they were in church.

Her father had, though — his Salvation Army special — and had left it draped over the back of a pew.

'Don't leave that there, Dad,' she said. 'Someone'll put it in the rubbish.'

Poor Daniel must be melting too, in his long, lacy christening gown. He certainly looked grumpy, waving his fists around and kicking out with little bootied feet.

Initially Allie was surprised that Pauline had consented to their mother's request that Daniel be baptised. She wasn't a particularly God-fearing girl, after all. But then she thought about it. They'd been brought up Catholic, and Pauline did go to church now and then, and after Johnny dying, and maybe even their nan, she supposed her sister might have had a bit of a think about religion and the afterlife and what have you. Or maybe not. Who knew? In the end she'd said yes and there they were, although it was half-past five on a Thursday and not a Sunday, the usual day for baptisms. Allie suspected Father Noonan might have chickened out of baptising an illegitimate baby on a Sunday.

And Pauline hadn't invited many people, just a couple of her girlfriends, the Apanuis and the Irwins — which did actually add up to quite a few — and the Leonards from next door, and a strange girl called Lee Bao she'd apparently met on the train. Allie quite liked her, to tell the truth. But still, they only filled the first few rows of the church, which was a massive place with a soaring, domed roof and pillars, an elaborate crucifix suspended behind the altar, and an old-fashioned pulpit that could only be reached by steps.

Apparently Pauline had asked Kura and Joseph if they minded their grandson being baptised into the Catholic church, when they were Anglicans themselves, and Kura said they didn't at all as long as he grew up knowing the word of God.

Best of all as far as Allie was concerned, Pauline had invited her and Sonny to be Daniel's godparents. Sonny was chuffed. Donna had said she was thrilled for them, and Allie thought she probably was, but then she was thrilled with everything at the moment because she'd just heard she'd passed all her nursing exams. Allie was delighted for *her*.

Gina was running up and down between the pews, her sandals clattering loudly on the floorboards, having a lovely time. Allie fetched her and brought her back. Father Noonan was ready now and they gathered around the baptismal font to one side of the altar.

He began: 'What name do you give your child?'

Pauline said, 'Daniel John Roberts.'

'What do you ask of God's church for Daniel John?'

'Baptism.'

'You have asked to have your child baptised. In doing so you are accepting the responsibility of training him in the practice of the faith. It will be your duty to bring him up to keep God's commandments as Christ taught us, by loving God and our neighbour. Do you clearly understand what you are undertaking?'

'I do,' Pauline said.

Allie cleared her throat as Father Noonan turned to her and Sonny. 'Are you ready to help the mother of this child in her duty as a Christian parent?'

'We are,' she and Sonny said.

And then Father Noonan did the bit with the water on Daniel's head, which he didn't like at all, then they were all invited to take part in the liturgy of the word. What a relief it was to sit down. Allie drifted off a bit after that, thinking random thoughts and surreptitiously fanning herself with an envelope from her handbag, until she suddenly realised something momentous.

She was three weeks overdue with her period.

*

On another very hot day, Allie drove Pauline and Daniel out to Waikumete Cemetery. It was quite a long trip and the interior of the truck was stifling even with the windows down.

Once inside the cemetery gates off Great North Road they knew exactly where they wanted to go, and drove slowly along the narrow roads through the resting places of many of Auckland's dead; those from the previous century who now lay beneath crumbling headstones and lichen-mottled angels; the war heroes, above whom uniform keystones marched in tidy formation as they once had themselves; the grand little mausoleums and follies eternally signifying the importance of their occupants; and the simple, neat rows of graves of ordinary people.

Allie felt quite strange. She'd visited a year earlier for her nan's funeral, of course, but the time before that had been in December of 1953, for the mass funeral of those who'd died in the Dunbar and Jones fire. She'd been looking for something then — an explanation for what had happened, perhaps? Some sort of resolution? Forgiveness? Whatever it had been she hadn't found it, but she had now, or at least enough of it to allow her to get on with her life.

She parked the truck on Acmena Avenue in the middle of the Catholic section, and they walked to Rose's grave. Daniel was fussing and a bit pink in the face so Pauline took off his cardigan and booties, leaving him in just a sleeveless romper. He was much happier after that.

Looking down at Rose's grave, Pauline said, 'It's sunk.'

Allie said, 'I think they keep topping them up till the dirt settles completely.'

'Yuck.'

'It is a bit. We should be able to organise a headstone soon, though.'

Pauline nodded.

Allie laid her flowers at the base of the temporary wooden cross marking the grave. She'd wanted stock, her nan's favourite, but they were out of season, so she'd picked some dahlias from Rose's own garden. They were a bit limp from the heat, but she didn't think Nan would mind.

'Can I talk to her for a minute?' Pauline asked.

"Course you can.'

'No, I mean by myself.'

'Oh. OK.'

Allie wandered off, stood under a tree out of the sun and lit a cigarette. It was very quiet in the cemetery, the air fat and still with heat, which is why, if she listened really hard, she could hear what her sister was saying.

'Nan? It's Pauline here. You know how you asked me once what I was looking for, and I said I didn't know? Well, I think I've found it. Here he is. His name's Daniel John.'

Author Notes

There are a few things I should probably point out relating to this story.

Flora MacKenzie was a real person, and her brothel at Ring Terrace, St Mary's Bay, was real too, not to mention famous. Flora appears to have been an interesting woman and has her own www.teara.govt.nz entry. She was born in 1902, came from a wealthy family, and was a very skilled dressmaker who had a boutique in Vulcan Lane off Queen Street, Auckland, specialising in 'society' wedding gowns she designed herself. She was also extremely partial to a drink, and apparently became a madam in the 1940s when she discovered that girls renting the flats she owned at Ring Terrace, where she also lived, were servicing American military personnel. Her establishment became quite exclusive and was elegantly furnished, attracting your wealthier type of customer. Flora appeared in court half a dozen times for brothel-keeping and was sentenced to gaol twice for periods of six months. She was loud, colourful, talented, and believed in equal rights for women, and she died in 1982, leaving all her money to the deaf.

Of all the characters who appear in this book who work at Smith and Caughey department store, only Miss Cato, the woman on the cash desk at the end of the Lamson tube, is real.

Miss Cato worked at Smith and Caughey for fifty-eight years. Apparently, 'The cash desk was her domain. She used to wear a black cardigan, a long black dress, her hair in a bun and she wore pince-nez spectacles' (Cecilie Geary, *Celebrating 125 Years 1880 — 2005: Smith & Caughey's*, p29). All the other characters I made up.

Smith and Caughey's original tearoom, called the Naumai Tearooms, opened in the 1880s but closed during World War I. After that there was nothing at all until 1958 when The Cedar Room opened. I've made a slight tweak and moved The Cedar Room back in time to 1955. Well, I had to — I wanted Pauline to work there. The Cedar Room served morning and afternoon teas and lunches, and had table and buffet service. It was very popular and in its first year served 106,000 customers.

A short note on hairnets in the kitchens at Auckland Hospital: I don't know if staff had to wear them or not in the 1950s and I couldn't find any information on the subject, so I decided they did wear them.

This one's a blatant lie: the Howard Morrison Quartet did not play at the Maori Community Centre at Freeman's Bay in 1956. They weren't even nationally known then. Howard Morrison was playing the Rotorua rugby clubs in a band called the Ohinemutu Quartet in 1955, and in 1956 he toured Australia with the Aotearoa Concert Party. On his return he formed the original Howard Morrison Quartet with his brother, Laurie, his cousin, John, and Gerry Merito. They were spotted by Auckland entrepreneur Benny Levin in December 1957, and joined Levin's touring show 'Pop Jamboree'. The following year they had hits with 'Hoki Mai' and 'Po Karekare Ana', and, after a national tour, signed with manager/entrepreneur Harry M Miller in 1959, who insisted the band become full-time professional musicians. Laurie and John, however, couldn't, and were replaced by Wi Wharekura and Noel Kingi. The Howard Morrison Quartet did actually play the Maori Community Centre in 1959 (if not probably before, and definitely in the 1960s), when the visiting

American band The Platters also played there — to the absolute delight of the audience.

Somervell's Milk Bar and Currie's Milk Bar are both real. Currie's, on lower Queen Street, was a favourite hangout of the Auckland Rebels Motorcycle Club, which was broken up by the police for being a pack of reprobates, but was soon followed by the Saints Motorcycle Club. Both groups were known as Milk Bar Cowboys or Currie Boys. Somervell's Milk Bar, 238 Victoria Street East, gained more notoriety after Frederick Foster shot his nineteen-year-old former lover Sharon Skiffington to death there in March 1955. Foster went to the gallows four months later on 7 July.

On an equally unjolly note, in the book the character Jack Leonard has a form of dementia. In the 1950s very little was known about this sort of illness — its causes, prognosis, or treatment — and all the variations of the disease were shoved under an umbrella called senile dementia. Those who developed dementia were cared for at home or sent to mental hospitals, where often they received no treatment other than very heavy medication in conditions that sometimes bordered on inhumane. But then, that would have been no different from the treatment frequently given in the 1950s to people with other mental health issues such as depression, schizophrenia and bipolar disorder. Someone like Jack, who couldn't be cared for at home because he'd become unmanageable, would very likely have ended up in the 'loony bin', where he'd probably have languished until he'd died — which is extremely sad.

Now for a word or two on New Zealand's Bethany maternity homes. By the turn of the twentieth century, the Salvation Army's late colonial rescue homes for girls had developed into Bethany homes for unmarried pregnant young women. There were eventually seven, one each in Christchurch, Dunedin, Wellington, Napier, Russell, Gisborne and Auckland, and they provided girls with a place to go, away from home, to have their babies. Some Bethany homes also took paying patients to offset the costs of non-paying unmarried patients, though evidently the two groups never mixed. The Auckland home in Grey Lynn was the last to remain in operation and was demolished in 2012.

Prior to the 1970s, many single women gave their babies up for adoption. The Bethany homes played a role in this process, as did other charitable maternity homes run by the Anglican and Catholic churches. While some women don't recall their time at Bethany and other homes as being unpleasant, others do, remembering awful food, being forced to do constant chores, judgmental and overbearing staff, and, worst of all, feeling they were coerced into giving up their babies.

During the 1950s there was a demand from childless married couples for babies to adopt. This led to the Adoption Act of 1955, which embraced the 'complete break' ideology, i.e. between 'natural' mother and child, and greater involvement of the state in the adoption process. The philosophy behind the complete break ideology was that, once adopted by two 'proper' parents, the bonding process would be organic and inevitable between an adopted child and its adoptive parents, the child had no need to know about its true origins, and the child's genetic relationship with its birth mother would be 'as if dead'. As for the genetic birth mother, she should do the unselfish thing and give up her baby so it could have a normal life, put her immature, unstable (as demonstrated by getting pregnant) behaviour behind her, and get on with her own life. (Paraphrased from an article by Keith Griffith, 'Adoption History and Reform in New Zealand', 1996.)

From 1955 state social workers were involved in facilitating almost all adoptions that weren't arranged among family. Mothers of babies were required to sign consent forms. Some women didn't get to see their babies at all before they were removed — others only after they signed the form. Some women kept their babies for a few days in the maternity home before they gave them up, and there are accounts on record of mothers refusing to hand their babies over and taking them home. This removal of babies from their birth mothers peaked in the 1960s.

In 1968 the Domestic Proceedings Act, and the Legal Aid Act 1969, made it easier for women to claim maintenance payments from their children's fathers, and in 1973 the Domestic Purposes Benefit was introduced. This gave women some economic independence. Also, by the 1970s the demand for babies for adoption had decreased, and social attitudes towards unmarried mothers were easing (slightly). Times were finally changing.

A brief comment about Three Eastbourne Road, Remuera, where, in the book, Kathleen and Jonathan Lawson live: this is a real house, which I spotted on Google Earth. If it's your place — sorry!

Finally, a note on several books I found particularly useful while researching this story. The first, an absolutely beautiful book, which was given to me by Paraparaumu PaperPlus (thank you!), is Bronwyn Labrum's *Real Modern: Everyday New Zealand in the 1950s and 1960s* (Te Papa Press, 2015). Also really helpful were: *Blue Smoke: the Lost Dawn of New Zealand Popular Music 1918–1964* (Auckland University Press, 2010) by Chris Bourke; *Dining Out: a History of the Restaurant in New Zealand* (Auckland University Press, 2010) by Perrin Rowland; Lindsay Neill et al's *The Great New Zealand Pie Cart* (Hodder Moa, 2008); *Kitchens: the New Zealand Kitchen in the Twentieth Century* (Otago University Press, 2014) by Helen Leach, because I don't have a clue about ovens pre-1980 — or post-1980, frankly; *The Loving Stitch: a History of Knitting and Spinning in New Zealand* (Auckland University Press, 1998) by Heather Nicholson; Margaret Sparrow's *Abortion Then and Now: New Zealand Abortion Stories from 1940 to 1980* (Victoria University Press, 2010); and *Wool: a History of New Zealand's Wool Industry* (Ngaio Press, 2003) by Bill Carter and John MacGibbon — which isn't as boring as you might think.

Acknowledgments

This is the important bit. Thank you to the HarperCollins Australia editing team, Katherine Hassett and Nicola Robinson, for making everything painless, and to my lovely freelance editor Kate O'Donnell, who as usual was spot on with all her comments, and to my agent, Clare Forster, for her encouragement and wisdom. A big fat thank you, also, to the HarperCollins New Zealand team, for constantly supporting and promoting my books. Special mention goes to Kelly Bold, who was responsible for turning the bleak wasteland that was my Facebook page into something that people actually click on now. Thanks, Kelly!

Thanks too to the staff of the Sir George Grey Special Collections at the Auckland Public Library, who were very helpful when I was looking for maps and photographs of 1950s Grafton. Sorry about the mess.

Finally, and as always, my enduring thanks and love go to my husband, Aaron. He's the one who has to put up with snippy moods (I'm working!), dinners gone cold (I'll be out in a minute!), and solo weekends (I have to get this finished!). And he always does.

HOUSE
of **SORROWS**

A Restless Years novel

Coming soon

Chapter One

Kings Cross, Sydney, 1964

Polly Manaia swore as she dropped her bag of groceries, watching in annoyance as several tomatoes rolled into the gutter. Oh well, too bad, they'd wash off. This would all be a *lot* easier if her flatmates weren't so insistent on getting their beauty sleep and managed to drag themselves out of bed before midday. *She* worked at night too, sometimes later hours than they did. And she had the dry horrors and a pounding headache, but there was absolutely nothing in the cupboard so someone had to buy food. She gathered up the tomatoes, wiped a bit of muck off one, and dropped it back in her bag.

It was half-past ten in the morning and the Cross was just waking up. The night people, which should include her, wouldn't be out for hours as the clubs and bars were shut, but the day people were in evidence, opening up the cafes and the delicatessens and the fruit shops. She waved glumly to a few people she knew, bought fresh rolls from the French bakery, and some cheese, and pastrami and salami from the deli. She ordered the spicy salami because she knew the girls didn't like it, which would teach them for lolling around in bed.

By the time she'd traipsed home she felt quite sick, and had been forced to eat a bread roll in an attempt to subdue her nausea. Nothing about her outing had cheered her up. It was a nice sunny October morning but the sun had been too bright and hurt her eyes and head. Every loud noise had made her jump then wince, it was warm and she'd sweated to the point that she could smell last night's booze coming out of her pores, and the crows and pigeons that seemed to be forever squawking and shitting round the Cross had got on her nerves. It was a relief to step inside the cool, dim foyer of the big old house on Bayswater Road in which she, Rhoda and Star lived.

They had the whole upper floor to themselves — three bedrooms, a small kitchen, a sitting room, a bathroom and toilet, another little room where they stored their costumes, and several balconies — though they did have to share a laundry with the people living in the two flats downstairs. There was a back lawn too, but not much of one, and no one cut the grass or took care of the shrubs and wildly overgrown flowerbeds, but there were a pair of jacaranda trees that bloomed gloriously in spring.

The house needed painting inside, some of the floors were on a lean, a couple of the windows wouldn't open properly, a dozen leadlights had been replaced with plain glass (or plywood), and mould grew on several interior walls in the winter, but she was still stately. There were fretwork arches, ceilings of fancy pressed metal — once white, now a bilious yellow — dark timber and panelling everywhere, picture rails in the sitting room and hallway, and great timber fireplaces that hadn't been waxed or cleaned for decades. The flat's shabbiness wasn't helped by the fact that it was filled almost exclusively with furniture and bits and pieces from the St Vincent de Paul shop down the road, but everything was comfortable and serviceable, if not exactly stylish.

Polly had moved into the house in 1956 when she'd arrived from New Zealand. She'd had different flatmates then. They'd left some time ago, to be replaced first by Rhoda the following year, and then Star in 1959. They'd shared the flat ever since, fairly happily despite their bickering, and had no plans to change their living arrangements. Polly counted Star and Rhoda as among her best friends, not that she had many. She had hundreds of acquaintances, but not many close friends. They worked in the same business, in the same part of town, during the same nocturnal hours, and they all knew the same people. Polly's only other really good friend, someone she really trusted, was Evie Palmer, whom she'd known in Auckland.

Polly headed up the stairs from the foyer, still enjoying the cool respite. Doors to the left and right of the staircase were closed, indicating that the downstairs flats' occupants were either out or still asleep. She plodded up to her own flat, wondering if Rhoda and Star were up yet, unlocked the door, and went in.

No, they weren't — she could hear them both snoring.

She unpacked her purchases, put the cheese, meat and tomatoes in the fridge, and left the bread rolls on the kitchen bench. She thought about waking the girls, but instead went into her bedroom and shook four ten milligram Valium tablets from an unlabelled medicine bottle, put them in her mouth, and washed them down with a slug of bourbon. Then she carried the bottle, a sticky glass and her cigarettes out to the balcony off the sitting room and gingerly sat down in a wicker chair. It was ancient and the wicker was unravelling and someone's arse was going to go through it one day. Rhoda's, probably.

She poured a drink, took a long sip, and waited for both it and the Valium to take effect. The Valium would help settle her jangling nerves, and the bourbon would at least postpone her hangover. The nerves, she knew, were left over from the Methedrine she'd had the night before, but she needed it, to work so late. She'd taken a couple of Quaaludes before she'd gone out this morning, to take the edge off her jitters, but all they'd done was make her feel confused about what cheese to buy at the deli. And she hadn't had a drink before she'd gone out because she didn't like to go up the street stinking of booze. She lit a smoke, sighed and wondered if she was getting too old for the life she was leading. It was too bad if she was, because she didn't have any other kind of life.

Eventually, as the rosellas flitted about in the jacaranda trees and the sun crept slowly across the long grass in the backyard, she nodded off.

*

She awoke with a start. Someone was banging about in the kitchen. She stretched, stood and wandered into the house. It was Rhoda, looking in the cupboards.

'Morning!' she said. 'Have you seen the frying pan? I'm doing eggs.'

'There aren't any,' Polly replied.

'Aren't there? Bugger.'

'But I went out and got rolls and a few things from the deli.'

'Thanks, darl.' Rhoda opened the fridge door. 'Ooh, pastrami!'

Polly sat down at the dining table in the sitting room. Her hangover had receded now, though her head felt as though it were stuffed with cotton wool. She watched Rhoda as she fluffed about, artfully arranging the food on a platter.

Rhoda was twenty-seven and stood six feet and one inch tall in her bare size ten feet. She had wide shoulders, a slender body and long legs. Her soot-black hair was shoulder-length, her eyebrows were plucked into dramatic arches, and this morning she had a hint of stubble along her jawline. As she moved about her pink nylon negligee and matching robe floated around her, creating an impression of casual glamour.

Star's bedroom door opened and she clomped out in her fluffy mules, satin robe fluttering, grumbling and scratching her head. Star was always in a shitty mood when she woke up.

'Morning!' Rhoda trilled.

Ignoring her, Star sat down at the table, lit a cigarette, then launched into a protracted spasm of phlegmy coughing, which she did every morning.

Once that was out of the way, she rasped, 'Is there tea?'

'Won't be a tick,' Rhoda said, setting the platter of food on the table. 'Polly went out and got all this. Isn't she a sweetie?'

'You look like crap,' Polly said to Star.

She did, too. Her hair was flat on one side and sticking out on the other, there were smudges of black kohl and mascara smeared around her eyes, a glowing red pimple had erupted on her chin, and she looked deeply tired.

'So do you,' Star said.

'I know.'

At five feet eight inches tall, Star was shorter and more compact than Rhoda. She'd been taking hormone pills — bought off the street — longer than Rhoda so barely grew a beard at all. She also had the beginnings of breasts, of which Polly knew she was very proud. Her wavy hair was collar-length and dyed platinum blonde, though her arched, plucked brows were still their natural dark brown. She was twenty-four, though very occasionally she behaved as though she were fourteen, which could be quite annoying.

Star and Rhoda were a double act at Les Girls night club: Rhoda was Jane Russell and Star was the late and very lamented Marilyn Monroe, and they were really extremely talented. They wore gorgeous costumes that cost them the earth and both did their own vocals, and were paid quite well for their efforts. They weren't female impersonators — they were men choosing to live as women, which is what they considered they truly were, and were both hoping, one day, to physically become women. Rhoda was known throughout the Cross as Rhoda Dendron, and Star as Star E Knight. Their 'past life' names were, respectively, Gary Hicks and Colin Jessop, which they loathed as relentlessly loutish and blokey. They were also camp, though neither currently had a boyfriend, and no one, Polly included, ever brought men back to the flat.

In fact, Polly hadn't been involved with anyone for a long time. When she'd arrived in Sydney she'd worked in a brothel for three years, and who had the energy or motivation for a love life while they were doing that? Then, after she'd saved a decent nest egg and chucked in the prostitution and gone to work as an exotic dancer, there'd been a man for about eighteen months, but that hadn't worked out and there'd been no one since. She was happier by herself.

'Good night at the club?' Rhoda asked, joining them at the table and lighting a cigarette.

'Same as usual,' Polly said. 'Busy. Rowdy. One of my pasties fell off.'

'Embarrassing!' Rhoda said.

Polly shrugged. It hadn't worried her. By law exotic dancers couldn't strip completely nude and were required to wear G-strings, and pasties over their nipples, but one coming off was hardly the end of the world. 'I didn't even notice. I was a bit hammered.'

'You're always a bit hammered,' Star said.

'Not *always*.'

Star took a big slurp of tea, then swore when she burnt her mouth. Eyes watering, she said, 'You know, love, if you keep going the way you are, one day you'll wake up and your lovely face and that beautiful body will be gone. And then you'll be sorry. You won't be Heliopolis the Dusky Maori Maiden any more, you'll be Heliopolis the Raddled Old Bag.'

Polly knew that — Rhoda and Star had told her often enough. And just as often she'd ignored their well-meant advice.

She hated her stage name. Heliopolis was actually her real name, after the hospital in Egypt where her uncle had died during World War I, but she'd always been known as Polly. The ridiculous Dusky Maori Maiden part had been thought up by her boss, Sam Adler, at the strip club. It wasn't fair; Evie worked there as well, and she hadn't been lumbered with a stupid title.

She changed the subject. 'How was your show?'

'Star sang flat during "Diamonds".' Rhoda said.

'Well, I couldn't hear the monitor. Anyway, *you* fell off your heels in the middle of "Bye Bye Baby".'

'That's true,' Rhoda said. 'Got a round of applause for it, though.'

'Crowd was good,' Star said, making a neat little stack of salami slices, popping them into her mouth and chewing enthusiastically. '*Shit*, that's hot.' She spat them out. 'God, girl!' she said to Polly accusingly.

'Is it too spicy?' Polly said. 'Sorry, my mistake.'

'Fucking hell.' Star shoved her chair back, clattered into the kitchen, ran the tap and drank a big glass of water.

'Water won't help,' Rhoda said after her. 'Milk's better for spicy food.'

Star opened the fridge, drank straight from the milk bottle, burped, then returned to the table.

Rhoda said, 'What a lady.'

Pointing at the salami, Star said, 'You try some. It's diabolical.'

'No thanks.'

Star bit into a bread roll, then glanced out the French doors opening onto the balcony. 'Nice day. I might go and get my nails done.'

'I might come with you,' Polly said. 'Later, though, after I've had a sleep.'

'Shall we go for coffee?' Rhoda suggested. 'There's a new place open on Darlinghurst and I've heard the cakes are divine.'

'I'm watching my weight,' Star said.

Rhoda said, 'You are not. You had two kebabs on the way home last night.'

'That was my tea.'

'No, it wasn't. You had a pie and chips for tea.'

'Did I?'

'We stopped at the chew and spew on Roslyn Street on the way to work, remember? *And* you had more chips at the club.'

'I don't remember that.' Star looked at her platinum and diamond Rolex watch, which she'd recently bought at the market for three quid. 'Shall we aim for two? I absolutely must shave my legs before I even *think* about going out the door.'

Rhoda said, 'Fine, but don't even *think* about using my razor. I'm fed up with you wrecking it on your hairy legs.'

Polly listened to them bicker while she finished her tea, then left them to it and went to her room, desperate for sleep. Opening the drawer of her bedside table, she looked through her stash for something that would send her off quickly. She sorted through bottles and packets of Methedrine, Dexedrine and Drinamyl — all amphetamines, or speed, so of no use — and considered Seconal, Mandrax, Quaalude, and the Valium again, which were sedatives. Valium never lasted long, so she chose the Seconal, which should give her a good couple of hours. She took four and lay on her bed, curling herself into a ball, then closed her eyes and waited for the drugs to draw her down into darkness.

*

Star knocked on Polly's bedroom door and opened it a few inches. 'Pol, darl? You awake?'

No answer. Behind her Rhoda said, 'She's probably knocked herself out.'

Star opened the door all the way. Polly was on her bed, lying on her side, knees drawn up, her long, dark hair fanned across her shoulder and the pillow. She lay very still.

Peering in, Rhoda asked after a moment, 'Is she breathing?'

Star crept into the room and bent down, her face inches from Polly's. Then she straightened, gave a thumbs-up and crept out again, closing the door behind her.

'Phew,' Rhoda said.

'Should we just leave her to sleep?' Star suggested. 'She must be knackered.'

'Full of drugs, more like.'

'Doesn't mean she isn't worn out.'

'That's true,' Rhoda agreed. 'I don't think she's very happy at the moment.'

'We'll bring something nice back for her,' Star said, collecting her handbag from the table and doing a twirl. 'How do I look?'

She was wearing a short-sleeved shirtwaist dress in blue and white-striped poplin, high-heeled navy-blue sling-back sandals, and one of her many blonde wigs. She prided herself on being able to buy her clothes straight off the rack, whereas poor Rhoda, being so tall, often had to sew her own. But then Rhoda was an excellent seamstress, which came in very handy when it came to their show costumes.

'Fabulous,' Rhoda said. 'Me?'

'Gorgeous.'

Rhoda's outfit was a teal-coloured shift dress with a cowl neckline, three-quarter sleeves and a matching fabric belt, and white court shoes with two-inch heels and a white vinyl bag, and she'd teased up her hair and curled the ends out in a jaunty bouffant style, all of which gave her the appearance of being almost six and a half feet tall.

'I couldn't decide between the teal and my new burgundy two-piece,' Rhoda said.

'We're only getting our nails done, aren't we?'

'And having coffee. Where is this new place, anyway?'

'Darlinghurst Street. Well, I say Darlinghurst but it's more like Williams. It *is* Williams, actually, near the intersection with Bourke.'

'Are we walking?'

Rhoda said yes.

Star looked at her feet. 'In these shoes?'

Rhoda made a face. 'Should we get a taxi?'

'Well, I'm not walking all that way in high heels.'

While Rhoda rang a taxi, Star re-did her lipstick, then they clattered downstairs to wait outside on the street.

'I feel a bit guilty now, leaving her behind,' Rhoda said.

'Polly?' Star said, lighting a cigarette. 'She's better off catching up on her sleep.'

'Has she heard from her brother lately?'

They were aware that Polly had a large family in New Zealand from whom she was more or less estranged, but not the reason why, though God knew they'd nearly killed themselves trying to find out. They suspected Evie knew, but she was as close-mouthed as Polly. They also knew Polly had a daughter, a girl named Gina aged eleven, who was being raised by her grandmother, because Star had once sneaked a look at a letter that had come from Polly's brother, Sonny, apparently the only member of her family who ever wrote to her. It was all a fascinating mystery and they couldn't understand how Polly could keep all those secrets to herself. If it was them they'd have told *everyone*. After all, a trouble shared was a problem halved, but Polly seemed to think that a trouble shared was a trouble doubled.

'I don't know, do I?' Star said.

'I thought you might have come across her mail again.'

'That was an accident. I didn't mean to look at it.'

'Well, wait till she goes out and have another accidental look. We might find out what's worrying her.'

'We could just ask,' Star suggested.

'Do you *want* your head bitten off?' Rhoda said.

'Not really.'

The taxi pulled up. Star took a last drag on her cigarette and they got in.

Rhoda said, 'William Street, please, intersection with Bourke.'

The driver eyed her in the rear vision mirror. 'Nice frock.'

'Thank you very much,' Rhoda replied, setting her handbag primly in her lap. 'I made it myself.'

The Smuggler's Wife series

**The bestselling saga of love and adventure
on the high seas of the Pacific**

The Convict Girl series

**The bestselling saga of four adventurous women
transported halfway around the world**